THE LONER

EMILY MARCH

Copyright © 2019 by Emily March

Copyright © 2008 by Geralyn Dawson Williams

All rights reserved.

No part of this book may be reproduced in any form or by any electronic or mechanical means, including information storage and retrieval systems, without written permission from the author, except for the use of brief quotations in a book review.

PROLOGUE

East Texas, 1871

He had a rocking horse named Racer.

On the front porch of his family's dogtrot cabin deep in the Piney Woods, he and Racer would ride and ride and ride. He wore his prized red cowboy boots emblazoned with a white Lone Star, a gift from his mama and papa for his fifth birthday two months ago. His brothers Alex and Sam had tanned the leather of the vest he wore, and his sister, Sarah, sewed it up in just his size. Nana Grey had sniffled a little when she gave him his white felt hat with its bright red string tie, but Nana cried at everything so that didn't much bother him. The tin sheriff's badge pinned to his vest was supposed to have been a present from Baby Joe—but he knew it really came from his parents. Baby Joe couldn't actually buy presents because he was only two.

He had a pistol, too. It was the prettiest thing. Papa had carved it out of a single hunk of oak and he'd stained it a golden brown and burned an *L* for Logan on the grip. It might be made all of wood, but in his hands it shot deadeye straight.

Today he and Racer followed a dusty trail chasing outlaws who had just robbed a stagecoach of its strongbox. Faster and faster he rode. "We're gaining on them, Racer. Keep going. We're gaining on them!"

The front door opened and Sarah stepped outside. She wore a traveling dress because the family was going to Louisiana to attend a wedding. She looked real pretty, but he didn't say so out loud. He was mad at her. At breakfast this morning, Papa had agreed it was time to get Sarah her very own pony.

"So where are you going, cowboy?"

He snarled at her. "Black Shadow Canyon. And there ain't no girls allowed."

"Oh, really?"

"Yeah. It's where the Apache live and outlaws go to hide."

"I see." Her lips twitched. "Hmm...that sounds like a scary place. Guess I'm glad I'm not allowed. So why are you going to Black Shadow Canyon? Are you an outlaw?"

"No, dummy." He stopped rocking long enough to point to his hat. "I have a white hat. I'm a lawman going to catch the villains and make 'em pay for their evil deeds."

His mother's voice sounded from the kitchen window. "You use that ugly word toward your sister again and you won't be able to sit down long enough to ride Racer. You'll have to wait until tomorrow to go kill villains, son. It's time to come in and change your clothes. Papa and the boys are almost through patching the fence, so we'll be leaving soon."

"Aw, Ma—"

"Don't 'Aw, Ma' me, young man. Rein in Racer right now."

"Yes'um."

Half an hour later, the entire family loaded up in the wagon and rode out. The road was muddy from all the rain they'd had in the past couple of days and the going slow. Papa drove the wagon with Nana sitting next to him. Sarah and Mama occupied the seats behind Papa with Mama holding the baby in her lap. His brothers sat in back with him playing cards. Mama, Nana and Sarah fretted on about getting to town in time enough to repair their hair before the wedding.

He couldn't see how it was broken, but he didn't care enough to ask because he was busy watching the trees for trouble. There were outlaws out there—he could tell. He had that black and dark and heavy feeling that let him know ahead of time that something bad was about to happen. He'd felt it right before his grandfather died. He'd felt it when Alex broke his leg. Every time he tried to tell his parents about it, but they never believed him—not even after the bad things happened. Papa called it coincidence and ruffled his hair.

So instead of trying to warn them, he pulled his pistol out of his pocket and watched the trees hard. It was silly to hold the pistol since it was really a toy, but having a gun in his hand made him feel better.

He was scared.

Time passed. The darkness grew stronger. Someone or something was out there. He knew it.

Finally, he had to try. "Papa? Something is wrong. I think you'd better stop."

"You sick, boy?" his father asked as his mother turned a worried look in his direction.

"Don't be throwing up on me, squirt," Sam said.

"I'm not sick. But I'm having my feeling..."

His mother's expression eased. "Oh, sweetheart. I know we've been traveling a long time, and you need to get down and run around, but we're running late. We don't have time to stop. Hear that thunder in the distance? We need to beat the storm to town." Addressing the other boys, she added, "Y'all keep your little brother occupied."

"But that's not it, Mama. I really do know that something bad is gonna happen."

No one listened and the feeling grew and grew and grew. His chest hurt and he wanted to cry and he had to blink away tears so that he could watch the trees for the outlaws. Maybe if he saw them soon enough, Papa would be able to shoot them first. Papa was a really, really good shot.

He stared at the forest, his gaze shifting from side to side to side. So intent was he on seeing the threat emerge from the trees that he didn't spot the one rising from beneath.

It happened in an instant. One minute the wagon was fording a shallow offshoot of Brushy Creek, and the next it was floating. Being swept away.

"Flash flood," called his father above the awful, horrible sound of rushing water. "Hang on, everyone. Hang on!"

The wagon spun, then began to tip. The women screamed.

He held his wooden pistol in a death grip and stood up tall in the back of the wagon. "I tried to tell you, Daddy. I tried to tell you."

He wet his pants right before he went flying. Something snagged his shirt. "Hold on, son," his father called.

He watched his father jump toward him into the rushing water, then something hit his head. After that, he knew no more.

Bodies were still being recovered from the Sabine River a week after the horrific flash flood that had decimated parts of East Texas. No one knew exactly how many people had lost their lives in the event, though estimates numbered in the dozens.

Ten days following the flood, a traveler spied a bruised and bedraggled boy sitting on a fallen log, constantly rocking back and forth, a wooden pistol clutched in his hand.

Try as he might, the traveler couldn't get the boy to speak more than two words. "Run, Racer, run. Run, Racer, run."

Aware of recent events in the region and mindful of the state of the boy's clothing, he surmised the youngster had survived the flood. In a hurry to continue his travels, but unwilling to leave the boy all alone in the middle of the woods, the man lifted him onto his horse and took him with him. They traveled for two days before reaching the home of old friends, the Jennings's, who had recently decided to open their home to orphans. Not once in all that time had he been able to coax a word out of the boy.

The traveler explained to his friends how he'd found the boy and his suspicions regarding the flood. Mrs. Jennings recognized emotional trauma when she saw it, and she promised her old friend that the boy would find a safe haven with them until his identity, and hopefully some family, could be discovered.

Her husband said, "That's a fine-looking pistol you have there, son. What's that on the grip?"

Without turning loose of it, the boy showed him. "Hmm, an *L*. Does your name begin with an *L*?"

When the boy didn't respond, Mrs. Jennings smiled kindly and placed a gentle hand on his shoulder. "He's alive. He's relatively uninjured. He's here safe and sound with people who are ready to care for him, ready to love him. I think that *L* might just stand for Lucky."

Her husband nodded. "Lucky. I like it. C'mon, Lucky, let's go raid my Nellie's cookie jar, shall we?"

Three months passed and though he never spoke, Lucky made friends with the other boys who'd come to live with Reverend and Nellie Jennings. One Saturday morning as Nellie made pie crusts, Lucky walked into her kitchen and said, "I had a rocking horse named Racer."

CHAPTER ONE

Fort Worth, Texas, Twenty-eight years later

"They say he's lucky," whispered a barrel-bellied man. "The luckiest man in Texas."

"If he's so lucky then how come he's caught in the middle of a bank robbery?" questioned a fellow sporting a red handlebar mustache.

"Because he's here and he can save us and probably earn a big reward for it. That's why!"

Logan Grey ignored the nervous murmurs and frightened whispers circulating behind him and concentrated on the matter at hand. Three gunmen. Seven potential hostages.

And he'd left his six-gun at the gunsmith's for repair.

Lucky, hell.

It was the same old story. Although he'd been known as Lucky Logan Grey for damn near his whole life, Logan knew that the only luck he truly possessed was bad luck. The trick to keeping it from rearing its ugly head was to keep folks thinking the opposite—that he *was* the luckiest man in Texas.

What a crock. Take this incident today. How lucky was it that he'd decided to put business before pleasure this morning? Choosing to look up the bank president and discuss his investment in a promising

East Texas oil field before dropping by Ella Jameson's Sporting House to end his dry spell had put him in the middle of this mess. He'd been three weeks without a woman, and the lack of relief was making him twitchy. He could be heating up the sheets with Ella right now, but no. Logan had no sooner walked through the bank's front door when he sensed trouble. It was a talent of his, a gift that came in handy for a man chock-full of bad luck, so he paid close attention to it. This time, however, he'd been a few steps slow. He'd just turned around to exit the bank when all hell broke loose in the lobby.

Five minutes ago, three men stalked into the bank brandishing guns and shouting demands. They'd shot the security guard dead, then forced the head teller to lock the doors and display the lunch notice. After herding everyone but the head teller into a group on the left side of the room, they'd handed the banker a bag and told him to fill it with cash from the teller windows.

"Hurry up!" demanded the outlaw leader, a lanky, bearded fellow missing his front teeth. He vaguely reminded Logan of Colorado Clem, a mean-assed bastard who'd died a few years back after being shot in a dispute over a faro game. Logan wondered if Clem had a brother.

"You need to move faster, banker," warned the outlaw. "My trigger finger's gettin' itchy."

Behind the teller's cage, the manager stuffed money into a bag with shaking hands as a bead of sweat dribbled down his temple. The scent of blood tainted the air, and to Logan's right, a child began to cry.

Within moments, the cries rose to wails and the mother's attempts to soothe her child grew frantic when another gunman took a threatening step toward her, saying, "Shut him up or I'll do it for you."

Logan took advantage of the distraction to scan the room in search of a weapon, any weapon. The level of tension inside the bank had escalated. Things were fixin' to turn ugly. His gaze settled on a brass paperweight shaped like an eagle sitting atop a desk about five strides away. A good throw could take out one of the gunmen. Wasn't enough, though.

Dammit, he needed his gun.

He'd have to take a weapon away from one of the bandits. Which one? Not ol' Gap Tooth, the leader. One of the others. Logan's gaze shifted between the other two thieves. He'd take the one by the door. He looked to be the most fidgety, probably the one who'd lose control and start shooting first.

"Here you are, sir," said the trembling head teller as he attempted to hand over the money bag.

"That ain't all," scoffed Gap Tooth. He leveled his gun at the banker's head. "Open the safe."

"But I don't know the combination! Only the president knows it, and he's at the rotary club meeting this morning." See, that proved Logan's point. He'd made the stop here for nothing. *Lucky my ass.*

The outlaw boss grabbed the manager by the necktie and said, "I reckon you'd better figure it out, then, huh?"

Logan sidled toward the twitchy outlaw. Judging by the look in the leader's eyes, Logan knew he needed to act fast. He took another surreptitious step toward his prey when a woman's voice broke the nervous silence saying, "Oh, darling, I'm so afraid!"

Then a female rushed toward him and burrowed her face against his chest.

Logan's arms reflexively wrapped around her and despite his surprise, he registered a number of facts in an instant. She was tall for a woman and not too young, maybe a couple years or so younger than he. Her breasts were full and soft. She smelled like lavender. Her hair was the color of a West Texas sunset, gold streaked with strands of red that glistened even in the muted light of the bank.

And her hands were fiddling with his belt.

In another reflexive reaction, his body stirred. Well, it *had* been three weeks.

Then something cold pressed the skin of his belly. Metal. Rounded. A gun barrel.

Well now. Logan stifled a smile. Things were looking up. Playing along, he replied, "Don't be afraid, my love. I'll protect you."

She nodded against his chest, then stepped back, leaving a gun stuck in the waist of his britches and concealed with the tail of his shirt, which she'd pulled free. He had a quick glimpse of violet eyes filled with courage and encouragement before trouble erupted back by the safe.

"That's all?" shouted Gap Tooth. "How can a damned bank have a damned near empty safe? What, is this place run by a bunch of outlaws?"

He took aim at the round globe of a lamp and pulled the trigger. Glass shattered. The child's screams resumed, and this time a couple of adults hollered along with him. "Shut up!" cried Gap Tooth. "Shut your trap or I'm gonna kill somebody."

Seeing the villain's gaze fix upon the crying child, Logan stepped forward and said the first thing that popped into his brain. "There's another safe."

Gap Tooth turned away from the child and pinned his black stare on Logan. "What?"

His mind raced as he concocted on the fly. He needed to separate the killer from that child, and fast. "It's hidden, but I know where it is."

"Who the hell are you?"

"A friend of Dair MacRae. I trust you've heard of the Bad Luck Treasure?"

Now he had the outlaw's undivided attention. The villain lowered his gun and took a step toward Logan. "All them jewels that was written up in the newspapers?"

"Jewels and gold, too. A fortune ten times over and it's right here in Haltom Bank. You let these people go and I'll show you where it is."

Avarice shone in the villainous trio's faces. Fidgety said, "I've heard of that Bad Luck Treasure. Didn't know it's still in Fort Worth."

It's not. Well, not the majority of it, anyway. Logan himself had helped transport a large chunk of it to more secure institutions in the East.

Skepticism dimmed the third gunman's expression. "How do we know that you're telling the truth?"

Logan tugged the gold medallion he wore around his neck over his head, then tossed it toward the leader, saying, "I helped my friends find the treasure, so they had this made for me in thanks."

The outlaw caught the gleaming medallion in a grimy hand. "Well damn my eyes. Look at those stones." Logan braced his hands on his hips, keeping the gun handy. "There are lots more of those within relatively easy reach, but you'll never find them on your own." Gap Tooth studied him with suspicion. "If you're that MacRae fella's friend, why would you up and volunteer to give away their treasure?"

Logan glanced at his fellow hostages on either side, his stare briefly meeting the violet-eyed woman's, before he said, "I'm offering to trade their treasure for the safety of these good people. My friends would never value money over lives."

The outlaw leader glanced at his partners. The third villain said, "You can't let anyone go, boss. We're all right so far because nobody outside has noticed there's trouble. The minute folks leave this building that'll change. The law will surround us."

"Which makes the secret tunnel leading away from the treasure vault all the more valuable," Logan observed, the lie spilling easily from his tongue.

"Tunnel?" Gap Tooth asked. "What tunnel?"

"The one Trace McBride had built to help protect the Bad Luck Treasure. He's an architect, you know. The man loves tunnels and secret passages. His home, Willow Hill, is full of them."

"I don't believe him," declared the third gunman. "A tunnel? That's a crazy thing to believe."

"I believe it." Fidgety scratched his chin. "I've heard talk about McBride. He's supposed to be pretty smart. A smart man would do everything possible to protect the Bad Luck Treasure. Wouldn't you think?"

After a moment's pause for deliberation, he added, "I say we do it. The Bad Luck Treasure would make us all rich for life." Obviously unconvinced, Gap Tooth scratched below his left ear. Then abruptly, he aimed his gun at a bystander. "Do you know about a tunnel?"

The man stuttered. "Um...no. Not...um...here." Then, perhaps seeing his chance of escape pass by, he added, "I do know that McBride likes to build secrets into his designs. His children played with mine, and I know his house has secret staircases and rooms. It makes sense to me that he'd build something secret to help protect his assets."

"Huh." Gap Tooth shifted his aim back toward Logan. "All right...what's your name?"

"Grey. Logan Grey."

"Wait a minute. I know you." The outlaw's eyes narrowed. "You're that range detective who works for the Waggoner Ranch out of Wichita Falls. The one they call Lucky. You kilt Two Dog Redmond. He owed me fifty dollars when he died, so I never got it."

Well, hell. His reputation struck again. "I'll make sure you get an extra emerald from the Treasure to make up for it."

Beady eyes narrowed even farther. "What sort of trick are you trying to pull? You're a range detective! A killer with a badge. This is a trap."

"No, it's not," Logan said with a shake of his head. That Killer-With-A-Badge label chapped his ass. He worked as a private lawman in places and at times where there weren't enough public badges to go around. Yeah, he'd killed his share of men, but only when arresting them wasn't an option. "I don't work for the Waggoner Ranch anymore. I'm just trying to get myself and these other folk out of here alive. I'm not on the job, mister. I have no legal authority. Frankly, it's no skin off my nose if you rob this bank, but I don't like seeing people hurt unnecessarily. Let these folks go, and I'll take you to the treasure."

The outlaw gave the medallion in his hand another long look. His boot tapped against the bank's green marble floor. "All right. Here's how we're gonna do it. First, you show me the escape route, then I'll let these good folk go."

Hmm. Not exactly what Logan had been hoping for, but at least it gave him a chance. Motioning toward the offices at the back of the building, he said, "It's this way."

"Wait," barked Gap Tooth. "You, there." He motioned with his gun toward the beauty who'd slipped Logan the weapon. "Pretty lady. C'mere."

"No, thank you," she politely said, smoothing her plain black traveling skirt.

The outlaw made a growling sound, then took three steps forward and grabbed her arm. He jerked her to him and put his gun to her head. He turned an evil smile toward Logan. "Make one wrong move and your lady pays."

Logan didn't doubt for a minute that ol' Gap Tooth meant what he said.

His gaze swept over the female. Look at her with her chin lifted, her eyes flashing. Full of bravado. Couldn't help but admire a woman like that. "I won't make any wrong moves," he assured the outlaw.

Every move he made would be exactly right. "Boys? Y'all keep everyone quiet here until I get back," Gap Tooth said to his cohorts. Then nodding toward Logan, he added, "Go on, then. Show me the tunnel."

As Logan walked toward the back of the bank, he mentally reviewed what he'd seen during his brief visit earlier. It was a damn shame this wasn't the bank where Dair and his wife located the Bad Luck Treasure. Trace McBride actually had constructed a hidden exit from the vault in the First National Bank of Fort Worth where a portion of the treasure remained. Logan could sure use a place like that at the moment to help trap this killer. Nevertheless, he was prepared to work with what he had.

Gap Tooth and the woman followed Logan out of the lobby into the office hallway. He'd take them to the president's office. On a previous visit he'd noted a large vent cover on the far interior wall. Unless a better idea occurred to him in the next thirty seconds, he'd try to lure Gap Tooth there and tell him it was the tunnel entrance. If he could get the outlaw to bend down, he could surprise him with an elbow to the chin followed by a gun to the gut. Once he had control of the situation, he'd force the bandit to—

Whoof. Thunk. While Logan turned toward the sound, Gap Tooth dropped to the floor like a stone. "What the—"

"If I'd known you'd be so slow to save us I'd have kept the gun myself," the violet-eyed virago hissed as she grabbed the weapon from Gap Tooth's hand.

Logan gawked at the gunman now writhing on the floor in pain. "What the hell did you do to him?"

"He loosened his hold on me, so I pulled away and kicked him in the private parts."

Logan braced his hands on his hips and grinned. On the floor, Gap Tooth let out a loud groan. She exhaled a snippy sigh, grabbed the handkerchief from Logan's jacket pocket, then knelt down and shoved it into the gunman's mouth to muffle the noise. Color stained her cheeks and frustration filled her eyes as she glared up at him. "Now, are you going to help me or do I have to do this alone?"

She was magnificent when in a snit. And she wasn't wearing a wedding ring. How handy was that? "What's your plan?"

"I don't have a plan. I thought you would develop one. You have much more experience at this sort of thing than I."

Logan used line cut from nearby window drapes to bind the would-be robber and secure the gag. "You know who I am?"

"Oh, yes."

"Have we met before?"

At that, she stared at him, her mouth slightly agape. Logan got the impression that for a moment, she considered pointing the villain's gun at him. Instead, she drew herself up, squared her shoulders and said, "Let's save the hostages now, shall we?"

"Sure." Logan nodded, frowning at the soiled spot on her stylish white blouse from the gunman's grimy hand. Seeing it made Logan want to follow her lead and give ol' Gap Tooth another kick in the balls. "That sounds like a fine plan, missy."

"Missy," she muttered.

A thought occurred to Logan that improved his mood. Maybe if he played his cards right, he wouldn't need to visit Ella's place after all. He could be charming when he wanted, and the woman had demonstrated that she knew her way around a belt buckle. Why, they could pass a right fine afternoon. Giving her a wink, he suggested, "After we are done with the rescuing, why don't you join me for lunch?"

A series of emotions flashed across her face—shock, surprise, consideration, then fury. "No, thank you."

Huh. Logan's brows arched in surprise. That put him in his place, didn't it? But he didn't understand the fury one bit. What was he missing here?

He wanted to find out. This gal lit his wick. Well, the sooner he took care of business here, the sooner he could see about getting his answers, so Logan turned his attention to matters at hand. Stepping into the bank president's office, he spied a walking stick with a metal handle. Testing its weight and strength, he nodded. It would do nicely as a weapon. Next, he made a quick phone call to Sheriff Luke Prescott's office and reported the robbery in progress. With the doors locked the lawmen couldn't storm the building, but they'd be waiting when access was provided.

Debating just how best to make that happen, he returned to where the woman waited with Gap Tooth in the hallway, the outlaw's gun in one hand, his medallion in the other. He nodded toward the gun. "Do you know how to use that?"

"I'm quite proficient."

"Have you ever shot a man before?"

"Only in my dreams, Logan Grey. Only in my dreams." The smile she wore when she said it made the hair on the back of Logan's neck stand up. She continued, "I am prepared, however, to shoot one of those criminals if necessary."

He didn't doubt it one bit. "Good. It's my hope it won't come to that. With any luck at all, your other weapon will do the trick."

"My other weapon?" she asked, following him back down the hallway toward the lobby.

"What weapon?"

"Your scream. When I give the word, I want you to scream as loud as you can and keep screaming until I tell you to stop. We're going to try to lure one of them in here."

At the wall separating the bank offices from the lobby, Logan peered cautiously around the door. Fidgety stood at the teller's counter. The third man watched the hostages from beside the front entrance. "Are you ready...what's your name?"

"I'm ready," she replied, ignoring his question. "Go."

She drew a deep breath, then let out a loud, long, shrill scream.

Though it was difficult to do, Logan tried to block out the sound of her voice and listen for the outlaw's approach. He raised the cane like a baseball bat ready to swing and hoped Fidgety would be the one to investigate. He sensed the third man would be less inclined to use his gun.

From the bank lobby, he heard the little kid join in the hollering. *No, kid. Hush up.* Beside him, the woman continued wailing on.

Time seemed to pass in slow motion. Logan saw a boot and he started his swing. The cane's metal handle caught the bandit at his temple, the blow sending him staggering. As Logan followed up by kicking the gunman's—the third gunman, not Fidgety's—legs out from under him, he heard a gunshot and new screams from the lobby.

"Hurry!" urged Violet Eyes when she darted past him as the gunman crashed to the floor. His gun went skidding from his grip and Logan grabbed for it. He heard the woman let out a yell that made her previous screams sound like whispers.

It was a battle cry, nothing less, and the sound of it caused his heart to lodge in his throat. The gunman attempted to rise, and Logan hesitated long enough to place one hard kick to the man's head and knock him into unconsciousness before dashing after the woman.

He reached the lobby just in time to see her launch herself at Fidgety at the same time his gun exploded. The bullet missed her and ricocheted off a center post, then slammed into the plaster wall.

Fidgety's yell was abruptly cut off mid-screech.

She'd knocked him down, grabbed him by the ears and beat his head against the floor until he passed out.

Hell, she hadn't needed backup.

Logan halted and observed the woman with blatant admiration as she rolled off the downed outlaw and climbed to her feet, then calmly brushed the dust from her skirt. What a fascinating female.

He stepped forward to help her—not that she needed help—as the head teller unlocked the doors and Luke Prescott and a half dozen lawmen rushed inside. Spying him, Luke called, "Lucky! You all right?"

"I'm fine."

"What happened here?"

Logan gave his friend a brief rundown of events, then showed him where to find Gap Tooth and the third gunman. "She was amazing, I'm telling you," he told Luke as he helped Gap Tooth to his feet. "Downright amazing."

"Who is she?"

"I don't know. I didn't get her name in the middle of things, but I aim to find out now."

But when he returned to the bank lobby and scanned the area, she was nowhere to be found. Logan strode outside and looked both up the street and down. Nothing. No violet-eyed Valkyrie in a simple skirt and blouse. She'd disappeared on him.

And she'd taken his medallion with her.

Well now, wasn't that just his luck?

CHAPTER TWO

CAROLINE TUCKED A STRAY STRAND OF HAIR BACK BEHIND HER EAR as she thanked the waitress who led her to an out-of-the-way booth in the Bluebonnet Grill. After this morning's contretemps she didn't want to see Logan Grey again until she was ready. "Mrs. Wilhemina Peters will be joining me shortly. Do you know her?"

The waitress almost hid a wince. "Everyone in town knows Mrs. Peters. I hope you, um, enjoy your afternoon tea."

Caroline intended to do just that. She and Wilhemina Peters shared a passion. It wasn't gossip; that was Mrs. Peters's milieu. No, she and Wilhemina were both newspaperwomen, two of very few in this great state of Texas. Though the Artesia *Standard* didn't have nearly the distribution or prestige of the Fort Worth *Daily Democrat*, Caroline had been able to use that connection to make this most important appointment. She intended to mine Fort Worth's self-acknowledged gossip queen for any and all information she possessed about Logan Grey. After all, knowledge was power, and Caroline needed all the help she could get in these circumstances.

"May I bring you something to drink while you wait for Mrs. Peters?" the waitress asked. "She is invariably late."

Caroline asked for tea, though she would have liked to order whiskey. It had been quite a day. Quite a week. For that matter, the entire year had been a trial.

On January first, she would never have guessed that in a few short months, she'd be on her way to beg the help of the dirty-dog scoundrel Logan Grey. But then, on New Year's Day, she hadn't known of the horrible events about to beset her family and leave her in these dire straits.

But here she was in April, in Fort Worth, Logan Grey's adopted hometown, filled with fear and willing to do anything—*anything*—in order to protect those she loved.

She had almost had heart palpitations when she saw him sauntering down the city street this morning as she walked from the train station to her hotel within minutes of her arrival in town. Her first inclination had been to duck into the General Store and hide. She hadn't been at all prepared to confront him at that point.

Still, she couldn't pass up the opportunity to observe him, so she'd followed him into the bank, taking care that he not see her. Then when circumstances required she act, she'd expected her plans to unravel.

But the low-down slimy toad hadn't recognized her. He'd looked right at her, spoken with her—held her in his arms!—and he hadn't known her from Adam. Shaken by that as much as the violence of the robbery, she'd slipped away from the bank at first opportunity, checked into her hotel and stewed for a good twenty minutes. Okay, maybe forty. All right, an hour.

The man truly got her goat. She wanted nothing more than to look him in those flirty green eyes and tell him what a lying, rotten, no-good, low-life, snake-breath, dirt-eating, overstuffed, ignorant, heartless, bug-eyed, stiff-legged, spotty-lipped, worm-headed dog he was. But doing so would jeopardize her mission and she simply couldn't allow that.

Dang it.

So she'd done physical exercises in her room until she'd calmed down, then she'd invited Mrs. Peters to tea.

Now she fiddled with her napkin and mentally reviewed the collection of half-truths, prevarications and flat-out lies she'd prepared for this meeting and the one she intended to have later tonight. Under other circumstances, the prospect of being so deceitful would prey upon her conscience. Her foster father, Ben, used to tell her she was too honest for her own good. Well, not today. Today she'd lie, cheat, steal— whatever it took to accomplish her purpose. She'd already lost one family member. Be hanged if she'd lose another.

The waitress walked by carrying a piece of pie and suddenly in her mind's eye Caroline was back in Ben and Suzanne Whitaker's kitchen on a Sunday afternoon not long after Ben had hired her to help his wife during her recovery from a buggy accident. Caroline was baking a peach pie for Sunday dinner. Suzanne, bruised and weak as a kitten, sat at the table drinking tea and telling her the story of her Past.

"I'm not proud of who I was, Caroline. I have regrets. Lots of them. No one forced me to ride with the Sunshine Gang. No one handed me a gun and said now go rob that train, then hightail it back to Black Shadow Canyon to hide. I did it for the excitement, for the money, and frankly because when I was your age I had a wild streak I simply couldn't tame. But I grew up and I recognized the wickedness of my ways, and ever since then I've made a real effort to make amends."

Suzanne smiled wistfully, sipped her tea and added, "Yet, for Ben, I'd do it all again. I guess that means I'm still not a good person, Caroline. Because I love him that much."

"Well, I love him that much, too," Caroline murmured, carefully aligning her silverware. Besides, she wasn't out to rob a train or steal a person's life savings. She intended to tell a lie that would save a life she valued. It was true that the lie she intended to tell wasn't nice, but neither was the man she intended to lie to. Logan Grey owed her. She'd simply come to collect.

"Get out of the way, you young whippersnapper," came a caustic voice from the front of the restaurant. "You should have more respect for an elderly lady who uses a cane."

"Uses it to hit people with," muttered the man in the booth behind Caroline.

With a prodigious bosom leading the way, Wilhemina Peters sailed through the restaurant toward Caroline's table. A stylish hat crowned silver hair and complemented her smart spring gown in shades of lavender and green. She did, indeed, carry a cane, an ivory-handled affair, and she made Caroline feel downright dowdy as she stood to greet her.

They exchanged pleasantries and small talk as they waited for their orders to be served. Then, her blue eyes shrewd and curious, Mrs. Peters cut to business. "So, Mrs. Whitaker," she said, using the false name Caroline had given when she telephoned earlier. "What made you decide to write an expose about Lucky Logan Grey?"

Caroline licked her lips, then launched into her story. "Logan Grey has become quite the folk hero in West Texas since he brought the Burrows Gang to justice. And yet, rumors persist that he is not the white knight his reputation allows. I think the Artesia *Standard's* readers will be interested to learn the truth."

"He is an interesting subject, that's true." Mrs. Peters pursed her lips and considered Caroline. "I'm curious. Do you intend to publish such a meaty piece under your own byline? Will your newspaper allow it?"

"My father owns and edits the *Standard*," Caroline replied. "He publishes my articles under my name."

"Indeed!" Mrs. Peters's eyes gleamed with approval. "You know, in the earliest days when I began my Talk about Town' column, I was forced to use a pen name, but times have changed. Women have more opportunity now than they did thirty years ago."

"Especially when the woman works with a man like my father," Caroline told her with a smile. "I can't tell you how many times I've heard him say that women aren't equal to men—they're usually superior."

Caroline had a vivid memory of Ben with his legs propped up on his desk, his weathered, wrinkled face alight with laughter as he read the editorial she'd written about the sanctimonious snobbery of a local church-women's group who refused a charitable donation of much-needed school supplies because the donors were women who worked upstairs at Artesia Saloon. *"You've a wicked pen, sunshine,"* he'd said. *"This is gonna ruffle plenty of feathers. Think I'll get me a sarsaparilla and sit on the front porch and watch the show."*

"Your father sounds like a man I would like," Mrs. Peters said.

"I love him madly. He is a forward-thinking, forward-looking man."

The moment the words left her mouth, Caroline knew they were no longer true. Ben Whitaker had quit looking forward in January when his beloved Suzanne died. He went crazy with grief. Nowadays, he only looked behind, and that way of looking was going to get him killed if she didn't do something to stop it.

Mrs. Peters nibbled at a lemon-drop cookie, then said, "Well, then. Yes, I'll be happy to help you. What would you like to know about Lucky Logan Grey?"

Caroline dragged her thoughts back to the business at hand. What did she want to know about Logan? Anything. Everything. The more the better. If she continued on the course she'd plotted, she'd be taking the biggest risk of her life. The more information she had about the man, the better.

Caroline smoothed the napkin in her lap. "I've done quite a bit of research on his professional successes. I'm curious about Mr. Grey's personal life."

Wilhemina Peters sniffed with disdain. "You want the dirt, the gossip." Then, a wicked gleam entered her eyes and she studied her fingernails. "That's why you came to me, of course."

Caroline simply smiled.

Leaning forward, Mrs. Peters lowered her voice. "Half the women in town have an infatuation for the man. Logan Grey is quite an intriguing fellow."

Of course he is. Caroline added a spoonful of sugar to her tea since it had taken on a bit of a sour taste.

"He is darkly handsome with a lean, muscular build that catches the eye of even a mature woman such as myself. He has a down-home style to him that doesn't hide his keen intelligence, and a ready wit that appeals to ladies and gentlemen alike. Since you're a married lady, I'll share this tidbit." She dropped her voice even lower. "From what I hear, the soiled doves find him appealing, too. He is said to have quite a sensual appetite and enormous stamina."

Definitely too much lemon in this tea, Caroline decided as her mouth puckered.

"The man reminds me of Trace McBride, back in the day. Do you know the McBrides? They've made regular appearances in print for years—oftentimes in my own column. They're one of the leading families in town today but years ago, Trace McBride was a scoundrel and a scapegrace. He owned a saloon in Hell's Half Acre and left his three little girls to run wild about town. Jenny Fortune saved that family by marrying Trace and taking those Menaces under her wing. You might have read about the Bad Luck Brides? That's what folks are calling the McBride Menaces now since they're all grown-up, married and making families of their own. In fact, one of the girls' husbands, Dair MacRae, is an old, dear friend of Logan Grey's. He's part of their circle of friends."

Caroline did know of the McBrides. The discovery of their family treasure had garnered quite a lot of newsprint, and since Logan Grey had been part of the event, Caroline had made it her business to find out everything she could about Fort Worth's leading family. "I've been a fan of your column for years, Mrs. Peters, so yes, I'm quite familiar with the McBride family. And of course, the Bad Luck Treasure made newspapers all across the state."

"The Bad Luck Treasure," Mrs. Peters repeated, clicking her tongue. "It's an amazing story...as is today's attempted bank robbery. Wasn't that something? Scuttlebutt says some mystery woman assisted Logan." The older woman bent her head to one side and studied Caroline. "Would you happen to know anything about that, dear?"

"No," she denied. The last thing she wanted was to shine the spotlight on herself, so she quickly forged ahead. "So, Mr. Grey is welcome in the parlors of Fort Worth's leading families because of his friendship with the McBride family?"

"That's how it started, but he's made his own place. Of course, his occupation as a range detective takes him away from town more often than he is here. That only adds to his mystique. You do realize that a range detective is little more than a hired gun with legal authority. He has all the wicked appeal of an outlaw, but with a badge to make it acceptable. Sets the young ladies in town all atwitter, though the fact he doesn't dabble there preserves his welcome by their fathers."

Caroline dumped another spoonful of sugar in her cup, then stirred and sipped her tea. The fact that he didn't dabble with daughters showed both self-preservation and intelligence—qualities she needed the man to have. She should be happy.

Nothing about Logan Grey made her happy.

After choosing another selection from the cookie tray the waitress offered, Mrs. Peters observed, "Yet, for all his popularity, Lucky Logan Grey keeps himself apart. There is a darkness about him that goes beyond his good looks. I happened to overhear the McBride girls speculating about him not long ago. They seem to think that something happened down in Mexico a few years back that continues to haunt him, but no one knows for sure. One thing they all agreed on was that he was a restless soul. They despair that he'll ever settle down and marry."

Caroline stifled a snort at that last bit, then turned her attention to the bit of news. "Mexico, hmm? That's interesting. I haven't run across that piece of information in my research."

"Apparently, he refuses to talk about it. Such an intriguing man." Mrs. Peters sipped her tea, then added, "I once overheard a society woman at a party say that Logan Grey is like a special dessert that makes only seasonal appearances on the menu. When it's available, a lady wants to indulge."

Caroline refrained from sneering. Barely. "So he is fickle? Disloyal?"

"Oh, no. He's fiercely loyal to his friends. He doesn't make promises he doesn't keep."

At that, Caroline couldn't stop the unladylike snort. Mrs. Peters rattled on through two more cups of tea, three cookies and two small slices of cake. She provided a gold mine of information which Caroline could draw upon when she approached Logan later that evening. When Mrs. Peters finally wound down, she asked a pertinent question of her own. "I trust you intend to interview Mr. Grey yourself before you write your story?"

"Yes. I hope to speak with him this evening, in fact." By then, surely she'd have worked up the guts to do so. "I understand he keeps a room at the Blackstone Hotel and takes his meals here in this restaurant when he is in town. I intend to join him for dinner."

"Then you'll need to go to Willow Hill," Mrs. Peters informed her.

"The Bad Luck Brides are hosting an impromptu dinner party there this evening in honor of Grey's heroics today at the bank."

Caroline's stomach sank. She hadn't anticipated that.

"The guest list is small—the McBride girls and their husbands, along with two of Grey's close friends, Holt Driscoll and Cade Hollister."

"Really," Caroline murmured, her thoughts spinning at the news.

"I found out because Kat Kimball came by the newspaper looking for the mystery woman so they could invite her to join them." The older woman dabbed her lips with her napkin. "My oh my. Look at the time. I must run. Thank you so much for the invitation, Mrs. Whitaker. I enjoyed our little visit tremendously."

Caroline pulled her distracted thoughts together. "Why, time certainly did fly. Thank you for joining me, Mrs. Peters. Your information has been a great help. I'll make certain you receive a copy of my expose."

"Lovely. I'll look forward to it." Then the older woman stood, gathered up her cane and handbag, and added, "Really, my dear. You should join them, you know. You won't get a better opportunity to gather information for your article. And besides, you have been invited. Am I correct?"

Caroline winced. Either Mrs. Peters was more astute than she had figured, or she herself couldn't prevaricate worth beans. Likely it was a combination of the two. *I have to do better than that.* "Yes, ma'am," she said with a sigh. "Apparently I have."

After Mrs. Peters left the restaurant, Caroline broke down and ordered a glass of liquid courage. She had her answers. Nothing she'd learned today either at the bank or from the newspaperwoman deterred her from her path. She didn't know whether that made her happy or sad.

"So, what in Sam Hill do I do now?" she murmured as she sipped her whiskey. Did she ambush him at the bottom of the hill after dinner? Did she wait until tomorrow and waste another day? Or did she forget this whole idea entirely and abandon the father of her heart to his fate?

Not hardly.

She would confront Logan Grey at the dinner party. He would have a harder time saying no if she did it in front of his friends, though the idea of it made her grimace. Facing the yellow-dog scoundrel was hard enough, but lying to him about something so important in front of perfect strangers? Could she do it? She hadn't fooled Mrs. Peters. What made her think she could fool people as clever as the McBrides were purported to be?

She had no other choice. Just think about Ben, about how he took her in and gave her a home and a family. Think about how much he loved her and about how much he needed her right now.

Caroline closed her eyes and recalled the day she had met Ben Whitaker. She'd had seventy-five cents in her pocket, no roof over her head, no food in her belly. After a full day of searching, she'd discovered there were only two jobs to be had in town—nursing Suzanne during her recovery or whoring upstairs at the Artesia Saloon.

"I don't know that you could do the job," Ben had said, his sharp gaze sweeping over her from head to toe when she inquired about the position in his household. *"My Suz is a substantial woman. You look as if a gust of wind could blow you down. There's another woman who—"*

"I'm stronger than I look, Mr. Whitaker," she interrupted. *"And there is no one in Texas who will take better care of your wife. I give you my word."*

He rubbed his hand along his jawline, his bushy salt-and-pepper brows lowered in a speculative frown. *"You're desperate, aren't you, girl?"*

"Yes, sir, that I am."

"Desperate then, and desperate now," Caroline murmured into her glass. Back then, she'd had another option. She could have whored herself.

Today, she had but one option. Lucky Logan Grey. "Heaven help me." Caroline finished her drink, then left the restaurant.

Four hours later, she stared up a hill toward the McBride family mansion, Willow Hill, her stomach churning with nerves. She'd second-guessed herself and her decisions all afternoon, but in the end, she didn't know a better way to achieve her goal.

"Oh for heaven's sake, Caroline. Just summon some grit and do it."

She started up the hill.

Upon reaching the house, she strolled up the front walk and onto the porch. There she smoothed the skirt of her favorite yellow dress—eerily similar to the one she'd worn that black day fifteen years ago—then patted the medallion she'd hung around her neck for safekeeping. Approaching the door, she raised her hand to the brass knocker just as a burst of laughter exploded from inside the house. Her nerve failed and she stepped away from the door. Her heart pounded like a drum.

Did she really want to do this? It would change everything. Life would never be the same if she went through with this.

Dear Lord, help her.

The sound of voices called to her, and she stepped toward them, peering cautiously through a sliver of space between the dining room window draperies at the group of men she'd known long ago. They were a handsome lot, she thought. All of them tall, all broad of shoulder, all hard and sculpted by the trials and dangers of the lives they'd led. Holt Driscoll with his icy-blue eyes; Cade Hollister, whose brown eyes had so often sparkled with mischief; Dair MacRae, the host of tonight's dinner party in his father-in-law's absence. Him, she barely remembered, though the intense silver eyes, now softened with love as he gazed at his beautiful wife, Emma, did strike a sense of familiarity.

Lastly, Caroline gazed at the green-eyed scalawag she'd come so far to talk to. Logan Grey. Lucky Logan Grey.

The rat. The lout. The bastard.

Look at him sitting there laughing at something his friends had said, even more handsome than before, curse his black soul. She could see why women acted the fool over him. He still had that thick, dark, wavy hair he wore just a little too long, still had those emerald eyes that gleamed behind sinfully long lashes. Though clean shaven, his heavy shadow of a beard contributed a scruffy look to the masculine angles and planes of his face that made him all the more appealing. His broad shoulders and lanky frame had filled out over the years, but the air of danger hanging about him hadn't disappeared.

Memories shuddered over her along with emotions she'd worked hard to bury—hurt, loss, fury and, young, reckless love. The first time she'd seen him she'd been all of eight years old, spending the summer with her maternal grandparents at their farm in East Texas. When she was twelve he'd used a wink and crook of a finger to lure her into the shelter of the pine trees for her very first kiss. Then the last time she'd seen him, those unforgettable eyes of his had burned with passion. Passion for her.

And she'd believed them, foolish female that she was.

Laughter again erupted from the dining room, dragging her back to the present. She identified the people inside from a photograph published in the newspaper on the occasion of the dedication of McBride Elementary. Inside, Emma MacRae's sister, Katrina Kimball, had stood in order to act out the story she was telling. Like Dair's wife and her other sister, Maribeth, who sat opposite her at the table, Kat was a beautiful woman.

It was good that the women were there, Caroline decided. Even though Logan was their friend, the fact they were females would likely make them sympathetic to her plight.

She stepped back and swallowed hard and returned to the front door. Her hand trembled as she sounded the knocker, but as she heard footsteps approach, a wind of righteousness swept through her and strengthened her. Her fear and her doubts subsided. This had to be done. It was a matter of life and death.

Dair MacRae opened the door and with a polite smile inquired, "May I help you?"

He didn't recognize her, either. Caroline wasn't surprised—or offended—since their acquaintance had been so brief, so long ago. "I am sorry to interrupt your evening, but it is imperative that I speak with Mr. Grey."

MacRae's gaze swept over her, though he gave nothing of his thoughts away. "May I ask who is calling for him?" She dodged the question by tugging the medallion from around her neck and saying, "I have something I suspect he'd like returned."

"Ah!" A smile bloomed on MacRae's striking face. "Today's mysterious heroine. We wanted to include you in tonight's celebration. I know Lucky will be thrilled you tracked him down."

I wouldn't count on it.

"Please, come in and join us." Dair opened the door wide and gestured her inside just as his wife joined them in the entry hall.

"Good evening," Emma MacRae said, her expression friendly but curious.

"I'm so sorry to interrupt your dinner party, Mrs. MacRae," Caroline said in an earnest tone. "But there is simply no time to waste. I must see Logan immediately." Knowing she might lose her nerve if she hesitated, she walked right past Emma MacRae into the dining room.

Everyone in the room looked at her. Caroline focused on the men's reactions as they politely rose to their feet. Cade Hollister's expression settled into a puzzled frown. Holt Driscoll's features warmed with appreciation. Logan Grey's green eyes lit with pleasure as he grinned. "Well, if it isn't my partner in crime-busting. What happened to you this afternoon? I turned around and you were gone. I never even caught your name."

"I'm Caroline," she said, watching closely for a reaction. She saw interest in his eyes, but not a hint of recognition.

The mangy dog.

She waited, counting silently to ten, before she accepted the truth. He *still* didn't recognize her. She'd told herself earlier to give him the benefit of the doubt due to the intensity of the circumstances at the bank. But now? After she'd given him the hint of her name? What excuse did he have now?

None. She found it totally humiliating.

Over the years, she'd dreamed about his reaction to seeing her again, fantasized how he'd fall at her feet and beg her forgiveness or maybe rush to hold her and confess that he'd searched for her for years. While she'd known better than to expect either of those outcomes, she had figured to see a spark of recognition in those emerald eyes, a flicker of shame. The total lack of remembrance floored her. It wasn't as if her appearance had changed overmuch in the past fifteen years. And heaven knew, he'd certainly enjoyed a good, thorough look at her then.

"It's a pure pleasure to meet you, Caroline. I'm Logan. Logan Grey."

Damned if he didn't finish with a wink. The same wink he'd used to charm cookies from her grandma. The same wink that had lulled her into the bushes for his kiss. The same wink he'd given her that night in the church in Odessa.

She wanted to rip off the offending eyelid, but instead of doing what she wanted to do, Caroline straightened her spine, squared her shoulders and with great restraint said simply, "Logan Grey, you are a sorry, no-good louse."

"Excuse me?"

She peripherally noticed speculative interest on every face at the table. "You don't recognize me, do you?"

Wariness entered his eyes. He blinked. "What do you mean? You were at the bank today."

"I mean before that."

He studied her, the furrows in his brow deepening. He was clearly at a loss. "I'm sorry, I don't recall having met you."

In that moment, Caroline decided she didn't mind lying to him at all. Not one little tiny teensy-weensy bit.

First, though, she'd tell him the truth.

She drew back her arm and fired the jeweled medallion at him. As it bounced off his forehead, she unfurled her dirty laundry right there in the McBride family dining room. "You should remember me, you dirty rotten mush-minded snake. You *married* me!"

CHAPTER THREE

Logan Grey was not a stupid man. He was not a forgetful man. He'd traveled a lot of places in his life. Done a lot of living. Met a lot of people. Bedded a whole lot of women. Loved and lost one. He'd lived a life packed full of adventures of every kind.

For the life of him, he couldn't remember getting married to this woman.

Unless... He remembered a gal one wild week years ago. "Wait. Are you the girl from New Orleans? We did that voodoo nonsense together which 'married' us for that week?"

He watched her rein in her temper, though her eyes continued to flash as she said, "No."

Logan studied her hard. He had sensed a glimmer of something this morning in the bank. He'd figured it for lust, not recollection. After all, with those magnificent violet eyes, her burnished gold hair and an hourglass figure that proximity had proved to be natural rather than created by a corset, she was a woman of infinite appeal. She was the type of woman who tended to stick in a man's brain instead of fading completely away.

Caroline. Hmm...

Logan admitted he had a tendency to block bad events from his memory, and something did tug at his mind, something unsettling. Those eyes. Where had he seen that color eyes? "Was it California? When I was tracking down the Watson Gang and I hired a 'wife' to help me—" She briefly closed her eyes. Color stained her cheeks— not anger this time, he thought. Embarrassment. "No."

Hmm...if not California, there had been those months in Mexico after Stoney Wilson destroyed his life when he'd pretty much lost himself in a bottle. There had been a woman then, too. About the only thing he remembered for certain was that her name wasn't Caroline. She'd called herself Señora Logan. He didn't remember at all what she looked like, but he wouldn't figure "Señora" Anyone as a fair-complected blonde. "I didn't meet you in Nuevo Laredo, did I?"

She smiled then, but Logan spied no amusement in it. In fact, he took it to be a warning. "We met when we were children and I visited my grandparents' farm in East Texas."

Sitting beside Logan, Holt Driscoll snapped his fingers. "That's it."

Across from him, Cade Hollister nodded once with gusto.

His friends' reactions gave Logan pause. What did they recall that he didn't?

"The last time I saw you before today was fifteen years ago," the beauty continued. She darted a quick, embarrassed glance toward the McBride sisters as she added, "After our wedding night in the Magnolia Hotel in Odessa."

Wedding night. Odessa. Violet eyes. Son of a bitch. Light dawned and Logan's own eyes widened. His gaze once again swept her head to toe as details came trickling back to him. This was Big Jack Kilpatrick's daughter. Caroline Kilpatrick. She'd been what, seventeen, back then?

He tried to remember. That was way back before Mexico, before the slaughter in Oklahoma, and he seldom thought about those years. It hurt too much to recall when his life—his soul—had still been clean.

But when he put his mind to it, he remembered a girl in a yellow dress. She had looked different then, too. For one thing, her hair had been white-blond, not this glorious burnished gold. Also, she hadn't been nearly this...curvy.

Cade leaned over and whispered, "How could you forget her?"

"I didn't recognize her," he murmured back, his gaze locking on her bosom. "She's grown breasts since then." Then he cleared his throat and said, "You're the Kilpatrick girl."

"Not for the past fifteen years. I'm Caroline *Grey.*"

Logan sat back in his chair. "You've pretended to be my wife all that time?"

Temper flashed. "I *am* your wife!"

Logan's gaze dropped to her hands as they continually made fists. She stood far too close to the carving knife beside the roast for his own ease.

"Don't you recall signing the church register?" she asked. "Mr. and Mrs. Logan Grey?"

"Oh, Lucky," Emma MacRae scolded, clucking her tongue.

"It was a long time ago," he responded defensively. The details of the day were slowly coming back.

"That's right." Caroline's tone dripped sugar, but her gaze shot poison darts. Her chin came up as she drew a deep breath, then declared, "Who could expect a man to remember the woman he tricked into marriage one night then deserted at dawn?"

Oh, yeah. He winced. Now he remembered.

"Lucky!" Kat Kimball gasped. "How could you?" She shoved to her feet and went to stand beside Caroline, looping their arms in a sign of solidarity. Having a history of marriage to a trickster, she was sensitive to the subject.

"Now wait just a minute," Logan protested as the events of the day came rushing back into his memory. "It wasn't like that. The whole thing was a lie."

Every woman in the room had folded her arms. All the men either grimaced or winced—except for Dair MacRae, damn his soul. That son of a bitch looked as though he was about to laugh as he drawled, "Since we're all done with dinner, perhaps we should move this conversation into the drawing room. It's more comfortable and the liquor is closer. Or, Logan, maybe you'd prefer privacy for this?"

"Dair!" his wife protested.

"No. I want everyone to hear this," Logan said, keeping his voice calm. "It wasn't like she said. It was a lie, a scheme concocted by her father. I was just a two-bit player."

Caroline's jaw gaped. "How can you say that with a straight face? You didn't even remember!"

"Well, I remember now," he fired back as the group moved into the other room. In his mind's eye he could see the tall, larger-than-life Texan with his granite jaw and steely demeanor saunter into the bar.

"Are you the fella who came looking for work at the K-Bar yesterday?" Big Jack Kilpatrick asked.

Down to his last two dollars, Logan glanced up from his card game. "I am."

"You the boy from East Texas? The one who said he knew my in-laws? Knows my daughter?"

"I spent a few years at the Pinery Woods Children's Home that bordered the Benson place. Your girl visited there in the summers."

A big, slow grin spread across Big Jack's face. "I see. Well, then, son. Looks like I might have a job after all. Cash out of your game, there, and join me for a drink."

"Here, Lucky," Luke Prescott said, shoving a glass at him. "Looks like you need it."

Logan shook off the memory and accepted the sample of Luke's father-in-law's whiskey. He was glad that a prior commitment kept Trace and his wife, Jenny, from being here tonight. He'd have hated to have this conversation beneath Trace McBride's overprotective-toward-females scowl.

Some of the details of the "wedding" remained hazy in his mind, but others had become crystal clear. Big Jack's hard eyes and careless manner as he made his shocking proposal was one of those clear moments. Joining Caroline Kilpatrick in bed was another.

Emma MacRae offered Caroline a seat in her mother's favorite chair before the fireplace and a choice of beverage.

"A glass of water would be nice. Thank you," Caroline replied.

After a consultation with the babysitter caring for the couples' children upstairs, the women took their seats—on the same side of the room as Caroline. Their husbands arranged themselves neutrally toward the center of the room. Cade and Holt stayed in close proximity to the liquor cabinet. Logan stood by the door, wondering if a quick exit might be necessary.

He took a long sip of whiskey, then because his friends' wives mattered to him, they were the ones he addressed. "I didn't remember at first because it wasn't a legitimate wedding. We didn't really get married. The whole thing was faked, a scheme of her father's to get around some legal issue he had. I think it was something about an inheritance that only kicked in when his daughter got married."

"That's a lie," Caroline declared, coming to her feet.

"No, it isn't. I specifically recall something about terms of your mother's will. Your father was quite adamant about his objections to—"

"The inheritance part is true," she interrupted. "I don't argue that. But the wedding was real. You married me."

Calmly, Logan took another sip of his whiskey, then with his voice ringing with sincerity, said, "I tried to hire on as a ranch hand at your father's place, but got turned down. Big Jack tracked me down in a saloon in Midland. The man was intimidating as hell."

He glanced at the women and explained, "I was just as tall as he was then, but I was a skinny runt. He had to have fifty pounds of muscle on me. He slapped me on the back and about knocked me across the room and offered me twenty dollars to go to Odessa and pretend to marry his daughter. I didn't think twice about taking the job. Legalities didn't bother me much then."

"They don't bother you much now," Dair observed.

"It *wasn't* a fake marriage." Caroline linked her hands and squeezed. "We said vows in First Methodist Church."

"In front of a fake preacher."

"We signed marriage papers."

"Fake papers your father promised to destroy after he used them with the lawyers."

This time it was Caroline who looked at the McBride sisters. "Reverend Harwell still preaches there today. The marriage is recorded at the Ector County courthouse. You can check."

"That would be easy enough to do. Lucky," Luke Prescott observed.

Now Logan felt his first real shimmer of unease. What if she *was* telling the truth?

No. Couldn't be. Being married would certainly qualify as trouble, yet this business had blindsided him, caught him totally off guard. His trouble-sense hadn't made a peep. She couldn't be telling the truth. "You knew it was a sham. You had to know."

"Excuse me, but do you remember that day at all?" This time Caroline looked toward Dair, Luke Garrett and Jake Kimball, the McBride daughters' husbands. "My father wanted me to marry a family friend, a rancher my father's age. He went forward with the plans even though I refused. I ran away but his men caught me and brought me back. He posted guards and summoned his friend and a preacher. He took all the clothes from my room except for a wedding gown made by—" she pointed toward their wives "—their mother!"

Maribeth Prescott glanced at her sisters. "Mama would remember. She remembers every wedding dress she ever made."

Caroline continued, "Fifteen minutes before I was supposed to go downstairs to marry some man I'd never met, Logan Grey knocks out the guard in front of my door and sneaks into my room."

Logan's stomach took a hard dip as he recalled that part of the day. He'd been the backup bridegroom. Big Jack had thought his goal might be accomplished easier if she thought she had a choice.

"Logan told me he'd heard about my plight in town and that he'd come to help me escape the ranch house. Then he convinced me to marry him by saying he'd always had a soft spot for me in his heart, and that marrying someone else was the only way to ensure my father couldn't make me marry that old man!"

He felt the censorious gazes of the females in the room as Caroline said, "I wanted to believe him. I'd had an infatuation for him ever since y'all built my Grandpa's barn. Remember that summer?" she asked the men. "You'd show up early before it got hot."

"You brought us lemonade," Cade recalled. "Cookies, too. I remember those ginger cookies."

Holt nodded. "Me, too. You went swimming with us in the river. Remember that swing we made over the swimming hole? No one else from the home had guts enough to try it. Just the three of us—" he grinned at Caroline "—and you."

"It was fun," she replied. "Being with the three of you was fun. And frankly, that summer, I'd have followed Logan Grey anywhere." She pinned him with a look. "You gave me my first kiss that summer. I don't suppose you remember that, either?"

Uncertain whether a lie or the truth would serve him best at the moment—he didn't remember that kiss at all—Logan simply shrugged.

"It's appalling to admit now, but when he offered me a way out of that marriage my father had arranged, I didn't think twice. I followed him out my bedroom window and to First Methodist Church, just like I'd followed him into his fort with its yellow bandanna flag in the Piney Woods forest. Only this time, he didn't stop after a few kisses." She met the gazes of each McBride sister before adding, "Fool that I was, I followed him to the hotel, too."

Kat gasped again. Emma winced. Maribeth frowned darkly at Logan and asked, "You consummated a false marriage, Lucky?"

Did she have to do this here in front of his friends? He shot her a look that combined a glare with a grimace and said, "Well, yeah, that wasn't supposed to happen. We were to stay in the hotel to make it look good, and I was supposed to sleep on the floor. But I was eighteen and she was..." *ripe* was the first word that came to mind, but he knew better than to use it in a room full of women "...irresistible."

Enthusiastic, too, once she got past her nervousness. Caroline made a little noise that was a cross between an embarrassed screech and an angry scream, and he eyed her warily. He could tell she wanted to strike out at him. Slap him. Punch him. Hell, she probably wanted to shoot him.

In retrospect, he couldn't say that he blamed her.

It was all coming back to him now. How *had* he forgotten that night? She'd been his first virgin, and as far as he knew, his last.

She glanced at the letter opener on the table beside her chair and Logan's eyes widened with alarm. He thought it best to move the conversation forward. "Look, Miss Kilpatrick—"

"Mrs. Grey."

"—I'll admit that wasn't gallant of me. In the heat of the moment I got carried away, and I'll apologize for that. But the rest—" he shook his head "—it was all your father's doing. He said he'd tell you everything that next day."

She folded her arms and stared at him. Studied him. He could all but see the wheels turning in her head. He knew she was considering that he might just be telling the truth when the light in her eyes changed and the color drained from her face.

A minute crept by, then two. Finally, in a quiet voice, she said, "When I awoke the following morning, Logan was gone. I thought perhaps he'd gone downstairs to order breakfast. The hotel owner told me he'd had bacon and eggs for breakfast, then climbed on his horse, and rode out of town."

Every last woman in the room now looked at Logan as if he were cow dung on the sole of a boot. He rubbed at the back of his neck and tried to ignore the headache beginning to pound at his temples. "Your father never told you it was all made up?"

"No." She closed her eyes and the cheeks that had gone ashen moments before flooded once again with color. "He was happy. He actually whistled in the wagon on the way back home. He told me he'd been wrong to try to force me to marry his friend and that he was sorry. He said we should look at life as a brand-new start."

Logan rubbed the back of his neck. "I'm sorry you went through that, Caroline," he said sincerely. "You deserved better than a make-believe marriage from both me and your father."

Again, time dragged out. Then she appeared to gather her defenses and strengthen her resolve. She lifted her chin. "You're right. I did deserve better. But I'm not the only one my father duped, Logan. The marriage *wasn't* all made up. It was all very, very real. It was legal."

Her claim echoed in the uncomfortable silence that followed.

Cade cleared his throat. "So why wait fifteen years to track him down?"

Yeah. Logan wanted the answer to that, too.

Caroline smoothed her skirts and visibly braced herself. The look in her eyes said she'd made a decision and Logan felt a shiver of apprehension race up his spine.

"I didn't need him before," she said, clasping her hands in front of her, squeezing so hard that her knuckles went white. She licked her lips, then met his gaze. For a second—just a fleeting second—he saw calculation in her eyes. Immediately, warning bells clanged in his brain.

"Logan," she said, "I need you now. I need your help."

Suddenly, it all made sense. Like father, like daughter. The woman must be playing a con. She probably saw the article in the Fort Worth newspaper last week about the reward he'd received from Wells Fargo for facilitating the capture of the Dodd gang who'd been terrorizing the West for years. The arrests had been the culmination of a six-month effort and the crown in his cap as a range detective.

Logan drummed his fingers against the glass in his hand. He'd come a long way since the days the flat-broke bronc buster had run across Big Jack Kilpatrick in a West Texas bar. His investment in the Corsicana oil field had paid off, and the one in East Texas was looking good. His only question was how much Caroline Kilpatrick would ask for. "So, how much money were you figuring to extort from me?"

She blinked in surprise. "I don't want your money."

"Then what do you want?" he snapped back. "Apparently you've already taken my name."

"You gave me your name. Believe me, there have been plenty of times I'd have loved to give it back. But in a way, I guess it is your name I need—Lucky Logan Grey. I read of your exploits in the newspaper, the gun battles you've won, the outlaws you've brought to justice. The *Daily Democrat* says that you're the luckiest man in Texas. That's what I need. I need luck, a lot of luck."

Luck. Well, hell. In his peripheral vision, Logan saw the McBride sisters—the Bad Luck Brides—share a significant look. He looked past Caroline Kilpatrick to the doorway, thinking he'd be smart to make tracks. Now that his trouble-sense had finally kicked in, it was telling him that his life was about to change.

Nevertheless, he asked the question. "Why?"

"Because you and I made more than a mistake that night at the Magnolia Hotel. We made a son. I named him William Benjamin. Will."

Holy hell. Even as shock rolled through Logan's system, he saw her swallow hard, watched pain flash across her face. Her next faltering words were a second punch that made his blood run cold.

"Two weeks ago, Will ran off to join a gang of outlaws. I need your help, Logan Grey, your good luck, to bring him safely back home."

CHAPTER FOUR

THE WILLOW HILL DRAWING ROOM WENT QUIET AS A TOMB IN THE wake of her shocking announcement. Waiting for someone to speak, Caroline thought her heart might just beat out of her chest. She'd never expected confronting him to be easy, but it had proved harder than she'd expected. Much harder. She hadn't thought she'd feel any sympathy for him at all.

But she did.

She believed him.

He had been just as big a dupe as she. She could see her father doing exactly as Logan claimed.

Big Jack Kilpatrick had been a difficult man. Demanding, oftentimes cold, he'd run the K-Bar with an iron fist and a ready draw. It took a hard man to wrangle a living out of the plains of West Texas, but Caroline suspected her father had been harder than most. For most of her life she'd felt as if he valued his cattle more than her. She'd simply never mattered to the man.

Well, except when he'd needed her money.

She'd been a means to an end. Logan, too. If she'd known then what she knew now, she wouldn't have grieved so much when Big Jack died after being thrown from a snake-spooked horse three weeks after her "wedding." He'd hit his head on a rock and lingered unconscious for three days before passing.

The next day the lawyer had arrived and informed her of her father's gambling habit. She'd been shocked to discover that not only had he used her inheritance to pay off a mountain of debt, a second mountain just as high remained. When the dust settled, she'd had next to nothing left.

That's when Ben and Suzanne Whitaker entered her life, and she thanked God for that blessing every day since.

The reminder of her purpose here gave her strength and allowed her to shore up her defenses where Logan Grey—a now-shaky, pasty-looking Logan Grey—was concerned.

He cleared his throat. "You want to run that by me again?"

She licked her dry lips, then told the truth. "You are the father of my son."

He closed his eyes for a long minute, but when he opened them, they glowed with fury. "I don't believe you. This is some sort of ugly extortion plot that you've invented because I've made money in the past few years. We are not really married, and you damn sure didn't have my child. This is some scheme you've cooked up. Guess you take after your father in that regard."

"This is no—"

"Listen up, sweetheart," he interrupted, taking a threatening step toward her. His voice was cold and mean, his eyes flat and hard as granite. "You are a liar and a fraud and I'll *be damned* if I'll let you pass off another man's brat as my own. Now you need to get the hell out of here!"

The room went quiet. The others' shock at his reaction was obvious.

Caroline's mouth was bone-dry as she went to open her suddenly very heavy purse, then hesitated. She could still back out. She could agree with him and make her escape and never see the man again. She wouldn't have to juggle the complications that involving him in their lives would invariably create.

But no, she'd already made this decision. She'd come too far to back out now, and she needed his help. Ben needed his help. Poor, devastated, crazy-with-grief Ben, who had taken in a homeless, penniless, pregnant girl and given her everything. Ben, who loved Will from the moment he was born, who protected him, provided for him. Ben who had stepped into the shoes of fatherhood because Logan was nowhere around.

Well, Ben needed her now the way she had needed him then, and Logan was their only hope.

She'd tried to hire someone else to do the job for her. She'd searched hard to find a man willing to brave the rumored evils of that place for the limited purse she had to offer. Quickly, she'd learned an undeniable truth: only a man with powerful motivation would voluntarily enter Black Shadow Canyon.

Logan Grey was the man. And because securing Ben Whitaker's safety simply wouldn't be enough, their son, Will, would be the motivation.

Which brought her here to this moment, offering up partial truths and a big fat lie. The lie provided Logan powerful motivation—saving his son. And the truth—the truth gave him Will!

Will was the greatest gift Logan Grey would ever receive. Will offset the price of the lie tenfold. A thousandfold.

Filled with righteous, maternal certainty, Caroline reached into her purse, pulled out the photograph and handed it to Logan.

"Holy hell," he breathed.

Gazing over his shoulder, Holt said, "He's your spittin' image."

Cade took a look, then blew out a long whistle. "Boy looks exactly like you did when you were his age."

"A son." Logan raked his fingers through his hair, his expression stunned and bewildered. He stared at the photograph, his jade eyes wide with shock.

He believes me now. Caroline nodded. "Yes."

At that, Emma MacRae stood. "Let's take a walk, shall we? I think Lucky and Miss...Mrs....umm...and Caroline deserve some privacy."

Caroline was grateful. After the women had stood up for her, lying to them didn't set well.

Logan poured himself another drink while the others exited the room. Kat Kimball looked as if she wanted to protest, but her husband ushered her from the drawing room while murmuring in her ear. Driscoll and Hollister each slapped Logan's back in support on their way out the door.

When they were alone, Logan took a long sip of whiskey, then said, "He's what...fifteen?"

"Fourteen."

"Fourteen," he repeated. He sounded a bit fearful when he added, "I have a fourteen-year-old son."

"He has your green eyes." At that his gaze flew to her face, and the quick flash of pleasure she spied in his eyes prompted her to add, "And your dark hair, your smile. I could never forget you, Logan Grey, because I see you every day in my son."

It was as true a statement as she'd made all night.

Logan blew out a heavy breath. "I can't quite wrap my mind around this. I never thought...Tell me about him."

Taking pity on him, she provided more detail than anyone other than a parent could possibly want. "He was only one week old when he smiled at me the first time. My friends told me that it was too soon, that it was only gas, but I didn't believe them. He got his first tooth at six months and began crawling at eight. He took his first steps in the aisle at the mercantile on his first birthday."

She spoke at length, and he listened raptly, asking occasional questions as she took him through the years until she told him about the Will of today. "He's a great kid. Everything a mother could hope for. He's smart and he's witty and he's kind. So kind. Oh, he's far from perfect—I can't tell you how many times he's late for supper—but it's his imperfections that make him all the more...well..."

"Perfect," Logan finished. At that point, he took his drink and walked to a window where he spent long minutes gazing outside without saying a word.

Caroline's nerves stretched so tight that when he finally spoke, she jumped.

"Let me make sure I have this straight. You claim you thought that we had a legal marriage, and yet you never bothered to inform me that I'd become a father?"

She refused to be battered by that argument. Suzanne used to scold her for not contacting Logan after she first saw his name in a newspaper when Will was eight.

Caroline didn't care. "I was seventeen, destitute and alone with a baby on the way. At that point, I was busy trying to survive. Tracking you down was not a priority for me. After all, you left me and never looked back."

In her mind, with that single act he had forfeited any rights he might have where Will was concerned.

"I didn't know I needed to look back. I mailed an address to your father, a way to reach me if it proved necessary." His brow furrowed. "Why *were* you destitute and alone? Did you tell him we bedded down together? Did he kick you out when he found out about the baby?"

"No. He never knew. He died before I discovered I was expecting."

Logan blew out a hard breath, then slumped into a chair. "I never thought...Hell. I've always taken care with the women I've been with. Except for that night, that is. When I never heard from Big Jack, I decided I'd dodged a bullet. Swore I wouldn't be careless again." The light in his eyes reflected how much the idea disturbed him, as he added, "I grew up without a father, and I promised myself I'd never do that to a child of my own."

A wave of compassion rolled through Caroline and prompted her response. "For what it's worth, Will doesn't hold it against you. He's proud that his father is a range detective."

"He knows?" Surprise lit his eyes. "What have you told him about me?"

Caroline squirmed a bit at that question. "Actually, I told him very little about you other than your name. Until recently, I didn't know how curious he was about you. I knew he spent a lot of time reading old newspapers, but I thought he was trying to learn the profession."

"Half of what has been written about me are lies."

"Tell him that when you meet him."

Logan leaned forward and propped his elbows on his knees. "So just how bad is it? Who is he riding with and what are they doing? Robbing trains? Rustling cattle?"

Well, shoot. She'd hadn't thought to research outlaw gangs, and she couldn't pull a name of one associated with Black Shadow Canyon from memory. "I don't know the name of the gang. He didn't tell me that in the note he left. What he did say is that he's gone to Black Shadow Canyon."

Logan went still. He cleared his throat. "Where?"

"Black Shadow Canyon."

He sat back in his chair hard. "No. Not there. Anywhere but there."

"I know it's not a nice place, but—"

"Not a nice place?" Logan shoved to his feet and reached for the whiskey decanter, refilling his glass with a hand that slightly trembled. "It's the roughest, meanest, most dangerous place in the West! It makes Tombstone, Arizona, in its heyday look like a Sunday stroll in a children's park. Hells bells, Caroline. Tell me my son isn't lost in that den of thieves and murderers!"

His son.

Caroline bristled at the idea. Will was *her* son. He had been hers and hers alone for the past fourteen years. Did Logan Grey truly think he could lay claim to a child so easily?

She folded her arms. What really made a man a father, anyway? The simple act of creation or the infinitely more complicated act of daily nurturing, teaching and providing? Caroline certainly had an opinion about that.

And yet, he'd accepted Will as his with little protest or resistance. She hadn't needed pressure from his friends as she'd expected. It wouldn't be necessary to shame Lucky Logan Grey into assisting her, not as long as he thought he was going to rescue his son.

His son.

Those two little words spoken with such caring and concern by this man—this same man whom she'd spent almost half her life cursing and despising and maligning—threatened to turn her world upside down.

The shame rested not with him, but with her. It appeared he wasn't as guilty as she'd thought him to be. He didn't deserve this worry she'd deposited at his feet.

"Caroline?"

She held herself stiffly. "I'm sorry, Logan. I wish I could tell you that Will hasn't disappeared into that place, but I can't." *It would ruin everything.* "I understand that you've gone into that den of thieves and come back out alive."

Logan ignored that. He shoved to his feet and started pacing the room. "How in the world did a fourteen-year-old boy make his way into that cesspool? Why would he want to? I need to know everything, Caroline, in order to formulate a plan to get him out. Start at the beginning. Tell me who influenced the boy and why."

Caroline gathered her thoughts, reminding herself of all the reasons she'd chosen this particular path. "After my father died, I had to sell the ranch to pay off his debts. By that time I was six months along, and I had nowhere to go, no one to help me."

Logan muttered an ugly curse.

She continued, "I found a job in Artesia helping the editor of the newspaper care for his wife, who was recovering from a buggy accident. I can't tell you what a miracle it was for me to find that job with the Whitakers. Not only did it save me from the whorehouse, it gave me a family. People to love who loved me in return. Then Will was born, and Ben and Suzanne fell silly in love with him at first sight. We made a family and—"

"Wait a minute. Ben and Suzanne Whitaker? *The* Whitakers? Not Gunslinging Suz. Surely you're not talking about the Whitakers who rode with the Sunshine Gang."

"They were retired." For the most part, anyway. She wasn't about to mention Ben's "little slips" as he liked to call them.

Logan braced his hands on his hips. "Are you telling me my son has been raised by outlaws?"

His son. Suddenly, she was real tired of hearing that. She straightened her spine and lifted her chin. "Suzanne was never convicted of anything, and Ben served his time in prison. He paid his debt to society. He's a good man who lived to regret some youthful indiscretions. Surely you can understand that."

"Ah, hell. The Whitakers!" Logan closed his eyes and after a moment made a circular motion with his hand, prompting her to continue.

Caroline found her determination strengthened by his reaction to the Whitaker name. She'd been correct in her assessment that he wouldn't be motivated to save Ben. She was doing the right thing, the only thing. "Everything was good, we had a fine life, until we lost Suzanne in January."

"Lost her?"

"She died. Fell down the stairs. Will found her when he came home from school."

Logan stopped pacing in front of the window. He shoved his hands in his pants pockets and once again stared outside. After a long moment, he said, "That had to be a hard knock for the boy."

"He suffered. We all suffered. Ben went a little crazy in his grief."

Logan whipped his head around and stared at her. "Did Whitaker mistreat the boy? Is that why he ran off?"

"Oh, heavens no. Ben adores Will. It's been a battle for me to keep him from spoiling my son silly."

"So why in the world would he want to become an outlaw?"

Caroline opened her mouth to talk about the appeal of rustling cattle, but she couldn't quite force herself to make Will look like a criminal in his father's eyes. "Well, that's not exactly what happened. It's more complicated than that."

"Complicated how?"

Caroline's teeth tugged at her lower lip as she tried to decide what truths to stretch. She hadn't intended to mention the gold until later, but maybe that was a mistake. After all. Logan had helped Dair MacRae and his wife and in-laws find the Bad Luck Treasure. The prospect of another treasure hunt might appeal to him. "Will doesn't want to be an outlaw, but he had to join a gang to be allowed inside Black Shadow Canyon. He wants access to the canyon to hunt for a lost gold mine."

"A what?"

"A gold mine. He has a treasure map."

"Not another treasure." Logan grimaced and let out a long-suffering sigh.

Oh, dear. That wasn't a particularly encouraging sign, but it was too late to back out now.

He pinned her with a stony stare. "Tell me about it."

Caroline concentrated on choosing her next words carefully, especially since this part of her story was heavy on falsehoods. "A few weeks after Suzanne died, Ben asked me to pack away Suzanne's personal belongings. He couldn't do it himself."

Actually, he had forbidden anyone from touching anything of his late wife's. Caroline only breached that privacy after Ben disappeared.

"I found a stack of letters from an old friend. One of them described his discovery of a gold mine called Sierra de Cenizas."

Logan grimaced and groaned. "Otherwise known as Geronimo's Treasure."

"You're familiar with the story?"

"Every cowboy who's ridden the trail in West Texas has heard that old yarn. An Indian guide showed the mine to Spanish explorers, who loaded down their mules with nuggets and ore to carry back home. They were all massacred in the great Indian uprising of 1680, but not before one of them left a document in the Palace of Santa Fe that described the discovery. Prospectors have been chasing that old legend and poking holes in the Guadalupe Mountains for half a century now."

"Apparently Shotgun found it."

"Shotgun Reese?"

"You know him?"

"I know of him. I know that he threw in with another bunch of pups after the Sunshine Gang broke up. He made quite a name for himself, participated in some sensational robberies. Wells Fargo wanted him bad. After a while, though, he disappeared from sight."

"That's probably because he didn't need to steal anymore since he'd found the gold mine."

"Of course he did." Logan's voice dripped sarcasm.

"He sent Suzanne some gold nuggets from the mine. She kept them in a little wooden box." She hesitated a moment before adding, "My mistake was showing them to Will. That and the map."

"The map to the gold mine," Logan deduced.

"Yes."

"And the mine is somewhere in Black Shadow Canyon."

"Yes."

"And Will has gone to find it." Logan dragged his hand along his jaw. "What a damned fool harebrained idea."

"He's fourteen," she said with a shrug. "Fourteen-year-old boys are full of harebrained ideas." *As are sixty-eight-year-old men.*

"He's gonna get himself killed!"

"No, he won't." She folded her arms and shot a fierce look his way. "Because you're going to save him, right? You're Lucky Logan Grey, the luckiest man in Texas."

"Heaven help us all," Logan muttered. He picked up the photograph of Will and studied it for a long minute.

Caroline held her breath.

Finally, thankfully, the anger drained from his expression, though frustration and concern filled his tone when he sighed, then said, "Yes, Caroline, I'll save him, but luck won't have anything to do with it."

Caroline saw the truth of his words glowing in his eyes as he met her gaze and said, "This is all about what is right. It is about what a man is supposed to do, what fathers do for their sons."

He excused himself after that to seek out his friends and ask their help in developing a rescue plan. Caroline sat in Willow Hill's drawing room fearing that she'd made a huge mistake.

Logan had proved he wasn't the dirty dog she had believed him to be. He was a man of integrity. A man of purpose. And he acted as if he cared for Will already. As if he felt a real fatherly bond.

That wasn't what she'd expected from the man she'd believed had loved her, then left her and never looked back. From everything she'd read about Logan Grey before coming to Fort Worth and based on her experience today at the bank and what she'd learned from Wilhemina Peters, she'd expected Logan to have a sense of responsibility toward Will that required he save the boy from the perils of Black Shadow Canyon. She never anticipated that he'd actually want to *be* Will's father.

As the repercussions of this revelation faltered through her mind, she murmured, "Heaven help us all."

"For the love of all that's holy, this is something I never thought I'd see." Cade Hollister turned to Holt Driscoll and said, "That's three.

Three! He turned down a freebie with Ella, an invitation from the librarian and he ignored a blatant proposition from twins. Identical, redheaded, brown-eyed, big-bosomed, saloon-girl twins!"

"The twins I don't understand," Holt observed. "However, Ella never makes him pay and the librarian is married. Lucky never plays with married women."

Cade pursed his lips, smothering a smile. "Except for the once—his own missus."

Logan made a vulgar gesture with his hand and his two friends laughed.

The three men sat at a table in their favorite Fort Worth saloon, the End of the Line, rehashing the events of the evening. Actually, Cade and Holt were the ones doing the rehashing. Logan was too busy brooding.

He was a father. He had a son.

A son who'd grown up without a father.

"I swore I'd never do that," he muttered, staring at the foam atop his beer. He didn't want the beer. Didn't want to be here at the End of the Line. He wanted to be asleep in bed with this entire evening being nothing more than a nightmare.

"Do what?" Cade asked, standing a poker chip on end and giving it a spin.

Logan could hardly form the words, so much did they shame him. "Desert a child of mine."

The other two men winced. More than anyone else, Cade and Holt understood the thought process behind the statement because they'd grown up in an orphanage along with him. They understood what it meant not to have a father. They understood that today's revelation was a kick to the gut that had knocked Logan on his ass.

Because he was a friend, Holt tried. "It's not your fault, Lucky. You didn't know."

"That's no excuse. She's right about that—I should have checked on her myself, taken responsibility. I shouldn't have waited for her father to contact me if there was a problem." He sat back in his chair, hard. "Problem, hell. There was a baby."

"She could have contacted you," Cade suggested.

"How? Stop and think about it. I didn't keep in contact with anyone those next few years. Not even you two." Guilt closed around his throat like a noose as he tried to imagine what she'd gone through. Poor thing—her apron riding high, no husband, not a nickel to her name. It must have been pure hell.

He should have been there for her. For the boy. Instead, he'd been...worthless. Both to her and the boy and to himself.

Just like in Mexico. Just like in Oklahoma. His stomach took a roll and he shut his eyes.

The piano player struck up a lively, upbeat tune. Logan wanted to throw his mug at him. Those years after he left the orphanage were lost years. Wasted years. He'd been a drifter, traveling from town to town, state to state, picking up odd jobs to support himself and moving on at a whim, always looking for something he never could define. Yet, in those days he'd never crossed the line. He was still a decent man when he married Caroline.

He had not yet hit bottom when he got tangled up with the Wilson brothers down south of the Rio Grande.

He'd never told another person about those dark months when his evil deeds had almost cost him his soul. He'd spent the past decade attempting to earn his redemption, and up until tonight, he'd believed his tab nearly paid. Now, he had to reassess.

"Lucky's right." Holt idly shuffled a deck of cards, then dealt them each a poker hand, though they weren't playing cards. "If not for Nana Nellie, we'd have lost track of one another completely."

Nana Nellie. Logan groaned softly at the memory. She'd be so ashamed of him today.

Officially, Nana Nellie had been the headmistress of Piney Woods Children's Home, but in fact, she'd been the orphanage's heart and soul. She'd lived the virtues and expected no less from those in her care. Growing up, Logan had chafed against her rules and expectations and upon leaving the orphanage he'd blatantly rebelled against them. What a dumbass he'd been. The one time in his life he'd had a run of good luck was the day he'd been turned over to Nellie Jennings's care. He'd just been too young, too stupid and too insecure to see it. Nevertheless, the lessons she'd taught had seeped into his bones, and on a mean, dark night in Saltillo, Mexico, he'd remembered them.

Standing over the body of the man—hell, the boy—he'd just killed, sickened and shamed by his behavior, he'd heard Nana Nellie's voice echo through his mind. *Prudence, justice, fortitude, temperance. Kindness, generosity.*

He'd walked out of the alley, bent over double, and vomited.

It had been a warning, but unfortunately, one he'd failed to heed for another year. What that year cost him...

For just a moment, Logan was back in Oklahoma, in that house, back with the bodies and the blood and smell of death and his own weakness. Pain flashed through him as keenly as a knife.

Finally, he had learned. From that moment on, he'd done his best to live up to her example, and he'd been somewhat successful. He'd sworn off alcohol and made it three whole years before indulging once again. While the notion of chastity had never caught on with him, somewhere along the way he'd realized that he was happiest when he attempted to live, if not a virtuous life, then at least one where he didn't have to hear Nana Nellie's voice scolding him all the time. The way it was now.

"A boy. I can't believe I have a boy."

"And a wife," Holt said. "Don't forget the wife."

"Which reminds me of a question I have." Cade leaned forward and gave Logan an incredulous look. "How the hell did you forget marrying a woman like that? Fake wedding or not?"

"I remembered," Logan protested.

"Not right away. Not until after you recalled the voodoo queen and the California whore."

Logan flipped over one of the playing cards his friend had dealt moments before. Considering that he'd met Stoney Wilson a couple of months after his "job" for Big Jack Kilpatrick, it was no wonder he put the whole incident out of his mind. But he would never make his friends understand unless he told them about Mexico, and he wasn't about to do that, so he didn't attempt to defend himself. He shrugged and said, "Too much whiskey after the fact, I guess."

Definitely some truth in that.

Holt took a long sip of his beer, then observed, "I can't get over how much the boy looks like you, Lucky. I know you're troubled by how it's happened, but at least he hasn't had to grow up trying to figure out which man in town was his daddy. That was always the worst part for me."

"Me. too." Cade agreed. "Remember that time we decided our fathers were riverboat gamblers who worked the Sabine River and we ran off to find them?"

"In February." Holt shook his head. "Dumbass kids. Never been so cold in my life."

"Yeah, well, I wish he'd come looking for me instead of going after Geronimo's Treasure," Logan grumbled. "What would possess a kid to do that?"

"Normal boyhood adventures?" Holt suggested. "He's just had a shock with his grandmother dying."

"Maybe it's a little bit of wanting to impress his old man, too. You said Caroline told you he read about you in the papers. He learned about your exploits, your adventures. He must know you helped Dair find his family treasure. Maybe he's trying to follow in your footsteps."

Great. That was just what he'd needed to hear. Logan snatched up the poker hand and scowled at the straight flush he'd been dealt. His son was trying to live up to a lie—Lucky Logan Grey. Wonderful. Just frickin' wonderful. "It's my fault that he's run off to that hellhole."

"Did I say that?" Cade looked to Holt. "When did I say that?"

Holt gathered up the playing cards, then shuffled them again. "The boy is fourteen and trying to be a man. Remember what we were like at that age? Some of the stunts we pulled?"

Cade's mouth twisted in a grin. "The riverboat incident?"

The memory brought a reluctant smile to Logan's face. "I thought Nana Nellie was gonna leave us in jail to rot. Damn, but she was mad."

"I'll bet your woman has a temper to her." Holt dealt poker hands again, this time practicing dealing from the bottom of the deck. "Got just a glimpse of it tonight when she pegged you with that necklace of yours."

"It's a medallion, not a necklace," Logan muttered as he tossed down the playing cards. His woman. That brought up a whole other opportunity for guilt. Again, he imagined how desperate she must have been, pregnant and penniless and alone, and the shame all but sent him to his knees.

"Wonder what Tom Addison is doing tonight," he mused, referring to the lawyer whose services he'd utilized for his oil field investments. "Think he's at the same shindig the McBrides attended?"

"Why?" Holt's brows arched. "You thinking about getting a divorce?"

Logan scowled at his friend. It was a natural question, he guessed, but he didn't like it. It didn't sit well, though he couldn't exactly say why. "Divorce? On what grounds? That I'm a prick?"

Cade snickered. "If that is grounds for divorce, no marriage in America is safe."

"I need Tom to write up a will for me before I head out for Black Shadow Canyon," Logan explained.

That observation sobered the three men and focused the conversation on the future rather than the past. "So what are you thinking, Lucky?" Cade asked. "Are we waiting for the westbound train on Friday morning or are we taking the noon train south tomorrow?"

Logan hesitated. "We?"

"You don't think we're letting you do this on your own, do you?" Holt said.

"I can't ask y'all—"

"Shut up, Grey." Cade flipped a poker chip like a coin. "You're not asking. We're telling you we're going."

Logan could not deny that the weight on his shoulders eased a bit at that. He could use their help. Holt's status as a Texas Ranger might come in handy, and Cade, a former Pinkerton man now working for himself, specialized in locating lost children. While a runaway wasn't exactly lost and they knew where the boy was headed, Logan figured Cade's skills could be of great assistance when they started tracking Will through the canyon.

And yet. he recognized that accepting their help created a bit of a problem. "I'll be glad to have y'all watching my back, but getting you two into the canyon might be sticky. You are both too well-known."

"And you're not?" Holt snorted a laugh. "Hell, Lucky, it'll probably be easier for us than for you. You made fools of 'em last time. They're gonna be gunning for you now."

"Then I can't let 'em see me coming."

"And how do you figure to do that?"

Logan swiped at the condensation on his beer mug with his thumb. "I don't exactly know, but I have five days to figure it out and, thankfully, you two to help me do it. I think it's best to wait for Friday's train—it's a more direct route and it'll get us there almost as fast as if we left a day earlier and went through San Antoine. We can use tomorrow to buy supplies and check with our contacts to see what news has come out of there in the last week or so."

"The Rangers should have declared war on that bunch and gone in and cleaned the place out years ago," Holt grumbled. "It goes against my grain to leave killers and thieves alone to do their dirty work just because they've holed up the middle of nowhere."

Cade tipped his chair up on its two hind legs. "I've missed seeing that part of the world. So, it's a four-day trip to Black Shadow Canyon?"

"About that. We take the train west, then go on horseback north to the Guadalupe Mountains."

"When did she say the boy left?"

"He took the train out of Artesia last Sunday. We'll be over a week behind him, but since he won't know where he's going, I'm hoping we'll make up time on him on the trail."

"He's grown up in town. Did she say if he's a good horseman? A good tracker?"

"We didn't talk about that. I know I should have asked a million questions, but I just...I needed time to digest the whole thing."

Cade and Holt nodded their understanding, then in an obvious effort to lighten the mood, Holt propped his boots on the empty chair at their table and said, "I've been wondering...what does this do to your reputation of being the luckiest man in Texas? I can't wait to see what Wilhemina Peters does with the news. Hell, she'll come out of retirement."

"Watch out, Fort Worth, if that's the case," Cade observed.

Holt grinned, then continued, "The way I see it, some folks might think your state of luckiness just took a hard hit. After all, out of the blue, you find yourself saddled with a wife and kid. How can that possibly be considered lucky?"

Cade flipped a poker chip into the air again and snorted. "Hell, all anyone has to do is get a gander at Mrs. Grey and they'll figure it out. Don't take this wrong, Lucky, but your lady is a looker."

"I won't argue that."

"And if the boy is all she told you he is, then you are doing all right there, too."

"No thanks to me," Logan grumbled, his mood remaining bleak. "She said he's bright. I hope she's right about that, and I hope it's more than book smart. He'll need quick wits and keen intelligence to survive in the hellhole of Black Shadow Canyon until I can get him out."

"Hunting a lost gold mine amongst the scum of the earth... The boy must have more nerve than a toothache," Cade said.

Holt nodded his agreement, then added, "Let's hope he inherited your lucky streak, Grey."

Logan didn't bother to respond to that. The whole lucky business had stuck in his craw ever since Nana Nellie first pasted the nickname on him. Out of respect for the woman he'd grown to love, he kept his opinions to himself, though he'd always wanted to ask her why she thought a person who had lost his entire family in a flood could be considered lucky. So what if his suspenders had caught on a log and kept his head above the raging waters until they receded? His entire family had died! He simply couldn't consider that being lucky.

Logan continued to keep his mouth shut about the idea because doing so suited his purpose. While he believed that people made their own luck rather than luck falling on their shoulders like fairy dust, he did recognize that having a lucky reputation often paid off. Opponents were easier to bluff in card games if they believed in his good luck. Folks were less likely to challenge his opinions if he tied them to his good luck tendency. Most important of all, he figured his reputation lessened the number of gunfights he got involved in by at least half. Men didn't mind matching their skills, but when it came to gun luck, superstition ruled the day.

Logan shoved back his chair and stood. "I'm going to try to catch Tom Addison. I'll look y'all up tomorrow."

He'd gathered his hat and started for the door when a stranger's voice brought him up short. "Lucky Logan Grey! I'm calling you out."

The piano music suddenly went quiet. As Logan turned to face a broad-shouldered stranger, he vaguely wondered when, if ever, he'd walked through a Saloon paying such little attention to his surroundings. Today's events certainly had taken a toll. "Who the hell are you?"

"My name is Bo Pilchard and I'm told that you're the man who put my brother in the hospital today."

Today? Who had he put in the hospital...oh. This morning seemed like forever ago. "Was your brother attempting to rob the bank?"

"Yes, I fear that is true. However, I made a promise to my mama that I'd have my brother's back. His brains are scrambled, so I'm afraid that puts you and me at odds. I demand retribution."

Logan noticed that friends rose from their seats and moved into protective positions as he asked, "You figuring to pull a gun on me?"

"No. That wouldn't be right considering it was a bank robbery and all." He held up two large fists. "I'm aiming to take my family vengeance with these."

"A rumble." Logan considered the idea. It had been a while since he'd indulged in a good old-fashioned bar fight, and the idea of throwing some good hard punches lifted his spirits. Maybe that was just the medicine he needed tonight. "You know what?" he replied, grinning. "Right at this particular moment, I can't think of anything I'd like better than a rumble."

Well, except maybe a tumble.

With his wife.

Distracted by the thought, Lucky missed his block and caught a hard jab to his jaw. As his head snapped back, he heard Cade whistle and Holt observe, "Now that's what I call a lucky punch."

Lucky, hell. Logan rolled up his sleeves and dived into the fight.

CHAPTER FIVE

Caroline glanced down at the note in her hand, then up at the placard on the door. Thomas M. Addison, Attorney at Law.

Her stomach took a roll. It had been rolling ever since the note from Logan arrived at her hotel this morning asking her to meet him here. Why would he want her to attend a meeting with an attorney?

To discuss divorce?

She swallowed a sudden bad taste in her mouth, then smoothed the skirt of her simple walking ensemble as her teeth tugged at her lower lip. It wasn't as if she hadn't considered the idea herself numerous times over the years, though she'd never followed through on it. It was silly for a woman in her circumstances to shy away from scandal. After all, she made her home with mostly reformed outlaws. Nevertheless, even in Artesia, where society was for the most part forgiving and accepting, the stigma of divorce was difficult to overcome. It was better to be a deserted wife than a divorced woman.

Besides, it wasn't as if she had a reason to need a divorce. She had no beau. She hadn't wanted one. She had Will and Ben and Suzanne. That was enough. And on those nights when she'd lain in her lonely bed and yearned for something more, well, she told herself it didn't matter. Nobody's life was perfect. She should be grateful for the blessings she had and not be greedy about it.

A divorce. Caroline's hand trembled as she reached for the doorknob. If that's what this was about, then she would deal with it. Maybe its time had come. Maybe the usefulness of this marriage had ended yesterday when she told Logan Grey he had a son—a legitimate son. Knowing she stood on solid moral ground regarding the marriage had given her the strength to approach the man. Now that she'd confronted the past, perhaps she'd feel free to move forward once Ben was safe and sound.

"Think positive," she murmured as she opened the door.

Warm walnut paneling lined the walls of the outer office. A large painting depicting the fall of the Alamo dominated the room, and as she viewed the graphic nature of the scene, Caroline wondered at the reasoning behind hanging such a picture in this particular law' office. Was it a warning? Something like *Beware, this is a place of slaughter?*

His gaze warm and admiring, a young gentleman stepped out from behind a desk. "May I help you?"

"I'm Caroline Grey. I believe Mr. Addison is expecting me."

"Yes, ma'am. Very good. This way. They're waiting for you." He led the way to a door at the end of a short hallway, then rapped on the frosted glass. "Mr. Addison? Mrs. Grey has arrived."

Seconds later the door swung open to reveal a dapper gentleman with kind brown eyes and a winsome smile that set her immediately at ease. "Mrs. Grey. It's a pleasure. I'm Tom Addison. So glad you could join us this morning."

Us? Caroline's gaze tracked into the office where she spied Logan standing at a window with his back toward her, a dark shadow framed by bright morning sunlight. Tension reignited and sizzled along her nerves. She pasted on a smile and said, "Hello, Logan."

He turned his head and her eyes widened upon seeing his black eye and the cut on his chin. What in the world had happened to him? He nodded, then turned back to the window without so much as saying good morning. *Well, that's rude.*

She tried to work up a snit, but failed. There wasn't room for any snit in amongst her guilt.

She'd barely slept last night because of it. All night long, images of Logan Grey's expressions as he'd listened to her accusations and revelations played across her brain. She'd misjudged the man. He truly didn't deserve the worry she'd dumped in his lap.

Logan believed his son to be in mortal danger when in fact, Will was happy as a pup with two tails getting to bunk with his best friend, Daniel Glazier, for a few days back home in Artesia. Not only was Daniel Will's favorite partner in mischief, but his mother, Ellen, was the best cook in the county. Her pot roasts were legendary, and she'd won the Best In Show blue ribbon for her desserts three years running at the Ector County Fair. Will was in far more danger of suffering bellyaches than bullet wounds at the moment, and it wasn't right that his father thought otherwise.

But it is for Ben. Don't forget that. You can't forget that.

"Would you care to sit down?" Mr. Addison's question jarred Caroline back to the present. He gestured toward one of a pair of wingback chairs in front of his desk. Caroline took her seat, smoothed her skirts and wondered if Logan would budge from the window and sit beside her. Instead, Addison sat in the chair and reached for the folder lying atop his desk. "We have some papers for you to sign."

"Already?"

That roused a comment out of Logan. "What do you mean, 'already'?"

"I thought it took more time to instigate a divorce."

"Divorce! What is this sudden obsession with divorce?" Logan scowled ferociously as he shook his head at her.

"Divorce is a huge undertaking, and even though it's possible to do, it's not at all common. Who the hell said anything about divorce?"

"Isn't that why you summoned me here?"

"No!"

The attorney smoothly interjected, "Mr. Grey has established a trust fund for your son, William. I need you to verify a few details for me if you would?"

A trust fund? Caroline sat back in her chair in shock. Absently, she responded to the attorney's questions while her mind spun. Logan wanted to give Will money? Oh, my. She'd never even considered the financial aspects of inviting him into Will's life. Foolish of her in hindsight, but this never had been about money.

"Will is well provided for," she said quietly. "I don't need your money."

"Don't make an issue of this, Caroline." Logan linked his arms behind his back. "Will is my son. I'll provide for him financially. It's my right and responsibility. Had I known about him from the start, I would have done so then."

"I didn't come to you for money."

"I understand that."

She folded her hands in her lap, squeezing hard. "Having you do this makes me feel...inadequate."

"That's stupid," he said with a shrug. "You shouldn't take this as a criticism or an attempt to usurp your authority. If I choose to do either of those, I won't beat around the bush. You won't have any doubt that's what I'm doing."

That, Caroline could believe. Logan did strike her as a forthright man who wouldn't play games. Still, the whole idea that he'd do this made her a bit...squirmy. She could better accept it if she weren't smack-dab in the middle of this big fat fib.

The attorney placed a flurry of papers before her and beneath Logan's glare of expectation, Caroline abandoned any effort to resist. She signed her name where he told her, initialed where he indicated and did her best not to think about the monumental change in her life these actions represented.

Not the money, though she'd have to think about that, too, at some point. No, what this did was indicate Logan Grey's intention to be part of Will's life. The boy wasn't hers alone any longer.

Maybe that won't be such a bad thing, she told herself. Contrary to all her expectations, Logan might be a good father for Will, although she wasn't ready to commit to the idea as of yet. There was that darkness in him Wilhemina Peters had mentioned. She'd like to understand that.

The man certainly was a puzzle. She wanted to ask him how he'd come about his black eye.

"Lastly," said the lawyer, interrupting her reverie, "Mr. Grey has asked me to give you a copy of this." He handed Caroline a long cardboard folder thick with folded papers and titled with a single word: *Will*.

"You want me to give this to Will?" she asked.

The attorney shook his head. "It's Mr. Grey's Last Will and Testament."

Caroline jerked her hand back and dropped the folder. As Mr. Addison bent to retrieve it, Logan shook his head in disgust. "It's just a precaution. Stick it away somewhere, Caroline. With any luck you won't need to look for it for years to come." Then, with a glance to the lawyer he added, "We're done here, right, Tom?"

"I believe so." He handed Logan's will to Caroline with a smile.

"Good. Thanks for your help, Addison. If you'll come with me now, Caroline, we have a few other errands to tend to." He hooked his arm through hers and led her out of the building.

Sunshine toasted her skin as Caroline ventured out onto Throckmorton Street. The aroma of baking bread floated on the gentle breeze and reminded her she'd neglected to eat breakfast. She'd been too nervous to stomach anything in anticipation of the law-office meeting, and while the bread smelled delicious, she still doubted that she could choke anything down. Not while Logan Grey held her arm, anyway.

His touch overwhelmed her. His presence overwhelmed her. Everything about Lucky Logan Grey overwhelmed her.

"My friends Cade and Holt are making this trip with me," he told her as they walked up the street. "We'll all leave on the eight-fifteen in the morning. I purchased you a ticket going as far as Artesia."

Caroline studied his casual expression, and deduced that he expected her to make a fuss about traveling with him all the way to Black Shadow Canyon.

Well, she wasn't a fluff-headed female with more emotion than good sense, and she knew she had no business going to Black Shadow Canyon. It wasn't a place for women, not even a woman who could hold her own during a bank robbery. It was one thing to challenge a trio of outlaws in the center of a city, but something else entirely to put herself in the middle of an isolated den of black-hearted killers and thieves.

Now, if her child truly were in danger, she'd walk through hell itself to save him, but she'd be smart about it. She wouldn't complicate the situation or escalate the danger by being hardheaded and going somewhere she shouldn't go. If Will truly had run off to Black Shadow Canyon, she wouldn't demand to tag along with those attempting to rescue him.

Probably.

Not all the way to the canyon, anyway.

Unless she thought he'd need her there. Then she'd go. Nothing would keep her away in that case. That wasn't being fluff-headed. That was being a mother.

But Will wasn't in danger. Ben was. At his age, in his condition, he wasn't equipped to survive the perils of Black Shadow Canyon. His past reputation would protect him only so far. He didn't have the skills or the total lack of conscience to survive in a place where it was said people killed on a whim.

Her friend, the father of her heart, was in danger.

Lucky Logan Grey was her best—her only—hope of getting him home safely.

That's why she intended to make the trip all the way to Van Horn, which was the railroad station closest to Black Shadow Canyon. Since the train made an hour-long dinner stop in Artesia, she had every intention of disembarking at that point. He didn't need to know that both she and Will would board on new tickets for a sleeping car before the train pulled out of the station, and that Logan and his friends wouldn't see them until they arrived in Van Horn.

That's when she would confess her lie, and she and Will would make their plea. Logan already cared about Will. His actions today proved it. In the time she had left this afternoon and tomorrow, she would do whatever she could to reinforce those feelings and to strengthen them. Then, when they revealed themselves and the truth, she had to believe that Logan wouldn't disappoint his son, not when he was so close to the canyon and not while staring into eyes so much like his own.

But he didn't need to know any of this now, so her only response to his comment about buying her a train ticket was a simple, "Thank you. It'll be good to be home."

He led her into the mercantile, where he piled his selections on the counter. Ammunition. Lots of ammunition. A campfire coffeepot. A new bedroll. Caroline's brow arched in surprise as she watched him dawdle over a baseball glove.

He picked it up, then set it down. He walked to another aisle and added a pack of playing cards to his purchases.

Then he wandered back to the sporting section and picked up the baseball mitt yet again. "Does the boy like baseball?"

"He does. He likes it very much."

He hesitated another moment, then tossed the glove onto the shelf. "He probably has a mitt."

He obviously wanted to buy Will a ball glove, so why the uncertainty? Did he think she wouldn't allow it? "He has a mitt, but it is worn near to pieces."

"Hmm."

Logan stepped down the aisle to a section of personal-care items and took half a minute to inspect a can of tooth powder. Caroline wasn't prepared to confront him about his wishes, but she decided to try once again with a subtle approach. "Last summer he and his friends played almost every evening. Will is wicked with the bat, but he says he needs more control throwing. He is always after Ben to play catch with him. Ben's rheumatism makes that difficult."

Logan glanced back toward the mitts, and the yearning on his face all but took her breath away. "Oh, for heaven's sake, Logan. Just buy him the danged thing."

His lips twisted in a rueful smile. "You don't think he'd throw it back at me? I should have been the one playing catch with him."

What was it about seeing a streak of vulnerability in a strong man that made a woman's heart melt? "He'll be thrilled with the glove, Logan. He'll probably ask you to play catch, then try to fire the ball so hard that it breaks your hand."

"Do you think?"

"Yes, I think."

It was like opening the floodgates of a dam. Logan bought the glove, then he added baseballs and a bat to a pile of purchases he built atop the counter. He added a slingshot, a checkerboard, marbles, another deck of cards and a new straw hat to the stack. When his gaze lingered on an advertisement for a bicycle, Caroline put her foot down. "No. You'll spoil him."

"It's not spoiling. I have fourteen years worth of birthdays and Christmases to make up for."

She tried to come up with an argument against that, and failed. After briefly debating color choice, he ordered a red bicycle for Will.

Logan didn't slow down until he wandered to the section of the mercantile that sold saddles. There, he paused. "When I was a boy, I wanted my own horse more than anything else in the world. I knew what he'd look like, right down to the white stockings on his legs. A few years after I left the orphanage I saw him. He was tied to a hitching post in front of a saloon in Big Spring, Texas, and he stepped right out of my imagination. I'd have done anything to own that horse."

Caroline's eyes went wide. "Did you steal it?"

"I'm flattered by the high opinion you have of me." He smirked. "I bargained as hard as I could, but the owner wanted fifteen dollars more than I had in my pockets. Couldn't get him down another dollar. I did talk him into giving me a week to get the cash."

"Did you raise the money?"

Logan reached out and trailed a finger across the saddle's supple leather. "Couldn't find any work in Big Spring, so I went on to the next town."

She put the pieces together. Big Spring wasn't far from Midland. "You met my father."

"Yep." He flashed her a sheepish grin. "The day I left you, I went back to Big Spring and bought myself my dream horse. Named him Scout. Happiest moment of my life. I thought I had everything in the world." He sighed and shook his head. "Scout was a damned fine horse. Saved my life twice while I was living down in Mexico. He took me all the way to California to see the Pacific Ocean. Had him for eight years."

"What happened to him?"

"I was working for the Long Bar Ranch in Eastern Colorado when we tangled with a gang of cattle rustlers. Bastards shot him right out from under me. What about Will? Does he have a horse?"

"You are not buying Will a horse."

"But—"

"No. Will already owns a horse, a bay gelding Suzanne and Ben gave him for his eleventh birthday."

"What about a dog? A boy should have a dog. I always wanted a dog when I was growing up. We adopted a stray one time, but something about him made one of the girls sneeze. Nana Nellie made us give him away."

"No dogs, either, Grey. You can give him all the baseballs you want, but I absolutely draw the line at things that breathe."

"But a dog—"

"He already has a dog. A mutt named Sly."

"Sly, hmm? That's a good name for a dog. But you know, dogs are often better behaved when they have a playmate of their own. Maybe we could get Sly a companion."

"No. Sly doesn't need a companion. One dog is plenty for our household."

"Spoilsport."

"Yes, it's another word for mother, I'm told."

He laughed and paid for his purchases, making arrangements to have what he couldn't carry with him boxed and delivered to the station in time for tomorrow's train. As they departed the mercantile, Caroline shook her head at the packages in his arms. "Your extravagance is ridiculous. I don't know whether to thank you or scold you."

He teased her with a wink, then suggested, "Instead, why don't you tell me more about our son. Is he a good student?"

"When he wants to be. He's quick at mathematics, and he has a curious mind that helps him excel in science. But he's a horrible speller, and don't even get me started about his Latin lessons."

"Latin? Why does the boy need to know Latin?"

Caroline halted abruptly. "Oh, my. That's amazing. You sounded exactly like him."

"Oh, yeah?" A smile hovered on his lips and the gleam in his eyes betrayed his delight at the thought.

Watching him, Caroline was once again struck by how wrong she'd been about Logan Grey. This wasn't a man who had turned his back on his child. Impulsively, she said, "I have a sketchbook. Suzanne had a talent for drawing, and Will was her favorite subject. Would you care to see it?"

He grinned with pleasure. "I'd like that very much."

"It's in my room at the Blackstone Hotel."

"Good. I can leave these packages there." He shifted the shopping bags into his left hand. "I don't know why I didn't have everything boxed up and sent to the train station."

"You weren't through playing with your new toys," Caroline observed as he brought the brass spyglass up to his right eye and pointed it toward the Texas flag flying atop the courthouse.

He shot her a wicked grin that she felt clear to her bones. When he followed the grin with another wink, her toes literally curled.

Oh, dear. With that one exchange, all the old feelings came rushing back. The desire she'd felt for one man, this man, welled within her, burgeoned and bloomed and heated her blood. Her cheeks flushed and her mouth went dry.

She was so ashamed. She should be beset with worry for Ben, but instead she was brimming with lust for Logan Grey. She'd be mortified if he noticed.

———

"Are you hot, Caroline?" Logan asked. "Your face is all red."

"I'm fine," she insisted. "Really. A little thirsty, perhaps." She gave a shaky little grin and increased the speed of her steps.

Logan ambled along behind her, his attention divided between the events of the morning and the saucy sway of Caroline Kilpatrick's—no, Caroline Grey's—hips. *His wife's* saucy, swaying, curvy hips. When she arrived at Addison's office, she'd expected to be served with divorce papers, and she hadn't been happy about it.

Interesting. Not as interesting as her curves, but still interesting.

What would happen after he rescued the boy? And he refused to think of any other outcome than that. Did she want to stay married? To maintain the status quo? Hell, what did *he* want? He had a financial responsibility, yes, and he'd see it through. But what about beyond that?

Divorce? No. Absolutely not. He knew the stigma divorce attached to a woman. Might as well call her a whore. He couldn't do that—wouldn't do that—to Caroline. Or to Will. But what was the alternative? Just walk away?

Or, maybe stay? The possibility floated through his mind like a dream. He could stay. Have a wife. Be a husband. Make a family. Make a home.

Whoa. He glanced up at the sky. Had he been out in the sun too long or what?

Logan didn't stay. He didn't want to stay. Never had, never would. He'd been a wanderer since the day he left Piney Woods Children's Home and the life suited him. His job suited him. He had freedom to go where he wanted, when he wanted. He lived in the here and now and that was the way it was gonna stay. He wasn't cut out for family life.

He'd learned that lesson all too well.

No, staying wasn't an option. Divorce wasn't an option. So what options did they have?

Logan veered around a broken jar of molasses lying on the sidewalk. Hell, he didn't know. This was all so fast. He was still digesting the fact that he had a kid.

His gaze fastened on the flash of bare ankle her swaying skirts displayed, and against his own better judgment, he indulged in the fantasy of having a wife—this wife—do all the wifely things a woman can do for a man.

Whoa. Don't go there, Grey. You're asking for trouble.

Yeah, but a little trouble sounds so good right about now.

He closed the distance between them as they approached the entry to the Blackstone Hotel, and with his hand familiarly at her waist, he ushered her inside.

Heavy doors and thick walls shut out the sounds of the city

outside. Dark paneling and upholstery in reds, greens and golds created a rich, wealthy atmosphere that encouraged muted voices. As they walked farther into the lobby, the heavy scent of lilies clashed with that of cigars. Logan wrinkled his nose. He never had liked lilies. Made him think of caskets.

Caroline dug her room key from her handbag as she led him up to the third floor. Her room was nestled against the staircase. Small, it contained only a bed, a little chest and a writing desk and chair. Her satchel sat in the chair, so Logan dumped the shopping bags atop the writing desk, then while Caroline removed her hat and set it atop the chest, he sat at the foot of the bed, thinking about how strange this situation was.

It was as if they were really married, having returned from a shopping trip for their child. They were comfortable with each other. Familiar. Easy.

Oh, hell. This was scary.

In the process of pouring a glass of water from the pitcher on the writing desk, Caroline's hand jerked and water splattered on the desk. "Oh, for crying out loud," she murmured, taking a handkerchief from the pocket of her skirt and wiping it up.

It flusters her, too, Logan realized. Ordinarily, he wasn't so slow on the uptake where women were concerned, but recent events would knock any man off his game. Now that he'd noticed, what would he do about it? What did he want to do about it?

Hell, Grey. You're chock-full of questions today. How about an answer or two?

"Water?" she asked, shoving a glass in his direction.

"No thanks."

She nodded, then tossed it back like a shot of raw whiskey. Yep, she was flustered, all right. And nervous about being alone with him in a hotel room. Did she think he'd lose control and ravish her?

He tucked his tongue into his cheek. The notion did have a certain appeal.

Come to think of it, that was what happened last time they'd been alone together in a hotel room. He'd certainly lost control and they'd ended up ravishing each other for most of the night.

Still, he'd like to think he'd gained *some* control in the past decade and a half. But then again, her beauty had ripened and matured in that time, too. Making her all the more desirable.

His body stirred.

Maybe she had reason for concern.

"I brought the sketchbook because I thought you might like to see it. Sketchbooks, actually. I brought two. I have a series of them. Suzanne started a new one every year on his birthday. I brought Will's first-year book and his sixth-year. Do you want to see them both?"

"Sure."

She opened her satchel and removed a pair of leather-bound books. Handing one to him, she said, "This is his baby book."

Logan's attention shifted from the mother to the son when he opened the book to see a rendition of a smiling infant with rosy cheeks and a tuft of red hair atop his head. "He has red hair? I thought you said it was dark."

"When he was born his hair was red, yes, but it didn't last. It darkened as he grew older."

Logan grinned and turned the page. "Plump little bugger, wasn't he?"

"He was hungry all the time and that hasn't changed. Keeping that child fed has been one of my greatest challenges."

Logan paged slowly through the infant pictures. Before this moment, he'd never had much interest in babies. He found it nearly impossible to relate to them. But with this little guy…everything was different. Look at that smile. Caroline said Will had his smile, but she was wrong. That smile was just like his mother's.

"I confess that little babies terrify me. They seem so fragile that I'm afraid I could break 'em."

"The McBride sisters all have little ones. Hasn't being around them gotten you past that fear?"

"Nope. I stay away from the infants—for good reason. When I was ten or so, someone abandoned a newborn at the orphanage and Nana Nellie asked me to give it a bottle. My hand shook so much that I put bubbles in the milk and gave the baby gas. Nana Nellie never asked me to help with him again."

Caroline laughed. "I was so young and inexperienced when Will was born that I did some of the dumbest things. It scares me now to look back on them. That poor baby—it's a wonder he didn't bleed to death from all the times I accidentally stuck him with diaper pins."

"Live and learn, I guess." In so many areas.

Logan continued to turn the pages of the sketchbook, watching his son grow up before his eyes. Will sitting up and playing with a variety of toys. Will chewing on a red ball. Banging a spoon on an overturned pot. Gleefully knocking down a tower of wooden blocks. He got a little gooey inside when he saw the drawing of his son holding a cowboy hat bigger than he was over his head, his green eyes alight with delight, his smile wide and showing off a pair of new teeth.

"He does have my eyes," Logan said, speaking past a blockage of some sort in his throat.

"Yes. Like I said yesterday, you certainly left your stamp on him. I knew he looked like you, but I didn't realize just how much until I saw you again."

"I'll bet he's not all like me." Curious, he glanced up at Caroline. "Tell me how he's like you."

She thought a moment, then shrugged. "Oh. I don't know."

"Come on. I know there's something." Logan wanted the answer as much to learn about his wife as about his son. "Tell me. Will is...?"

"He has a temper like mine," she finally said, a rueful tip to her smile. "It flashes hot and fierce, but we tend to get over it fairly quickly."

"What else?"

"Will inherited my sweet tooth. I'm a fool for chocolate, and Will is just as bad." Smiling, she added. "We have contests to see who gets the last piece in a box of chocolates."

Logan studied his wife, then glanced back down at one-year-old Will. "He has your smile, Caroline. Bright and open and infectious. That's a real nice gift you passed along to our boy."

Color stained her cheeks. "He's a happy child. Or at least he was. I haven't seen his smile very often since Suzanne died."

He detected a glimmer of guilt in those gorgeous eyes of hers. "You can't blame yourself. From what I can see, you've been a good mother. That's all any kid could ask for."

"I love him. He's hurting and I can't fix it. That makes it hard for me."

Logan took her hand and gave it a comforting squeeze. "We'll bring him back safe, Caroline. Don't doubt it."

After she gave him a shaky smile, he resumed his perusal of the sketchbook and saw his son learn to crawl, then walk. Four of the drawings included sketches of Caroline, and Logan lingered over those. She'd been young to face all that she'd faced. Seeing her in these drawings drove that point home, and admiration at how well she'd managed washed through him.

"Can I see the other one?" This time when she handed over the book, he grabbed her arm and tugged her down beside him. "Tell me about the pictures as we look at them."

"I can do that standing up."

"I'm getting a crick in my neck from looking up at you. This way is more comfortable."

Unsettled, Caroline shifted her weight on the thick feather mattress and established a good foot of space between them. Logan countered by closing the distance as he opened the sketchbook, propping it half on his lap, half on hers. He breathed in her lemony scent and studied the first drawing, which depicted Will playing with a dog. In his mind's eye he saw another child playing with a different dog, but he ruthlessly buried the memory, cleared his throat and said, "Now, that's a cute kid. You say he's six years old in these pictures?"

"No. I thought I had a different book. This is actually his five-year-old book."

"Gunslinging Suz was quite an artist."

"I have a beautiful watercolor of a sunset back home that she painted, but she always said that Will was her favorite subject."

"She loved him. You can see it." Logan carefully thumbed through the pages, stopping at one that showed Will staring at a barber pole, his expression etched with horror. "Tell me about this one."

Her smile turned wistful. "He'd just had his first haircut in the barbershop. What a battle that was! Will has a cowlick right here—"

She gestured toward the crown of her head. "It got to where no matter how I tried, I only made it worse when I cut it. I decided I needed professional help and, oh my stars, that turned out to be a mistake. Will took one look at the barber's chair and turned and started screaming."

"He was afraid?"

"Terrified. I was shocked. Up until that point, he'd been Mr. Fearless."

"What did you do?"

"The barber sat down on the floor and asked Will to sit in front of him and that was that."

"I've known a barber or two I wish I'd run from," Logan said, chuckling, as he turned the page, then froze. His breath rushed out in a whoosh.

The drawing depicted a day at the swimming hole. Will knelt beside the water playing in mud, his face streaked with dirt, his grin wide and a little bit ornery. Suzanne had drawn herself seated on a quilt, a sketchbook in her hands.

"Oh, dear." Caroline grabbed at the book. "I forgot about that drawing."

Logan kept a death grip on the page. Caroline lay against another quilt, her long, lush eyelashes resting above rosy cheeks as she slept. Her hair was mostly dry, pinned in wild disarray atop her head, though a few straggling curls lay in damp ringlets against her cheeks. From the neck up she looked like a Madonna in repose, a peaceful, resting angel.

From the neck down...one word came to Logan's mind. Sin.

Her bathing costume would have gotten her arrested in a public venue. Instead of one of those navy-blue bloomer girl uniforms he'd seen women wearing on California beaches and along the Texas Gulf Coast, she wore what appeared to be her underwear—white, lacy, thin. Transparent.

"Please, Logan." She tried to yank the book from his grip.

Yes, it pleased him.

The wet fabric clung to her skin, outlining the shapely length of her legs, the curve of her hip, the fullness of her breasts. Motherhood had softened her body and given it a lushness that she carried still today.

He reached out with an index finger and traced the line of her figure from her bare feet up her calf to her thigh and—

Caroline yanked hard and successfully snatched the book away and slammed it shut. "Really," she muttered. "I don't know why I didn't tear that page out of the book. Suzanne had no business..."

His gaze locked on hers and in her wide violet eyes he watched both awareness and trepidation bloom. She moistened her lips. The air between them thickened and went hot. "No business what?"

"M-m-making me look like that."

"Like what? Beautiful? Alluring? Sultry?" When she closed her eyes and shook her head, he focused on her lips. "You were all those things, Caroline. You *are* all those things...and more." He leaned forward, pressed a butterfly kiss against her lips. "Tempting." He touched his lips to hers again. "Tantalizing."

Her mouth opened on an evocative little gasp and Logan rimmed her lips with his tongue. "Tasty."

She shivered. "Oh, Logan."

He laid claim to her with his kiss, plundering her mouth, tasting her, taunting her, demanding she respond. For a brief moment, her spine remained stiff, her muscles tense, but when he made a low-throated sound of encouragement, the dam broke.

She returned his kiss with a fiery heat that seared him to his bones. The sketchbook slid to the floor as her hands lifted to rest upon his shoulders, then clutch him there as he took the kiss deeper.

Logan speared his fingers through her heavy curls. Her lips moved firmly beneath his, and her tongue met his with a heady passion. Desire pulsed in his blood and instinct took over. Fitting his hard frame against her soft curves, he pressed her back...back...then he rolled them both until she lay full and flat against the mattress. At his mercy.

He settled in beside her and lifted his head just enough to breathe. "Caroline."

Her eyes were closed, her breathing shallow and fast. Her lips, swollen from his kiss. Beautiful. So damned beautiful.

His hand tugged at the buttons lining the high neckline of her suit until he revealed the creamy skin he sought. Then he skimmed his mouth across her cheek to her neck where he nibbled and licked and sucked on her skin until she shuddered. Boldly, his fingers trailed down her bodice, exploring the luscious swell of her breast. Her breath caught and she squirmed beneath his touch, shaking her head back and forth as he cupped her fullness, kneaded her, teased her nipple to a turgid peak. Mentally, he cursed the layers of fabric separating his palm and her sweet skin.

He wanted her naked. He wanted to see her bounty revealed, to touch and taste and sample at his leisure. He wanted to free his aching erection and thrust inside her hot, slick passage, to take her and claim her and slake his lust and hers until they both collapsed in exhausted bliss.

And yet, the small part of him that retained possession of his wits recognized the danger in pursuing the pleasure his body so fervently demanded.

It was too soon. He and Caroline had too much left to settle. Indulging themselves here and now would only complicate an already complex situation.

Knowing this delightful interlude must end, he captured her mouth once more in a hard, deep kiss that communicated his need and frustration and desire. Then with a groan, he wrenched himself away from her and lay on his back beside her, gritting his teeth and breathing as if he'd run ten miles in five minutes.

Caroline lay without moving for a full half a minute, then abruptly levered herself to a sitting position. "Oh my."

She scrambled off the bed and whirled on him, her eyes wide and wild. "Oh my," she repeated.

With jerky fingers, she buttoned the neck of her blouse. Embarrassment bloomed on her cheeks like roses.

She went to the door and opened it. "You need to leave now."

He sighed and rolled to a seated position. "Caroline…"

"Just leave. Please, just leave." A shrill note entered her voice as she added, "You know how to do that. I know. I was there."

He stood and took a step toward her. "Honey…"

"Stop! Go! I've done this once. I'm not doing it again."

What was she talking about? Sex? "Have you not had sex again in all this time?" Hell, he'd been young, sure, but... "Was I that bad?"

"No. I haven't been with another man, but that's not what I mean. I've raised one child alone. I'm not going through that another time. Do you hear me? Not again. Never again. Get out of here now, Logan Grey, or I'll...I'll..."

"Wait a minute." Logan dragged his mind away from the fact that she'd remained virtuous all this time and thought about what she'd said. His own temper flared. "Wait just one minute. I'll take a lot from you—heaven knows I deserve it—but give me some credit here. I learn from my mistakes. Don't be talking like I'd walk out on you again if you turned up pregnant, because I wouldn't. I won't. Take that as a promise or a warning, however you wish."

He grabbed his hat and headed for the door, pausing at the threshold to say, "I don't know how things are going to settle between us, Caroline. I figure we both have some thinking to do. I know that I want you. It took every ounce of discipline I possess to roll away from you just now, but I did it. I want credit for that."

"This isn't a contest, Logan Grey."

"Right about now it feels like a war, to be honest. And speaking of honest, you need to be honest with yourself and admit that I was the one who pulled back today. Blame me and curse me, but you were right there with me."

She sucked in a breath as the color faded from her face. Quietly, she said, "I know that."

Logan dragged a hand through his hair. "Look, Caroline, I don't want to hurt you. There's a fire between us, and there's no denying that. How we choose to deal with it...well...it seems a shame to waste it. Heat like that doesn't come along very often."

"I shouldn't be thinking about heat. I should be thinking about fear and danger and rescue. I won't be ruled by my passions, Logan Grey."

"Seems to me that indulging in and being ruled by are two different things. And you can't think about Will's trouble all the time. That will drive you crazy. Believe me, I have plenty of experience in such things. That aside, I reckon we should both spend some time deciding what we want and how we intend to deal with one another. But, Caroline, when you are doing your thinking, you need to know this. No matter what happens to us, I aim to be part of that boy's life from here on out. You invited me in, now you're going to have to deal with me."

Logan expected her to slam the door behind him. He wasn't disappointed.

CHAPTER SIX

From her hotel room window, Caroline watched dawn break in a symphony of pinks, oranges and golds. She'd slept maybe an hour over the course of the night and that was spent curled up in a fetal position at the head of the bed—as far from the spot of her stupidity as possible.

She couldn't believe what had happened. Couldn't understand how she'd left her brain in the hallway when she brought Logan Grey into her room. What was it about that man that sapped every bit of sense she possessed? He was like a vampire who sucked away her intelligence rather than her blood. That he turned into a hot, pounding pulse of sexual desire.

"Leave it to Lucky Logan Grey to be different from all the other vampires," she muttered.

She butted her forehead against the cool window-pane. She wasn't being fair. Her behavior wasn't Logan's fault. None of this was Logan's fault. Not really. She was the one who was here under false pretenses. She was the one who brought him into her room.

The fact of the matter was she'd had an infatuation for Logan Grey since she was in pigtails. "Will I never grow up?"

Actually, she might well be forced into such a state when they reached Van Horn. Logan might not forgive her lie.

Maybe she shouldn't regret what had happened as much as what had not happened. That may well have been her last chance to enjoy marital relations with her husband.

"Aargh!" She banged her head against the window-pane three more times.

An hour later, bathed and dressed and with her defenses shored up, Caroline left the Blackstone Hotel. The downtown street bustled with activity as workers hurried to begin their business day. The aroma of freshly brewed coffee and bread right out of the oven drifted on the cool morning breeze. Caroline stopped at the bakery owned by the McBride sisters' aunt Claire and purchased a cinnamon roll for her breakfast and a scrumptious-looking chocolate cake she intended to take home to Will. Then, fifteen minutes before the train's scheduled departure, she arrived at the Texas and Pacific Depot.

Logan and his two friends waited outside. Caroline greeted Mr. Driscoll and Mr. Hollister before turning to her husband. She had to force herself to meet his gaze. "Good morning, Logan."

"Mornin'." Without betraying any remembrance of their encounter the previous day. He peered into the shopping bag she carried and whistled. "Look here, boys. Caro brought us a treat."

"No, it's for..." Oh. Wait. She couldn't say Will. This lying was absolutely a problem for her. "Lunch. The cake is for dessert after lunch."

"Oh, that's one of Claire McBride's cakes," Holt Driscoll observed, eyeing the printing on the bag. "You know, ma'am, lunch is an awfully long time away. How about we make it a midmorning snack?"

The hopeful waggle of his eyebrows made Caroline smile and reconsider. After all, these two men were risking their lives for her family. If they wanted Will's cake, they could have it.

"Here." She handed Holt the bag. "Have it whenever you want."

"What a woman," Cade said, snatching the bag from his friend's hand. The two men scrapped like little boys over the sweet and set the tone for the first few hours of their trip.

With passengers in the railcar surprisingly sparse, the men stretched out on one bench apiece, allowing Caroline a seat of her own, also. Conversation remained light and easy, and none of Logan's comments to her ventured into personal matters. Thank goodness.

Cade talked her into breaking out the cake in the second hour of the trip. They'd finished the entire thing by the time the train reached Abilene.

Caroline drifted into sleep shortly after lunch, and she dreamed that she was home and that Suzanne was still alive. It was a lovely fantasy; she stood at the stove stirring a pot of stew while Suzanne worked flour into bread dough on the counter. Will's laughter rang out from the other room and moments later, a man's hands gripped her waist, a mouth nuzzled her neck. *Logan.*

Awareness trickled in. She was warm. Comfortable. Secure. The scent of starch and bayberry tickled her nose. Mmm. She didn't want to wake up.

So she didn't. She snuggled against the warmth, drifted and dreamed.

This time her dreams turned dark.

She is alone in the middle of a vast plain. Something bad is happening, something terrible, and she needs to get home. She starts running but she doesn't know what direction to go. Fear is a big black raven that sinks its talons into her shoulders and flaps its wings, creating a violent wind that makes it harder for her to run. Suddenly, the raven screams and the plain transforms to a mud bog that sucks her feet until she sinks to her knees.

Then on the horizon, light dawns and reveals a shadowed figure standing with his arms outstretched. Thunder booms and from behind her comes the pound of hoof beats headed her way. She twists around and as lightning flashes against a red sky, she sees a horseman riding out of the black void. His horse is black. His clothing is black. Beneath the broad brim of his black hat, red eyes glow.

Caroline wants to scream, but she can't make a sound.

Lightning blazes and thunder rolls and bitter cold wind whips over her as the devil-rider rides past, flying toward the light. The figure on the horizon begins waving his arms.

Caroline hears a cry, a shrill keening sound. Then laughter. Harsh, maniacal laughter that causes the raven's claws to dig deeper.

She struggles, battles against the mud that now threatens to swallow her.

Thunder cracks and booms as the horseman rides straight for the figure that shouts out, "Ma!"

"Will!" she cried, breaking through the dream, fighting her way free of the mud, which upon awakening proved to be Logan Grey's arms.

"Shush, sweetheart," he murmured, nuzzling her temple. "It's all right. Everything is fine. You were dreaming."

"What...?"

"It was a dream. Probably the storm brought it on."

Caroline's head felt thick, her thoughts slow as cold molasses. Deep within her she felt a bone-chilling fear. "Will."

"I thought it might be something like that." Logan gently brushed her hair away from her face. "I know you must be frightened half to death about him. This is a difficult burden to bear."

A dream. It was just a dream. Caroline drew in a deep, shuddering breath. "It was dark and loud. Someone was after Will."

It was so real, she thought, her heart racing. So terrifying. The coppery taste of fear coated her mouth, and she thought that if she had needed to stand up, her knees wouldn't have supported her weight. She'd never had a dream like that before, so clear, so threatening.

Probably her guilty conscience acting up. That's what lying would do to a person.

Better that than a premonition.

"Oh, dear." She shuddered, and Logan patted her knee.

"It's been dark and loud outside," he said. "We went through a thunderstorm while you were sleeping. Looks like we're heading into another one now. They tend to come in waves this time of year."

Only then did Caroline become aware of the view outside the railcar. They were passing through a part of Texas that was flat from horizon to horizon. Off to the west she could see a thundercloud that seemed to fill the entire sky.

"West Texas always needs rain," she murmured. Then, when the fact that Logan had his arm around her finally dawned on her, she added, "You switched seats."

"Couldn't stand to watch your head bobbing any longer. 'Fraid you'd get whiplash. Besides, some rough-looking characters from the other car joined us. Didn't like leaving you alone."

Caroline knew she should straighten up and put some distance between them, but she couldn't summon the will to do so. Her dream lingered like a hangover, and Logan provided that unique comfort she'd wished for thousands of times over the years. He was Will's father. He could share the burden of her worry. What would that hurt? "How long did I sleep?"

Logan slipped his right hand into his pocket and pulled out a gold watch. His left arm didn't budge from around her. "A couple of hours. You must have been tired."

"I didn't sleep well last night," she admitted.

"More bad dreams?"

Due perhaps to the lingering effects of her dream combined with the constant presence of guilt about her lie, Caroline was compelled to answer honestly. "I couldn't stop thinking about what happened."

"In your room," he clarified.

"It just...I don't know what happened."

"I do. Desire sizzles between us like that lightning flashing out there on the prairie. We had it fifteen years ago and we have it still today."

"It's not normal."

He chuckled. "Sure it is, honey. It's nature at its finest, although from my experience, it's rare as bluebonnets in October." He traced the whorl of her ear with his index finger as he added, "I think we would be doing ourselves a great disservice if we fail to take advantage of it."

"Of course you think so. You're a man."

"And you are a woman who is missing out on one of life's greatest pleasures. I told you yesterday we needed to think about our situation and I spent some time doing just that. I have to tell you, honey, the fact that you've been celibate all these years knocked me for a loop right at first. Someone with your fire and passion and beauty—it's a damned shame. I figured that men must have come calling from time to time—after all, you're as beautiful as a summer sunset—so for you to sleep alone all this time means you must have some powerful convictions regarding sexual relations outside of marriage."

That managed to clear the remaining cobwebs from her brain. "It's called adultery, and yes, I do believe it's wrong. The Bible makes that very clear."

"See? That's not a problem for us. You can do it with me free and clear. You won't have to waste yourself anymore." He patted her knee and smiled with satisfaction.

She almost took a swing at his jaw. *Waste myself? Waste myself!* "Of all the egotistical..." She literally bit her tongue, took a deep breath, then continued. "So what are you suggesting? Are you proposing we live together as man and wife in every sense of the word?"

"In the sexual sense, definitely. Beyond that, well. I'm not a home-and-hearth kind of man. My job prevents that, if nothing else. However, I do intend to keep as close an eye as possible on Will, so I will be around whenever it's possible. I think it's a good solution, honey. Your life won't have to change hardly at all, but you'll have the benefits of the bedroom."

"Lucky me," she muttered beneath her breath. "You don't have a clue about family."

He went stiff. "Mine died when I was five, so no, I don't have a lot of experience."

Caroline folded her arms and studied him, the details she'd learned of his past rolling through her mind. She could see him all too well, a bedraggled little boy who'd lost everyone he'd loved. It broke her heart to imagine, and it also gave her a bit of insight into how he could be so clueless when it came to women, marriage and family.

She shook her head. "You have a point, Logan. I'm not at all certain I agree with it or accept it, but I can see why you would think what you do. The good thing is that nothing needs to be decided now. We're on a train, not in a hotel room. You're dangerous in a hotel room."

"Hell, honey." He chuckled and lowered his voice even more. "I could be dangerous right here if you were of a mind."

She scooted all the way over against the window and he laughed out loud. "All right. Don't fret. I'll behave...for now."

Caroline looked away from him, staring out toward the oncoming storm. She didn't know what to say to him. Logan Grey was a constant surprise to her. When she had decided to come to Fort Worth, she had known he might want a relationship with Will. She'd never expected he'd want one with her.

She had never dreamed she would like the idea so much herself.

"I've been thinking about Will, too," Logan continued. "I grew up without a father so I know how difficult that is on a boy. I decided that I'm glad that Will has had your friend Ben as another male he could look up to—even if he is an old outlaw. I had Reverend Jennings so I know what a blessing that can be. Still, that's no substitute for a flesh-and-blood father. Will is fourteen. These next few years are important for a young man. They're the years he'll need a father the most. I can't be around all the time, but I can be around enough to matter."

"That would be good for him."

"It would be good for you, too."

Caroline listened to the rhythmic *click click click* of the railcar wheels and tried to put her emotions into words. "It's just that this is all happening too fast. You and I don't know each other."

"We know each other as well as some other married couples I know." He gave her hand a squeeze, winked at her and added, "I can guarantee you that we will set the sheets afire, and I doubt there are any other couples who've been married fifteen years who can say that. Well, except for maybe Trace and Jenny McBride. Those two still have some special sizzle going on between them."

She rolled her eyes. "I think you are spending way too much time thinking about one subject."

"Maybe if I got to do more than think about it I wouldn't be so focused."

She ignored that. "We haven't spent enough time together. Once we do, we might not like each other at all. I have a temper, Logan."

He gave her a droll look. "I did pick up on that little fact when you threw my medallion at me."

"And you drank a lot that night. I don't care for drunkards, Logan Grey."

"Hey, I had every reason to toss back the whiskey that night."

"I won't argue that. However, for all I know it's an everyday occurrence for you."

"It's not. I admit I had a bout of trouble with whiskey years ago, but nowadays, I'm damned near a teetotaler." Logan glanced over his shoulder. "Hollister. Driscoll. Have a question for you. How often would you say I overindulge in spirits?"

Cade sat with his long legs outstretched on the seat, his back propped against the side of the railcar, his arms folded and his hat pulled low on his brow. After Logan asked his question, he thumbed the hat back and said, "You're kidding, right?"

"No. My wife wants to know if I'm a drunkard. She noted that I drank quite a bit at the dinner party at Willow Hill."

Holt rubbed his whisker-shadowed jaw with the palm of his hand, his blue eyes twinkling as he snickered. "Mrs. Grey, that night was a special circumstance. He needed some liquid courage. That's the most I've seen Lucky drink in years. See, ordinarily, the man can't hold his liquor."

"He's good for two drinks, then he falls asleep," Cade agreed. "I figure all the excitement the other night kept him awake."

Logan shrugged sheepishly. "I've taken a lot of ribbing for it over the years. You don't need to worry about me being a drunkard. Now see, you know something more about me. What else do you want to know?"

Caroline shook her head. "I don't know. I haven't thought about it."

"Oh, c'mon now. Are you trying to say you've been married to me for fifteen years and you haven't spent some time wondering about me?"

"It's different wondering about such things when you are sitting beside me."

"You want me to go back to my other seat? That'll mean Cade and Holt will be able to hear our entire conversation, but if that's what you want..."

Caroline didn't know what she wanted—except that she'd rather this all be happening without The Big Lie hovering between them. That was the real problem here. No matter what Logan said and no matter what ideas she'd be happy to consider, she knew that the situation was likely to change once Logan learned her true purpose.

She shook her head. "I guess it wouldn't hurt for us to have a conversation—a private conversation. It'll help pass the time."

"I can tell you anything and everything you'd want to know about me between here and Artesia. I'm not that interesting of a person."

Now that was an out-and-out lie. Nevertheless, his casual attitude put her at ease and allowed Caroline to ask a few of the questions she had wondered about from time to time over the years. "All right, then, tell me this. I'd like to hear your version of how you came to be known as the Luckiest Man in Texas. I know how the Fort Worth *Daily Democrat* told the story, but I'm curious to hear it from your point of view."

Logan's smile of satisfaction at her agreement dipped into a grimace at her request. "Shoot, Caroline. Can't you ask me something more exciting than that? Like maybe how I like my eggs cooked in the morning?"

"No. I don't think so. You see, I believe there is something to it. Considering what I've asked you to do, I need to believe it."

He rubbed the back of his neck. "I guess I asked for this, didn't I?"

"Yes."

After taking a moment to gather his thoughts, he said, "I think luck is like a snowball that starts rolling downhill. Once it gets going, it picks up more speed and more snow and that makes it harder to stop. That's why I haven't tried to discourage the talk, even though most of what is said about me is pure nonsense."

She didn't like the sound of that. She truly needed him to be lucky for this whole scheme to succeed. "Oh? Like what?"

"I haven't been in thirty gunfights without being wounded."

"How many gunfights have you had?"

"It's not the number of gunfights. It's the wounded part. I have a nice little scar just above my hip bone." He waggled his brows. "I'll be happy to show it to you later."

She ignored that and pressed. "So you're saying you're not the Luckiest Man in Texas?"

"Exactly. That's just silly sensationalism for the newspapers to have something to write about. Damned newspapers make up half of what they print."

"That's not true," she protested. "My family runs a newspaper and we don't make things up. But back to this snowball. There must be something at its center to send it rolling downhill. You *must* be lucky."

He *had* to be lucky. Otherwise, she couldn't ask him to go into Black Shadow Canyon after Ben.

His intense green eyes studied her. "It's important to you that I'm lucky."

"Yes!"

"You'd think I'd be accustomed to this by now." His mouth twisted in a crooked grin. "All right, then, Caroline. I guessed the correct number of pickles in the barrel at the general store and won a new hat when I was fifteen, so I guess that makes me lucky."

"Oh, stop it. I'm not talking about pickles and new hats. I want to know what is at the heart of your reputation." He sighed heavily. "You don't want the legend, you want the truth."

"Exactly."

He frowned at her and delayed by checking his pocket watch again. She could tell he really didn't want to take the conversation in that direction. "You're the one who suggested we get to know each other. The only way to do that is to share the important things."

He repeated his sigh. "Oh, all right, but I want you to understand that I'm sharing something I ordinarily keep to myself. It sounds strange to say, and I'm not asking you to believe in it, but the truth of the matter is that I...well...I sense trouble."

"What do you mean?"

"I can't explain it other than to say that more often than not, I get this feeling when trouble is headed my way. It's like my senses grow sharper. The hair on the back of my neck stands up. Sometimes it even seems like time slows down. I'm totally aware of everything going on around me, and because of it, I'm able to get out of the way of trouble."

"You have a Guardian Angel."

"Could be. When I was young I liked the idea that my mother was up in heaven watching out for me. That notion grew troublesome once I started romancing the women, so I decided instead that I have an extra sense. A trouble sense. I pay attention to it, and as long as you're hanging around with me, I hope you will, too."

She eyed him suspiciously. "That depends. It appears to me as if a man could take advantage of such a claim."

"I could." He stretched his legs out into the aisle and crossed his ankles. "However, I won't. That's just wrong. As soon as I start using my gift to manipulate people, I'm liable to lose it."

"You are superstitious."

"Sure am. What man who is still standing after thirty gunfights wouldn't be? Look, I don't know if this thing I have is a gift from God or a quirk of nature or the result of my tuning into something every one of us possesses, but whatever it is, I appreciate having it. It's saved my life more times than I can count, and it's helped me save the lives of other folks. I'm not going to jinx it by using it wrongly." He paused, stared her straight in the eyes and added, "I don't need my trouble sense to get you back into my bed. I have other weapons for that."

Staring into those mesmerizing green eyes, Caroline didn't need a sixth sense to know that he intended to use those weapons at the first opportunity.

Heaven help me.

LOGAN FIGURED he'd come up with the perfect solution to the problem. He wanted this woman. Badly. And he didn't need his sixth sense to know it. She fascinated him. It was more than her beauty, more than the sexual attraction that hummed between them. Caroline Kilpatrick Grey had backbone, and he found it infinitely appealing.

Look at what she'd accomplished in her life, all that she'd overcome. Many women would have folded in the face of the adversity that had come her way. Not Caroline. When life knocked her down, she'd climbed right back onto her feet, dusted off her skirts and made a home and family for herself that from all appearances made her happy. A man had to respect that.

Logan respected it. He respected her. She had those same qualities that made the McBride sisters such strong women. She was intelligent and courageous and determined. She was generous, kind and committed to those she loved. Nana Nellie would have called her a virtuous woman.

Logan didn't need to know more. Fate and her father had given him this opportunity. Only a fool would allow it to pass him by, and Logan was no fool. He would use these hours between now and their arrival in Artesia when they were simply man and woman, husband and wife, to win her.

"I need to stretch my legs. Care to walk with me, Caroline?"

"I'm fine here."

He stood and grabbed her hand and pulled her to her feet. "Walk with me."

"Where? There are only two passenger cars to walk through."

"So we'll turn around and walk them twice."

He led her out to the open vestibule where the two cars connected, but instead of opening the door to the second car, he stopped. He backed her against the railcar and boxed her in, one arm on either side of her. "I didn't really want to walk," he told her, moving close. "I felt the urge to back up my words, and I didn't want witnesses."

Her eyes were round and wary, but he didn't miss the excitement flickering within their depths.

"Which words?"

"I'm flashin' one of my weapons."

Then he kissed her.

And made it count.

Logan branded her with his mouth, pouring every bit of talent and technique he'd developed over the years into the act. He tempted them both by lingering over her lips, ravishing her with his teeth, his tongue. He wanted her boneless and aching and aware of all he had to offer.

When his control stuttered, he knew it was time to pull back. He nipped her bottom lip as he lifted his head away, then spoke in a deep-throated, gravelly tone. "You are the most intoxicating woman, Caroline Grey. You make me lose my wits. We are going to be so good together."

"That's manipulation."

"No, darlin'." He touched her soft cheek and smiled into those sea-blue eyes. "That's seduction, and you're as guilty of it as I am."

"I'm not trying to seduce you."

"You don't have to try. You just do. It's a natural happenstance." He stepped close to her and inhaled her citrus-and-spice scent. "Since I'm married to you, maybe I should rethink the whole snowball idea. Maybe I really am the Luckiest Man in Texas."

But as he bent his head to take her mouth once again, something stopped him. A black sense of foreboding swept over him. *Oh, hell.*

Immediately, he went on alert, one hand going for his gun as he turned to shield Caroline with his back and take stock of the situation. He didn't have far to look.

The threat was real and ugly and as frightening as anything he'd ever seen. The dark cloud of the thunderstorm had turned a shimmering shade of green and now bore down on the train.

But what brought Logan's heart to his throat was what he saw dipping, churning, twisting toward the ground. On the ground.

Tornado. Big and black and violent.

It was headed right toward them.

CHAPTER SEVEN

Logan's thoughts fired like rounds from a Gatling gun. The people on this train were sitting ducks, but stopping the train and getting off wouldn't do them any good. There wasn't a damn bit of shelter anywhere on this plain.

Yet, the damned thing could change directions. Twisters were known to do that. Or, it could lift back up into the cloud. It could miss the train entirely.

But that wasn't going to happen. He knew it.

The dark cloud churned toward them. It had to be a mile across in width. They had to prepare, to protect themselves as best they could and hope for a measure of good luck.

Caroline cried. "Oh, my. Logan. Look!"

"Yeah. Let's get inside."

He led her back into the railcar saying. "We got trouble. A twister is bearing down on us. A big one. We don't have much time."

Cade and Holt came to their feet as a woman passenger cried out in fear. Nervous conversation rose around him as Logan made a quick head count. Ten people total in this car. Probably fifteen or twenty in the other car, plus the railroad crew. Could be a lot of hurt folks before this was over.

Cade said, "What do we do, Lucky?"

"Not much we can do. I think—" Logan broke off as he sensed a change in the momentum of the train. "They're braking."

They heard the squeal of brakes as the train began to slow.

Holt stared out the window and murmured, "It's huge."

Caroline spoke in a calm, collected voice. "We should protect ourselves from flying glass."

"True." What Logan truly feared was that they'd need to protect themselves from flying railcars. A storm like this one had the capacity to lift a train and toss it about like a stick.

One of the passengers cried out. "We're all gonna die!"

"No, we're not," Caroline insisted. She gestured toward Logan. "This is Lucky Logan Grey, the Luckiest Man in Texas. He will not die in a tornado today, so we're lucky to have him with us."

"Come stand by me," a man called.

"Nobody needs to be standing." Holt shifted his gaze from the window to Logan. "The twister isn't changing direction. It's time for us to move."

"Move where?" Cade asked. "Under benches?"

Logan focused on the cloud and listened to his instincts. "If we stop soon enough, I think we're better off underneath the railcar as long as we have time to get there."

"It'll be close," Holt said.

"Well, I'm not going anywhere," another passenger said.

Logan glanced at Caroline. "Go stand at the front of the car, honey. Be ready to move at my word."

Brakes continued to squeal. The railcar's speed continued to slow. Logan watched the twister advance and was awed by the display of nature.

The thunderstorm stretched from north to south and moved in an easterly direction. Away from the tornado, lightning flashed from cloud to ground. Rain fell in inky-blue sheets from green clouds that so often indicated hail. The twister hooked down from the southern edge of the storm, a black, twisting vortex with a peculiar kind of beauty. At the base of the funnel where it touched the ground, dust and debris billowed up into the air. It was chewing up everything in its path.

"It could miss us," the female passenger said, hope in her tone. "I'm gonna pray that it misses us."

"You do that, ma'am," Cade responded as she hit her knees. "Prayers never hurt."

Logan figured the angles. Nope. It wasn't going to miss. It was just too big a storm and its path hadn't changed in the two or three minutes since he'd first spotted it.

The air around them had gone hot, sticky and still. Heavy. Ominous. In that moment, he knew. "Let's go. We have to move now."

Cade and Holt didn't hesitate and they pushed Caroline along with them. Logan jumped to the ground behind his friends and wife, vaguely noting that only one of the other passengers accompanied them. The railcar's wheels rolled a slow half turn, then stopped.

They scrambled beneath the train as a roar, the loudest sound Logan had ever heard, bore down upon them. Lying between the rails, Logan climbed on top of Caroline, shielding her as best he could while he dug the toes of his boots against the railroad ties.

Cade positioned himself at Caroline's head, Holt at her feet. Both men grabbed hold of Logan, an unspoken testament to their faith in his good luck.

Logan could feel Caroline trembling beneath him, and in an attempt to distract them both, he spoke into her ear. "I've thought about lying on top of you, but I was hoping for better circumstances."

She made a gurgling noise that might have been a laugh or could have been a scream just before the roar of the twister drowned out all other sound.

Logan braced himself as the world started to shake. Seconds passed like hours. He closed his eyes and hunkered down and prayed that his luck would hold. He and Caroline couldn't die here and now and leave their son orphaned and in trouble.

Logan quit thinking as hell descended upon them. The noise—a huge, howling, earsplitting roar unlike any he'd heard before—rolled over them as the twister ripped and tore and destroyed, the unholy wind battering everything in its path. Logan's ears popped as the railcar above them rocked once. Twice.

It lifted from the rails and flew away.

Exposed to nature's fury, Logan pressed himself into Caroline, into the ground, his hands gripping the rails as he tried desperately to hold on and anchor them to solid ground. Something hit his shoulder hard. He heard Cade shout out in pain. The wind tore at him, sucked at him. It went on and on and on.

He couldn't hold on much longer.

Logan felt his grip slipping. His left arm stung as something pierced it deep. His legs lifted. Caroline screamed.

He lost his hold and went sailing into the storm. Something hit his head and blackness descended.

THE WORLD FINALLY WENT STILL.

Her breath sounded harsh to her own ears as Caroline cautiously lifted her head and opened her eyes, and gasped.

Death and destruction surrounded her. Railcars lay smashed and peeled open like tin cans. Scraps of metal, wood, paper and cloth scattered the area like oversize confetti. Black smoke rose from a fire burning west of her.

The bodies of horses and of humans littered the ground.

"Logan." She eased up onto her knees and looked around. Holt was giving his head a clearing shake. Was he hurt? She didn't see Cade or Logan anywhere. "Logan?"

The fear that had eased a bit upon the tornado's passing came pulsing back. He had lain on top of her— protected her—and now he was missing. "Logan!"

No response. The only sounds to be heard in the eerie, deathly silence were keening wails, broken sobs and cries of pain.

Holt muttered a curse, then climbed to his feet. "Lucky! Cade!" he yelled out, his voice just a little bit shaky. When no one answered, he closed his eyes for just a moment, and when he opened them again, the fierce determination Caroline saw in them reassured her.

"You all right?" he asked, helping her to her feet.

"I think so. Yes. I am. Holt..."

"We'll find them," he said, his smile grim. "They'll be all right, too."

She covered her mouth with her hands as she stepped off the railroad track and identified the nearest prone figure with unseeing eyes as the man who'd joined them beneath the railcar.

"Help me. Help me," came a weak voice.

Caroline followed the sound and spied the woman who'd stayed in the railcar to pray lying pinned beneath an unidentifiable scrap of metal some yards away. Beyond her a good twenty yards from the rails sat the other passenger railcar, flipped over onto its side. She heard a child's cry coming from inside. "We have to help these people," she told Holt.

"We need some organization, a system. We need to assess all the injuries then determine who needs help first."

"While we look for Logan and Cade," she said.

"Exactly. We'll cover more ground if we split up. You okay with that?"

She nodded. "Most of the debris is north of the track. How about I take east of here and you go west? We'll meet back here as soon as—"

She broke off abruptly when movement off to the northeast caught her notice. Someone ran toward them, coming fast, the figure too far away to see clearly. Nevertheless, she knew. "Logan. Logan!"

She picked up her skirts and started running. He cradled one arm against him as he ran, but when he saw her, identified her, he opened his arms wide. She ran into them, wrapped her own arms around him, buried her face against his chest and sobbed. "You're alive!"

"Yeah. How are you? You okay?"

"I'm fine. Frightened, but okay. Logan, was Cade with you?"

He stilled. "No."

Holt caught up with them. "You're covered in blood, Grey."

He glanced down at his left arm. "It's just a poke. Nothing important." He met his friend's gaze. "Cade?"

Holt shook his head. "We were just headed out to look for you two." He gave Logan a quick rundown of their plan.

"Please!" came a weakening female voice. "Somebody help me! I can't stop the bleeding."

Caroline made a quick decision. "You two go. I'll stay here and do what I can to organize—"

A loud explosion ripped through the air.

Logan moved to shield Caroline, hollering, "It's the locomotive. I could see it burning from where the wind dropped me."

"Fire," Holt breathed as flaming debris launched into the sky, then fell back onto ground. In some places, rain-dampened ground failed to catch fire. In others, brush kindled and burst into flame. "Jesus. What next?"

Tornado survivors screamed and ran as chaos reigned. Logan shrugged out of his jacket and took charge. "We have to stop it before it gets out of hand and kills us all. Caroline, check the woman. Holt, come with me. You, there!" he called toward two men who stood around in shocked inactivity. "Help put out these fires!"

Caroline rushed toward the wounded woman's voice and found her bleeding profusely from a cut in her upper thigh. She stripped off her petticoat and tore it into strips which she used for bandages, first on the woman, then on a child she pulled from the railroad car and finally on the puncture wound in Logan's arm.

Under his direction, the men succeeded in containing the fire. He then directed efforts to assist the wounded and free those trapped inside the railcars and beneath large pieces of debris. As soon as his conscience would allow, he left in search of the missing.

With the fires put out, an uninjured passenger took a quick count which showed they had seven dead, fourteen injured and four unaccounted for. Eight passengers and one crewman had made it through the storm relatively unscathed. Caroline was thrilled to discover that one of the injured was a physician. He had a lump the size of a small fist on his head, but once his thoughts cleared, he set about sewing up cuts and splinting broken bones.

A half hour after the tornado struck, Holt returned to the site of the wreckage with the discomforting news that he'd located two of the missing, both dead. Of Cade, he'd seen no sign.

He turned right around to continue the search in another direction when a shout alerted them to a rider approaching from the east, a second riderless horse trailing behind him. "It's Logan," Holt said. "I can tell by the way he sits a horse."

"Where did he find a horse? Two horses?"

"There's no telling. He's lucky that way."

As Logan drew closer, Caroline realized that he wasn't alone. "Look, Holt. He has someone with him."

This time it was Holt who took off running, but when he halted abruptly, Caroline's heart sank to her toes. The figure riding in front of Logan was slumped over double. Like deadweight. Caroline recognized the green plaid shirt. Cade.

"Doctor? Doctor Barnes? We need you!" she called as Logan rode up. She wouldn't believe that Cade was dead. She wouldn't! She hurried to make a place for him. spreading out a blanket, then urging the doctor to hurry along as Logan rode up to them.

He handed Cade down to a waiting Holt. "He's alive. He's still alive."

"What happened to him?" Holt asked.

Caroline's breath caught. He was covered in blood from head to boot. In a day of horrific sights, this was one of the worst she'd seen.

"Damned barbed wire." Logan slid from the saddle and helped Holt carry their friend to the blanket. "He was wrapped in it completely."

"How did you get it off?" Caroline asked even as her gaze went to his bloodied hands.

"It was bad. I didn't have any clippers of any kind. My knife wasn't any help. I started to leave him and ride back for a tool, but then I heard a pack of coyotes." He briefly closed his eyes. "I had to unroll him."

"Oh no," Holt murmured.

Logan cleared his throat. "Think his legs might be broken. One of 'em for sure."

"Let me have a look," the doctor said.

Cade's skin was torn in too many places to count, everything from slight scratches to deep, ugly gouges. The doctor cut away his trousers and revealed that not even the heavy denim had protected him. Standing by with wash water, Caroline felt the tears rolling down her face.

"Let me do this," Logan said, taking the bowl from her hands.

"I've been nursing other men..."

"I know. But I know my brother, too. He wouldn't want you to see him this way."

His brother. These men were brothers, weren't they? They were family. And Logan's and Holt's hearts were sick with worry. She gave his shoulder a squeeze, then turned away. There were plenty of people who needed help.

Caroline lost track of time as she tended to those unable to tend to themselves. She spent a few extra minutes with the train's engineer, who said he'd experienced a religious conversion and asked her to pray with him. He thanked the Lord for numerous blessings, including the fact that the train had carried fewer passengers than normal. As he spoke, Caroline realized that today's disaster could have been much worse.

Maybe Logan's Guardian Angel existed after all.

"Hey, lady?" a man called. "I can use some help here."

Caroline turned to assist him and while she kept a smile pasted on her face, her heart sank. He sat propped against the back of a seat that had been ripped from one of the passenger cars, and she recognized him as one of the rough-looking men whose entry to their railcar caused Logan to change his seat. Despite his grimace of pain, something about the look in his eyes made her uneasy.

"What is it?"

"I have this pain." He winced and rubbed his thigh, then shifted his hips as if trying to get comfortable. "Think you could take a look at it for me?"

"Are you wounded? Bleeding?"

"I'm aching something fierce."

She tangibly felt the avid gazes of his three companions and in that moment, she knew to beware. "Let me get Doctor Barnes."

He reached out and grabbed her skirt. "I want you, pretty gal." He tugged hard, pulling her to her knees, then he grabbed her hand and shoved it onto his crotch. "Rub my ache."

The gunshot bit the dust at the man's feet. "Let her go now or the next one goes in your head," Logan said.

The villain's grip loosened enough to allow her to snatch her hand away. Logan leveled a deadly glare on the man as he helped her to her feet. "You all right, honey?"

"I'm fine." She smiled down at the vermin while tugging a knife from her pocket. "Consider yourself lucky that my husband showed up. I grew up on a cattle ranch. I learned castration at an early age." It startled a laugh out of Logan, which Caroline considered a victory.

"C'mon." He pulled her away, saying, "You are some woman, Caroline Grey. A little scary at times, but damned fine."

"You wanted to know more about me, know this. I don't let anyone push me around."

Once they'd moved beyond earshot of the men, the smile slipped from his face. "I need to talk to you about something."

That sounded ominous. "Cade?"

"He woke up, so that's a relief. He said just enough so that we could tell his brains aren't scrambled. Doc thinks only one leg is broken, but all those cuts..." He shook his head. "Infection is a serious concern."

"Did you let Doctor Barnes look at your arm?"

"It's nothing. Piece of wheat stuck into me, that's all. Look, Caroline, we need help. When we don't show up at the next station they will send someone out to search for us, but the telegraph lines are down and the storm ripped up track both ahead of the train and behind it. No telling how long it will take for help to arrive, or how close they'll get to us."

Caroline realized where he was going with this. "Some of our injured can't afford a long delay."

"I won't have Cade survive the storm only to die from infection." He rubbed the back of his neck, and asked, "How well do you ride, Caroline?"

She blinked hard. "You want me to ride for help?"

"I'm going for help, and if you can keep up, I want you to come with me. I can't kill these peckerwoods who insulted you—much as I'd like to. Holt needs to concentrate on Cade, and I don't want to leave you here without protection."

"I can keep up, but I don't know about leaving. Doctor Barnes might need my help."

"There are others here who can fill in for you. Caroline, there is another aspect to this. This storm has delayed my arrival at Black Shadow Canyon by at least a day."

Her gaze swept over the scene and she got a sinking sensation in her stomach. "I did think of that."

"My first priority has to be sending help to these people here, but I'll keep going just as soon as that's done."

Caroline's head fell forward and she stared at the ground. "Holt will stay with Cade. Of course. I didn't think it through." Her gaze locked on a single wild dandelion, one spot of beauty amidst so much ugliness. "You plan to go into Black Shadow Canyon alone."

"Yes, but I'm not worried about that. It may well be safer that way."

The reminder of the reason why Logan, Holt and poor Cade had been on this train, part of this disaster, brought the guilt roaring back. The urge to confess all hovered on her tongue.

"I spoke with the engineer and pinpointed our location," Logan continued. "The closest town is about a four-hour ride south of here. Next one on the rail line is twice as far away. We'll get word to those who need it fastest if we head south, so that's where I'm headed. What do you think, Caroline? Are you able to ride and ride hard?"

The question he asked wasn't the one that mattered. The question was, what was she willing to do? Was she willing to tell Logan the truth when he would undoubtedly abandon her cause?

She stared around at the death and destruction spread out on the plain. She spied Holt Driscoll's weary, worried face as he sat next to the still figure of his friend. So much trauma. So much despair.

What a mistake she'd made thinking that her family's suffering mattered more than that of anyone else.

Shame all but brought Caroline to her knees. She didn't need to think about it any longer. She had to tell him the truth. She *would* tell him the truth.

But not here, not now. He had enough to deal with now.

Caroline eyed the pain etched across Logan's brow, the weary stoop to his shoulders, the worry dimming his eyes. Yes, not now. Later, once they'd gotten help for Cade and the other injured people, she'd confess.

And then she'd watch him walk away.

CAROLINE SWALLOWED HARD AND ASKED, "When do we leave?"

According to its residents, Parkerville was a town that refused to die. Ignored by the railroads, it should have gone the way of other small towns by becoming little more than a ghost town. However, a small core of determined families had kept it alive and thriving, and Parkerville remained the center of activity for area farmers and ranchers.

With a population just under six hundred, the town boasted three churches, one school, a post office, a hotel and two saloons. While everyone knew that the two-storied house on the south end of Main Street was a brothel, no one talked about it.

Most important, Parkerville had a telegraph.

The sun had set by the time Logan and Caroline rode into town, and as he'd expected, he found the telegraph office closed up tight. "Let's try over there," he suggested, gesturing toward a well-lit building sporting a sign that read Parkerville Dining and Drinking Emporium.

He peered through the window to ensure it was a suitable establishment for his wife to enter, then led her inside. He wasted no time before announcing, "A twister hit the rail line north of here. Where can I find the telegraph operator?"

That's all it took to mobilize help. Within minutes, the telegraphs had been sent and a relief effort was being organized on the church steps. Half an hour after Logan and Caroline rode into town, the first of the supply wagons headed out.

Caroline breathed a sigh of relief. "What wonderful people. I knew we'd find help here, but I never expected half the town to drop what they were doing and ride to the rescue."

"Salt-of-the-earth folks," Logan agreed, placing a hand at her back to lead her into the Emporium, where he'd been told they'd find a meal. "The minister's wife told me that five years ago a tornado killed three people and destroyed the church and two buildings in town, so they know what it's like."

The aroma of bread fresh from the oven greeted them as they entered the restaurant, and a friendly young man waved them over to a table. "Mr. and Mrs. Grey? I'm Harry Tompkins. This is my folks' place. Ma said for y'all to have a seat, and she'll get you supper right out. Special tonight was chicken fried steak with mashed potatoes and fried okra. Does that sound all right to you?"

"That sounds wonderful," Caroline said with a warm smile for the boy.

"Thank you, Harry. Chicken fried steak is my favorite." Logan waited until the boy had disappeared into the kitchen to add, "I wouldn't care if they were serving shoe leather as long as I could choke it down. I'm starving."

"Me, too."

But Caroline's actions didn't fit her words. When their supper came, she only picked at her food. Well, it had been one helluva day.

He wondered if she might be worried about sleeping arrangements. When he'd inquired into hotel rooms, he'd learned that the county fair had the town bursting at its seams. Logan had managed to talk his way into a room upstairs—one room with one bed. Caroline's eyes had rounded when he informed her of the fact, but she hadn't voiced a protest. Honestly, he couldn't tell what thoughts ran through her head right now. Maybe she was just too tired to think. Heaven knows he was exhausted. He couldn't wait to go to bed. With her.

Be damned if he'd sleep on the floor. She was his wife, after all. That at least got him half a mattress, the way he viewed it.

Not that he expected sex from Caroline. While he wouldn't turn it down, he didn't anticipate that she'd offer. Today had been a bitch of a day that had worn them both to a frazzle. Although, maybe after a good night's sleep...

"Eat your meat, Caroline," he instructed. "You need the nourishment. Besides, it's damned delicious."

She took an unenthusiastic bite. "Logan, if it weren't for the situation with Will, would you ride back to the train to be with Cade?"

"Tonight?" He frowned and took a sip of sweet tea. "Another four hours in the saddle? Can't say I'd look forward to it. I wouldn't be able to walk for a week. It's a good thing I don't have to try. I'm whipped."

"This is the first time you've stopped since the twister hit," Caroline observed. "Of course you are exhausted. You need to rest."

"I won't be sorry to see my pillow."

She pursed her lips and studied him. "You wouldn't do your friend any good if you dozed off to sleep in your saddle and fell off your horse."

"I don't fall off my horse." He glanced up from his plate, affronted. "Why are you fretting about this, anyway? I told you I'd make this delay as short as possible. I understand better than anyone how important it is to get Will away from Black Shadow Canyon as fast as possible."

She drew Xs in her mashed potatoes with her fork. "You'd be better off sleeping before you make a journey of any kind."

He sat back in his chair and frowned. "Is that what this is about? You're worried about our sleeping arrangements?"

She blinked, her expression suggesting that wasn't her concern at all. Nevertheless, he attempted to reassure her. "Look, Caroline, I know that we have a risky history regarding hotel rooms, but tonight you don't need to worry. After the day we've had, the only thing on my mind is sleep."

Hell, Grey, you are such a liar.

Her cheeks stained pink as she shook her head. "That's not what I meant. Oh, my goodness." Now she was flustered, and she hid it by concentrating on her chicken fried steak. She ate a third of her serving before speaking again in a rush. "I intended to talk to you about Will and Ben and the whole situation, but I'm just so...like you said, after the day we've had...I'm so tired, Logan."

His lips lifted in a half smile. "You've been a real soldier today, Caroline. You're an amazing woman. Now, why don't you take your amazing self upstairs and have your bath and climb into bed. I intend to linger over my meal, then I'll probably take a walk to work the kinks out of my muscles. I'm sure you'll be sound asleep before I make it upstairs."

"Yes. I think I'll do that." Her smile was both grateful and relieved. She dabbed her lips with her napkin, then pushed her head back and stood. "Goodnight, Logan."

"Goodnight, Caroline. Sleep tight." Watching her hips sway as she walked away, he murmured, "Don't let the bedbugs bite."

Now, husbands were something else, entirely.

———

CAROLINE FELL asleep in the bathtub and woke when the water cooled and left her chilled. As the events of the day came roaring back, she sat up abruptly and all but leaped from the tub. How long had she been asleep?

Swiftly, she dried herself, then donned the nightgown and robe one of the churchwomen had provided her. *Please don't let Logan already be in the room.* She couldn't face him again tonight. She simply couldn't!

She exited the bathing room and spied a matron waiting in the hallway. "Finally," the woman said with a disapproving sniff.

Caroline smiled sheepishly as she rushed past, saying, "Sorry. I fell asleep."

At the door to her room, she paused and listened, but could hear no sounds from inside. *Please oh please oh please.* She stuck her key in the lock, drew a deep, bracing breath and opened the door...to an empty room. "Thank you, Jesus."

She left her robe on and crawled in bed. She wanted to turn on the light and check the time, but knowing her luck, he'd pick that moment to walk into the room. So she pulled the covers up to her chin, closed her eyes and went to sleep. At least, she tried to go to sleep, but the day's events twisted through her mind like colors in a kaleidoscope. Not wanting to think about that, she attempted to focus her thoughts on Will. That only made her think about tomorrow, and the inevitable confrontation when she told Logan the truth.

She didn't want to think about that, either.

"I am such a coward. Putting this off."

I have good excuses. He does need his rest. He can't help Cade if he is half-dead from weariness himself.

"Still, excuses are all they are. I *am* a coward."

She sat up, punched her pillow, took half a dozen deep breaths to calm herself down, dropped back onto her back and started counting sheep. She'd jumped one hundred twenty-seven fluffy white animals over the fence when the door opened. She peered through slitted lids as Logan stepped inside.

The hall light shining behind him shadowed his broad-shouldered form before he shut the door, plunging the room into darkness. She opened her eyes wide at that point and stared in the direction from which the sounds were coming. Rustling-of-clothing sounds. The thunk of a belt buckle hitting the floor. More clothing rustles.

She couldn't see a thing in the darkness.

Floorboards squeaked as he stepped toward the bed. Caroline slammed her eyes shut. She lay stiff as a board, which she knew would give her wakefulness away. She must relax. Loosen her muscles.

The covers moved and the bed dipped.

She waited, pretending sleep, bracing herself to ignore his advance.

He stretched out, moaned softly with delight.

She sensed the heat from his body and her pulse pounded. She breathed in the scent of soap, not lavender like the bar she had used, but something different. Something cleanly masculine.

She waited.

He started to snore.

Well. Her eyes flicked open. She scowled into the inky darkness. Well. He's keeping his word. That's good. Right?

That's what she wanted.

She hadn't expected him to keep his word. She'd expected him to at least try something. He had every other time they had passed time together in a hotel room.

Shamefully disappointed, Caroline rolled over, punched her pillow and summoned the sheep once again. Her last conscious count was three hundred forty-seven.

At some point, she was back in her dream.

Back on the dark plain, at the center of a circle of swirling, churning white tornadoes. She stands on a pitcher's mound, a baseball in her hand. Will is at the plate with a bat. He is smiling and laughing and calling for her to make a pitch.

She doesn't want to throw the ball. She holds it in a fierce grip, her right arm stiff and heavy as lead.

"Come on, Mom. Throw it. Watch me hit it halfway to Oklahoma! Hurry, Mom. Throw the ball."

"No, Will. It's dangerous!" *She doesn't know how she knows, but the knowledge burns her heart like a brand.*

The baseball grows warm, then hot. Its temperature continues to rise until her skin begins to burn. Pain radiates from her hand, but still, she holds the ball in a death grip. She dare not let it go.

Then her hand burns away and the ball drops. But instead of falling to the ground, it slowly circles her. Once. Twice.

She tries to run, but her feet won't move. She tries to call out to her son, but she can't draw a breath. The baseball bursts into flames and picks up speed, swirling around her, faster and faster and faster. Beyond her the circle of white tornadoes moves closer.

Will's voice calls, "Mama. Throw the ball, Mama."

The tornadoes chant, "Liar. Liar. Liar."

"Mama! Throw the ball."

"Liar. Liar. Liar."

The flaming baseball whirls and twirls.

"Liar. Liar. Liar."

"Mama!"

The baseball circles her ankles so closely that it singes her skin. Then it travels up her body in a widening circle as if climbing a funnel until it rises above her head. At that point she can breathe again and she screams, "Will! Run!"

But it is too late. The flaming baseball leaves its path and shoots straight toward her son.

Filled with terror, she watches him draw his bat back. Like a comet, the ball hurtles toward him. He starts his swing.

"Will...no!" she sobs.

His bat connects, the ball explodes, and when the fire dies, her son is gone.

"Will!" She wrenched herself forward and awoke to find herself sitting up in bed, her heart pounding, her mouth dry. "Will!"

"Shush, Caro. You were dreaming again." Beside her, Logan sat up, switched on the bedside lamp and pulled her into his arms. "You had another nightmare. Understandable after the day we've had."

The events of the afternoon came rushing back. The tornado. The dead passengers. Poor, broken and bloodied Cade. She trembled like a leaf in a gale.

Logan stroked her hair and spoke in a soothing tone. "It's okay, sunshine."

"No. No, it's not."

"Look, I know you're worried sick about Will, but you need to listen to me. I will save our son." He pressed a kiss against her head.

Despair welled up inside her. He didn't understand. He *couldn't* understand. He didn't know the truth.

In her mind's eye, she saw Cade Hollister wrapped in barbed wire spinning through the sky, and at that, Caroline did something she very rarely did. She started to cry. "I'm so sorry, Logan."

"Shush, darlin'," he said, his hands continuing to stroke her, to comfort her. "Don't do that. Don't cry."

"It's my fault."

He chuckled softly, then pressed a kiss against her temple. "Your fault? I know you're a strong woman, Caro, but really, I don't think you command the winds."

"Cade wouldn't have been there if not for me."

"Now, don't do that." His big hands stroked up and down her arms. "There's no call for you to feel guilty. He was there for me, and because that's the kind of guy he is. Cade wouldn't want either of us to feel guilty."

"But that's because…Will. I have to tell you about Will."

"Ah, baby." He kissed away a tear. "It was just a dream. Let it go." He kissed the tears on her other cheek.

"You're shaking like a hen in a dust bath. Don't go back to that place."

His warm care and tenderness pierced the chill of her shame and guilt, touching a place inside her that had been frozen and lonely for so long. Fifteen years had passed since this man—since any man—had held her this way. Fifteen long, hard, lonely years.

She was too tired, too weary, too heartsick to resist the temptation. "Then keep me here, Logan. Make everything else go away. Just for tonight. Just let me have tonight."

CHAPTER EIGHT

Yearning glowed in her eyes and Logan knew he couldn't resist the quiet plea. He ran a finger along her cheek, her expression pale in the dim lamplight.

So pretty she was. So unique, unlike anyone else he'd ever been with. Strong, yet vulnerable. Surprisingly brave. A fine woman. A fine mother for his child.

Of all the too-many-to-count mistakes he'd made in his life, leaving Caroline Kilpatrick Grey alone in that hotel room fifteen years ago had been one of the worst.

And here, now, she wasn't asking for tomorrow. Tonight all she wanted was escape. She wanted a few hours here in the darkness where she could escape the horror of the day, her fear for their son and the nightmares that plagued her sleep. Logan desired the same escape that Caroline craved, but as he stared into those lovely, liquid violet eyes, somewhere deep inside himself, he knew she needed...she deserved... more.

She needed a husband. A real husband. One who didn't play at it part-time.

What if...

It floated through his head like a fantasy. What if it wasn't just for tonight? What if he put the past behind them and made a future with her? Made a life with her? It could be so sweet....

Stop it, Grey. You know better. You reached for that once before and look where it got you. You've been there, lived it and dug the graves to prove it.

He pushed fruitless fantasies from his mind, then stroked the hair away from her face and kissed her.

A sigh caressed his lips in return, and she pressed against him ever so slightly. Taking the cue, he moved his hands from her shoulders to the gentle dip of her waist. He explored her with lazy precision, reveling in her softness. As her body melted into him, he deepened the kiss, touching his tongue to hers, as he laid her back against the bed.

Unable to help himself, he made a low sound of desire and need as he trailed kisses up her neck. "Touch me, Caroline."

Tentatively, she touched his bare chest with trembling fingers. Featherlight at first, she grew bolder with his whispered approval. The heat of her hands stoked embers deep within.

My wife, he thought. If only for tonight.

Feeling an emotion he wasn't certain he could name, Logan lowered his mouth to Caroline's once again. This time, she matched his hunger.

He gave over to her completely, soaking in the smell of soap and warm woman, letting the sensations surround him. His body strained against her thigh, nudging, tempting. The need to make her his again was so powerful that Logan was certain that even another tornado wouldn't stop him.

He steeped himself in sensation. She tasted sweet, so sweet. The brush of her hair draping over his arm and shoulder and the lovely softness of her cotton-clad breasts pressing against him. The sounds she made, the perfect little moans of need, never in his life had he wanted a woman this badly.

Nibbling on her earlobe, he brushed his fingers along her breast and pulled at the ribbons on her robe, then the buttons of her gown to seek the warm skin beneath. Tentatively, he palmed the rounded softness, then rubbed a lazy thumb over her nipple.

"Oh," she gasped, arching into his hand.

As she gripped his shoulders, something in Caroline's voice gave him pause. Meeting her eyes, he froze when he noticed a fresh teardrop trail down to her pillow. "Caroline?"

"It's all right. Don't stop." Grabbing at his hand, she stayed his retreat. "Please don't stop. I'm just...feeling so much. It's been so long."

He hadn't forgotten that she'd named him as her one and only lover, and the knowledge filled him with a fierce, possessive satisfaction. "You think you're feeling now?" he asked, his voice low and rough. "Just wait."

He pulled the robe from her completely. He wanted her bare. He wanted her beneath him. He wanted her body one with his own.

So he stripped off her gown and left her naked. Skin on skin, he kissed her with more insistence, their tongues meeting and caressing. Remembering. Rediscovering. How could he have forgotten this warm, wondrous woman? She was like a song whose melody he'd remembered, but the lyrics remained forgotten.

Until now.

Now he remembered her. He would remember all of her all over again. Covering her supple breasts with both palms, he rubbed and teased the responsive tips with his fingers, enjoying every moan, every gasp.

Kissing her jaw, her throat, he blazed a path down to one straining nipple and took it between his lips.

She cried out, lacing her fingers in his hair.

Pleased, he licked and sucked, switching from one breast to the other until the soft and needful sounds she made broke on a sob. He loved that she was so responsive. Hearing her pleasure tightened his body and fired his blood even more.

What sort of noise would she make if his lips traveled even lower?

With a sharp intake of breath, Logan pressed his forehead against hers. He needed to gain a measure of control and thinking about tasting her...Whoa. He swallowed hard; the image was more than he could bear. *Get hold of yourself, Grey, before you lose it here and now.* They'd wasted too many years for this to end too soon.

He levered himself away from her, standing just long enough to strip off his pants and pull the medallion over his head, before joining her again in their bed. In their marriage bed.

It was heaven on earth, the feel of her. The heat. The magic. With moonlight spilling across the bed, the desperate urgency of two souls reconnecting filled the air. Looking down at her shining eyes, Logan let himself fall into her abyss.

"I need you, Caroline," he said in a low, breathless tone. He nuzzled her ear. "I have to have all of you."

"I'm yours," she whispered. Tracing a hand over his face, she let her finger run over his bottom lip. "All these lost years, I've always been yours."

"Mine." He grinned, slowly, wickedly. "Am I a lucky man, or what?"

Caroline laughed at the smug satisfaction in his tone. She couldn't help it. Joy sizzled along her nerves as heady as desire. When he caught her finger in his mouth and sucked hard, the heat coiling within her nearly burst. "Make love to me, Logan Grey."

And so he did.

His hot mouth covered her breast again, making her moan and arch and beg as his hand eased down, touching her where she ached the most. With light fingers, he brought her to the very brink of madness, only to leave her there.

Bereft when he drew back his hand, she protested, "Logan."

"I know, sweetheart. Let me give you what you need. What we both need."

He positioned her beneath him, lying between the cradle of her thighs. Instantly, the solid tip of him probed at her wetness, seeking an entrance she was helpless to deny. Above her, his jade eyes were hooded in the lamplight as he pushed inside.

He caught her cry with his mouth. It had been such a long, long time. The pressure of his body sinking fully into hers was deliciously illicit, and Caroline wanted more. Blindly, she reached around and gripped his back, pulling him closer. Wanting him deeper. Wanting to lose herself in him. But he remained still, as if trying to savor the moment.

"Caro," he mumbled against her mouth. "You feel so good, Caro. So very good."

She couldn't respond. It was all she could do to breathe. The feeling, the sensation of where they were joined overwhelmed her. She didn't want to talk. Didn't want to think. All she wanted was to feel.

Moving ever so slightly, she tilted her hips and spread her legs a notch farther. It was his turn to gasp, and feminine power coursed through Caroline. Encouraged, she lifted her body, taking more of him inside.

The look of exquisite pleasure that crossed Logan's face would be burned upon her memory for the rest of her life.

He'd closed his eyes, but his hands moved over her, holding her, pulling her closer. He couldn't seem to get enough of her, and again Caroline felt the unaccustomed well of tears. Resting her cheek against his shoulder, she hid her brimming eyes.

They moved together as if they'd never been apart. He whispered to her, mindless words of praise and encouragement. He told her she was beautiful, that no woman had ever made him feel like this. He said other things, too. Erotic things. Forbidden things.

During all this, he kissed her with such passion that for one moment in time, Caroline let herself believe in the impossible.

He said everything a woman wanted to hear from her man. Words that meant something. Words that mattered. Maybe that was part of it, Caroline thought as she returned his kiss. All her life, she'd wanted to matter. And right now, to Logan, she did.

She moved with him, matching his tempo and reveling in his deep-throated groan when she wrapped her legs around him. He knew how to touch, how to tantalize, when to slow, when to quicken. The swells of pleasure between them built higher as his thrusts increased.

It was the sweetest torture Caroline had ever known. Had it been this good before? she wondered. Had she been too young and too foolish to realize? How could she have lived without this for so many years?

How would she live without it after tonight?

Not wanting to think about tomorrow, Caroline banished her musings. She wanted more. She wanted him. She wanted to forget everything but the here and now.

Urging Logan with her hands and lips, the first ripple threatened, and on its heels, the wave. The intensity she'd almost forgotten washed over her, and the sharp, unmistakable pang of need pulled her under. Her mind empty of everything but Logan, the hard tremor snatched her breath and rocked her from head to toe.

Her last bit of control forsaken, she sobbed out her release, hearing him call out her name as he followed.

When their bodies cooled, Logan turned and settled her against him in a heartbreaking embrace.

She couldn't stop trembling. Their encounter had been so passionate, so amazing. The way he'd touched her, the things he'd said. For long minutes, she tried to calm herself, but the myriad of emotions fan far too high.

He seemed to sense her distress and gently kissed her temple. Rubbing his cheek against her hair, he asked quietly, "You all right?"

She could only nod.

"Good. Because I'm certainly all right. More than all right. Caroline, that was wonderful. You're wonderful. I can't think of a better ending to a totally lousy day."

"Logan...I want...I need..."

After a moment's hesitation, he chuckled softly. "Again? Ah, sunshine, I'm right there with you, but I'm afraid I'm not eighteen anymore. After the day I've had, I'm gonna need a few minutes to get my oats back." Curling his arm around her again, he smiled. "Until then, I'll just hold you."

She closed her eyes against the pain and the shame and the guilt. "I'd like that."

Within minutes, he was asleep.

Caroline lay awake and miserable. She didn't deserve this, to lie here with him, cradled in his arms as if she were someone special. As if she were someone he could care about.

She didn't deserve his intimacy or his concern. She'd lied to him, played the part of a terrified mother to appeal to his sympathy and heartstrings and it had all worked like a charm. Better than she could have ever hoped.

An image of Cade flashed through her mind. Look what her lies had cost him. Logan would never forgive her.

He will hate me. Come morning, he'll walk away and never look back.

Self-loathing ripped through her, stealing her breath and freezing her blood. Why? Why had she asked him to make love to her? Why had she allowed it? Why had she clung to him, practically begging him to make it all go away? Had she lost her mind?

She could tell herself it was insanity. Or even the human need to reconnect after the tragedy they'd experienced at the crash site. But deep down, Caroline knew it was far more than that. She'd needed to feel again what he'd made her feel all those years ago. Wanted. Cherished. Desired.

Loved.

She kept her head on his chest, counting his heartbeats, knowing the steady rise and fall of his breathing indicated the deep sleep of a sated man. Her man. If only for this one night.

Wishing morning would never come, Caroline lay in her husband's arms and cried silent tears of loss.

A BEAM of morning sunshine streamed through a gap in the window curtains and woke Logan from a dreamless sleep. His first thought was of the warm bundle of woman in his arms. Dammit, he'd fallen asleep without a second go-round. He must have been even more exhausted than he'd realized.

But damn, hadn't the first been fine.

He opened his eyes, a satisfied smile stretching across his face as he contemplated waking her up with lovemaking. That would be another first for her. He'd discovered he liked the idea of introducing her to a whole lot of firsts.

He propped his head on his elbow and stared at her, his smile going tender. Such beauty. Such strength. What a soldier she'd been yesterday in the wake of disaster.

Disaster. The events of yesterday intruded on his peace and worries came roaring back. He thought of Cade and the other injured passengers. He imagined Will moseying up to outlaws. With those two realities lodged in his mind, duty dimmed his desire.

He'd slept later than he'd intended, and he had a lot to do before they boarded the stage that would take them to the rail stop where they could continue their trip west. He'd better get over to the telegraph office and see what replies to the telegrams he sent yesterday awaited him. Among other things, he'd asked the young Fort Worth doctor who'd been such a help when Dair MacRae was ill to make himself available to Cade. Logan needed to know Dr. Peter Daggett's reply as soon as possible in case he needed to clear the way of any obstacles that might prevent the doctor from assisting his friend.

He hated being pulled in two directions like this—fear for his son and for his friend, as well. Despite the reassurances he'd given Caroline last night, he felt the same guilt as she had over Cade's injuries. Under any other circumstances, he'd be hightailing it back to the scene of the wreck right this very moment, but Will had to be his first priority right now, and Logan knew Cade wouldn't want it any other way.

Black Shadow Canyon. Its very name gave him the sweats. Though he tried hard to hide it from Caroline, Logan was worried sick about their son. He knew that hellhole and the villains who called it home. Killers without conscience. Men who thought nothing of murder, rape and rampage. Imagining his boy in the midst of their evil scared Logan to the bone and made him curse every hour of this delay.

He reached for a curl of Caroline's sunburst-colored hair and twirled it around his index finger. His son. His wife. These new responsibilities weighed upon his soul. Talk about firsts. This was the first time he'd woken up with a woman, thinking about more than his own wants and desires. It changed a man. For the better. Despite all the worries and concerns, it filled an empty spot inside him he hadn't even known existed.

I'll find him, Caroline. If it's the last thing I do. I'll bring our boy home to you.

With that, he decided to let her sleep. They had another hard day of travel before them, and the more rest she had ahead of it, the better. He placed a gentle kiss against her bare shoulder, then eased from the bed. Ten minutes later, washed and dressed and ready to face the rigors of the day, he exited the hotel.

It was a fine spring morning, and Parkerville bustled with activity even at the early hour. Logan tipped his hat to a woman who'd assisted

Caroline the night before, then detoured toward the church where volunteers were gathering for the trip to the spot of the train wreck. He approached a slim, balding man who carried a clipboard and checked items off a list as they were loaded into a wagon. "How's it going, Reverend Marshall?"

"Good. We'll be ready to pull out in twenty minutes or so, I suspect."

"Any word from the railroad?"

"Yes, and it's not good. That storm threw off a half dozen or more twisters yesterday and it tore up chunks of track over a wide area. What's good for your group is that track to the east of your accident was easily repaired. A crew out of Fort Worth should be reaching them soon. Of course, our first wagonload will have arrived by now, and this next load of supplies should set everybody up just fine until we can get folks out of there and on their way."

The news lifted Logan's spirits and he continued toward the telegraph office with lighter steps.

The bells of a door chime announced his presence when he opened the door and stepped inside. The office was a single room divided by a wooden railing with two desks behind the railing, and a table and chairs where customers could sit and compose their messages.

The operator sat behind the railing at his desk munching on crisp bacon while he pored over the morning newspaper. "We don't open until eight," he said without looking up. "A man has the right to have his breakfast in peace."

"I can't argue with that." Logan took a bill from his wallet, leaned over the railing and tossed it onto the table. "Although I am a man who appreciates extra service."

"Oh, Mr. Grey." The operator swallowed his bacon, snatched the bill and stood. "I thought you were another one of the fairgoers. Folks are driving me crazy because I'm head livestock judge and there was a problem with the pig panel yesterday."

"Sorry to hear that. Do you have anything for me?"

"Sure do. A whole stack. My overnight help had them ready when I came in this morning. He was worried that we didn't deliver them, but I told him you'd said you and the missus needed your sleep." He grabbed a pile of envelopes off his desk and handed them over. "He put 'em all in individual envelopes for you."

"Thanks, I appreciate it." Logan flipped through the envelopes, noting the senders. Dair. The doctor. His banker. Tom Addison. Wilhemina Peters. He opened the doctor's telegram first.

Excellent. Dr. Daggett promised to make Cade his number one priority.

It took Logan about ten minutes to read and respond to all his messages. He settled his bill, then turned to leave when the operator said, "Oh, I almost forgot. Your wife has a reply waiting, too. Do you want to take it to her?"

A telegram? Logan's sense of foreboding leaped to life. "Caroline sent a telegram? Last night?"

"Sure did. Came back not long after the two of you left here. Since you said to hold the others, we held it, too."

Logan recalled that she'd gone off with some women last night to help gather supplies. Must have done it then. "Sure, I'll take it to her."

She probably sent word to Ben Whitaker that she was all right, Logan thought as he exited the office. "I should have thought about that last night when I was sending all the others," he muttered to himself.

He stuck his telegrams in his back pocket, slipped hers into his shirt pocket and headed for the general store where he planned to replace the necessities he'd lost in the storm. Traveling by himself meant a bit different approach: less food, more ammunition, for instance. While Parkerville's store didn't have as big a selection as he'd found in Fort Worth, he was able to get what he needed. After that, he went by the livery to make arrangements for the horses they'd ridden to town last night.

He didn't think anymore about Caroline's telegram until he was on his way back to the hotel half an hour later. At that point, he pulled the envelope from his pocket and for the first time, looked at the sender's name listed in the upper left corner.

Not Ben. It was from a woman. Mrs. Ellen Glazier. Logan's stride slowed as an ugly thought occurred. What if Ben didn't reply to Caroline's telegram because he couldn't? What if something bad happened to Ben?

Son of a bitch. Caroline didn't need more bad news. She didn't need more stress and upheaval. He stared at the envelope, his mouth set in a grim frown. She was a strong woman, but everyone had a breaking point.

The instinct to protect welled up strong inside him. That's what husbands did, right? Logan opened the telegram and read:

Have tried to reach you, stop.
    Bad news, stop.
    Will disappeared two days ago, stop.
    Is he with you, stop.

"What the…" He read the telegram again. This made no sense. Had another Will gone missing? Couldn't be his Will. His Will had been missing for a lot more than two days. Unless…

Had Caroline lied?

Something cold washed through his body as the questions shot like bullets from a gun. Was it all a lie? Were they even married? Did he actually have a son? Had his son really gone missing? Or was everything she'd said to him a slick and sick lie?

No, surely not. He couldn't believe that. That would just be too…much. Especially after last night.

Maybe the woman mixed up her words. Maybe the telegraph operator interpreted them wrong. Maybe this message wasn't even meant for Caroline.

Then in the whirlwind of his thoughts, Cade came to mind, and the chill inside him turned to frost. Had he dragged his friends—his brothers—into the path of a cursed tornado for no good reason? What possible reason could Caroline have to tell such a filthy, destructive lie?

You'd better find out.

Logan refolded the telegram and idly slapped it against his other hand as he mentally reviewed events and conversations that had occurred since Caroline had waltzed back into his life. What, if anything, was suspect? Nothing he could put his finger on. Sure she'd acted strange a time or two, but considering the circumstances, that was to be expected. Try as he might, he could not recall a single word or action that suggested she wasn't being truthful.

No sense in being paranoid about this. There must be another explanation. There must be another Will among her friends in Artesia. After all, William was not an uncommon name. Hell, he could probably yell it out right here and a half dozen people would come running.

And yet, if the telegram didn't portend trouble, why had the hairs on the back of his neck risen to attention?

Logan shoved the telegram back into his shirt pocket. He didn't have enough information.

He knew of only one place to get it.

Picking up his pace, he hurried back to the hotel. He glanced into the Emporium as he passed by, hoping she hadn't gone to breakfast in his absence, and was glad to see no sign of her. This was one discussion he thought should take place in private.

He entered the hotel and bounded up the stairs. He gave a cursory knock on the door before he entered their room. She was up, dressed and standing by the window that overlooked the street. She would have seen him heading this way.

Logan opened his mouth to speak, then hesitated. Under different circumstances following a night like last night, he'd have crossed right over to her, pulled her into his arms and kissed her silly. But the telegram burning a hole in his pocket and the troubled expression on her face stopped him, and he said simply, "Good morning."

"Good morning, Logan."

Well, this was awkward. "I hope you slept well."

Color stained her cheeks. "I did. Thank you. I see you've been out."

"You were sound asleep when I woke up. I ran a few errands."

Following a few seconds of silence, they both spoke at once. "Caroline, we need to talk."

"Logan, I need to talk to you." She closed her eyes, then brought her hands up and clutched her head. "Please, let's not discuss last night. I can't do that, not now."

His temper flared at that. She didn't have to act as if making love with him had been the biggest mistake of her life. "Fine. Then let's talk about this."

He grabbed the telegram from his pocket and tossed it onto the bed. "What's that?" she asked.

"Telegram came for you. The operator gave it to me when I picked up mine this morning." He folded his arms and waited.

"I sent word to my...loved ones...last night that I wasn't hurt. I thought they'd want to know."

"Understandable."

She reached for the envelope and noted it had been opened. "You read it?"

"I was afraid it was news about Ben. Thought that as a good husband, I should try to protect you."

She set her mouth, making it clear she didn't care for his action, but once she started to read the telegram, her pique was obviously forgotten. Her complexion drained of every drop of color.

"What the hell is going on here, Caroline?" She looked up at him, her eyes round and wild. "Will. It's Will."

"Whose Will?"

She dropped the paper and rushed toward him and the door. "I need to find out...Send a telegram...Oh my..."

He grabbed her arm as she attempted to rush past. "Hold on just a minute."

"No! Let me go!" She wrenched herself away and dashed into the hallway, then down the stairs.

Logan muttered a curse and followed her. Once outside, she lifted her skirts and ran.

"Be damned if I'll run after her," Logan muttered, though he lengthened his stride and picked up his pace. She reached the office a full minute before he did, and by the time he entered, she was handing over a telegram for the operator to transmit.

"Oh, and please add the words 'Request Immediate Reply,'" she told him. "How long did it take for the reply to come last night?"

"Well, let me think." The operator pursed his lips and rubbed his chin. "No more than fifteen, twenty minutes, I expect."

"Fifteen minutes!" Her voice went shrill. "You should have delivered it to me. We've wasted a whole night."

"Now, little lady. Your husband said to hold 'em, that y'all needed your rest."

Caroline paced the small floor space in the office, her hands fisted and nervously hitting her hips. "At least it shouldn't take too long for Ellen to reply today."

Logan spoke up. "Is there somewhere my wife and I could wait in private? We have things we need to discuss."

"How 'bout y'all stay here?" The operator pushed away from his desk and reached for his hat. "I'll mosey over to the cafe and see if Mrs. Gillespie's raisin muffins are out of the oven yet."

"No! You can't leave." Caroline blocked his exit. "You need to be here when my reply comes. It might not take twenty minutes."

"I know Morse code," Logan responded. He dragged Caroline to his side, allowing the older man to pass. "I can handle it."

When they were alone in the office, she resumed her pacing, her focus somewhere other than on him. From the looks of it, she didn't care that Logan had discovered her perfidy. The information she'd received in that telegram was all that mattered. Her son was all that mattered.

Her son. His son. His son?

That was one little detail he wanted cleared up right away.

She started muttering to herself, and with every sentence, her tone grew louder, more shrill and tinged with hysteria. "Where did he go? What happened? I shouldn't have left him. What was I thinking?"

She whirled toward him. "They took him, didn't they? Will."

She steepled her fingers in front of her face and rocked forward and backward. "Will."

"Caroline, talk to me."

She ignored him, speaking to herself and making little sense to him. "A bad idea. Should have listened to my mind instead of my heart. Oh, Will. Will."

Logan stepped toward her, took her arm and yanked her down into a chair. "Start making sense, Caroline."

She bounced right back up. "I can't sit down. I'm too nervous."

"About your son? Is the boy who that telegram says has gone missing your Will?"

"Our Will."

"Is he?" Logan snapped back sharply.

"Yes. He is." She briefly closed her eyes, then said, "I didn't lie about that, Logan."

Bitterness washed through him. "But everything else...?"

"I was going to tell you." She halted and lifted her chin, meeting his gaze square on with earnestness shining in her violet eyes. "I swear. First thing this morning."

He didn't believe her for a second. "Right."

She didn't protest his disbelief. In fact, she barely seemed to notice as her thoughts went right back to the boy. "Oh, Logan. I'm so afraid. This isn't like Will. Not like him at all. He's so responsible and he promised me he would behave for Ellen. Will doesn't break his promises."

"Maybe he takes after his mother." Logan folded his arms. "Maybe he lies."

That got her attention. Pain rippled across her face at his words. "All right. I deserve that. I owe you an explanation, and I'm prepared to provide it, but I just can't think right now. I'm too worried."

"If you can't think then maybe I'll have a better shot at getting the truth," he fired back. He took a step toward her and braced his hands on his hips. "Talk to me, Caroline. Why did you want me to go into Black Shadow Canyon?"

She closed her eyes and sighed. "This isn't how...I'm sorry, Logan. I didn't mean for you to learn it this way."

"I haven't learned anything yet! Except that my wife is willing to lie to me. Hell, she's willing to screw me to get what she wants!"

Caroline turned white at that, but Logan was too angry to care. She lifted her chin and said, "I will not take that."

"Yeah, you damn sure will. You'll take it because you deserve it, and you'll start telling me just what the hell was worth all this."

"It's Ben," she said, wincing. "Will didn't go looking for Geronimo's Treasure. Ben did. Sort of."

It took a moment for her words to sink in, but once they did, white-hot fury whipped through Logan. "Ben Whitaker? This is all because of Ben Whitaker? Cade is...is...."

He closed his eyes as he relived the horrifying moments when he removed the barbed wire from Cade Hollister's body. Logan was so angry that he couldn't see straight, as furious as he had ever been in his life, so enraged that articulating his thoughts and emotions proved all but beyond him.

He took a deliberate step away from her, putting her beyond arm's reach. "You turned my life upside down—lured my brothers into danger—because an old, washed-up outlaw decided to prospect for gold?"

Caroline whirled on him, her own temper blazing. "You watch what you say about Ben, Logan Grey. You have no cause to say such ugly things."

She really is something, isn't she? Stands there and defends that old outlaw like he's some kind of saint? He braced his hands on his hips. "No cause? Cade Hollister is fighting for his life because that old bastard decided to get greedy again and you say I have no cause?"

"Ben Whitaker is a fine man. He was there to hold your son the day he was born. He provided us food and shelter when you weren't around to do it. He was there for me at the lowest point of my life, and he saved me. He saved Will."

"I didn't know—"

"That's right, you didn't know," she interrupted, her eyes flashing fire. "You didn't try to know. Yes, Logan, I lied to you. Yes, I used you. But you know what? You owe him because he was there and you were not!"

"I don't owe him shit! Okay, fine, he took care of you and Will, but it was *your* choice to keep me out of my son's life when you *knew* he was my son. You took my choices away."

"But—"

He wouldn't let her talk. "I should have looked for you, yes—and for that I'll take the hit—but you were just as much a parent as me. You made the choice to raise Will without me, and you chose an old gunslinger to take my place. Just like you made the choice to come to Fort Worth with a sob story about a missing child to pull me into your damned deceitful web. Had you not done that. I'd have never boarded that damned train. Cade and Holt would not have boarded that damned train."

"Don't you try to blame me for the tornado! I feel terrible about Cade, and I was going to tell you to go to him this morning, but now you can't because this time it is not a lie. This time Will really is missing!"

"Is he? How the hell can I be sure this isn't just another story? How do I know that this isn't some wild-ass scheme you've cooked up with Whitaker?"

Her eyes went wild with fury and fear, and he waited for her to strike out at him. Instead, she crumpled. She folded in on herself like a broken doll, slipped to the floor and wept with despair. With defeat. With terror for her son.

Watching her, Logan recognized that she was telling the truth. He didn't soften—not much, anyway—but he did realize that Will was, indeed, in trouble.

Logan reached down and grabbed her around the waist, then lifted her back onto her feet. He gave her a firm but gentle shake. "Stop it. Calm down, Caroline. It doesn't do any good to lose control. Look, I believe you, okay? Now explain to me what is happening here so I can start to fix it. Let me hear the story from the beginning."

"But I can't think about anything other than my baby!"

"Sure you can." He stared deeply into her tear-filled eyes. "Focus, Caroline. It will help pass the time until you get a response to your telegram from Artesia."

She pulled away, wresting from his grip as she wiped the wetness from her face. She went to stand beside the window, and, gazing out into the street, she finally began to speak. "About six weeks after Suzanne died, Ben received a letter from Shotgun Reese's companion, a woman named Fanny Plunkett."

Logan gritted his teeth. Fanny Plunkett. Great. Just frickin' great. Fanny Plunkett was a black-hearted bitch of the first water. Before she retired to Black Shadow Canyon, she was the brains behind the biggest gang of train robbers Texas had ever seen and she had no qualms about killing—man, woman or child. This story kept getting better and better.

"Fanny wrote that, even though Shotgun was terminally ill when he died, she didn't believe he'd died from natural causes. She believed he'd been murdered. When she read about Suzanne's tragic fall in the newspaper, she considered it suspicious, too."

"Why?" Logan asked, even as he put the clues together. "Did Suzanne know something about Geronimo's Treasure?"

"Apparently she did. According to Fanny Plunkett, Shotgun corresponded with Suzanne in the months before his death. She believes he sent her a map to the mine shortly before he died."

"Why would he do that? For safekeeping?"

"For love. Ben won Suzanne away from Shotgun. Fanny said he loved Suzanne until the day he died. Ben thinks it is definitely possible that someone who knew Shotgun's intentions came into the house, stole the map and pushed Suzanne down the stairs."

Logan took a seat across from Caroline. He drummed his fingers on the table as he considered what she'd said. Why would a woman like Fanny write to Ben Whitaker about this map? It didn't make sense. There had to be more to this, more than either of them knew right now. "Did Ben know about the map? Had he ever seen it?"

"No. He knew Shotgun and Suzanne corresponded—the letters were as much for him as for her. But the idea of a map was news to him and the impetus to finally go through Suzanne's things. I did it for him. He couldn't face it. I found the stack of letters and some gold nuggets that Shotgun had sent, but nothing else. No map and no letter that sounded as if it might have accompanied a map."

"Maybe there never was a map."

"That's what I thought until I found a simple gold necklace in an otherwise empty envelope. Ben recognized it as the necklace Shotgun had given to Suzanne years ago, the one she had returned to him once she decided to marry Ben. Ben believed it was entirely possible that Shotgun would have sent it along with the treasure map. Since the necklace was there and the map wasn't, he believed there was something to Fanny Plunkett's claim."

"So, has he gone looking for a gold mine or for his wife's killer?"

"The killer! He's gone hunting a killer when all he's done for the past twenty years is be a kind, gentle newspaperman. Someone will die, but it won't be Suzanne's killer. It'll be Ben." Tears flooded back into her eyes as she continued, "And you know what? I'm afraid that's what he wants. That's what terrifies me the most. He may well have marched into that canyon with his guns blazing, begging someone to shoot back. Ben was not in his right mind when he left. You need to understand that he has been lost without Suzanne. He didn't eat. Didn't sleep. He hardly spoke—not even to Will."

"So he left, and you cooked up the scheme to get me to go after him."

"I tried to find someone else to go, but I didn't have any luck. I was desperate, Logan." She sighed with defeat, then said, "I didn't know what else to do. Ben was the father I should have had, despite all his faults. He was good to Will. I owed him. I love him. Maybe I should have handled it differently, but let me ask you this. Would you have helped me had I come to you with the truth?"

"I wasn't given the choice."

"That wasn't what I asked you."

"I can't answer that, Caroline," he snapped back, his anger flaring up hot and fierce all over again. He'd let himself be taken in by a woman. Hell, he'd even let himself dream a little again. All based on a lie.

Her explanation sat in his gut like a piece of bad meat. He couldn't abide liars under any circumstances, but this, what she did, it went way beyond a lie. This was a betrayal.

Logan cleared his throat, then spoke in a tone that was low, flat and cold. "I might not have awakened crying on a train or screaming in bed, but I've had my share of nightmares about Will. You gave me a son, Caroline, and placed that son in the gravest of danger in the very same breath. I've never experienced the joy of fatherhood without harrowing fear accompanying it. Maybe I can't rightfully accuse you of stealing the first fourteen years of my son's life from me, but I can damn well accuse you of stealing my joy."

Her expression stricken, she reached for his hand. "Logan…I don't know what to say."

"There isn't anything you can say that I'd want to hear or even believe at this point."

He pulled his hand away. "I understand love. I understand wanting to help your friend. But this...Your excuses don't wash with me."

"It isn't an excuse! I just didn't know what else to do."

"You could have tried the truth, Caroline. It all comes down to honesty. You lied. Again and again and again. You had plenty of time, plenty of opportunities to tell me the truth and you didn't. Hell, last night you—"

"I don't want to discuss last night. Last night has nothing to do with Will or with Ben."

"Oh, but I think it does. Thought you might soften me up a bit, didn't you? Thought you'd work your wiles and draw me in a bit more? Well, damn, honey, you should be an actress. Your performance was flawless. I just wonder how long you would have strung me along...and for that, I'll never forgive you. You used me, used my fear and my feelings and wormed your way into my bed. Hope it was worth it for you."

She sucked in a breath and grimaced with pain and defeat. Logan recognized that he had wounded her, recognized that he was acting like an ass, but he was so angry with her. Hell, he was angry with himself, too, that he was spouting from his gut rather than his head. Still, he couldn't find it in himself to be sorry for it. Not yet. Maybe not ever.

The telegraph key began to click. Logan rose, stepped behind the operator's desk and picked up a pencil. The letters and words that he scratched out on the paper only increased the sickness in his stomach and inflamed his fury.

"Is it from Ellen?" Caroline asked when he set down his pencil. She stood beside the table, her hands linked in front of her mouth as if in prayer.

"Will went home to get his baseball glove. He never returned. They've searched the town and surrounding area. Checked the water wells, the creek. Set someone's bloodhounds on the scent. Will disappeared without a trace."

"His baseball glove," she murmured, rocking back and forth. "My dream. Oh, my heavens. He was playing baseball in my nightmare. It *was* a premonition!"

She looked fragile, as if she were about to shatter into tiny pieces, but Logan's heart was hardened against her. Yesterday, he would have gone to her, held her, offered her comfort and reassurance. Today he could barely stand to look at her.

He shifted his gaze to the door and focused his attention on the facts as he knew them. "Who is this Ellen?"

"She's a neighbor. A friend. Her son Daniel is Will's best friend."

"Is this the first time he's stayed with them? Any chance he could have had trouble and run off?"

"No, I'm sure that's not it. He and Daniel often stay at one another's houses. Will has never given Ellen any cause for concern. He always does what he's supposed to do. I've threatened him with dire consequences should he do otherwise."

Gone for two days. Not a good sign. Not a good sign at all. Damn it to hell and damn Caroline. What had she been thinking to leave Will? "Why the hell didn't you bring him with you?"

"I was protecting him! I didn't want him around you until I knew more about you. Judged firsthand what sort of man you were."

"You were protecting my son from me? Damn you, Caroline!" His temper threatened to flare out of control once more, so he wrestled it down. As much as he wanted to throttle her, he had to calm down and think.

So, what had happened? Had Will run off? Such an act might not be in character for him, but Logan wasn't ready to dismiss it as impossible. Or, was he hurt, injured in a way that prevented him from being found by those looking for him? That, Logan had a hard time buying.

Most likely, his son had been taken, probably against his will. Logan would bet his bottom dollar that Will's disappearance was somehow tied to this gold mine debacle. The very idea made him feel mean as a demon from hell, and if Ben Whitaker were in range of a bullet, he'd pull his gun and plug him. Shotgun Reese, too, even though he was already dead. Man like that could never be dead enough.

Hang on, son. I'm coming after you.

Logan checked the clock on the wall. Just enough time to get his things and grab some breakfast before catching the stage. Without another word to Caroline, he headed for the door, his mind on tracking and travel schedules.

"Logan? Logan, where are you going?"

"To find my son." He stepped out onto the sidewalk and put his hat on his head.

Caroline scrambled after him. "But...what about me? What should I do?"

He stopped, glanced over his shoulder. "Honestly, Caroline, I don't give a flying rat's ass what you do."

He saw her jaw drop before he turned away. "Excuse me? What did you say?"

"You heard me."

He took one step away, then two. A part of him expected to hear her screech or protest. Another smaller portion thought she might run after him and beg.

Nothing—not even his sixth sense—gave him warning of the clay pot that hit him square between the shoulders and came damn close to knocking him down. *What the hell?* Glancing down, he spied the head of a red geranium propped atop his left shoulder. He slowly turned around.

Caroline stood in the street, mayhem in her eyes, her chest heaving, her complexion almost as red as the flower she'd whacked him with. Heedless of the pedestrians around them who stopped and stared, she snapped, "You can walk away from me, Logan Grey. You can ignore me. You can divorce me, for that matter. But I'll be hanged if you're going to talk to me like I'm cow dung on the bottom of your boot. I'm the mother of your son, and for that alone I deserve more respect than that."

"You throw something at me again, woman, and I'll put you over my knee and tan your hide."

"Try it. Go ahead. Just try it."

He took a step toward her. "You really, really don't want to test the last shred of my patience, Caroline. Trust me, it's about gone."

Apparently she heard him, because she sucked in a deep breath, then said, "I apologize for that. I lost my temper."

"I've had enough of your temper, your lies, and I've had enough of you."

"Fine. That's just fine. You and I truly don't matter."

"That's right. We don't matter. We never did and we never will. I didn't matter enough for you to tell me that you gave me a child, and you don't matter enough for me to care right now that you were the one who did. All that matters is Will. He deserves better than us as parents, but we're all he's got. So I aim to find my son. And I'm warning you, lady, so help me, if something has happened to Will because of your lies..."

"Please, just find him, Logan. That's all I want." She took a step toward him, her eyes filled with fear and pain and hope, such hope, that it damn near brought him to his knees. "Find our son. Save our son. I beg you."

"I intend to, Caroline." And then, because his own fear rode his blood along with the white-hot fury at the people and circumstances that had put his child in danger, he added, "And once I do, I'll be taking him away with me for a while so I can get to know him."

"Taking him away?"

"Yeah, away. Away from outlaws and liars and schemers. You've had him for fourteen years and because of your choices, he's in more danger than any kid should ever have to face. I'm taking him away from you, Caroline. You don't deserve him."

She swayed beneath the force of the blow, but she didn't fall. Watching her, Logan couldn't help but think that she was still the most beautiful woman he'd ever known.

He expected her to beg him not to take her child, but once again, Caroline surprised him. "If that's the price, then so be it. Just find him, Logan. Keep him safe. Will is my whole world."

Logan walked away with another emotion joining the fear and anger riding his blood.

Logan walked away feeling shame.

CHAPTER NINE

Caroline stood in the rail car's vestibule and covered her ears when the whistle blew as the train pulled into Artesia a day and a half after she'd left Parkerville. A day and a half since she and Logan had exchanged so much as a single word.

He had slept, or pretended to sleep, during the entire stagecoach ride to the depot in Midland. After buying a ticket—one ticket—for the next westbound train, he'd disappeared during the two-hour wait for the scheduled departure. Caroline had watched him board a different car than her own just before the train pulled out of the station, and the only time she'd seen him since was when she left her car to get some air and peeked into the one in front of her.

He'd been talking to a woman. Smiling at her. That no-good rotten, overstuffed, pigheaded, rogue.

Caroline deserved his anger, she knew that. She'd earned every word. Now what she hadn't deserved was his accusation that she'd used sex against him. She hadn't planned to make love with him. She wasn't trying to work her wiles or soften him up. Not that he'd ever believe it.

So now he was chatting with that woman, perhaps thinking to make her jealous? Well, that was a waste of time. She didn't care about anyone or anything but Will.

Now as the train began to slow, she put her husband out of her mind and focused entirely on her son. Maybe she'd hear good news from the Glaziers. Maybe Will had come home since her last contact with her friends during the wait in Midland. Her gaze frantically searched the platform for Will and hope formed a lump in her throat. There was Ellen, dressed in her favorite blue gingham gown, her dark hair hid by her sunbonnet. Her husband, Daniel, wore a dark suit befitting the town's most prominent attorney. Anxiousness filled both their expressions. Caroline didn't see their son Danny. She didn't see Will's dog, Sly.

She didn't see Will.

Well, she'd known in her heart not to expect a miracle, though she always hoped for one. At least she was home now, and soon would have the comfort of friends at her side, rather than hostility from her husband.

Brakes squealed and the wheels slowed. Caroline was second off the train. One car ahead of her, Logan was the first. Ignoring him, she ran toward Ellen. "Any news?"

"No, I'm sorry." Lines of concern creased Ellen's full face. "I'm so sorry, Caroline. We were responsible for Will and—"

"Stop it. This is not your fault." Caroline wrapped her friend in her arms and hugged her as tears pooled in both women's eyes.

Behind her, she heard Logan ask, "I take it you are the Glaziers?"

"Dan Glazier," Ellen's husband said, extending his hand for Logan's handshake. "My wife, Ellen."

"I'm Logan Grey. I'm Will's father."

"Well, now," Ellen said with a smile. "Of course you are. He looks just like you."

Dan said, "Pleasure to meet you. Sorry it's under these circumstances."

Logan accepted the welcome with a nod. "I have a number of questions. Is there somewhere we could speak privately?"

"You're welcome to come to our house," Ellen offered.

Caroline debated just a moment before saying, "Mine is closer. The sooner Logan can begin his search for Will, the better."

Dan Glazier nodded. "You'll want to speak with my boy, I'm certain. He's the last person who saw Will before he disappeared."

"Is Danny in school?" Caroline asked.

"Yes, I'll get him and bring him to your place."

So, without exchanging a word with her husband, Caroline led the way home.

Even though she knew Logan would want to go through the story step-by-step, Caroline's concern and curiosity caused her to pepper Ellen with questions about the search for Will as they walked. Hearing of the outpouring of support from townspeople overwhelmed her, support echoed in the well-wishing of friends and acquaintances who stopped them on the street. Everyone expressed their worry and concern for Will and offered their encouragement, which in turn gave Caroline a measure of comfort. If good thoughts and prayers could keep her son safe, then Will would be all right.

With the delays, the walk home took a little more than ten minutes. As they arrived at the two-story house painted in Suzanne's favorite color of robin's-egg blue, Caroline's gaze swept the gabled roof, the dormer windows and the wraparound front porch and waited for that usual sense of homecoming to descend. It didn't come.

Ellen slipped her arm though hers in support as they stepped up the front walk and onto the porch, Logan trailing silently behind them. Caroline blew out a heavy breath, unlocked the front door and walked inside her home. Her empty, lonely home. "This is harder than I expected," she murmured. "Is Sly at your place?"

"Yes. If I had known we'd be stopping here, I'd have brought him over to welcome you properly. Let's put the teapot on, shall we?" Glancing over her shoulder, she added, "Mr. Grey? Will you join us in the kitchen?"

"No." His gaze had focused on the stairs. "I want to take a look at the boy's room."

Ellen waited until Logan had disappeared upstairs and she and Caroline were alone in the kitchen to say, "Glory be, Caroline, I've never seen such an ugly look on such a handsome face. What is going on?"

Caroline gave her friend an expurgated account of recent events as she filled the teapot with water and placed it on the stove. "He despises me, but that doesn't matter. Will is all that matters."

Ellen wrinkled her nose. "Well, I don't like it. He might have a right to be a bit peeved, but honestly, Caroline. Your motives were pure, and that tornado was horrible. How frightened you must have been!"

"Ellen, I had relations with him."

Ellen nearly dropped the cup she was holding. After a moment of shocked silence, she whispered, "Before or after the truth came out?"

"Before."

"Oh, Caroline."

"I didn't mean for it to happen. It just did."

"You're still in love with him."

"No!"

"I know you, Caroline. You wouldn't have done that with him if you didn't have feelings for him."

"You're right." Caroline's shoulders slumped and she grimaced. "It's all a mess. Honestly, I can't put a word on what's in my heart right now. The tornado changed everything. I was scared, Ellen, but Logan was so protective. I trusted him. I knew in my heart that he'd keep me safe."

"What does your heart tell you about Will? Do you think he'll find him?"

"I'll find him." Logan strode into the room carrying a ball glove. "Is this what he headed home to get? It was sitting on a shelf in his bedroom."

"Yes."

"So he never made it home," Caroline observed, her gaze locked on the worn and tattered baseball mitt. The memory of the visit to the General Store with Logan floated through her mind and her heart twisted.

"It's hard to tell. I see no obvious signs of struggle or intrusion, but this isn't my house. You'll need to take a look around and see if you notice anything different or out of place."

Well. Apparently he was speaking to her again. At least to give her orders. Caroline smothered the urge to stick out her tongue at him, reminding herself that she needed him and his expertise more than ever.

"Mrs. Glazier, was your husband at your house when the boys decided to play catch?"

"No, he was still at work."

"Then I'd like to go ahead and get started. Would you please describe the events as they happened, providing as much detail as you can recall?"

Ellen nodded and took a sip of her tea, collecting her thoughts. "Storms blew through three afternoons straight. While rain is always a blessing in this part of the world, it does tend to make the children stir-crazy. When the boys came home from school, they were raring to go. They intended to take the horses out onto the prairie for a run, when another boy from school came by the house with word that their friends were gathering at the school yard to play baseball. Our boys decided to go."

"What time of the day was this?" Logan asked.

"Between four and four-thirty."

"Will and your son left the house together?"

"They did. Danny said they walked together as far as the Baptist Church before splitting up."

"I'll ask your Danny to describe what happened after that," Logan said. Glancing at Caroline, he asked, "Do you have a street map of town?"

"No, but I can draw one."

He nodded, then addressed Ellen once again. "At what point did you learn that Will had gone missing?"

"Well, not until Danny came home looking for Will a couple hours later. He'd never showed up at the school yard and they played the game without him. At that point, Danny, his father and I started looking for Will around town. We figured he had met up with another friend and decided to do something else. That sort of thing has happened before. No one grew particularly worried until he failed to come home at dark. When he wasn't home by ten, we sent for the sheriff."

Ellen reached for Caroline's hand. "I'm so sorry we didn't realize sooner that he had disappeared. I feel so awful, Caroline. He was my responsibility."

"Please stop, Ellen. I would have done the exact thing you did. I've never thought twice about allowing Will the freedom to roam. Artesia is—or has been, anyway— a safe place for our children. How many times have our boys gone off on an after-school adventure and lost track of time? You had no reason to think this was anything different."

Ellen blinked back tears and squeezed Caroline's hand, a silent thank-you. Logan continued his questioning, asking details about the search. Ellen was describing the search grids when Dan and Danny arrived.

The boy took one look at Logan and fainted dead away.

HE KNOWS SOMETHING.

Logan sat back and waited while Caroline and the Glaziers fussed over the boy. For the first time since arriving in town, he harbored a measure of hope. The boy knew something, and once he pried the information out of him, Logan would have a place to start looking. Will was still alive; he knew it in his bones.

Ellen Glazier gave her son a glass of water as his father helped him into a chair. "Have you eaten today, son?" Dan asked after Danny had gulped down half a glass of water.

"No, sir. I'm just not hungry."

"Ellen, fix Danny a sandwich." As his wife bustled to make their son a sandwich, Dan Glazier continued, "Son, I know you are worried about Will, but making yourself sick over it isn't going to help. I know you want to help."

"Yessir."

"Then you need to eat."

"Yessir."

Dan nodded, then said, "Now, introduce yourself to Will's father, Mr. Grey."

Danny set down his glass and rose to his feet. He wiped his hand on his shirt leaving a smudge of dirt behind, then held it out to Logan. "Pleased to meet you, sir. I'm Danny."

Logan shook his hand and wondered if anyone else noted that the boy didn't meet his eyes. "Hello, Danny. I understand you are my son's best friend."

"Yessir."

Ellen Glazier set a ham sandwich in front of her son, and Logan gave him time to eat. For a kid who wasn't hungry, Danny chowed down on his food, disposing of half the sandwich in three big bites. When his mother set a glass of milk in front of him, he drained it in a single gulp.

Logan grinned at Danny's father. "What is he like when he *is* hungry?"

The adults all smiled, and when Logan judged the boy to have boosted his constitution adequately, he said, "I'd like you to tell me what happened when you and Will left your house to play baseball that afternoon."

Danny stopped chewing mid-bite. Then he swallowed hard. "Sure thing, Mr. Grey. We was going to play ball."

"We *were* going to play," his mother corrected.

"Will hadn't brought his mitt along to my house, so he wanted to go home to get it. I went on to the school and we started playing without him." He set down his sandwich and added, "I was mad at him for being so late. I thought he ditched me for something more fun."

"I understand," Logan responded. He did not, however, believe the boy.

Caroline asked, "Did he seem upset about anything, Danny?"

"No, ma'am." He darted a look at Logan. "He was looking forward to meeting his pa."

"Was he really?" Logan resisted the urge to glare at Caroline. She'd be expecting it, and he found he preferred to keep her guessing.

He was rather curious about how she had intended to pull off that feat when she'd first instigated her plan. At some point she would have had to tell him she'd sent him looking for Ben Whitaker rather than his son.

That was a question for another time, however. Now he needed to deal with young Danny, so he addressed the boy's father. "I'd like to walk the route between here, the schoolhouse and your home, and I'd like your son to act as my guide. Is that all right with you?"

"Sure. Anything we can do to help." Dan slapped his son on the shoulder. "Right, Danny?"

"Right," the boy replied, though his smile looked a shade sickly to Logan.

"Caroline, while I'm gone I need you to search this house from top to bottom looking for anything at all that is missing or out of place. Check everything from Will's dirty clothes hamper to the number of pickle jars in the pantry. See if he might have taken anything with him."

"All right."

"Is there anything you'd like us to do?" Ellen Glazier asked.

Logan nodded. "I need to speak with your sheriff and any other official who was involved with the search. Perhaps you could arrange a meeting with them for me? Say in about an hour?

"Be glad to handle it," Dan replied.

"Thanks. Danny, you ready?"

He nodded and stood and shuffled out the door. The minute they stepped outside, Danny shoved his hands in his pockets. He scuffed his shoes with every step. Logan might not be an expert on kids, but he knew how a guilty teenage boy acted. He could all but hear Nana Nellie's voice in his mind. *What has your dauber down, Lucky? Pick your feet up and stand up straight.*

"So, you like baseball?" he began as they turned north onto the street. "What position do you play?"

"Catcher."

Logan pursed his lips and nodded sagely. "Important position, catcher. You must have an arm."

"I can throw," the boy replied, shrugging.

"What sort of arm does Will have?"

"He's all right, but he's real good with a bat. Will is strong. He can hit a ball like nobody's business." *Strength is good. The boy might need it.*

At the first intersection, Danny paused. "Do you want to see the school or my house first?"

"The school yard, I believe. Unless..." Logan stuffed his hands in his pockets, too, and adopted a casual tone. "You know, when I was about your age, my best friends and I had a special place. A secret hideout. I don't suppose you and Will have a spot like that?"

Danny Glazier blinked. "We have a fort, but he's not there, Mr. Grey."

"You checked it?"

"Um...yeah."

Another lie. "I'd still like to see it. I might pick up a clue or two. I'm a range detective, and I'm excellent at tracking people. Did you know that?"

He nodded. "Will has newspaper clippings about you. Did you really track the Burrows gang all the way to Wyoming?"

Logan thought of the scrapbook he'd found in Will's room. That he'd shared the stories with his friend gave Logan a warm feeling inside. "I did. I'm smart, Danny, and I'm very good at what I do. I could track a minnow through a swamp. On top of that. I'm the luckiest man in Texas. I will find my son. You can count on it. Show me your fort, Danny. I'll keep your secret."

The boy frowned and tugged at his earlobe. Logan pressed the point by adding, "You can trust me."

After a long moment, the boy sighed heavily. "It's down along the creek that runs behind Will's house. It's not really a fort...more just a shack we've built from scraps. We go down there and gig frogs and catch crawdads. If my ma finds out about it, she'll tan my hide. She worries about snakes."

"Women tend to do that." Logan held the rest of his comments and questions as he followed the boy across a stretch of vacant lots toward a tree-lined creek bank. At the first sight of the shack, he grinned. The structure looked eerily similar to something he, Cade, and Holt had built years ago.

Danny fished a key from his pocket and slipped it into the padlock on the shack's door. "I don't know why we keep it locked. We don't have nothin' that's worth anything inside."

"My friends and I kept our hideout locked to keep the girls out." He gave the boy a wink, then added, "Later on, we invited them in."

Danny's face flushed, the tips of his ears turning beet-red as he busied himself opening the shack's door.

Logan ducked inside. A quick glance around revealed a couple of bedrolls, a lamp, cane fishing poles and a bag of marbles. Marbles. Perfect. Except, he needed more room.

He scooped up the bag of marbles and carried them outside, where he hunkered down beside the creek. "How about a game of square ring?"

Danny hesitated. "Don't you need to look around and search for clues?"

"I have time." Logan knelt on one knee and drew a square in the dirt. He spilled the marbles onto the ground outside the circle and gestured for Danny to make his choice. Taking turns, they divided up the marbles. Logan chose a gold-banded aggie as his shooter, then placed a marble in each corner of the square and one in the middle.

Danny chose a jade-green sphere for his shooter, then placed marbles beside Logan's inside the square. "You want to lag for who goes first?"

"Sure."

Danny drew a line some ten feet away. On his hands and knees, Logan took aim and flicked his shooter out of his fist with his thumb. It stopped six inches from the line. Danny's shot halted within an inch.

"You're up," Logan told the boy.

He waited as Danny made his first shot, sending one marble out of the northeast corner and leaving his shooter inside the square. The second shot cleared the southwest corner, but the shooter stopped outside the square making it Logan's turn to shoot. As he eyed his shot, he casually asked, "What really happened that afternoon, Danny?"

"'Scuse me?"

Logan knocked two marbles out of the box. His shooter stayed inside. "You know why I have the nickname Lucky? It's because I have a sixth sense that warns me when something isn't right. My sixth sense started talking to me the minute you walked into my wife's kitchen."

The boy neither spoke nor lifted his gaze from the marble game.

Logan took another shot and a blue aggie rolled out of the square. "You and Will didn't split up and go your separate ways, did you, son?"

The boy's tone betrayed a slight note of panic as he said, "Yes, we did. It happened just like I said."

Logan rolled back on his heels and pinned Danny Glazier with a piercing stare. "Why would you lie about your best friend, I wonder? Put him in danger?"

"I'm not lying!"

"I suspect you have powerful motives, and I reckon those would go two ways. Either you made a promise you don't want to break or you're being threatened in some way."

Danny tossed down his marbles and scrambled to his feet. "You're crazy. I'm not going to talk to you."

"Sit down, Dan," Logan ordered in a tone that brooked no argument.

"You can't make me. You're not my father!"

"That's right." Logan rose and braced his hands on his hips. "I'm not your father. I'm Will's father and I'll do anything...*anything*...to bring him home. Now, I didn't want to threaten you, son, but you need to understand that I mean business."

At the word *threaten* the boy's eyes went round and fearful. His breaths came as shallow pants. "You have it all wrong."

"Then make me understand."

"You don't know what you're doing. Can't you just leave it alone!"

"He's my son."

"And he's going to be all right! If we just leave things alone, Will is gonna be just fine. He swore it."

"Will swore it?"

"No. The man who—" Danny broke off abruptly when he realized what he'd just said. "Oh, no. No." He dropped his chin to his chest and linked his hands behind his head.

"He isn't here to save you right at the moment, so I suggest you start talkin'."

But Danny Glazier had another round of resistance in him. "The man from the Wild West Show. He came through town looking to hire marksmen for the show. Once he saw Will shoot, he hired him on the spot."

Logan stared at the boy for a few beats, then grinned. "I like you, Dan. Damned if I don't. You've given it a good effort. However, it's time to let it go. Tell me about the man."

When the tears pooled, then overflowed, Logan knew the boy had broken. Considering the circumstances, the words Danny finally spilled didn't shock him or even surprise him. They did, however, make Logan go grim.

"He said he'd kill my ma if I told. He told me how he'd do it. It was awful. I gotta protect her, Mr. Grey."

The mother, of course. The one thing the kid would protect at all costs. "No one is going to hurt your mother, Dan. You have my word on that. Who was he?"

"I don't know his name. He isn't from around here, Mr. Grey. But, I don't know about my mom. I think he could get her. He said he killed Mrs. Whitaker, that he pushed her down the stairs and that no one is the wiser and if I didn't keep my trap shut he'd see to it that my ma got the same treatment as her!"

"Tell me exactly what happened."

Dan swiped the back of his hand across his cheeks, wiping away the tears- "My ma..."

"He'll never get close to her, Dan. Look at me." Logan waited until the boy had met his gaze. "He's a dead man. The moment he laid a hand on my boy, he forfeited his life. You hear me?"

Danny stood frozen for a long moment, then as Logan's vow seeped in, his tension drained like beer from a brand-new tap. "You won't let him near my ma?"

"That's right."

"Nothing against my pa, but he's a lawyer. He'd want to arrest him and put him on trial and send him to jail. Mr. Grey, I looked that man in the eyes. The only time he won't be a danger to my family is when he's in the grave."

"I respect the law, Dan. One of my best friends is a Texas Ranger. But a big chunk of Texas is still as wild and uncivilized as a peach-orchard boar. Out there, men like myself sometimes have to take a shortcut to justice."

"Sometimes range detectives put men in jail."

As much as Logan wanted to push him, he could tell the boy needed the extra reassurance. He swallowed his impatience and said, "Not this time. He confessed to murder and he's guilty of kidnapping. He's earned a death sentence and I aim to carry it out."

Danny gave his eyes another wipe, then began his story. "I didn't go on to the school yard like I said. That was a lie. I went home with Will and we walked inside and there was a man sitting at the dining room table drinking a glass of Mr. Ben's best whiskey. He looked at Will and then at me and said, 'Which one of you is Ben Whitaker's grandson, Will?'"

The boy closed his eyes and shook his head. "I've been thinking ever since that I should have said it was me. Maybe we could have confused him and distracted him and somehow got away. But for a minute there, we thought maybe Ben had come home. We thought maybe he was a friend of Ben's. After all, he was in his house and making free with his whiskey."

"That's understandable," Logan said in an effort to encourage.

"Will stepped forward and said, 'I'm Will,' and then—" Danny blew out a heavy sigh "—the man stepped forward like he was going to shake Will's hand but instead he drew his gun and put the barrel right up against Will's head."

Bastard is dead, Logan silently repeated. *Stone-cold dead.*

Danny continued, "That's when he looked at me and asked me my name. Again, I did the stupid thing and told the truth. He said, 'Here's the deal, Danny Glazier. I need Ben Whitaker's help with something and he's not cooperating. Will is gonna come along with me and help the old man to listen to reason.'"

Danny dropped his gaze to the ground and gave a red marble a hard kick. "That's when Will got his mule look on and—"

"Mule look?"

"Will can be stubborn, sir. Real stubborn. Mr. Ben likes to say that the way to handle Will is to treat him the way you would a stubborn mule you're fixin' to corral. Don't try to drive him in, just leave the gate open a crack and let him bust in."

Logan's stomach took a hard dip. "What did he do?"

"He tried to get away. Fought the man. The son of a bitch hit him on the head with his gun and knocked him senseless."

Stone-cold graveyard dead.

The tears welled up in the boy's eyes once again, but he valiantly blinked them away. "I didn't know what to do, sir. For a minute there, I was afraid Will was dead. Damned near pissed my pants. The outlaw started cussin' a blue streak and he drew back his boot, so I threw myself in front of Will. Took the kick for him. At least I did that much."

Stone-cold graveyard worm-eaten dead.

"He was mad," Danny said, then the words came in a torrent. "He started muttering how he'd tie Will to the saddle if he had to. He ordered me to go get a glass of cold water, that if I wasn't back in fifteen seconds he'd shoot Will. Then he threw the water on Will's face and he woke up and the man yanked him onto his feet and his voice got mad-dog mean and he told Will if he tried another stunt like that he'd come back here after he turned Will over to the others and give Will's mom the same treatment he gave Mizzus Suzanne. That's when he said he'd pushed Miz Suzanne down the stairs. He described how she lay there all crumpled and broken, her eyes open and staring and glassy. It was like listening to the devil himself speak. Then he looked at me and promised to k-k-kill my ma if I said anything about him coming for Will."

"Did he ever say his name, son?"

"No, sir."

"Describe him as best you can."

Danny dragged the back of his hand across his mouth, then nodded. "Okay. He was tall, but shorter than you. 'Bout my dad's height. He had brown hair and brown eyes and a mustache. He didn't look like a killer. Could have been a banker if he was in a suit rather than denims and a shirt."

Logan needed more than that. "Anything unusual about him? Think hard. Did he wear something peculiar? Was his hat shaped funny? Did he have any unique scars or markings?"

"No, sir. Not that I noticed."

Well, hell. Guess that would be too easy. "All right, then. He said he needed Will's help to convince Ben Whitaker to cooperate. Did he mention Black Shadow Canyon at all?"

The boy's eyes widened at the question. "Black Shadow Canyon!" He shook his head rapidly. "No. No, sir. He didn't say a word about that."

"Tell me the rest of it."

"He asked what Will and I were supposed to be doing and Will told him we were supposed to meet a whole bunch of friends to play baseball and that they'd miss us and come looking for us if we didn't show up. The man told me to git and not to say a word about seeing him. He said to think about my mama, that it's a son's duty to do whatever was necessary to protect her. He said that one time this fella threatened his mother with a knife and he tracked the fella down and skinned him alive."

Logan stiffened, but the boy didn't notice and continued without a break. "I believed him, Mr. Grey. He had the devil's own look in his eyes when he said it. It occurred to me afterward that since he'd just threatened my mama it was a stupid thing for him to say, but at the time, all I could think about was him taking that knife of his to a man."

"Deuce Plunkett," Logan murmured, putting the clues together. Of course. The pieces were all there. The letter from Fanny Plunkett to Ben Whitaker had been enough to lead Logan in that direction; skinning a man alive sealed the deal. The Plunkett twins were famous for their devotion to their mother. The rumor about Deuce and the man who had once cut Fanny Plunkett's arm had floated around for years.

"You know him?" Danny asked, his eyes going round and wide.

"I do. You've given me the information I needed. I know the identity of Will's kidnapper and I have a good idea where they've gone."

"So you can go save him. Save Will. And my mother will still be safe."

"Exactly."

The boy exhaled a heavy sigh. "Good. That's really good. Except that..."

"What?"

"I don't suppose we could keep this to ourselves?"

"Worried about your folks'!"

"They're gonna be pur-dee unhappy with me. Pa will probably tan my hide to where I can't sit down for a week."

"Well." Logan rubbed the back of his neck. "I'm new to this father business, but it seems to me that the reason you kept your mouth shut just might spare you a whippin'. It would if you were my boy."

"Really? It might help if you'd say that to my pa."

"Hey, I have your back, Dan." Logan slung his arm around the boy's shoulders. "Shall we head on to the house, then?"

Danny shoved his hands in his pockets and gazed in the direction of Caroline's house. "I wouldn't mind finishing our game of square ring first."

Logan considered the idea. "Does another westbound train come through today?"

"No, sir."

"Then I can't do anything more for my boy this afternoon. Waiting is the hardest part. I can use the distraction." He cocked his head and gave the marbles on the ground a speculative look. "I like the looks of that blue aggie of yours. Wouldn't mind winning it."

Danny snorted. "Like to see you try."

They ended up playing the best two out of three. Logan figured the boy had earned a respite, considering he'd been carrying the weight of the world on his shoulders for the past few days. Besides, he did need the distraction, and he'd enjoyed learning more about his son through Will's best friend's eyes. For instance, Caroline probably didn't know that Will could spit a watermelon seed farthest of any boy in school and that he'd kissed Jo-Ellen Knautz behind the Knautzes' barn on Christmas Eve.

Danny pocketed the final marble in the third game, thus securing the victory. "You wanna go four out of five?" he asked hopefully. "You might have better luck gettin' my aggie."

Logan might have agreed—he honestly did like the looks of that aggie—but during Danny's final shot, he'd noted movement up the creek. Caroline stood watching them, her hands on her hips and storm clouds in her face.

"Sheet-fire," Danny breathed. "That makes me damned sad. Last time Mrs. Grey stood there looking like that, Will told me he was in for a whippin' for sure. You gotta get him back, sir. He's my best friend."

"I will, Danny. You have my word. I'll bring him home or die trying."

WILL Grey eyed the killer's knife and considered making a grab for it. After days in Plunkett's company, he'd grown a bit numb to the fear. His rage, however, had yet to abate.

He wished Deuce Plunkett to the lowest levels of Hell. He'd killed Suzanne. He'd caused Ben to go crazy. By now Will's mother probably knew that he'd been kidnapped, and she'd be worrying herself into the grave—all because of this cussed Deuce Plunkett.

I could kill him and not feel an ounce of guilt. He'd been watching for an opportunity ever since they'd stopped and made camp an hour ago. Or rather, since Will made camp. Plunkett just sat and watched him do all the work.

Although Will hadn't been told where Plunkett was taking him, he'd bet his beloved baseball bat that they were headed for Black Shadow Canyon. The idea made him shudder. It wasn't bad enough to have one criminal to handle. In Black Shadow Canyon, he'd have dozens to deal with.

He tried to tell himself that maybe it wouldn't be as bad a place as rumor made it out to be. No one really knew what went on in that canyon. Could be the bad stuff was all talk. Criminals had to take a break from rape and pillage and murder sometime, didn't they? Maybe they didn't like to take their work home with them.

And maybe it'll snow in Artesia on the Fourth of July, too.

Damn, he wished he was home. They'd left Artesia by wagon, his kidnapper driving, Will bound, drugged with some bitter-tasting brew and stuffed in a trunk. The next day or two had passed in a drug-induced fog. He'd had the sense of traveling by train, but he hadn't gotten his wits back entirely until he woke up in a livery in Van Horn. Plunkett had put him on a horse, tied his hands to the saddle and kept a gun trained on him until they'd traveled well out of town into the desert.

They'd ridden hard, not stopping until dark and starting again at dawn. Yesterday about noon, he'd spied the mountains rising in the distance to the north and that was when his suspicions were confirmed. It was also when he'd decided to watch for a chance to escape. He'd searched his heart and decided that if the situation presented itself, he could…and would…kill Deuce Plunkett.

It would be a righteous killing. No one could argue otherwise. If he did it, he would be following in the footsteps of his father. Wonder what his mother would think of that?

"What are you thinking about, boy?" Plunkett growled. "I don't like the look in your eyes."

"Nothing, sir," Will hastened to say, dropping his gaze toward the ground, his tone cowering. It was a persona he'd developed right after getting his wits back, acting timid and scared, thinking ol' Deuce might relax his guard if he thought Will was a yellow-bellied coward.

"You better not be gettin' any funny ideas, boy."

"No, sir. I'm not thinking anything about anything. I'm too tired to think." That last bit had some truth to it. He'd been both surprised and grateful when the killer stopped early today.

"Good. Not that you'd get very far in this damned desert. No place to hide, no water to drink unless you know where you're going. Now get to cookin'. I want beans with that smoked pork and pilot bread and some of them dried peaches."

"Yes, sir."

Will quickly went through the familiar motions of building a campfire, glad to have the chance to move around with his hands and feet free. Although Plunkett appeared to watch him closely, he managed to squirrel away a few items he thought he might possibly use as weapons. A stone, a sharp stick. A hunk of cactus. He spied a scorpion scurrying toward a rock and made a note of its location. No telling what might come in handy, when.

Will pictured himself throwing a panful of hot beans into the bastard's face and stealing his gun. He imagined kicking hot coals at him and grabbing his knife. He imagined leaping at the peckerhead and stabbing him in the eye with a stick.

He wondered how Lucky Logan Grey might act in a similar situation.

It was an exercise he practiced on regular occasions, imagining how the range detective who'd fathered him might react in various circumstances. Will had long harbored a secret fascination with Lucky Logan Grey. He'd read every newspaper account of the man's exploits that he could find. The story of how' he'd captured a member of the Burrows Gang and used him as bait to lure the others into a trap was so exciting that somebody should write a book about it. At times he hated his father, at times yearned to know him.

His mother didn't like his preoccupation with Grey. She got a sour look on her face every time Will mentioned him, but she didn't try to prevent him from learning about him, either. The one thing she wouldn't do, however, was talk about him.

Will felt a sting when a stone the size of a walnut hit him in the shoulder. "Move faster, boy," Plunkett growled. "I'm hungry."

Let me stuff a yucca down your throat. "Yessir. I'll do my best, sir."

"Damn right you will." Plunkett rolled to his feet and rummaged in his saddlebags, then pulled out a bottle of whiskey.

That's good, Will thought as he watched his captor take a long sip. Maybe he would drink himself sloppy.

Instead, he started talking.

"I hate this damned desert. It's either burning hot or freezing cold. Trip I made in January was a bitch with all the snow and ice. Damned wind was raw as a whip and blowin' hard enough to turn a prairie dog hole inside out."

Will was uncertain about whether or not to respond. A number of times on this trip the killer had displayed a hair-trigger temper, and he didn't want to spark it. But if response would encourage him to keep talking, to keep drinking, that could prove helpful.

While Will debated with himself, the outlaw continued, "Traveling in it put me in a sorry-ass mood. Stupid woman should have noticed." He took another sip of whiskey. "She should have accepted my request at face value. Should not have argued with me. Damn sure shouldn't have threatened me."

Will stirred the beans. Who was he talking about? Suzanne?

Minutes passed and Plunkett continued to drink. Will attempted to plan.

"Sure, I made a mistake, killing her like I did. I knew the moment she hit the floor and lay there with her head all caty whampus and her eyes open and glassy that there would be hell to pay back home because of it. Damned troublesome female. Why couldn't she have given me what I asked for? Tell you what, boy. Neither one of us would be here in this godforsaken spot right now if she had just cooperated."

Yes, he had been talking about Suzanne. Grief twisted like a knife in Will's gut and he wished Plunkett would keep his big mouth shut.

"Gunslingin' Suz," the outlaw muttered. "That's what they called her back in the canyon. Folks still talk about her. Said she could give Annie Oakley a run for her money. A person didn't lose her shootin' skills just because she retired and went straight. Only a fool would have let her get to a gun when she went running for one, and I'm no fool. I thought Mama would understand."

He took an extra long pull on the bottle. "I was wrong."

HOPE STIRRED in Will's heart. Plunkett's eyes looked to be going a little glassy. Maybe he would drink himself into a stupor.

"I didn't mean to push her down the stairs. I was simply trying to stop her. Who would have expected an old woman to be so strong?"

That comment brought the sting of tears to Will's eyes. Suzanne had been strong in many ways. She'd taught him a lot and he'd miss her until the day he died. *Which hopefully won't come too soon.*

"Damn that old good-for-nothin' Shotgun Reese. This entire mess is all his fault. He's the one who cheated his family. He's the one who stole what was rightfully Mama's. I hope he is burning in hell right this very minute." He drank his liquor, then frowned toward Will. "How much longer till the food's ready?"

"Just a few more minutes. The fire is slow. I should have scrounged for more wood."

Plunkett snorted, then settled back to brooding. When next he spoke, Will thought he detected a slur in his words. "I found the map, though, didn't I? I had to hunt through her underwear and old shoes, but I finally found the stack of ribbon-tied letters."

Another sip of whiskey. Good. He'd downed a quarter of that bottle in the last twenty minutes. He definitely had to be feeling its effects by now.

"What's a woman her age doing with silky, skimpy underwear like that, anyway? Downright shameful, if you ask me."

Plunkett's fingers drummed against the bottle. When he looked as if he were going to set it aside, Will asked, "How did you know the map was with the letters?"

"'Cause I'm smart, that's why," Plunkett said, his words beginning to slur in earnest. "I recognized Shotgun's handwriting on the envelopes and knew I'd hit pay dirt. I figured the map would be in one of the last letters the old fart wrote. Sure enough, the December letter was pure gold."

Curious despite his better sense. Will asked, "What did it say?"

"Why should I tell you?" Plunkett belligerently demanded.

Will shrugged. "No reason. Just to pass the time."

The gunman snorted, then fell quiet for a time, but for a few drunken mumbles into his bottle.

Will had given up on learning anything more when Plunkett suddenly sat up and started spewing words.

"Shotgun told Suzanne that he was dying. He said he'd enclosed his Last Will and Testament, which gave all his worldly riches to her. He called her the one true love of his life—that really stuck in my mama's craw. She spent a lot of years with the bastard. But she forgot about it quick once she saw the third piece of paper. It was Shotgun's map to the lost Sierra de Cenizas gold mine."

"Geronimo's Treasure," Will said.

"Yeah. When I saw that, I thought Mama wouldn't be too upset that I killed Gunslinging Suz. In fact, I thought she might be glad considering how her man held a torch for Suz until the day he died." He sighed heavily. Hiccuped. "I was wrong."

"Your mother cared about Miz-Suzanne?"

"Hell, no! She cared because the damned map is written in code."

"Code?" Will asked. "What kind of code?"

"Hell if I know." He fell silent again and Will thought he was done talking, but he had one more spurt in him. "Code was something Shotgun figured Suzanne would understand. With both of them dead..." He shrugged. "That's why you are here, boyo. Mama needs Ben's help, only once he figured out what had happened he quit cooperating. Him and his wife—damn their stubborn souls. That's why I'm back in this damned desert. You are our hostage to motivate Ben to decipher that map and find us the gold mine. Now, quit your lollygagging around. Feed me my supper."

"Yes, sir." Will piled Plunkett's food onto his plate, then walked toward him. The urge to throw the plate in his face made his hand tremble. Was hot food his weapon?

He didn't know. He simply didn't know what to do. He was four steps away, and he had a mouthful of his own heart and about as much guts as a skeleton. *Don't be chicken. Don't be spooked. You can do this.*

Three steps.

Mom will kill me if I do something to get killed.

Two steps. Bet Lucky Logan Grey wouldn't hesitate. *Yeah, but he's the luckiest man in Texas.*

One step. *I'm Lucky Grey's son.*

Deuce Plunkett reached for the pan...and Will let him have it.

"Shee-it!"

The killer screamed, bringing a hand up to his face even as Will lunged for his gun. He got his hand on it, sensed the sun-warmed steel of the barrel before Plunkett yanked it away.

"Damn! You little bastard." Plunkett backhanded Will with the gun and sent him sprawling. "I'll kill you now."

Now that he'd started the battle, Will refused to go down without a fight. He threw himself at the killer, his fists pummeling and scrapping for all he was worth. But Plunkett was older, bigger and meaner, and he overpowered Will. A hard elbow to the temple knocked him backward and made him see stars.

"You stupid shit," Plunkett said as he rolled to his feet. He stood over Will, scowling down at him as he wiped bean juice and blood off his face.

At least I bloodied his nose. Will saw the gun come up and tried not to cower. He absolutely, positively refused to pee his pants.

He watched Plunkett cock the trigger, then he closed his eyes. *Guess when it comes to luck, "like father, like son" has nothing to do with it.*

Sorry, Mama.

CHAPTER TEN

AFTER GIVING ELLEN ONE FINAL HUG, CAROLINE STEPPED BACK inside her house and shut the front door. Only then did she drop her brave facade and allow her fear full rein. She collapsed against the door, shaking like a willow in a whirlwind as her mind replayed Danny Glazier's confession.

Her family. Oh, no. Her family. How had they come to this? Suzanne murdered. Ben in some sort of trouble with Shotgun Reese's paramour. Will kidnapped by a crazed killer.

Her estranged husband sharpening his Bowie knife in her kitchen.

Suzanne's voice echoed in her mind. *Pull yourself together, Caroline. Tears and fears won't help Will one little bit.*

"You're right," Caroline murmured. She made herself stand up straight. She drew a deep breath and squared her shoulders. She needed to talk to Logan, and she'd be a fool to approach him while acting like a weak-kneed female.

You're the same woman who brought down a bank robber. You're the same woman who stayed strong in the face of a tornado. You can face anything Logan Grey has to throw at you.

"Questionable choice of words there, Suzanne, considering that last time I saw him he was sharpening his knife," she muttered as she walked toward the kitchen door. She wasn't quite sure how to react when she saw that Logan had set down his knife.

Now he was oiling his gun.

At least the weapon was in pieces. "How did you know Danny was holding back?" she asked.

He didn't look up from his work, nor did he respond. Caroline tapped her foot.

"Did he say something that tipped you off?"

He lifted the gun to the light and stared down the barrel.

Caroline folded her arms. "So, you're not talking to me again? I swear you are acting like a five-year-old."

"Actually, I'm acting about as adult as I've ever managed," he replied. "I have a powerful anger on toward you, Caroline. It's even stronger than what I felt the other day in Parkerville. I figure it's best I speak to you as little as possible, otherwise it might all bust out. Trust me, that would be very ugly."

"Fair enough. I'm not feeling all that generous toward you right at the moment, myself. Nevertheless, we share a son and I do believe that his safety is the first priority for us both. So I'll skip the small talk and cut straight to the information I require. Do you intend to depart for Van Horn on tomorrow's train?"

"Wait a minute. Back that wagon on up. What possible reason do you have to be angry at me?"

Caroline wondered if this was a direction in which they really needed to go. Her emotions were as raw and jumbled as she could ever recall. She'd probably say some things she'd invariably regret, and he had warned her of his own emotional state, had he not?

Yet, maybe it was best for them to clear the air. After all, Logan didn't know it yet, but they would be spending lots of time together. She had no intention of staying behind while he rode off to the rescue.

"I have fifteen years' worth of reasons to be angry at you, Logan Grey. You can be angry at me all you want about the way I chose to handle Ben's disappearance, but the fact is that I did what I thought was best for my family just like I've done since the moment I realized I carried a child."

His mouth flattened into a grim line. "You made a damn fool decision, didn't you? You knew what kind of people Ben Whitaker tangled with by going into Black Shadow Canyon, and yet you chose to leave my son unprotected and at the mercy of a coldhearted killer. That's unforgivable, Caroline."

"That's bullshit, to put it bluntly," she fired back. "I didn't leave my son unprotected. I didn't invite Deuce Plunkett inside my home. Sure, I wish I'd done some things differently. I'd give anything to go back in time and bring Will with me to Fort Worth to keep him out of a kidnapper's clutches. But it's awfully easy to say 'should have' and 'would have' with the benefit of hindsight. It's awfully easy for you to look at my choices and say you'd have done it differently—you would have done it *right*—when you weren't there walking in my shoes at the time."

"Easy! You think any of this is easy for me?" His eyes snapped and flashed. "To know that I have a son who is almost a man and I've never laid eyes on him. I've never spoken to him. I know that if I don't do everything right for the next week or so, I might never get the chance to do either one. I know my friend is lying in a hospital bed fighting pain the likes of which I can't imagine. I know that I'm actually married and that my wife is a liar and that I can't trust a thing she says or does. What's easy about any of that?"

"Trust? You want trust?" She braced her hand on her hips. "You wanted me to trust you with the truth based on what? The way you treated me with such honor and honesty fifteen years ago? You know why you're so angry, Logan? Because deep down, you feel guilty. It's not my actions that have you so infuriated, but your own. You know that none of this would have happened if you hadn't turned your back on me all those years ago."

A muscle worked in his jaw. "Dammit, Caroline."

She was on a roll. "Yes, I lied to you. Yes, I made mistakes. But every lie I told, every mistake I made, was motivated by love."

"Oh, really?" His voice rose to nearly a shout. "What about the other night in Parkerville? That was both a lie and a mistake and love had nothing to do with it."

The words echoed in the sudden silence and Caroline closed her eyes, absorbing the blow. A full minute passed before she responded, her voice low and calm, her heart bruised and battered. "You will think whatever you want to think, so I don't know why I'm even wasting my breath. As far as I'm concerned, our night together wasn't a lie and it wasn't a mistake. And love? Well, you obviously haven't learned anything about me because I wouldn't have been with you if my feelings weren't involved. If my heart wasn't involved at least a little bit. Not fifteen years ago, and not the other night."

He gave a scornful laugh. "Am I supposed to believe that? Come on, Caroline."

"I don't guess it matters what you believe, does it?"

But it did matter, more than she wanted to even admit to herself. But he was so angry with her, and now that the initial blast of fury had dulled to this sullen ebb of ire, she wouldn't be able to reach him. Not now. Maybe not ever.

"You know, Will is well-known for being muleheaded, and now I see that he comes by it honestly. If you could set your snit aside for a few moments, I think that even you will agree that it does Will no good for us to be at odds. I have some information about Ben and his connection to Shotgun Reese and the Plunketts that might be helpful as we search for our son. If you will—"

"Whoa." Logan held up his hand, palm out. "Just hold on there a minute. What do you mean, *we?*"

She braced herself and gathered her thoughts. She had expected this discussion, so she had her arguments prepared. "I'm going with you."

His scowl turned thunderous. "The hell you are."

"He's my son. I have to be there."

With forceful, jerky motions, Logan reassembled his gun. "Don't be stupid, Caroline. You are a woman. You would be more hindrance than help."

Typical man. "Oh, like I was more hindrance than help to you during the bank robbery?"

"That was different."

"How? You needed my help then and you need it now. You no longer have Cade to watch your back—"

"Who's fault is that?" he snapped.

"One more time, I'm sorry I caused Cade to be on that train. I feel terrible about it. I'd give anything to change what happened, but I can't. But you need to be done with that now, Grey. It's not helping matters." He sneered at her then, but she ignored it and continued, "I've been thinking about this. When Cade got hurt it made your job a whole lot more difficult. Not only do you need someone to watch your back, you need someone to help you slip into Black Shadow Canyon. Last time you pulled off that feat, no one knew who you were. That's not the case anymore. You'll need a disguise. What better one than me?"

He set down his gun, folded his arms and sighed heavily. His eyes flickered with reluctant interest. "What do you mean?"

Well, fancy that. For the first time since everything fell apart between them, he had actually listened to her. "I can ride into the canyon publicly and make a real spectacle of myself as Ben Whitaker's adoptive daughter. We can make a few changes in how you look—bleach your hair, cut it short, hide your eyes behind some glasses—and I can introduce you as my, well, I don't know. Not my bodyguard because that would be too close to who you are, but you get the idea."

"But—"

"I'm good with a gun, Logan. I'm smart and Ben and Will will trust me from the very beginning. That could be important if the situation were to go south."

Logan rose and walked to the back door where he stood staring out toward the creek for a long few moments. When something in his stance told her he was about to refuse her help, Caroline added, "I won't stay behind, Logan. I'll follow you anyway."

He twisted his head and met her gaze. "You would, wouldn't you?"

"Count on it."

"Do you have the slightest clue as to what you'd be letting yourself in for? The only women in that place are whores. The men are violent, lawless animals. They're no strangers to rape."

Caroline understood that, and she acknowledged her own fear of the possible dangers she might encounter. But Will was her child. "I am willing to take any risk for my son. I will sacrifice my life for him if necessary. I know you think I'm a poor excuse for a mother, but you are wrong, Logan Grey. I am a good mother to Will. A loving mother. A caring mother. Believe me when I tell you, I am not staying behind. I know I'll have to be careful. I also know that just like I'll be there to watch your back, you'll be there to watch mine."

After a moment's pause, he muttered, "I have to be crazy to even consider this."

"I was of assistance during the bank robbery, don't forget. I was calm and cool and helped save the day. Our boy needs his parents, Logan. Both of them."

He muttered a curse, then added, "Tell me everything you know about Ben Whitaker and the Plunketts."

"So, you agree? You won't fight me about coming with you?"

"I'll have a few conditions and some rules you have to agree to follow."

"Rules? What sort of rules?"

"I'm not sure. I need a little time to think about them. Now, talk to me about Ben so I can figure out a plan on just how we'll get into Black Shadow Canyon."

Two days later in the hotel room he had rented upon arriving in Van Horn, aware that both he and Caroline needed a good night's sleep in preparation for the grueling combination desert-and-mountain trip ahead, Logan planted his feet, folded his arms and gave his wife a bulldog look. "For the last time, I'm not shaving my head."

They'd argued the point off and on since they started planning the trip into Black Shadow Canyon. Logan couldn't believe some of the crazy ideas his wife had spouted while calmly sitting and sewing on a dress. He wondered if Will had the same outrageous imagination as she did.

Caroline responded to his declaration with a disapproving frown. "I never guessed you'd be so vain."

"It's not vanity!" he fired back, knowing he lied. "I simply don't agree it's the most effective way to change my appearance."

"Oh? And your plan to switch from a black shirt and hat to a white shirt and hat is?"

"I've always worn black."

Was that a little smile of satisfaction that flashed across her face?

"I agree that if you won't make a major change to your physical features, then changing your costume is the next best thing. However, I'm afraid your color choices aren't bold enough to make a real difference, and since our mission is so vital—our son's life is at stake—I want you to have the best possible disguise."

Caroline pulled a stack of clothing from one of the carpetbags she'd toted along from Artesia. "You'll need to go with these, Logan."

His chin dropped. "Orange britches? Where the hell did you get those?"

"They're not orange, they're pumpkin. The pants and the vests are costumes from the Artesia Playhouse. The actor who wore them is similar to you in size, so they should fit well enough." She held a purple vest against him and measured him with her eyes.

When she pulled a lavender scarf from the bag, he scowled and took a step backward. "Hell, why don't you just put me in a dress?"

"I'm afraid that would attract too much attention."

There. He saw it. Her lips twitched again.

"The idea is to make the new you look as different from the old you as possible," she continued, reaching once more into her bag.

When she pulled out a little bowler hat, he put his hands on his hips. "That's going too far."

"Actually, I'm afraid it's not far enough." She placed the hat atop his head, then studied him. Her teeth tugged at her lower lip as she worriedly shook her head. "Maybe if you wore your medallion outside your shirt rather than inside as is your habit...but no. We want the outlaws' eyes to skim, not focus."

"They'll take one look at me and shoot me!"

She clucked her tongue. "It's almost impossible to make you look effeminate. You will need to work hard to look less manly. You need to slump more, Logan. Try to look...limp."

He swiped the hat off his head. "I knew I was making a mistake listening to you," he grumbled. He still wasn't certain exactly why he had. He was still furious with her, wasn't he? Still angry about her lying and scheming ways?

Yes, except he couldn't quite work up the mad he'd had on before she'd let him have it with both barrels. Damned if he couldn't see her side of the argument. He didn't have to like it, but that didn't mean he couldn't see her point.

When it came right down to the nut-cutting, didn't he want his boy to have a lioness for his mother? Would he respect any woman who wouldn't go to any lengths to protect the ones she loved? Just because she loved that old geezer Whitaker, whom he didn't consider worthy of that love, didn't lessen the value of her gift.

In a moment of brutal self-honesty, he'd come to realize that his fury was rooted not in guilt as she'd charged—he'd pretty much made his peace there—but rather in bruised and battered pride.

Ego. Hurts like a son of a bitch when it comes out swinging.

She'd fooled him, sold him possum hide for rabbit fur and slept with him, to boot. No man worth his salt liked it when a woman played him false, and he'd not been willing to look past his anger until...well, to be honest...until she'd thrown the idea of love into the mix.

Hell, maybe he ought to wear a dress. Since when had his emotions gone and gotten all female?

Since that moment in her kitchen, he admitted. She'd gotten to him with that big-eyed declaration of "feelings being involved." It was stupid that he even paid attention. After all, lust was a "feeling" wasn't it? His own "feelings" had damned sure been involved that night.

But, she'd also said "heart." Her heart had been involved.

It wasn't just lust for her, but something more, and once he'd calmed down enough to realize it, the fact had soothed his battered pride. Being a man, he also knew she wasn't free with her favors. If she'd been honest about anything, it was that she hadn't been with anyone but him.

So, now what?

They continued their arguing and bickering, but the sharp edge was missing in their interactions. The sizzle, however, had returned the minute the haze of anger faded away. At least, from Logan's point-of-view, it had. He couldn't tell what Caroline was thinking—they hadn't exactly kissed and made up.

"Oh, don't be such a grump," she scolded. "I'm not saying you have to wear them all the time. Just when we get close to the canyon. You still have a few days to work up to the indignity of wearing puce."

His brows arched in alarm. "Wearing what?"

She laughed and only then did he notice the teasing glint in her eyes. "It's a color. Sort of a reddish-brown."

"How can you be so cavalier about this?"

"We're closer to finding Will. That brings my spirits up immeasurably."

Her spirits weren't the only thing rising at the moment. Dammit, what was it about the two of them and hotel rooms? At least he'd been able to rent two rooms this time. As much as the idea appealed, he didn't think that another roll in the sheets would be in their best interest at this particular moment.

It didn't help that he remembered how she felt. How she melted in his arms. How she smelled—like lemons and sunshine. It didn't help that she smiled at him, either. Or that she laughed.

The trail ahead of them was long and dangerous and it required focused attention and clear thinking. In his experience, sex blurred a man's focus and clouded his mind.

As his gaze made a lingering journey down his wife's curvaceous figure, he further admitted that sex with Caroline just made him stupid. *Time to get out of this hotel room.*

Although, she *was* his wife. He did have every right…

That would be a big mistake. Huge. Colossal.

Stupid.

I'd be satisfied, but stupid.

He cleared his throat. "Give me the damned britches. We'd both better hit the hay. We need to be up, fed and ready to ride at first light. Can you manage that?"

She handed him the clothes. "I promised you I wouldn't slow you down. I meant it."

"Good." He tucked the offensive garments under his arm, and tipped an imaginary hat. "Good night, then. Hope you rest well."

"You, too, Logan."

Dammit, did she have to lick her lips like that?

The vision haunted him as he tossed and turned in his lonely bed the rest of the night. What little sleep he did get was haunted by dreams of Caroline, naked and lying amidst rumpled, pumpkin-colored sheets. He woke up hard and aching and tired—not an auspicious way to begin the next grueling part of this journey.

Pulling on those damned orange britches only made him feel worse. Even though their destination was a hard two-and-a-half-days' ride away, he expected to run across others going to or coming from the canyon. From this moment on, both he and Caroline needed to be prepared to dive into character at a moment's notice. So he donned the white shirt and purple vest, tucked his medallion out of sight and looked into the mirror.

"Holy crap." He couldn't go out in public like this. He'd die of embarrassment long before an outlaw's bullet reached him. Nope, a man could only be pushed so far.

Half an hour later following a detour to the hotel kitchen where he did business with one of the cooks, he sat on a bench in the lobby waiting for Caroline to come downstairs. He didn't look up when he heard her door shut and her footsteps descend the staircase. When she walked right past him, he knew he'd made the right choice in costume.

In Spanish, he said, "*Senora*, may I buy you breakfast?"

"No, thank you," she said, turning with a smile. "I'm waiting for my hus—"

Logan forgot all about his own costume as he lurched to his feet. "Where the hell is the rest of your dress?"

She ignored the subject of the extreme low cut of her altered neckline as her gaze swept him from head to toe. "A serape and a sombrero? Excellent choice. It'll be hot, but—"

"Better to die of a heatstroke than embarrassment."

"Yes. I knew that with enough motivation you'd come up with an acceptable disguise."

Enough motivation? Why, the little witch had manipulated him. Scowling, he grumbled, "While I'm having a heatstroke, you are liable to freeze to death, no more than you have on."

She shrugged. "I did a few alterations. We need attention to be on me, not you."

"Attention is one thing. If you start a riot, I'll be forced to pull my gun."

She laughed. "Don't be silly. Sit down and have a cup of coffee. You'll feel better once you're good and awake."

He was already good and awake. Any more awake and he'd have a helluva time riding a horse.

The coffee, bacon and eggs the waitress brought over did ease his grouchiness somewhat. The shawl Caroline draped over her bountiful charms went a long way toward improving his mood. It wasn't exactly "out of sight, out of mind," but more "out of sight helps."

By daybreak, they were mounted and ready to ride.

Logan had purchased four horses upon their arrival in Van Horn the previous evening: two sorrel mares, a black and a bay gelding. One supply horse would have been enough, but he figured bringing along a mount for Will made a statement Caroline would appreciate.

He had warned his wife that he intended to set a hard pace from the beginning. He did just that, knowing their speed would slow once the desert heated up in the afternoon. The land between Van Horn and the Guadalupe Mountains was desolate and forbidding, at first glance barren, but in reality teeming with life. Agaves, prickly pear cacti, yuccas and walking-stick chollas grew in abundance, while lizards, snakes, coyotes and mule deer populated the desert. Caroline lived up to her word, traveling without complaint and not slowing him down. He was proud of her.

Twice they met riders coming at them on the trail who barely spared him a glance. It was almost noon when a third rider approached riding a paint whose markings Logan knew well.

Calvin Hornbeck had made a career of robbing banks, trains and stagecoaches. He was a killer wanted in two states and the Arizona territory. He had a three-thousand-dollar price on his head and enough bounty hunters after him to field a baseball team. He had busted out of jail in Kansas six months ago—the same jail where Logan plunked his ass three months before that.

Logan's hand shifted toward his gun. He could—probably should—

kill him outright. Heaven knew, he deserved it. It hadn't been three years ago that he'd ambushed a stagecoach in South Texas and killed an eight-year-old girl.

Except, he hated to kill a man in cold blood in front of Caroline. He'd have to explain and that would waste time—as would burying the body in this hardscrabble ground. After that nightmare in Mexico, Logan had made an unbreakable personal rule about burying the bodies of the men he killed. Digging would be a pain in this dry dirt. Killing Calvin Hombeck could easily cost him half a day.

So he waited, his sombrero pulled low, watching alertly as the killer approached. "Beware, Caroline," he cautioned softly. "This bastard and I know each other."

"Then keep your hat down," she warned.

Damned if the woman didn't adjust her bodice so that it drooped a little lower.

When they'd drawn within speaking distance to the other rider, she called out, "Hello! It's a beautiful day to ride, isn't it?"

Hombeck's gaze focused on Caroline, darted quickly toward Logan, then returned to Caroline where it remained locked on her cleavage. "Right beautiful, I'd agree," he said. "Lucky day, too. A fella doesn't often run into a pretty woman on this stretch of the road."

"My name is Caroline Whitaker, and I'm on my way to meet my uncle Ben in Black Shadow Canyon. This is Pepe." She waved a dismissive hand toward Logan. "Are you coming from Black Shadow Canyon? Do you by chance know my uncle Ben?"

"Ben Whitaker? You're Ben's kin?"

"Yes."

"I see. Well, yeah, I know him. Haven't seen him lately, though."

"He and a number of his old friends are supposed to meet us near here... Where is the spot, Pepe?"

Hell. What is she doing? Picking the landmark closest to their present location, he said, "Chimney Rock in the Sierra Diablo."

"Yes, Chimney Rock." She flashed a brilliant smile. "Well, we'd best be hurrying along, then. I don't want to keep Uncle Ben and his friends waiting. I understand they're not the most patient crowd of men. You have a nice afternoon, sir."

She finger-waved, kicked her horse and rode off.

Logan waited a moment and made sure Hombeck rode in the opposite direction. Watching him go, Logan sighed. It went against the grain to let a cold-blooded killer with a bounty on his head ride away, but he had to keep his priorities in order. *One of those priorities better put her damned shawl back on before she gets sunburned.*

Catching up with her, he said, "Remember those conditions and rules I mentioned? I have another one to add to the list."

She arched a curious brow.

"Don't you ever up and do something stupid like that again!"

She blinked. "Excuse me?"

"What were you thinking, Caroline? You don't get friendly with strangers you meet on the road. Especially not this road. That man was a killer. He could easily have taken your friendliness as an invitation to rape! Where we're headed, you need to be aware of just how dangerous these men are."

"I recognized the risk, Logan. I also considered that this was a heaven-sent opportunity to test your disguise."

"Nothing about Calvin Hombeck is heaven-sent," he grumbled, removing his wide-brimmed sombrero and wiping his sweaty brow.

"Maybe not, but it is good to know the disguise works, isn't it? I know I'll feel safer now when we ride into Black Shadow Canyon."

"All right. All right. It's over and done. But from now on, Caroline, I want your word that you won't pull another stunt like that again."

"So you'll trust my word?"

Well, now. She'd certainly boxed him in with that, hadn't she? Trapped him like a possum up a tree. "Are you giving your word?"

"I will if you'll agree to accept it."

"Fine. From now on just keep your mouth shut and your top pulled up. Got it?"

She rolled her eyes, sighed loudly, but nodded.

They pressed forward toward Chimney Rock, arriving about an hour ahead of schedule. Logan asked Caroline how she was holding up. "I had intended to camp here tonight, but we made excellent time and have a few more hours of daylight left. The next water is an hour away. We can keep going or settle here. It's up to you."

She smiled tiredly and lifted her gaze to the rugged peaks that rose abruptly from the desert floor. "How far are we from the canyon?"

"About a day to the Guadalupes, another few hours to the canyon's entrance. The trail into the canyon to the settlement they call Devil's Rest will take half a day more. We will have some time to look around for Will and Whitaker, then after dark, I'll hit the saloons and see what I can learn."

"Let's keep going. The sooner we can start looking for Will, the better."

By the time they finally stopped for the night, Caroline looked ready to drop. Logan chose a campsite beside a clear spring that bubbled at the base of a mountain. It was a pretty spot with cactus flowers in bloom and dotting the landscape. Soon, the crackle and scent of burning brush filled the air as Logan lit the fire. They ate beans and bacon with campfire coffee.

"I wonder if Will has enough to eat and drink," Caroline said as she set her tin plate down beside her. "I imagine him out here in this scorching heat without enough water to drink and it tears me to pieces inside."

"Don't think about it."

"I can't help but think about it."

"Then think about what a resourceful young man he is. He knows how to take care of himself." Then, in an effort to distract her, he said, "Look at the sky."

She leaned back on her elbows and lifted her gaze to a brilliant sunset. "Oh, my. Isn't it beautiful?"

"Yeah." Watching her, Logan got hungry all over again.

"The sky at home is bigger than this, but there is something about being out away from town that just makes the colors seem brighter and richer."

"Hmm," he said in a distracted response. The sunset—as gorgeous as it was—didn't hold anything on her. Her burnished-gold hair glistened in the dancing firelight, her eyes gleamed with the purple-blue hues of dusk. Her curves rose and fell like the mountains to the west, as intriguing and tempting as water to a thirsty man.

She watched the sky without further comment until the last of the light faded away. Then she stood, stretched and said, "I'd like to wash up if you think it's safe."

He had an instant, vivid image of Caroline walking naked into the spring which gave him an instant, vivid erection. Christ. Just the image he needed in his head. He'd get no more sleep tonight than last.

"Sure. I'll keep an eye on things." The sharp look she shot his way made him realize how his words sounded, so he gestured toward the landscape away from camp. "That way."

"Thank you," she said drily. She pulled soap and a towel from one of the saddlebags, then gave him a pointed look until Logan turned his back toward the creek.

He heard the rustling of clothing. A splash. A sigh.

Hell.

He rolled to his feet. "Think I'll find a high spot and see if anything's moving."

"I won't be long."

"Neither will I." He couldn't get away from the spring fast enough.

Logan hiked up a hill and stared out into the deepening night where stars popped out like freckles in the moonless sky. He saw no sign of other campfires, heard no sounds of human proximity. It was as if he were out here alone on a beautiful evening, under a star-filled sky, with his wife.

His beautiful, naked wife.

The wife who'd played him for a fool.

Yet, he couldn't resist looking. He turned his head and sucked air past his teeth. Damn.

Illuminated by starlight and firelight, she was something right off a grand master's canvas. He watched as she soaped herself, her hands stroking her neck, her breasts, her hips. Between her legs. His own fingers moved instinctively as he imagined that her hands were his hands.

It was wrong for him to play the voyeur. He knew it. He didn't particularly care, however, except that it only made his own physical position more painful.

He wondered just how cold that creek water was.

When she finally dipped down to rinse, he managed to pull his attention away. He heard a coyote howl off in the distance, and when he turned toward the sound, something made him pause. That long-familiar sense of knowing filled him.

Trouble was on its way.

Logan went still and focused on his surroundings. There. Behind another hill a short distance away. Was that the faintest of glows coming from behind another rise?

With urgency humming in his blood, Logan hurried down the hillside taking care to move as quietly as possible. By the time he reached the campsite, Caroline was out of the water and toweling herself dry. She gasped and covered herself with the towel when he appeared inside the circle of light. "Get dressed fast, honey. I'm getting a bad feeling. I need you stashed away somewhere safe while I check it out."

"But—"

"Please, Caroline."

Thankfully, she did as he asked, moving quickly and efficiently while he gathered his pistol and extra ammunition. "Try to move quietly," he said, leading her away from camp. He'd chosen a spot about a hundred yards away from the campsite, a place he'd noted upon their arrival for just such a circumstance. Surrounded by tall walls of rock on three sides, it offered Caroline both concealment and security. "I'll call out when I come to get you. If you see any movement in the meantime, shoot first and ask questions later."

"I'll be fine. Don't worry about me. Go take care of the problem, Logan."

"You'll stay here?"

"Yes, Logan, I'm not a fool."

He hesitated, then leaned down and pressed a quick, hard kiss against her lips before turning away. "Neither am I."

He took a route that angled away from both their campsite and the nook where he'd hidden Caroline, stopping every few minutes to listen and to concentrate. Nothing.

Yet, his antennae continued to quiver. Something was out there. A threat.

To the north, he again heard a coyote's howl. Was that the threat he sensed? A four-legged variety?

Could be. His trouble sense didn't differentiate between species when it came to threats. But it also didn't thump on minor dangers, either. This was two-legged trouble and he needed to track it down.

Moving like a ghost, Logan headed for the area where he'd detected the glow of firelight. The rising moon cast a silvery light across the desert landscape and made his passage both easier and more open to detection. He walked with his gun drawn and his senses alert.

The coppery scent of blood stung his nostrils long before he reached the spot where dying campfire coals turned gray.

What if it was Will?

His mouth went dry. His heart pounded. He braced himself to move forward. At first glance, all he could see was a prone shape, and he couldn't tell if the body was man or animal. He made a quick survey of the surrounding area. The site had an empty feel to it. Whoever—or whatever—had been there wasn't there now.

Logan moved closer, summoned his courage and took a good look at the body. It was a man, thank God, not a boy. Not a boy. *I don't have to go back and tell his mother...*

The poor bastard had been cut and stabbed dozens of times. For the first time since he'd begun this hunt. Logan was glad of the absence of strong light.

It's possible that animals got to him after he was dead, but Logan considered that scenario doubtful due to the relatively undisturbed condition of the campsite. No, a human did this. A human animal. *Sick. Just sick.*

So, just where had the depraved bastard gone and how long ago had he left?

Then, to Logan's shock and surprise, the body on the ground let out a groan. *Sweet Jesus. He's alive?*

Poor bastard. Logan took half a step forward just as the man's eyes opened. Glazed and glassy, the plea was obvious even in moonlight. Even as Logan debated his decision, the hair on the back of his neck rose.

The first gunshot hit the dying man right between the eyes.

The second spat up dirt at Logan's feet.

CHAPTER ELEVEN

Caroline heard the gunshot and flinched. When she heard the second gunshot, she jumped.

She shifted her index finger onto the revolver's trigger and watched the area in front of her like a hawk even as she listened hard for any and every sound. Seconds ticked by...minutes ticked by....

The third gunshot shocked an inadvertent squeal out of her.

Her heart pounded, her mouth went dry as sand. The urge to move was strong, but his words echoed in her mind. *You'll stay here?*

She'd promised. She wouldn't go back on her word, not after everything that had happened.

Come on, Logan. Call out to me. Let me know you are all right.

She heard nothing. No scuffle of boots against rock. No voices. No horse's hoofbeats. Nothing.

She tried to count the passage of time. One minute, two. Then five. Then six.

Go to ten, Caroline. Get all the way to ten. If he hadn't reappeared ten minutes after the third gunshot, then she would leave here and go look for him. After all, she had also told him she would watch his back. Staying hidden away in her safe little hiding spot wasn't exactly doing the job, now was it? On reflection, she'd be breaking her word to him either way, wouldn't she?

She made it to the eight-minute mark, then could wait no more. She took a deep breath, kept her gun up and her finger on the trigger, and eased out of her hiding place.

She hadn't a clue of which way to go.

"Oh dear," she whispered beneath her breath. "Oh dear oh dear oh dear."

Make some noise, Grey. Unless it's a scream. I don't want you to scream.

She decided to make a circle around their campsite. It took all her discipline not to call out for him, but better sense prevailed. If someone other than Logan had fired those shots, then she very well might need the element of surprise.

She'd traveled almost halfway around her circle when she heard the sound. She halted mid-step and listened hard. There. Again.

Male laughter. Ugly male laughter. Not Logan's laughter at all.

Caroline swallowed hard.

All right. What to do? She had to sneak up on whoever it was and see if he was keeping Logan prisoner. She absolutely, positively wouldn't think that those gunshots meant anything uglier than…well…that man's laughter.

Keeping the pistol at the ready, she made her way toward the sound. Perspiration trickled down her back as she heard that horrible cackle. All right, that was a good sign. He wouldn't be laughing like that if someone wasn't around to hear him. Would he?

Maybe there were two gunmen. Maybe they were laughing at each other. Over Logan's… "No!" she shouted in a whisper.

Caroline continued toward the sound, moving quietly, but not silently. Tomorrow before she and Logan resumed their journey, she'd make him take five minutes and show her how to walk like a ghost. That was a skill she could use. One she needed.

Dear, God. Please, let him be all right.

Moving forward, her foot slid on loose gravel, and she swayed, losing her balance, making way too much noise. She reached out and grabbed at the thorny branches of a bush, saving herself from a fall at the sacrifice of her skin. She clenched her teeth against an expression of pain as the spikes gouged deep into her hand and stood silently for a moment, hoping—praying—that her mishap had gone undetected.

For a full minute she waited, holding her breath. Then when she heard the stranger begin speaking, she moved steadily forward. "Just take a look at the Preacher there if you doubt that I know how to make you talk. I'm famous in the canyon for my knife work," cackled the voice. "Stubborn fool wanted to take the secret of Shotgun Reese's stash to his grave. Well, didn't happen, did it? Lookee here."

Close now, Caroline stopped when he quit talking. She saw a flare of light and heard the crackle of burning brush. Then the man continued, "I aim to win this fight, boy. I want that gold. You might as well tell me before I hurt you like the Preacher here. I'll be happy to slit your throat nice and quick like. That's a sacrifice for me, I might add. I do enjoy my knife. So, talk. Where is she?"

She? Did he mean me? Surely not. Though she hadn't seen his face, judging from the sound of his voice she'd never met the man. What could he possibly want with her?

"Whatever you think Caroline knows, you're flat-out wrong," Logan said.

Logan! A tidal wave of relief washed over Caroline as she listened to his strong voice continue, "Ben Whitaker never mentioned the damned treasure to her. She doesn't know squat."

Her sight of the men was blocked by the same crag of rock that hid her. The rocks also deflected the voices, making it impossible to know which man was standing where. She did, however, smell blood and the fact frightened her half to death.

"Doesn't matter. Whitaker told the Preacher the location of Shotgun's stash in exchange for a promise to guard over the woman. He knew she'd be coming after her boy once the Plunketts snatched him."

"Which they did in order to use the boy to threaten Whitaker?"

"Yep. Just like I'm gonna do with your lady. Now, where is she?"

"Go to hell."

The stranger cackled his evil laugh. "Now, that was a mistake."

Only because she was listening hard did Caroline hear Logan's quick intake of breath.

"That feel good? It's just a warm-up. Although, since I've already tested my skills tonight, I'm already pretty warm. Maybe I'll skip straight to your pecker. Ever thought what it would feel like to bleed out from your pecker?"

"Screw you."

"'Fraid that'd be difficult to do, though, since you won't have a pecker. Last chance. Where is she?"

Caroline drew a deep, bracing breath, then stepped forward, the pistol leveled at the villain's heart. Logan was seated, his hands bound behind him, his legs tied at the ankles. The stranger knelt beside him.

She hadn't expected this. How had he gotten the jump on Logan? He was young, younger than Logan, but lanky and slim, not broad and muscular like her husband. Even as the stranger noted her arrival, she snapped in a tone filled with bravado, "She's right here, you thug. Drop the knife."

The stranger moved like lightning and had his knife at Logan's throat even as she prepared to pull the trigger. "You drop the gun, bitch, and I'll let him live."

"You cut him again and you are dead." Inside, Caroline quavered with fear and nervousness, but she used the lessons she'd learned from living with Ben and Suzanne to keep those feelings off her face.

Tension hung in the air thick enough to taste. In the flickering firelight, Logan's eyes snapped with frustrated anger. The man dragged the knife, and Logan's blood beaded against the silver blade. Caroline gritted her teeth as the outlaw said. "Last warning."

He laughed and the sound sent shivers up her spine. In the dim light, his eyes took on a maniacal glow and they telegraphed his intent. Caroline's finger tightened on the trigger just as Logan let out a yell and threw himself toward the man and knocked him over.

They rolled and grunted and bucked, but Logan's ability to battle was limited by the ropes around his wrists and ankles. Caroline's throat went tight. She took a step closer as the men rolled again. This time, the stranger ended up on top and as he rose up and lifted his arm, the knife flashed in the firelight.

Caroline pulled the trigger. Once. Twice. Three times.

The stranger slumped on top of Logan, who cursed and bucked the body off. "Dammit, Caroline!" he hollered.

"Are you hit?"

"No! I'm fine. What the hell were you thinking?"

"Excuse me. I need to be sick." She turned away and that was when she saw the body lying on the ground.

She stumbled around a rock and fell to her hands and knees. Her stomach heaved and she vomited until she was empty.

A hand touched her back and she jumped. "Caroline," Logan said.

He's all right. Logan is all right. I'm all right.

No. I'm not all right. I just killed a man.

She gave her head a shake, hoping to clear it. "You're loose, Logan. How did you get loose?"

"Fellow left a knife lying around. C'mon, let's go back to our camp."

"He's dead, isn't he? I killed him. I killed a man."

"Somebody other than me. Imagine that."

Somewhere deep inside, she appreciated his attempt at humor, but she couldn't summon so much as a smile. She felt shaky and sick and afraid. She'd killed a man.

Logan put his hands at her waist and lifted her onto her feet. "Let's go back, honey. I can use a dip in the creek."

Caroline went along with him blindly as reality settled in. Halfway to their campsite she started to shake violently. She stumbled and he caught her to keep her from falling. In her mind's eye she relived the moment she pulled the trigger and her head began to spin. "I need to sit down."

Instead, he lifted her into his arms and carried her like a child back to their campfire. When the tears started, he held her, rocked her and murmured comforting words against her ears until she slipped into sleep.

LOGAN HATED TO LEAVE HER, but he needed to go bury that poor man the killer had called the Preacher. Besides, he had a powerful anger riding his blood that simply wouldn't stop.

He carried the camp spade and a blanket back to the scene and went to work digging a single grave between a cholla cactus and a flowering agave. Since Caroline had been the one to shoot the bastard, he didn't feel obligated to bury him. In fact, in this instance if he had been the one to pull the trigger, he'd probably make an exception to his rule. He couldn't think of anyone he'd rather see picked clean by the buzzards than this sorry snake.

Rage pulsed through Logan's veins as he methodically turned the hard dirt. Rage at the killer, rage at the circumstances, rage at himself. He had a lot of rage at his own missteps in this fiasco. He deserved to have his throat slit for letting that son of a bitch get the better of him.

He deserved to have his nuts cut off for putting Caroline in the position to kill.

Come to think of it, he was a tad bit furious with her, too.

When she'd stepped into the firelight, he'd about had a heart attack. The one positive he'd held on to during the debacle was the knowledge that she was stuck away somewhere safe. Seeing her reveal herself had struck fear into his bones unlike any he'd known before.

He'd have to think about that later.

Now he just wanted to get this damned job done. One positive result of his fury was the energy he had to put into his digging. The desert ground was hard and dry, but it couldn't withstand his temper.

He'd dug half the grave before the rolling boil of his rage lessened to a simmer and he was able to think straight once again. He spent a few moments considering the information he'd learned from the killer.

First, he'd confirmed that the Plunketts had Will. Logan had been ninety-five percent certain of it, but it was nice to know for sure. Second, he'd learned that Whitaker expected Caroline to come looking for her son, and that he believed strongly that she needed protection. Logan's gaze drifted to the bag of gold promised to the Preacher in payment for such protection. He might have to reconsider his opinion of Whitaker. He'd given away a fortune in gold to protect Caroline. Not exactly the behavior one might expect from an outlaw'.

Finally, he thought about his own plans in relation to tonight's events. Had anything changed? Should he reconsider how he intended to take Caroline into Black Shadow Canyon? One piece of information he dearly wished he'd gotten from the killer was just how he'd known what this Preacher fellow was up to. Was the whole Geronimo's Treasure search common knowledge in the canyon? He hoped the hell not. Caroline would be a target for every man out there.

Shoot, she was already a target for every man. Her beauty assured that. What the hell had he been thinking letting her come along?

Logan stripped off his shirt and medallion, then sank his shovel into the dirt and repeated a litany of curses until a new thought occurred. Maybe tonight's troubles would have given her second thoughts. Maybe she'd be so upset over having taken a life, she'd be willing to return to Van Horn and wait for him and Will.

He struck rock, and the jar on the spade rattled his hand and shook some sense into him. Caroline, leave without her son? The lioness give up? When hell froze over, perhaps.

No, if anything, once the shock cleared from her mind, she might consider continuing her killing ways by plugging a bullet into him. He couldn't argue that he didn't deserve it.

He couldn't remember the last time he'd made such a stupid, green mistake as to let the bastard get the drop on him. The fact was that he'd let himself get distracted by playing Peeping Tom at his wife. Lust had clouded his mind like a dust storm, and he hadn't had a single clear thought until the bastard's bullet kicked up the dirt at his feet.

Hell, he'd load Caroline's gun for her if she wanted to shoot him.

Judging the grave to be deep enough, Logan approached the mutilated body and wrapped it in the blanket. "God have mercy on your soul, Preacher," he said as he covered the corpse's face. "I thank you for trying to help my wife. Wish I had been around to be of help to you."

He tugged the body into the grave, then began the process of filling it with dirt. Once that was done, he piled stones atop the dirt, stood at the head of the grave and said the Lord's Prayer.

He grabbed up his shirt and medallion, then took a circuitous route back to camp, keeping a sharp eye out for the presence of any other intruders. He returned to find that Caroline continued to slumber. With any luck, she'd sleep straight through the night.

Feeling gritty, grimy, and sore, Logan grabbed a bar of soap and a towel from his supplies, stripped off the rest of his clothes and waded waist-deep into the cold spring. He soaped himself, scrubbing hard to wash off the blood, both his own and that of others, then submerged his entire body beneath the water. The cuts and scrapes from the fight burned like fire, and he gritted his teeth against the pain.

Pushing out of the water, he gave his head a shake and set droplets flying. The movement pulled at the cut across his throat and he winced. He felt the dribble of liquid down his neck and touched it, hoping it was water. Thick. Warm. Sticky. Hell.

He'd have to get Caroline to sew it up for him in the morning. The idea pissed him off. Reminded him how stupid he'd been. How reckless Caroline had been. He tossed her sleeping form a fulminating look.

They couldn't let it happen again. He needed to keep his mind out of his pants and she absolutely had to follow his instructions. To the letter! It had worked out all right tonight, but they could not count on being lucky like this again. Not with his luck.

Logan waded out of the stream, both physical pain and mental ire heating his temper once again. Naked and dripping, he reached for the towel he'd left draped across a bush and wiped himself dry.

He slung the damp towel around his neck and put pressure against the cut hoping to stop the bleeding. It was then that he noticed that Caroline was awake, sitting up and watching him.

Absently, she licked her lips.

Blood rushed immediately to his crotch, dammit. *Hell, no sense keeping pressure on the cut—no blood in my neck left to lose.*

The fact that he was so painfully aroused, so quickly, made him furious. He lashed out at her saying, "Dammit, Caroline."

She blinked. Her gaze lifted to his eyes. "What?"

"What?" he repeated. He wrapped the towel around his hips, shielding himself from what looked to be a hungry gaze. The fact that he did it when what he really wanted was to march over to her and bury himself in her charms only flamed the fires of his anger hotter. "You ask me *what?*"

"Um...yes."

"You can't look at me like that!"

"Like what?"

"Like I'm cream and you're a thirsty kitten."

"Oh. Did I do that?"

"You damned sure did!"

"I'm sorry. I was asleep. I woke up and there you were. All...naked."

"For goodness sake, Caroline."

She smiled sheepishly, then said, "You're all scarred and bloody. A warrior. You make me feel safe."

"Safe? Christ, Caroline. I almost got you killed tonight."

"No, you almost got yourself killed, which I admit does stir my temper. You need to be more careful with yourself."

"Careful with myself?" The tucked-in towel slipped a bit as he brought his hands up, held on to his head and repeated a frustrated, "Careful with myself! This from the woman who left a perfectly safe hiding spot after promising me she wouldn't?"

"You can't hold that against me, Logan. I also promised I would watch your back. After hearing three gunshots, I determined I had no other choice."

"I didn't ask you to watch my back!"

"Nevertheless, I promised I would."

He turned away and started pacing back and forth. Frustration had him slapping a towel-clad thigh as he attempted to rein in his temper. He'd damned sure better get hold of himself, or else...

Or else he'd be taking hold of her.

"Grrrr," he growled. Then he stopped, braced his hands on his hips and said, "Look, we need to talk."

A smile briefly flirted with her lips. "You say that to me rather often, do you realize that? I don't want to talk, Logan. Come here."

"No."

"Why not?"

"It's not safe."

She sat up straighter and her eyes went round. "Are you worried about another intruder?"

Hell, he hadn't meant to scare her. "No, we're okay. I checked things out before I took my bath."

"So, why aren't we safe?"

"You're safe. I'm not!"

"I don't understand."

"Yes, you do. You damned sure do. You're dangerous, woman!"

"Because I killed a man tonight?"

"No, because you make me want to forget everything I'm supposed to be doing and thinking. That's what got me into trouble earlier tonight and I'd have to be a cotton-headed fool to let it happen again."

"I want to forget, too, Logan. It's been a really awful... " Her voice cracked slightly as she added. "Horrible night. Please come here and help me forget."

"No."

Caroline's reply was to stare at him for a long moment, then rise gracefully to her feet. She took hold of the hem of her gown and whipped it over her head.

In the end, Logan was simply a man. He didn't have the fortitude or the desire to withstand a woman—*this* woman—bent on seduction.

To hell with it. Yet, even as he closed the distance between them, his anger at himself and at her simmered on his nerves. As a result, when he grabbed her hand and yanked her into his arms, the gentleness he'd shown her before was missing.

He buried his fingers in her hair and yanked her head back. His heartbeat raced as he ravaged her throat. His mind fogged as he savaged her mouth. The need to take her pounded through him like a drug.

Caroline didn't appear to mind his harsh treatment.

She met his rough kiss with a wildness of her own. When his hands gripped her hips and kneaded the soft, supple flesh, her hands streaked up and down his back. Her nails scraping. Her fists pounding. Her voice demanding more even as it whimpered.

Their lips fused in a desperate kiss, their tongues battling, their teeth scraping. The heat of his desire burned through any restraint, any self-control. He stumbled forward, backing her against a hard, rough wall of rock. She lifted her legs, wrapped them around him. He tore his mouth free of hers, hoisted her higher and fastened it on her breast.

He suckled her greedily, feasted on her sweet flesh, and hot, electric lust pumped through his blood like a drug. Through his own haze, Logan heard the desperate, wild sounds she made. Madness had hold of him. He had no gentle caress to give her, no soft words. Yet, judging by every fevered response, Caroline didn't need that. Didn't want that.

Her hands grasped and grabbed, her fingernails bit into his skin. She cried out in pleasure as his tongue and teeth scraped roughly over her. Her legs gripped his waist like a vise.

He spun away from the rock wall and strode toward the bedrolls. She nipped at his jaw, pressed a sweet, gentle kiss against the cut on his throat, then sank her teeth into the spot where neck and shoulder met. The flash of dark, erotic pain made everything inside him go tight.

He lowered her onto the bedroll, then himself on top of her.

Her body was soft, smooth and hot. She trembled, strained against him, and Logan surrendered to the desperate desire to have her, to take her. To conquer her. He surged into her deep and hard, her hot, wet sheath gripping him like a glove.

The sense of coming home shocked him.

"Logan," she breathed, her voice needy, demanding his attention.

He covered her mouth with his and plundered with his tongue even as his hips began to pump. She tangled her fingers in his hair as she arched her hips up, meeting his thrusts, matching his rhythms, driving him further into madness. Their bodies turned hot and slick and fused into each other as one. He could barely breathe for wanting her...needing her. A forgotten emotion tugged at his heart and in the midst of passion Logan felt vulnerable and afraid.

She dazzled him. It was more than simply her beauty, as irresistible as that was. It was her generous, giving nature. Her fierce, loyal spirit. And her passion. Such passion.

Beneath him, her body vibrated. He watched with blatant male satisfaction as he drove her up, higher and higher, toward the peak. He murmured words to her—dark, shocking, erotic words not meant for the light of day, and Caroline responded with a high-pitched, needy keen. Then with a gasp, she fell, crying out her pleasure as her muscles gripped him, contracting around him in that torturous rhythmic pulse meant to pull the life force from a man.

When she opened her eyes, he met her gaze and let himself drown in the violet sea. With one final thrust, he surrendered, and as the molten pleasure erupted through him, an emotion he refused to name and never expected to feel fluttered in his heart.

Fear rolled over him like a tidal wave. *This can't happen. I won't let it.*

Ruthlessly, Logan shored up his defenses. He crushed the flutter and strengthened his walls.

He told himself he absolutely, positively had not fallen in love with his wife.

Somewhere in the back of her mind, Caroline knew that reality did indeed exist. For the time being, however, she was happy to live inside the fantasy.

The sky was huge with the moon high and bright. Stars painted the sky. The night was still; the cool, desert-scented air kissed her sweat-dampened skin. Somewhere up on the mountain, a cougar roared.

Caroline didn't even shiver. The bedroll beneath her lay scrunched and rumpled. She had anvils for arms and lead poles for legs. A fallen redwood lay splayed across her, dead to the world but for the steady beat of his heart.

For a minute there, she'd worried they might have killed one another. The intensity, the heat—a time or two in the middle of things she'd halfway expected to burst into flames. She sighed, content and sated, and a half smile played upon her lips as the haze of desire slowly faded from her mind. *What a way to go.*

Logan shifted, disengaged and rolled off her onto his side. Caroline murmured a protest, mournful at the loss.

He cleared his throat. "I don't know what to say."

"Just don't ask me to stand up."

"Caroline, I tossed you down and plundered you."

She didn't try to keep the smug satisfaction from her voice. "Yes, you did, didn't you?"

"I was angry and I treated you roughly."

"We treated each other roughly and I'm not complaining. I'm not a fragile prairie rose, Logan. I enjoyed what we did. I didn't know it could be like that. It was...exciting. I don't know that I'd want it so rough-and-tumble all the time, but it fit the mood tonight. Don't you think?"

He laughed reluctantly. "I don't know what to make of you, Caroline Grey. You are one surprise after another."

Boldly, she trailed a finger across his chest. "I like that. I like that you see it in me, too. I have a theory about that. Would you like to hear?"

"Chatty little thing tonight, aren't you?"

"I need to keep my mind occupied. I don't want to think about what I did or what our son might be going through at this moment. I need to not think about bad things right now. Is there something else you would like to discuss?"

Logan tucked her head against his shoulder. "Actually, I'm not so sure I'm ready to let my thoughts wander where they will, either. Tell me your theory."

Caroline stretched her legs, then cuddled against her husband. "I think that as a rule, Texas women are a bit different from women from other states. Ellen and I have discussed this at length. See, women of the West are independent by nature. They've had to be to survive. Texas women have that added bravado that comes from Texas having once been an independent republic. But as the West is tamed, civilized society is established and it attempts to mold women into what it considers acceptable. For the most part, women are ready for it, but while a woman can tame her independent streak, she'll never remove it entirely."

Amusement laced his voice as he said, "That makes a bit of sense, I guess. Although, I wouldn't say that you've exactly tamed your independent streak."

Caroline sighed. "It's finishing school."

Logan waited a moment. "All right, I can't follow that one."

"I didn't go to finishing school. My mother intended to send me. My father married her during a visit back East, and she was a consummate society lady. I don't know that she ever adjusted to being a rancher's wife. Anyway, she died and I stayed home, so I never had the independence—"

"Otherwise known as stubbornness," Logan interjected.

"—polished over," she continued, ignoring his comment. "Then, of course, I had Will and moved in with Suzanne and Ben. That pretty much cemented my independent streak, and it's probably why I don't respond the way you expect me to."

He lifted his hand and palmed her breast. "Caro, your response is more than I've ever dreamed of."

Without another word, she pushed her body up against his, pressing against his chest. The warmth of his skin upon the points of her breasts sent another wave of need through Caroline that reached all the way to her toes. Their mouths opened to each other, his tongue gently caressed hers, coaxing her to wander back into the flames that smoldered between them.

His palms moved slowly up over the sides of her breasts until his thumbs came to rest on her nipples. Drawing circles around the aching buds, he teased and taunted as he kissed her, his touch lazy yet with veiled intent. He wanted her again, and the nudging hardness against her thigh pressed with more insistence.

A tingle of feminine power stroked Caroline's ego. The feel of his arousal, the idea that she could make him lose control as he had, it was thrilling and satisfying and a bit scary, truth be told. But she didn't want to think hard about tomorrow. Didn't want to think at all. For these few stolen moments, she was going to be a woman with a man. A wife with a husband. A lover with a lover. The rest would all take care of itself.

As if Logan read her mind, he let his hands reach down to her hips and slipped her beneath him. When he claimed her this time, it was sweet and gentle, the rhythm between them almost poignant. With tears unshed, Caroline kissed the side of his neck and sighed, laying her head upon his shoulder as he loved her. Wrapping her arms around him, she looked up at the blurry stars and let herself be consumed by the magic of Logan Grey.

She awoke to the scent of frying bacon and coffee. Stretching to work the soreness from her muscles, she glanced around for Logan and finally spied him bedecked in his big hat and serape on a rise above the campsite with field glasses up to his eyes.

Caroline quickly made her morning ablutions and dressed, then tended the bacon and poured herself a cup of coffee. By the time Logan came down the hill, the bacon was ready.

She turned to him with a bright smile and said, "Good morning."

He didn't meet her gaze. "Mornin'."

He busied himself pouring his coffee and shoveling down his breakfast. Caroline ate, steamed and stewed. She'd expected more from him, expected better from him. How could he be so attentive last night and so chilly this morning?

Whatever the reason, she was tired of it. It hurt her feelings, to be perfectly honest. He'd made love to her last night! Or at least, that's what she had thought he'd done. Maybe for him it was nothing more than sex. Just like on their wedding night.

The dirty flea-bit dog.

Well. She debated whether or not to bring the subject up. Maybe he expected her to question him so he could say it didn't mean anything to him. Was that his game?

The dirty rotten flea-bit dog.

Caroline had just worked up the nerve to tell him exactly what she was thinking when he said, "We need to get a move on. I want to be far away when somebody stumbles across the evidence of last night's troubles."

With that, the memories Caroline had tried so hard to block from her mind came rushing back and pushed her pique at Logan right out of her mind.

She helped Logan break camp and each time she reached for something, she halfway expected to see blood on her hands. In the light of day, the events seemed surreal. A nightmare. She stole a glance at Logan and at the cut on his neck. Fresh blood smeared his skin. "Shall I stitch that for you?"

He touched his neck and grimaced. "I don't want to take the time now. It can wait until we stop for lunch."

Within twenty minutes, they rode out of camp, Logan leading the way. They traveled steadily for two hours, conversing only when necessary. The heat rose with the sun and became visible waves against the flat horizon, creating lakes where none existed. Mirages. It made her thirsty just to look at them. A couple times Logan dropped back and attempted to instigate a conversation, but Caroline wasn't in the mood. Eventually, he took the hint.

It was during the fourth hour of travel that he reined in his horses. "Rider coming," he warned.

He tugged the field glasses from his saddlebag and trained them on the approaching figure. After a long moment, he said softly, "Well, damn my eyes."

Then he turned a look on her that was fiercer, more ferocious, than anything she'd ever seen from him before. "Caroline, listen. You absolutely must follow my lead this time. Got it? I need you to swear. Swear on Will's life that you'll let me do the talking here. It's that important. And get your gun out. Keep it hidden in your skirts, but at the ready."

"All right," she said as her stomach took a fearful dip. "I promise. But why?"

"The rider who is heading toward us? He's Deuce Plunkett. He's the man who kidnapped our son."

CHAPTER TWELVE

CAROLINE GASPED. "I DON'T SEE WILL. DO YOU?"

"No." Logan lifted the field glasses once again, and gave the area a second sweep to confirm. "Plunkett is alone."

"Is that a good thing or a bad thing, do you think?"

Logan focused on the killer's face. A red mark marred Plunkett's left cheek. Looked like a burn. A recent one.

"Does he know you?" Caroline asked.

"No. We never met face-to-face." He'd watched the bastard beat a man to a pulp, however, in a saloon brawl in Black Shadow Canyon. He'd go to his grave remembering the expression of pure evil in Plunkett's eyes.

"Then how do you know that this man is Plunkett? Maybe you're mistaken."

"He has distinctive features, Caroline. Women think he's a real pretty boy." Or at least, they did. That burn on his face might change that.

Although, chances were good that Deuce Plunkett wouldn't have the chance to be showing off his scar to any women. Logan would need a real good reason to let the killer leave the upcoming meeting alive.

He wondered just when and how ol' Deuce had received the burn.

Was Will responsible? The idea both frightened him and gave him hope.

"Tell me what to do, Logan," Caroline said calmly as Deuce's approach brought him to within fifty yards or so.

"Let me answer all the questions unless he speaks to you directly. Watch his eyes, honey. If you have to shoot, shoot to kill."

"We can't kill him. We need to find out about Will."

"Oh, I'll find out about Will. Don't worry about that."

Plunkett reined in his roan a short distance from Logan and Caroline. Adopting a friendly smile, he tipped his hat. "Howdy, folks. Plenty hot day to travel, isn't it?"

Following Logan's instructions—for once—Caroline smiled, nodded, but kept her mouth shut. Logan thumbed back his sombrero and replied in a deceptively pleasant tone, "It's hot enough to melt the shoes off a horse out here amongst the cacti, but I expect it will cool off once we reach the mountains."

Plunkett nodded sagely. "Yes, it will, but you have to climb pretty high to beat the heat." He turned his gaze toward Caroline, and gave her a smile. "I'm surprised to see a lady out and about on such a day in this hardscrabble part of the country."

Logan said, "It's the shortest route to her parents' place north of here. Her mother is ill."

"I'm sorry to hear that." Plunkett frowned and added, "I'm on a grave mission, myself. My son...well...he had a disagreement with his brother. He's run away. I'm hoping you might have seen him."

"Your son?" Caroline blurted out.

"Yes, ma'am. He's a good boy, but he and his brother... they're twins. You know how brothers can fight. The boy took off and now he's wandering around this desert. I'm desperate to find him."

"I'll just bet you are," Logan murmured, meeting Caroline's questioning gaze. He both warned and reassured her with a look, before turning back to Plunkett. "How old is your boy? What does he look like?"

"He's fourteen. Tall and lanky. Boy eats like a horse. He has dark hair. When he ran off he was wearing denims and a dark brown shirt."

"Did he have a hat?" Caroline asked. "This sun can be brutal. And water? Did he take water with him?"

Calm down, Mama. Those weren't questions a stranger would ask. Caroline must have realized that, too, because she hastened to say, "I'm a mother, so I understand how worried you must be. The idea of a child...any child...being out here ill-prepared. You poor man."

"Um...yeah...well. He had a hat and some water."

She offered Plunkett a trembling smile that passed for comforting. "That must relieve you."

Logan cleared his throat, dragging the killer's attention away from Caroline. "You think he's in this area? How long has your son been missing?"

"He ran off north of here a ways. A couple of days ago."

Two days? Logan eyed the bastard's burn, analyzed the amount of visible healing and stifled a grin. *Good job, son.*

The boy was a pistol. Logan couldn't wait to meet him.

"And you've been looking for him ever since?"

"Yeah. It's hard to believe he could disappear so completely. That's why I'm so worried about him."

"Maybe he's hiding from you." At Logan's casual suggestion, Plunkett narrowed his eyes, and the cold, dead look Logan remembered flashed in their black depths. "He must know you'll be forced to punish him once he's found."

Plunkett rolled his tongue around his mouth. "Well, a father can't let his kid run roughshod over him, now can he?"

"You know, mister, I think we might have some information for you." Logan rubbed the back of his neck. "We didn't actually see him, but a man who stopped by our campsite last night looking for a meal claimed he'd run short of food because he'd shared his noon meal with a boy who had eaten everything in his saddlebags but the leather. The boy's name was Will Grey."

"That's my son. Will Grey."

Logan saw Caroline stiffen, and her hand moved surreptitiously in her lap. He shot her a warning look. *Don't shoot the bastard. That's my job.*

Plunkett asked, "Where did you camp?"

Logan made a show of twisting around in his saddle. "Well, not many landmarks in sight. Let me draw you a map."

He swung down from his horse, and walked toward a sandy spot of ground about twenty paces away. Plunkett followed, but when Caroline started to dismount, Logan called, "Stay where you are, dear. This won't take long."

He hunkered down and drew a few *Xs* and lines and a circle or two. When Plunkett approached, he pointed at one of the *X*s. 'This is where we are now." Gesturing toward another *X,* he added, "That's the hill about an hour back that...Wait. I know something that will make better sense of this. Wait here."

He walked twenty paces, then with his hands hanging loosely at his sides, Logan turned. When he spoke, his voice was hard. "Deuce Plunkett?"

The killer's head came up, alarm in those awful eyes.

Logan's countenance was hard and implacable. "I'm placing you under arrest for kidnapping."

Slowly, Plunkett rose, his hand hovering over his gun. "Who the hell are you?"

"I'm a range detective and you're under arrest. Lay down your gun."

"The hell I will!" The second Plunkett's hand moved toward his gun, Logan drew and fired. Scarlet blossomed on his chest and he clutched a hand to his heart. "Son of a...You killed me!"

Plunkett dropped to his knees on the desert floor. Hatred blazed in his eyes as he struggled to bring his gun up, but Logan stepped forward and kicked it safely away. He leaned over the fallen man and added in a tone cold as the grave, "I'm also Will Grey's father."

Plunkett's eyes widened, then turned to glass. He fell forward onto the dirt.

Stone-cold graveyard worm-eaten dead.

Logan smiled.

THEY LEFT him for the buzzards to deal with, and Caroline couldn't find it in herself to care. She was rather numbed by the entire incident, in fact. Two days. Two dead men. It was simply a bit much for her.

She let Logan lead the way as her focus turned inward. She felt wounded, even worse today than she'd felt yesterday, which didn't make sense considering she knew that Will was safe from that evil man's clutches. Underneath her numbness, she continued to worry over Will. As if from far away, she fretted about where he was and whether he had enough water and shelter and food. She brooded over the fact he was alone in the desert—or at least, she hoped he was alone and not caught up with killers like the two she'd run across in the past two days.

Two days. Two dead men. Add in the death and destruction brought about by the tornado, and she'd seen more blood in the past week than she'd seen in her entire life. Perhaps she'd reached her limit on violence.

Perhaps she'd reached her limit, period.

Her mind fogged. She wanted to crawl under one of the million rocks around here and go to sleep. Her hands started shaking, her legs began to twitch. Thirst was suddenly a raging need within her. When the world started spinning, she managed to rein her mount to a halt.

She slid down from the saddle, then sat on the ground. Her gaze focused on a prickly pear less than a foot away. *I almost sat on that.* Giggles bubbled up inside her, strangled her throat, then spilled from her lips.

She still had just enough sense left to take notice of the hysterical note to her laughter. *I'm addled. I've lost my marbles. I've gone crazy as a bullbat.*

"Caroline? Sweetheart?"

Logan's shadow blocked out the sun. She continued to laugh. She tried to stop, but she couldn't. The laughter bubbled and burbled and gurgled and somewhere along the way tears joined the mix. Imagine that. More tears. Tears and blood. Blood and tears. Funny how they went together so well.

"Shush, honey." Logan knelt beside her. "It's okay. Everything is okay."

"No. It's really not." Abruptly, as if a candle had been snuffed or a bullet pierced a brain, the laughter died. "I'm thirsty, Logan."

He rose and reached for her canteen, unscrewed the cap and put the spout to her lips. She drank swallow after swallow after swallow until he took the canteen away. "That's enough, honey. You'll make yourself sick."

He must have been right, because her stomach immediately began to roll. Her skin went clammy, sweaty and cold, and the tremors renewed.

"Heatstroke," Logan murmured. "But it's not that hot. Have you been drinking any water, Caroline?"

Water? She didn't know. She shrugged. "I'm sick of blood, Logan."

"I know, baby."

"I think Will is probably safe. Don't you? He got away from that man, didn't he? He's a good boy. A smart boy. He has to be safe. He has a hat. Surely he has it with him."

"A hat?"

"The sun is very, very hot. Don't you think? But a hat will protect him. He needs to be protected."

"I'm sure that Will has a hat, Caroline," Logan said, sending her a concerned look. "Now, let's find us a spot to rest for a bit. Look, see the trees up ahead? We'll reach the mountains and that nice shade and probably some water, too, in ten or fifteen minutes."

Caroline gazed up at the horse. The saddle might as well have been a million miles away. "I'm fine here."

"You pitiful little thing."

Logan rose and left her side, but she didn't know what he was doing. She couldn't quite work up the energy to care. A few minutes, or maybe a few hours, later, he returned.

He didn't say a word, just slipped his arms beneath her and lifted her against him. He carried her to his horse, then slung her up into the saddle, following right behind. He wrapped one arm around her and snuggled her back against him. "You just relax, Caroline. Try to sleep if you can."

Surprisingly, she did just that. She stirred, but didn't fully awaken when he dismounted and settled her beneath a tree beside a clear stream running between the cliffs rising high all around them. She had the sense of cooler air, of a pine-scented breeze, of the clatter of a chickadee above. They must be in a canyon. *The* canyon? Then she sank back into oblivion, not waking until the scent of roasting rabbit tickled her nostrils.

Her eyes fluttered open, and she sat up, taking stock of her surroundings. Meat broiled on a spit over a rock-ringed campfire. A glance toward the sky told her it was mid-afternoon. She'd slept for hours. Logan sat propped against a tree trunk, his long legs outstretched and crossed at the ankles. He was reading a book.

Noting her movement, he looked up and smiled. "Hey there, sleepyhead. How do you feel?"

Caroline blinked and rubbed her gritty eyes like a little child. "I'm fine. I...Oh dear. I don't know what happened to me."

"You shut down. I've seen it before." One corner of his mouth lifted in a lopsided grin. "Hell. I've done it before."

Well, she'd never done anything like that before. It embarrassed her to recall how she'd trembled and cried. It made her feel like a weak little kitten. "I'm sorry I slowed us down, Logan."

"Hey, I was ready for a rest myself. We've been going at it awfully hard. Now that we know Will was smart enough to get himself away, we can afford to take a break. I figure that a good meal, a relaxing afternoon and evening, and a good night's sleep will help us shake off the events of the last few days. We can head into the mountains toward the canyon with our energy restored."

"So this isn't Black Shadow Canyon?"

"No. You didn't sleep that long," he teased.

She eyed the fire. "The rabbit smells good."

"I did my job as hunter-gatherer pretty well," he said with a wink. "I found us two rabbits, and I foraged for some onions and carrots and potatoes so we can have roasted meat soon, then a delicious rabbit stew later."

She smiled. "It's amazing what a skilled hunter can find in supply saddlebags."

"Hey, now. I did catch the rabbits, didn't I? In this barren part of the universe, that's saying something."

"And I am grateful for it."

"I'm the grateful one, Caroline," he said, following a moment's pause. "I need to tell you...well..."

She braced herself. While he'd begun this on a positive note, she couldn't help but be wary. The peace they'd established since leaving Artesia was a fragile one. She didn't want to see it destroyed. "Can we not talk about serious things, please?" she asked, feeling tired all over again. "I'd like—"

"You need to hear this. Caroline, I want you to know that I know I was wrong about some of the things I said to you. Most important, I know that you are a good mother. Hell, you are a great mother. You are loyal and loving and ferocious in Will's defense. I couldn't ask for more or for better for a child of mine."

Caroline blew out a breath. His words threatened to put her right back into shock. "You said—"

"I know what I said, and I was wrong. That's what I'm trying to tell you. Caroline, I wasn't fair to you. My anger blinded me and I was wrong to let it happen." His smile, his voice and the light in his eyes were solemn and sincere as he added, "I was wrong to threaten to take Will away from you."

Her breath caught. "You won't take him away?"

"Shoot, I don't know that I could have made that happen even if I wanted to." Amusement flashed across his expression. "The boy got away from Deuce Plunkett. I wouldn't stand a chance of keeping him around if he didn't want to be there. But that's not why I changed my mind, Caroline. That would be wrong and I can see that now that my eyes aren't seeing red. Hell, I could see it that night. It was bruised pride talking and I apologize for it."

Well. Maybe this peace between them wasn't so fragile, after all.

"Now, that doesn't mean I intend to abandon him," Logan continued. "I want to be part of his life if he'll have me. If you'll allow it."

Her pulse doubled its pace. "What are you thinking?"

He shrugged and looked away, not meeting her gaze. "I don't know. I guess when all of this is over, the three of us—four if you want to include Whitaker—will need to sit down and hash it all out. For all I know, Will might not want to have a thing to do with me. I'm not saying I'll take it as his final word. I'll fight for him, Caroline, even if it's him I'm fighting. But you have my word that I'll be conscious of his wishes, and I'll do my damnedest to do what is best for him in the long run."

"He won't reject you, Logan. At the very least he'll be curious about you, and he'll want to get to know you."

"I wouldn't be so certain. He's fourteen. At that age, he's between being a boy and a man. This experience he's gone through may well have knocked what's left of the boy right out of him. He may tell me to hit the trail, that he's a man now and he can take care of you, and that the two of you, don't need me."

"He'd be wrong." Caroline's smile was tremulous. "I don't know what I would have done without you these past few days. If you hadn't agreed to come with me…" She shook her head. "It frightens me half to death to think about it. I couldn't have survived all this without you."

"Sure you could have. You are one of the strongest women I have ever known."

Caroline's heart melted. He was saying all the right things, but even more, he said them as if he truly believed them. The words were balm for her wounded heart, salve for her soul, and they left her open and vulnerable to emotions that, despite everything, had never truly died.

She had feelings for Logan Grey. Feelings that, if she didn't guard against them, might deepen into love.

Maybe that wouldn't be such a terrible thing, Caroline thought as she watched him tend the roasting rabbit. They *were* married, after all. They could make a home, live as a family. Logan could play catch with Will in the evenings and shower him with as many gifts as he wanted—well, within limits. Maybe she could even have another child, a little sister for Will. He'd be such a fine big brother. She shouldn't forget that it was entirely possible that Will's sister already could be on the way.

It was there, just beyond her fingertips. Everything she'd never dared to want. All she needed to do was to reach out and grab it—as long as Logan wanted to grab for it, too.

That was the real issue here, wasn't it? What did Logan want? He'd said all the right things, acted with passion and promise, but he'd never once suggested a future where they lived together as a family—even after he'd made love with her on two separate occasions. In fact, the closest he'd come to discussing the future was that humiliating conversation on the train when he'd suggested what amounted to drop-by sex.

She should ask him. Before she allowed her heart—and be honest, her body—to get any more involved with him, she should find out what his intentions were. So, all she needed to do was to work up the nerve to ask him.

All right, do it. She cleared her throat. "Logan?"

He glanced up from the rabbit. "Yeah?"

She licked her lips. "I was wondering...um...is the meat almost ready?"

"Hungry? Me, too. It'll be ready in another few minutes or so, I figure."

Disgusted with herself, Caroline figured she shouldn't be allowed to have lunch. After all, chickens didn't eat rabbits, did they?

His words echoed in her mind. *You are one of the strongest women I have ever known.*

Prove it, Caroline. Be strong and courageous. Ask him.

But try as she might, she couldn't work up the courage to voice her questions. She managed small talk while she watched him lift the meat off the spit and set it aside to cool, and they had a rousing discussion about upcoming statewide elections as they lunched on the rabbit. When their meal was finished and cleanup accomplished, he removed a book from his saddlebags, sat with his back against a pine tree and stretched out his long legs, crossing them at the ankles. She decided to try again.

Just do it, Caroline. Ask him. She licked her lips, then cleared her throat. "Logan? I want to...I guess I need to ask..." She blew out a heavy breath. "Logan, when you think about filling the role of Will's father, what do you have in mind for...well...what about me, Logan? Where do I stand?"

After a frozen moment, he asked, "What do you mean?"

"You've made it clear that you intend to be a father for our son. What I am not clear on is where you stand on being a husband."

When he grimaced in response, it gave her a real good hint.

He didn't want her? It was a painful, emotional punch to the gut that sucked the breath right out of her. Caroline wished she'd never brought the topic up. And yet, she needed to know. She deserved to know what his intentions were. Didn't she have some intentions herself?

Well, not really. Not yet. She'd been waiting to see what he intended to do. But apparently it didn't matter what she wanted, did it? Apparently Will was all he was interested in.

He let out a long, heavy sigh and set his book aside. "I reckon we should talk about it. We probably should have an understanding before we find Will. I owe you that, don't I?"

Owe her? For what? The sex? Caroline's back stiffened even as her heart broke a little. "I don't want to think in terms of 'owing' one another. Whatever happens in the future, I think we should put our past behind us once and for all."

"Hell, Caroline, I can't think of anything I'd like better." He rolled to his feet and stuck his hands in his back pockets. "Unfortunately, that doesn't seem to work for me. My past is my present is my future—it's a full circle no matter what."

What did he mean by that? What didn't work? Couldn't he settle for just one woman? Was that it? A cold chill settled over her. She didn't want to believe that. It hurt too much.

Was it something else, then? Wanderlust, perhaps? Was he a range detective because he couldn't stay in one place? She recalled that first night in Fort Worth when he'd mentioned California and Louisiana. Did the travel mean more to him than home and hearth?

She waited a moment, debating with herself before asking, "Why not? I don't hold what happened between us against you, not anymore."

"You don't understand."

"Obviously." She began to feel a bit grumpy now and needed to be on more equal footing. She she rose to her feet. "Thus the need for an 'understanding.'"

His mouth twisted in a crooked smile. "You are a good woman, Caroline. A wonderful woman. You deserve to have…well…whatever you dream of having."

I deserve you. I want you. Why don't you want me?

She folded her arms and waited. This was sounding very much like a goodbye. While he could easily ride off into the sunset, under the circumstances she didn't see that happening. Their son was still missing and they were in the very middle of nowhere.

He shoved his fingers through his hair, then started to pace. "I think I've come to know you pretty good in the past week or so. In some ways you are quite unconventional, but when it comes to home and family, I reckon you're about as traditional as they come."

He halted, faced her. Sincerity rang in his voice as he said, "I can't be a traditional husband, Caroline. I can't get up and go to work in the morning, come home for supper and play ball with the boy until it's time for bed. I admit I see some appeal in a life like that, but it is simply not in the cards for me."

Her knees wanted to tremble, but she refused to allow it. "Because you don't want it to be. You want travel and adventure and other women."

"No, that's not true." He punctuated his words by jabbing his finger in the air, his green eyes flashing. "That's absolutely not true! It doesn't matter what I want, because when I take a chance and reach for it, the people I care about end up paying."

The vehemence in his tone caused her to realize that he'd said something of import. It took a moment for his words to sink in, but once they did, her eyes rounded with alarm. "Oh, for crying out loud. What are you saying, Logan? Are you telling me that Will and I are not your only family? Do you have another wife and child stashed away somewhere?"

"Not anymore," he shot back. Immediately, regret flashed in his eyes, and Caroline knew he'd said more than he'd intended.

Shocked, she studied him. hurting for the both of them. She saw guilt in his expression plain as day and her stomach sank to her toes. "We're back to the 'I don't understand' part."

He drew in a deep breath, then let it out in a heavy sigh. "It's a long, ugly story, Caroline. You don't need to hear it."

"I think I do. I think that might be the only way I can understand what is in your head when it comes to our family."

"We don't have a family!" he shouted. "We can't have one."

She leaned back against a tree, folded her hands and met his stare. "Then tell me why. This much you do owe. You're married to me and, like it or not, we have a child. The least you can do is explain why we can't be together."

"Dammit, Caroline." When she didn't relent, his mouth flattened into a grim line and his eyes took on a stoic light. He hissed out a defeated breath. "You know I grew up in an orphanage. My family all died in a flash flood."

"That's how you got your nickname. People called you Lucky."

"Yeah, well, Nellie Jennings and I had different opinions on what was and wasn't lucky. I spent about a decade at Piney Woods Children's Home, and I left because I wanted to see the world. I was in the process of doing that when I met up with your father in that saloon." He shot her a sharp look and made his point. "Look at what getting tangled up with me did to you."

"I have Will," she responded in a quiet, even tone. "I consider him the luckiest thing that ever happened to me."

"Yeah, well, I suspect the rest of the world might think differently considering the way you had to scratch and scramble to provide for him," he said with a self-directed sneer. "But you weren't the last person whose luck went bad after I entered her life.

Her life. The pronoun didn't escape Caroline. She closed her eyes. She knew what was coming now. He was fixing to tell her about another woman with whom he'd been involved.

"It was a year or so after our meeting in Artesia. Remember, Caroline, I didn't think we were married."

Wonderful. Simply wonderful. Just what every woman wanted to hear—stories about her husband's other lovers. "In all honesty, I think I'd just as soon skip this part of your story."

"It *is* the story. Look, I'm more than happy not to tell it if you're willing to let this whole discussion lie."

"No." Movement above caught her attention and she watched a blue jay flitter from tree to tree. "I want to understand."

"It'll probably make better sense if I start at the beginning." Logan bent and scooped a handful of gravel from the ground. As he told his story, he threw one rock after another at random targets. "After leaving Artesia, I had wandered down south. I had a vague intention to go all the way to Mexico City. I drifted along, taking odd jobs when I needed cash. I entered a shooting contest in Laredo and won twenty dollars. A couple of men watched me shoot and offered me a job. They said they were range detectives working for ranchers in the area. Jack and Stoney Wilson. That's how I got started doing what I do."

"I've wondered about that," she said.

"I liked the life. It suited me. I did a few things that shame me now when I look back on them, but at the time...I was playing cowboys and outlaws, Caroline. Just like I had when I was a kid. Sometimes I wore a white hat, but sometimes the damned thing was black as midnight. I didn't much care."

"You were young."

"Young and green and I didn't cotton on to the more serious crimes this pair were running. Took me a year to figure that one out—a year and a couple of ugly deeds." He shut his eyes and dropped his head back. His voice dipped. "Ugly deeds."

Caroline waited, her heart softening as she watched the inner struggle evident in his features. He would speak when he was ready— whether she wanted him to or not.

"The Wilsons sent me to Saltillo to bring in a man who had rustled some cattle from them. I rousted him from a bar and dumped his drunken butt in a wagon to take him back to Texas when his partner showed up and took a shot at me." He looked at her then, and the pain in his gaze shook her to the core. "I shot back and killed my first man —only he wasn't a man. He was just a kid. Younger than Will is now. His face haunts me to this day."

"Oh, Logan."

His voice flattened. "But I didn't quit. Didn't leave. Told myself that it was self-defense and he deserved it. Nevertheless, he was still a boy and I didn't feel good about what I'd done. Couldn't justify taking a youngster's life on account of a handful of cows."

He threw the last, the biggest, of the stones he'd collected and it pinged off a boulder some twenty feet away. "It was still eating at me a couple months later when I overheard a conversation between the

Wilson brothers and figured out that they had lied to me. The man I went looking for in Mexico wasn't a rustler. He was a father who was searching for his daughter, who had gone missing. The boy I killed was his son."

Caroline didn't know what to say to him, so she walked over next to him and attempted to take his hand. He pulled away, rejecting her comfort, and she tried not to let it hurt.

"I attempted to find out more about the family, but doing it without tipping my hand was hard. It took a couple of months before I discovered what scheme the Wilson brothers played, but when I did...Jesus."

This time he gave the loose rocks at his feet a good hard kick. "They kidnapped women, Caroline, and sold them into Mexico as whores."

Her mouth gaped. She recalled Ben warning her about such events maybe eight or ten years ago when two young women disappeared without a trace from a town not far from Artesia. "Oh, no. What did you do, Logan?"

His eyes went ice-cold and granite hard. "I played along with them. Told them I wanted in on their game. Next time they took a string of fillies—that's what they called them, fillies, the bastards—I went with them. I wanted to kill them outright, but they were part of a much bigger organization. I realized early on that I wouldn't stop the practice, that I'd just slow it down if I took them out without learning who all the players were. I went to the Rangers and told them everything. They formulated a plan to bring down the entire group, and I went along on the next sale."

Caroline made a quick mental review of the newspaper stories about Logan that she had read. She didn't recall any about him helping the Rangers bring human traffickers to justice.

"That time they brought eight women," Logan continued. "Eight women and..." he paused, visibly braced himself "...and one beautiful little girl. She was six years old with dark brown curls and big brown eyes. Her name was Elena."

Caroline bit her lip. She didn't know what he was going to say next, but she could tell from the pain in his expression that it wasn't going to be a pretty story.

"Her mother was a young widow who had worked as a housekeeper for a Hill Country rancher. Maria was fierce like you trying to protect Elena. Once when she was at her most desperate, she said she'd kill her baby and herself before she'd let her daughter meet the fate that we had planned for her. I couldn't stand it, Caroline."

"You helped them escape, didn't you?"

"Yeah. In the end, I didn't trust the Rangers to get them out safe. The night before the Rangers were scheduled to arrive, I took 'em and ran. I thought we got away clean. I kept my eyes on the newspapers and saw that the raid was successful. We thought the trouble was all behind us."

The agony that dimmed his green eyes told her that wasn't the case.

"I wanted away from South Texas, so I took us to Oklahoma. I bought a farm. We settled down." He grimaced. "I married Maria, Caroline. I didn't know that you and I…"

"I get that." She had trouble speaking past the lump in her throat. The pain in her heart made her want to lie down and cry. "You loved her?"

He hesitated over his words. "It's complicated. I adored Elena. She was cute as a button and so full of life. When Elena smiled, the rest of the world grinned with her. She was an innocent, an angel, and I loved her like I had never loved anyone before. Maria was…well…she tried, but she still mourned Elena's father. Too much had happened too soon for her to really take it all in. I think in time, we might have been fine. Time was something we didn't have."

"What happened to them, Logan?"

"The Wilsons happened, that's what. They escaped the Ranger's trap—which was my fault, I should add. I tipped them off by stealing Maria and Elena away. I heard they swore revenge on me, but I honestly thought we were somewhere safe." He gazed off into space, then shook his head. "Damn their souls to everlasting hell."

Caroline couldn't stay away from him now. She put her hand on his shoulder, offering the little bit of comfort she thought he would accept. When he didn't shake her off, she said, "You were a long way from South Texas."

"We used different names, too. For all the good it did. If it had just been me, they might not have looked so hard. They needed Maria. The bastards ordinarily took any woman as long as she was young and healthy. Maria was different. Her beauty sucked a man's breath away. A wealthy Mexican don had seen her in the marketplace in San Antonio, but she rebuffed his advances. He wasn't willing to accept that, so he placed an order for her."

"What an evil man!"

"I won't argue that. The Wilsons took a lot of money for Maria, so after she escaped, not only were the Rangers after them, the don's men were, too." He dragged the back of his hand across his mouth. "I never thought they'd live long enough to find us."

A long moment passed in silence. Logan turned his head away. His throat bobbed as he swallowed hard. "I'd gone into town to buy a gift for Elena's birthday. I came home to..."

He closed his eyes. His muscles betrayed a slight tremble. She wanted to stop him, to tell him that she understood, that he'd said enough. But she remembered how Suzanne always used to say that a lanced sore needs to drain for healing to begin, so she clenched her teeth and remained silent.

"It was obvious that the Wilsons had tried to take her again, and that Maria wasn't having any of it. I don't know what they did to her, what they said to her, but I think she must have gone a little crazy."

Again, a pause. Then he cleared his throat and said in a low, flat tone, "She got a pistol and shot Elena, then turned it on herself. I arrived home no more than five minutes too late to save them."

Caroline sat in stunned horror. That poor mother. What an insane choice she had faced. To kill her own child or let her be sold into sexual slavery? Caroline couldn't imagine.

And Logan. To have to walk in on the aftermath. Just a heartbeat too late. No wonder he didn't believe in family. And that little girl...

The tears that had welled in Caroline's eyes spilled at the horror of the picture he had painted. She wrapped her arms around his waist and hugged him. At first he held himself stiff and aloof, but he didn't push her away. Caroline took that as a positive sign.

He needs me. He doesn't know it, but he needs me.

"You killed the Wilsons, I hope?"

"Oh, yeah. Emptied my gun into their cold black hearts. Too damned late, though." His voice broke. "Too damned late."

"Logan, I—"

Apparently he'd reached the limits of his willingness to accept comfort because he pulled away from her, whirled on her. "I learned my lesson, Caroline. Lucky Logan Grey? That's a crock. Twice now I've had my family taken from me. Third time is no charm for me. So now do you understand, Caroline?"

Oh, Logan. He needed her. She needed him. She needed to show him that there was another chance for him, another family. People who would love him and heal him. But how to tell him? How to show him? How to make him see?

Before she could find the solution, he braced his hands on his hips and declared, "I can't be the husband you want. I *won't* be the husband you want. Hell, I can't even be the father Will deserves."

"Logan, don't say that."

"I am saying it and you damned well better hear it. I'll give you my money, Caroline. I'll give you my care and concern. I'll gladly give your body pleasure any time you'd like. But, don't ask for more from me. I don't have it to give, and even if I did, I wouldn't visit my bad luck on you. I care about you too much."

She understood, all right. Even brave, courageous men could have a fear they could not conquer. Logan was terrified of the past—he'd lost his family twice. He was fearful of what the future might bring—he couldn't bear another devastating loss. For over a decade now he had lived only in the present, sinking no roots, protecting his heart. Living alone.

This poor, sad man.

Bravely, she approached the wounded animal to whom she was married. She took his face in her hands and stared up into his eyes. "I care about you, too, and now I understand. I do. That doesn't mean that I agree with you, however."

"What do you mean?"

Now the time had come for her to jump off the cliff, so to speak. She didn't want to do it. She hated the thought of making herself vulnerable this way, but Caroline knew that reaching a man this badly wounded required a great show' of faith. And more.

"I love you, Logan Grey."

The words echoed in the silence that followed. For the briefest of instants, something flared in his eyes—hope or happiness or joy. Then he flinched as if in pain and his entire body went stiff. "Ah, Caroline, don't."

She ignored his protest and pressed onward. "I love you and you don't have to be alone any longer. I can understand why events in your past have made you think it's necessary, but it's time to stop being afraid."

"Hell, Caroline..." His inner struggle played across his face. He wanted to believe her, to take the chance, she could see it. But his fear was a monster, and it would take some time, some doing, for her to convince him that he deserved another chance at a happy ending.

She put a finger against his mouth. "Just let me say this. In fact, I'd rather you didn't say anything at all. You are my husband, Logan Grey, and you're the father of my son, and if nature warrants, the father of the child I could even now be carrying."

"Oh, hell," he muttered against her finger, panic brimming in his eyes.

"We already are a family, albeit one of an unusual circumstance, so it's really too late for you to say it can't happen. You have a family and I intend to make a home for you."

"Dammit, Caroline! Didn't you hear a word I said?"

She'd heard. She'd also seen the battle he fought in the pain on his face, the anguish in his eyes. He wanted to walk away because he thought he was trouble for her and Will. Yet, he obviously didn't want to walk away.

"I heard it," she replied, her smile bittersweet. "But I choose to be optimistic. You are a courageous man at heart, Logan. You've survived things that would have killed a lesser man or at least made him bitter and mean. You've allowed this fear to rule you for too long, but it can be overcome. I am willing to give it some time. I'm willing to bet on myself and on our home and family...I'm willing to bet on you."

He dipped his head, rested his brow on hers. "You're crazy, Caroline Grey."

"Crazy in love with you." She lifted her face and went up on her tiptoes. "Kiss me, Logan. Show me what I know is in your heart—even if you can't say the words just quite yet."

He groaned his defeat and touched his lips to hers. It was a kiss unlike any other they had shared. A kiss filled with tenderness and tears, a kiss filled with yearning, so sweet that she couldn't help but weep at the beauty of it.

The menacing and nearby *sha-shuck* of a round being chambered in a shotgun shocked both Caroline and Logan from their sensual fog. Then came the sound of the sweetest words Caroline had ever heard.

"You have half a second to get your filthy paws off my ma before I shoot you dead, you sorry son of a bitch."

CHAPTER THIRTEEN

"Will!" Caroline tore out of Logan's arms and darted toward the boy, squealing with joy and relief. "Oh, Will."

Logan's heart about stopped as he watched her rush toward the gun, and he didn't breathe freely until he saw the barrel shift toward the ground. Then she was in the boy's arms, weeping and laughing and squealing like a mashed cat.

"Mama!" The single word conveyed both concern and embarrassment as one arm wrapped around his mother and the other kept the gun handy.

Smart thinking, Logan thought as he studied his son. Will was almost as tall as Logan, skinny as a rail, but with broad shoulders that promised a full frame. Looking into his face was like staring into a magic mirror that took years off Logan's own visage. Except the eyes that glared at Logan were full of protective fury and awkward awareness.

Great. What a wonderful way to make a first impression—my hands on his mother's ass.

Caroline babbled. "Oh, sweetheart, I was so scared. Are you all right? Did he hurt you? Oh, baby."

"I'm fine. Are you all right, Mama?" Again, he shot Logan a glare hot enough to spark a fire.

"I'm fine, too. I'm wonderful, Oh, Will." She stepped back, gazed at her son, then burst into blubbering tears and collapsed, overcome with emotion.

"Caroline!" Logan said, taking a step toward her.

"Get back!" Will snapped. He hovered over her, shielding her from Logan. "What did you do to her?"

Logan debated the best way to handle the situation. Did he assert himself as the leader of their little pack here and now, or did he step back and allow the boy time to adjust?

Caroline took the decision out of his hands by lifting her head and saying, "Be nice, William. Just give me a minute. I need to cry a little more."

"But you never cry." He shot an accusing glare toward Logan. "She never cries!"

"She's been worried sick about you. Plus, it's been a difficult trip. She's a little wobbly right now, but I suspect she'll be right as rain once she waters herself out."

Will scowled and rubbed the back of his neck, his gaze flitting between his mother and his father. "I don't like it."

"Can't say I like it much, either. Few things in the world scare me like a female's tears." He waited a beat, then casually asked. "Are you hungry? The rabbit stew needs to cook a while longer, but I can rustle up something to fill the hole in the meantime."

The boy was obviously torn. It was clear that he didn't want to accept anything from Logan, but hunger was a powerful motivator—especially since the boy had been on his own for a bit.

"I guess I could eat," Will finally said with a shrug.

Logan strode over to the supply bags and pulled out a can of peaches. He held it up, Will nodded and Logan tossed first an opener, and then the can to him. The boy caught them, then as he opened the can, he stated, "You are Logan Grey, aren't you?"

Logan tensed. "I am."

But Will didn't say any more. He focused his attention on the peaches, devouring the entire can in half a minute.

His mouth twisted in a wry smile, Logan handed over a second can.

"You want me to heat some beans or do you like them cold?"

"Cold is good."

Logan nodded and fished a can of beans out of the supply bag. Before Will was through, he'd polished off a second can of beans, an apple and two strips of beef jerky. Logan watched in fascinated wonder until his son washed down his meal with half a canteen of water and curiosity compelled him to ask, "Did Plunkett feed you at all?"

The boy froze. "You know about him?"

"That was a mighty ugly burn he was sporting on his ugly mug. I assume you were responsible for it?"

"You saw him?" Every drop of color drained from Will's face. He glanced around, searching for the shotgun he'd set aside in order to eat. He didn't realize Logan had picked it up and stuck it in the supply bag. "Is he near here? Look, we need to hide. He's dangerous. He's—"

"Dead."

His head snapped up. His eyes were round as saucers. "What?"

"Our paths crossed this morning. I killed him. Deuce Plunkett will never hurt you or anyone else you love ever again."

With that, all the fear and all the fury drained out of the boy. He stumbled backward a step and for a moment there Logan thought he might collapse just the way his mother had. Instead, he bent over, put his hands on his knees and sucked in a heavy breath. "You killed him."

"Yep."

"Did you shoot him?"

"I did."

Will nodded. "I threw hot beans in his face."

"Good choice. Those suckers stuck to his skin. Burned him bad."

"Made him slow down on the trigger. He thought he had me, but I jumped him and managed to get away."

"Smart thinking. I'm proud of you, son." When Will shot him a sharp, disgruntled look, Logan added, "Maybe it's a little soon for me to use the term?"

The boy shrugged, then glanced toward his mother as if looking for help, but Caroline appeared to have cried herself asleep. Logan gave her a hard look. He could use a little help here, too. Was she playing possum?

"I don't mean to sound ungrateful," Will finally said. "It's just that... well...this feels mighty peculiar. I mean, I hadn't eaten in two days, then I get a whiff of rabbit and I follow it to find my mother and your hands...well...I want to skip that part."

"Good idea. Great idea."

"Then you tell me you killed him...I feel like it's last year when my mama made me join the local theater group and I was living someone else's life."

"Caroline must really like that theater. She tried to make me wear a costume as a disguise. Orange pants and a purple vest." Logan made a show of shuddering.

A grin flickered on Will's lips. "She once tried to talk me into being a girl character in a play. A while back I had a real high voice and they needed another singer. I had to threaten to run away from home to get her to let it go."

Logan shook his head. "You could have been scarred for life."

Will filled his cheeks with air, then blew out a slow breath. "I have a million questions, but I don't really want to ask them. I have a few things I want to say to you, but I can't seem to work up the mad to do it. Like I said, it's peculiar."

"Like a dream," Logan agreed. "I understand that. It's the same way for me."

"It is?"

"Yep. Ever since your mother dropped the bombshell about you. I've imagined meeting you." Logan stuck his hands in his pockets and rocked back on his heels. "Never once did I imagine you'd be pointing a gun at me."

"You had your hands on my mama's—"

"We're skipping that part, remember?" Logan interrupted quickly. Hurriedly, he continued, "It's extra strange that you look so much like me."

"I do not." Will sneered. "I'm skinny."

Logan snorted. "You have more meat on your bones than I did at your age, and you're the spittin' image of me. My friends who knew me back in the day recognized it in the picture your mother showed us.

Looking at you now...it's unsettling. Not a bad unsettling, but like you said—peculiar."

They both nodded sagely, and silence fell between them. Almost a full minute passed before Will said, "I probably ought to tell you that I've gone a lot of years without having a pa. Don't know as I think I'm ready to think of you that way."

"Fair enough. I'd like to think of you as my son, though, if it's all right with you."

Will shrugged. Shoved his hands in his pockets. Shuffled his feet. Logan thought of something to fill the quiet. "Your mother says you like baseball."

"I do."

"Do you only like to play yourself or do you follow the Texas League at all?"

"I love the Texas League. Ben has put me in charge of collecting the scores to print in the Artesia newspaper. I got to go to a Fort Worth Cats game once—Ben and Suzanne took me a couple years ago."

"Yeah? What did you think?"

"The Cats needed pitching bad, but it was a good time."

"Recently a fellow approached me about buying into the team."

"Into the Cats?" Will's eyes went round and wide. "Really? Oh, wow. Are you going to do it?"

"I'm thinking about it. I see some problems with the League, however. It's desperate for some organization."

With baseball, father and son found common ground and they spoke at some length about teams, players and Will's dream of playing in one of the pro leagues someday.

Neither of them noticed that Caroline sat watching them, a smug smile of satisfaction pasted on her face.

LATER THAT EVENING, long after the stew was consumed, the topic of baseball exhausted and summaries of the days since Will and Caroline parted ways exchanged, Logan left camp to make a guard circuit before turning in for the night, leaving Caroline and Will alone for the first time since his appearance at the campsite. Caroline was grateful to have the chance to talk to her son. She was finding it difficult to tell what he was thinking and feeling where his father was concerned.

Sitting cross-legged beneath a tree, she used a stick to draw a game of tic-tac-toe in the dirt, then she tossed the stick toward her son. "Come play."

Will showed her a tired smile, then did as she asked, taking a seat beside her and drawing an X in the upper right-hand corner of the grid. "What is it, Mama?"

She wanted to brush his hair away from his face but she stifled the urge. He'd already fussed at her once for hovering. "I want to talk to you about Logan. I imagine you have some questions."

He nodded. "Is he going after Ben? No one has said a word about him and I was afraid to bring it up."

"I don't know," she replied. "That's a discussion for tomorrow, I think. Personally, I need a good night's sleep before I fight any more battles."

"So you think it will be a battle?"

"Honestly, I'm not sure." Though she'd never say it to Will, she wasn't at all certain what she wanted Logan to agree to do. These last few days—the violence and the killings and Will kidnapped—had shaken her. Her love for Ben had not diminished one whit, but her maternal protectiveness had tripled. Quadrupled. And for that matter, she didn't want Logan risking his life in Black Shadow Canyon, either. "One thing I've learned about your father, Will, is that he has very good instincts when it comes to danger. We need to carefully consider everything he says in regard to rescuing Ben."

"We're too close to just abandon him now."

"I know, honey. But... let's save all that for tomorrow, shall we? I'd like to hear your impressions of Logan."

The boy shrugged. "I don't know. He seems all right, I guess." A slight hint of bitterness entered his voice as he added, "You certainly seem to like him."

Okay, time to tackle this bull by the horns. "I do like him, Will. Considering my past attitude toward him, I imagine that surprises you, but I learned some things about him and our past that I never suspected." She gave him a synopsis of what she'd discovered regarding her marriage, then added, "He was shaken to the core to learn about you, Will. He didn't turn his back on us. He honestly didn't know about us."

"Wow." He blinked and a smile played across his mouth. "I always wondered... It didn't make sense that he'd be so heroic as a range detective, but such a louse in his personal life."

Caroline drew a circle in the center square of the neglected game grid. "He's definitely not a louse and he wants to be part of your life, Will."

The boy marked his X in the dirt and with studied casualness said, "Oh yeah?"

"Yes. Let me tell you about our trip to the general store."

Her description of the gifts Logan had purchased and the tornado destroyed had Will bemoaning the cruelty of nature. Still, he was a bright enough young man to look past the presents to the heart of the matter.

"So where do we stand, Mama? Is he going to live with us? Is he going to be a real father to me? Is he going to be your real husband?"

She hesitated and drew a circle without paying attention to the game. "It's complicated."

"Didn't look complicated when he was all tangled up with you." He jabbed his X into the ground, then slashed a line through the row of three indicating a win. "You've been lonely a long time, and I'm afraid that when it comes to men you are as green as grass."

Her first instinct was to snap at him and tell him her private life was her own business and she wasn't all that green thank you very much, but she recognized she needed to step carefully here. She and Will had been a pair for a long time and naturally he was protective and probably a little jealous.

"I understand you want to watch out for me, but you keep in mind that I am not a fool, young man. The situation we have with Logan is this." She ticked her points off on her fingers. "We have a number of different relationships going on—one between you and me, one between you and your father, one between me and your father and one between the three of us as a family. With you and me—our relationship doesn't change. You are my son, and nothing and no one will ever affect my love for you. Now, while I might have opinions and concerns about your relationship with Logan, I am staying out of it. It's your relationship, not mine, and the two of you will need to work it out however is best for you. It's the same way with my relationship with Logan. It's our business, Will. Not yours."

"I wasn't trying to..." He shrugged.

"I know, honey. You care. But I am an adult and I am responsible for my own decisions, just like you are."

That distracted him. Surprise lit his eyes as he asked, "Did you just call me an adult?"

"Well, don't get too big for your britches, young man." She gave in to temptation and smoothed back his hair. "But I do recognize the changes in you. You are certainly adult enough to decide just what sort of relationship you want with your father."

While he digested that, she hurried on to the one in which the two of them would need to work together. "Now, that last one—the family—is more complicated, like I said. Will, I think Logan wants to be a part of our family more than anything else in the world."

"You do?"

"Yes, I do. I could be wrong, but I honestly don't think that's the case. Unfortunately, he has reasons—good reasons—to believe it is better he not try."

Will's brow furrowed. "What reasons?"

"It's not my place to tell you, honey. That's information that needs to come from him. What I need to know is how *you* feel about the idea of us living as a real family. I know you've just met the man and you might not know the answer yet, but it would help me to know what you want. Would you like the three of us to be a family, Will?"

He drew idle circles in the dirt with the stick. "I dunno. I guess so. If you want it. And as long as he treats you right."

Caroline recognized yearning in the shrug of his shoulders and deliberate insouciance of his manner. Smiling, she reached over and gave him a hug. "I do want that, yes. So, what I think we need to do to work on that family relationship is for us to treat him like he is the head of the family."

Will's head jerked up and he shot her a worried look. "Does that mean we have to mind him and do everything he wants us to do?"

"Oh, heavens no." She kissed his cheek, then added, "We just have to make him *think* that's what we're doing."

"You have to be kidding!" As the sun ascended in the eastern sky, Logan stood with his hands braced on his hips, his incredulous gaze shifting from his wife to his son, then back to his wife again. "Haven't the two of you had enough trauma, drama and danger to last you for a while? Jesus! I swear, if you think I'm going to cart you two into Black Shadow Canyon then you don't have the sense God gave a turnip."

Caroline smiled impishly. "Actually, I thought we'd ride horses, or maybe walk. No need to take a cart."

"Very funny."

Will spoke up. "Sir, we can't simply leave when we're this close to Ben."

"Sure we can."

Will looked him straight in eyes and said, "He's family, sir. You don't just abandon family."

It was a shot through the heart, and the boy knew it. Logan couldn't help but admire the effort. He nodded his acknowledgment of the hit, then said, "Nor do you consciously put family in danger. From what I know about Ben Whitaker and from everything your mother has told me, I doubt he'd disagree. If he'd wanted you with him in Black Shadow Canyon, I suspect he'd have taken you along when he left."

"Ben wasn't thinking straight," Will explained. "He wouldn't have gone himself if he'd been right in the head."

"Which doesn't help your argument at all." When Will glanced toward his mother for help, Logan sighed. "Look, here's what I'll do. Let me take you and your mother back to Artesia, where it's safe. Then I'll come back out here and find Whitaker for you. Fair enough?"

Will scowled. "But that will waste so much time. You were going to take my mother into the canyon, weren't you?"

"Yes, but only because I knew she'd go on her own if I didn't take —" Seeing Caroline and Will share a look at that, Logan knew he'd put his foot in it. "No," he continued. "I won't have it. Do you hear me? Caroline, I'll have your word right here, right now that you will stay put where I put you."

"But, Logan—"

"No buts."

Will said to his mother, "I don't know that I like this head-of-the-family stuff."

Caroline rolled her eyes at her son, then said, "What if you 'put' us somewhere in the canyon that's hidden away? It's a large place. Isn't there a place where you hid when you went into Black Shadow Canyon before?"

Yes, there was, and Logan had already thought of that possible solution. In fact, the hiding place was so good that he credited it with getting him out of the canyon alive. While fleeing from men determined to kill him, Logan had chosen to forge his own path up to the canyon rim in the hopes that they'd lose his trail.

Halfway up, one of them had clipped his leg with a lucky shot and he'd feared he was a goner.

When he'd spied the dark slit in the rocks, he'd expected to find a bear or coyotes or, at the very least, a snake. Instead, he'd escaped into an underground cavern. A huge underground cavern. He'd explored a very little bit and damn near couldn't find his way out, which was why he didn't want to stash Caroline and Will there.

He realized he had given himself away when Caroline said with triumph in her voice, "There is a place!"

"It's a cave. It's enormous and confusing and if one of you wandered off we might never find you."

"But no one found you."

"No."

Will spoke up. "Let me understand this. You know of a great hiding place but you don't want us to use it because you're afraid Mama or I will get lost?"

"You don't understand just how enormous this cavern is. I'm lucky

I found my way out at all. If it hadn't been for the trail of blood I left behind, I might still be down there."

"But you wandered off. We won't do that."

"But—"

"Sir, I give you my word."

"I appreciate that, Will. I truly do. The problem I have with the idea is that the other night, I stashed your mother somewhere, and she gave me her solemn word that she'd stay put. That didn't happen. She came looking for me when she thought my life was in danger."

"It *was* in danger."

"And you almost got yourself killed saving me."

"That's easy enough to prevent," Will quipped, before Caroline could voice her protest. "We won't try to save you."

When both Logan and Caroline gazed at the boy in surprise, he said, "Seriously, sir. You make a list of rules, and I'll make a solemn vow that we will uphold them. If that means not leaving the cave, even if you're outside and begging us to save you from a bear, we won't do it. It's whatever you say. Your rules, period. It will be the first commitment I'll ever make to you as son to father, and it will include my promise to make my mother mind the rules, too. Even if I have to physically restrain her. I'm bigger than she is now. I could do that if I had to."

Caroline gasped. "Why, William Benjamin Grey."

Well, hell. The boy—the young man—had just maneuvered him between a rock and a hard place. How could he possibly begin their relationship by telling Will no and effectively calling him a liar?

Logan narrowed his eyes and studied his son. "You are a pretty sharp fellow, aren't you?"

"Yes, sir. Maybe I take after you."

A reluctant grin flirted with Logan's lips, then he said. "Caroline? Do we have a pencil and paper anywhere in our supplies?"

"I carry a small notebook in my handbag."

"Excellent. Get it for Will. Son, you ride next to me so I can dictate my list of rules."

Will's expression lit with delight. "You'll take us with you into

Black Shadow Canyon? Will we get there today? Will you begin your search for Ben today?"

"After you and your mother sign my rule book—in blood, if necessary—then yes." It didn't escape Logan's notice that Will didn't protest his use of the word *son* that time, so he guessed he'd handled that all right.

He knew it when the boy extended his hand for a handshake and said, "Thank you, Pa."

Logan shook hands, then had to turn his head away to blink back tears. Damned blowing dust was stinging his eyes, he told himself.

Himself didn't believe that for minute.

CAROLINE EYED the dark slit between the rocks and pasted a smile on her face. She wasn't about to let either Logan or Will know just how much she dreaded the thought of hiding in a cave. Ever since she'd spent an afternoon trapped in a dry well on her father's ranch where she'd fallen when she was eight years old, dark, enclosed spaces made her skin crawl. But the men in her life were counting on her, so she would do her part and be a good little soldier.

"Let me check it out and make sure it's still safe." Logan squeezed between the boulders and disappeared.

He was gone a good ten minutes and Caroline got antsy. "Maybe I should go after him..."

"No, Mama."

"But—"

"Rule number three."

She scowled at her son. "We're not there yet so the rules don't apply."

"Don't be difficult, Mother."

She shot him her best mean-mother glare, but Will proved steadfast and impervious. In a switch of roles, she wrinkled her nose and made a childish face at him. He laughed.

Another incredibly tense five minutes ticked by. "What is he doing in there? This was a bad idea. Logan was right. He should have taken us back to Artesia. Or, we should have waited where we camped this morning. Just because he was safe there once before doesn't mean it's automatically safe now."

Will eyed her warily, then suggested, "Would you like a drink of water? It might help you calm down."

"I don't need to calm down. I am calm. I'm calm as a horse trough in a drought. I am a veritable sea of tranquility, do you hear me?"

He blinked. Twice. "Yes, ma'am."

She put her hands on her hips and stared at the entrance to the cave. "If he doesn't come out of there soon, I'm going to kill him."

She knew she wasn't making any sense, but that was beside the point. She was a wife and a mother; she didn't have to make sense.

Just when she was about to explode with fear-filled frustration, she saw Logan's hand emerge from the narrow black slit. Relief washed over her—until she got a good look at his face. "Something is wrong."

"No," he said. "Well, yes, I guess it is. We've an unexpected complication."

"Did you find someone dead inside?" Will piped up.

"Not another body!" Caroline exclaimed. "I can't deal with that tonight."

"No, I didn't find anybody dead. Come inside, you two. There is something you have to see."

CHAPTER FOURTEEN

CAROLINE TOOK HOLD OF THE HAND LOGAN OFFERED AND LET HIM guide her through the slim opening and into the cavern, Will following on her heels. The interior was cool and dark, the air fresh and clean. She grabbed Logan's hand a little tighter as he waited a moment for their eyes to adjust to the dim light.

Off to their right, a soft glow of light provided a beacon in the darkness, and she wanted to cheer when Logan headed that direction despite the fact that the cavern appeared to narrow to the space of a doorway. The cave lent her voice a hollow sound as she asked, "What's there, Logan?"

"A surprise."

"I can't say I've enjoyed the surprises I've had lately."

"You'll like this one—though I have to say it's as prickly as a cactus."

"A prickly surprise?" At the passage, he stopped, then motioned for her to go first. Caroline gave him a long look then said, "Only because I trust you..." She stepped through, then stopped abruptly in shock.

Behind her. Will gasped with pleasure. "Ben!"

Ben Whitaker stood at the center of a lantern-lit area the size of a small church, his arms spread wide and a warm smile on his face. "Hello, squiggles."

Caroline heard Logan murmur, "Squiggles?"

She ran into Ben's arms and inhaled his comfortable, familiar scent. "You're safe. Oh, thank God, you're safe." She cried and blubbered in his embrace for a bit, then pulled back and stared up into his pale blue eyes. Anger pulsed in her veins. "I could kill you, Ben Whitaker, for running off like you did."

"I'm sorry, sunshine."

"Well, you should be. When I think of all that's happened since you left Artesia, it makes me a little crazy."

Ben cleared his throat and repeated, "I'm sorry. I never thought you'd try to come after me. That was a damned fool thing to do. And to involve the Sum-beetch?" he said, using the name he'd settled on Logan years ago. "I can't believe you did that. What the hell were you thinking!"

"Now wait a minute. Ben," Will said, his obvious relief transforming into a flash of anger. "This isn't about Logan. It's about you. You wouldn't believe what all my mama has been through because of you. Ben. It's been awful, just awful, for her."

Unspoken, but understood by everyone were the words *and for me.*

Regret rolled across the older man's face. "The Sum-beetch sketched it out for me. You're right. You all's being here is on my shoulders. I feel terrible about that, William. From the moment I realized just what was going on. I've been working hard to right the wrongs and make that woman pay."

"What is going on, Ben?" Caroline asked. "What do you know? And what are you doing here?" With a glance around at the cavern's walls, she added, "Is it the gold mine? Have you found it?"

"No. Jim and I haven't been looking for the gold mine."

"Jim? Who is Jim?"

"That's me." A voice spoke from out of the shadows and a figure Caroline hadn't previously noted moved into the light. *He's not much older than Will.* The young man continued, "I'm Jim White. Ben and I are partners."

"Partners in what?" Will asked suspiciously.

"That's not important," Ben declared simultaneously. "I want to hear about what happened to you, Caroline."

Logan spoke up for the first time, folding his arms and narrowing his eyes at the older man. "Whitaker, you need to answer their questions first. Start at the beginning and tell us what happened to bring you to this place at this time."

Ben bristled at being told what to do by the "Sum-beetch," but when Caroline folded her arms, too, he acquiesced. Much of what he said at first, Caroline either knew or had surmised. He spoke of receiving the letter from Fanny Plunkett that suggested Suzanne had been killed by someone looking for the map to Shotgun Reese's gold mine.

"I knew I had to come after the bastard," Ben explained. "I had to avenge my Suz's murder, even if it killed me. Hell, to be honest, I was hoping it would kill me."

"Oh, Ben," Caroline murmured, her pique melting away.

He continued. "You know, it was strange. It's been twenty years since I made this place my home, but as I traveled the old trail, it was like I slipped into my old skin. By the time I made my way to town and sauntered into the saloon, I felt mean as hell with the hide off. I tracked down Fanny Plunkett and her boy Ace, and he told me he'd already found both the man who'd killed Suzanne and Shotgun and the map to the lost mine."

"Ace Plunkett?" Caroline asked, alarmed. "I thought his name was Deuce."

Jim White popped up. "There's two of 'em. Twins."

More Plunketts. Caroline could have done without this bit of news.

Ben continued, "Ace told a detailed story about tracking the killer down and killing him to avenge the murders. I believed him until Fanny showed me the map and asked for my help deciphering it. See, it was more a puzzle than a map, written in a code of sorts that used incidents in our past as clues."

"What sort of incidents, Ben?" Will asked.

"Ah..." The old man scratched his beard. "For instance, one of 'em said Wilbur's poker north two hundred yards. Only me and Suz and Shotgun would have known he meant the campsite where we played cards with Wilbur Burlington the night before he rode off to die trying to rob a stage. They were those sorts of clues."

"So Fanny needed your frame of reference," Logan observed.

Ben nodded. "I might have fallen for the whole story if she hadn't given the game away. She said all the right things, but the hard gleam in her eyes didn't match her words. Neither did her impatience to start the treasure hunt. She wouldn't allow me the time I needed to digest what had happened to my Suz and why. Made me suspicious and when I dragged my heels..."

"She sent her son to kidnap Will in order to blackmail you into cooperating," Logan said.

"Yep. She wants the gold and will stop at nothing to get it." Ben gazed apologetically at Caroline and Will. "I'm so sorry. I never dreamed you two would have to pay for my problems. Was it horrible for you?"

Will looked to his mother to respond, so Caroline gave a censored synopsis of events up to the point that Will found her and Logan. However, Ben knew her well and his expression revealed that he knew she'd glossed over a lot. He turned a proud gaze toward Will and said, "I'm sorry you got dragged into this, son, but I'm not surprised you outsmarted Deuce Plunkett. He's cruel, but stupid."

"He's dead," Will replied. "My pa shot him."

Ben dropped his chin to his chest. Caroline took a step toward him, ready to assist, when he swayed and it appeared as if he might fall. "Ben?" she inquired.

"Deuce was the one. He's the one who killed my Suzie." Lifting his head, he met Logan's gaze. "Dammit, I am in your debt."

"There is no debt. The bastard kidnapped my son." Ben acknowledged the sentiment with a reluctant nod.

When the familiar brooding look settled onto Ben's features, Caroline knew he needed to be distracted from memories of Suzanne's death, so she asked, "What happened after Deuce left to get Will?"

Ben grimaced and rubbed the back of his neck. "Well, I wasn't too happy for one thing. I came close to killing the bitch...Pardon my language, honey, but that's the cleanest word I can think of to describe her. First time in my life I've hit a female. Ace would have killed me, but Fanny wanted the gold more than she wanted revenge."

"Thank goodness for that," Caroline observed.

Ben shrugged his shoulders. "I came up with a plan to get away from the Plunketts and hide until Deuce showed up with Will. Jim, here, has been my secret weapon."

The boy grinned like a coon on a trash can. Ben continued, "Shotgun's map indicated that the gold could be found in a cave, but I told Fanny I'd need help locating 'em because my eyes aren't so good and I'm not familiar with the canyon anymore. Fanny was rightfully wary of sharing word of the treasure with the men who call Black Shadow Canyon home, so she went outside the canyon to one of the nearby ranches where a young cowboy—" Ben hooked a thumb toward Jim "—spent all his spare time exploring a huge underground cavern north of here. It was a lucky day for us when she hired Jim."

"Lucky for me," Jim offered. "I'm a rich man now."

"You found the mine!" Will exclaimed.

"Not a mine, but a stash. That's getting ahead of the story, though. Let me tell it my way."

Will rolled his eyes. "You're so slow!"

Ben ignored him, saying, "The second day we followed the clues in earnest, the map led us to a cavern about a quarter mile from here. When I studied the next clue, I had a hunch we might be about to find the gold, so I called a halt for the day and spent the evening concocting a plan." As Ben continued, the gift of storytelling that made him such a good newspaperman took them into the cave with him.

JIM, Ace and Ben arrived back at the eastern-facing entrance of the cavern around midmorning when the sun was in just the right direction to shine into the hole. In addition to their kerosene lanterns, Jim had several coils of rope looped over his shoulder while Ben toted wire and a hand ax. Plunkett carried only his light.

"Where do we go now, old man?" Ace said, gesturing toward the map in Ben's hand.

Ben had memorized the next clue. El Paso Run, twenty ticks. Bullet's mistake. Seventy-three paces. Beware. N—thirty-seven. Waiting for the Abilene score. "See that tunnel? We walk into it for twenty minutes."

Staring at the tight space where light went to near naught, Ace's eyes went wide and he broke out in a sweat. Jim smothered a smile as Ace exclaimed, "Twenty minutes! Hell, that's the middle of the mountain!"

"Maybe the bottom of it, too," Jim piped up cheerfully. "Sometimes these caverns go straight down."

"Damn." Ace rounded on Ben. "Let me see that clue. How do you know you're right?"

"El Paso Run refers to the time ol' Shotgun got belly sick after eating at a cantina just over the border. His gut got to rumbling, and he ran for the john, but too late. Man left a trail behind him...just like that." Ben pointed toward a trail of bat guano. "We follow the droppings twenty ticks of the clock."

Ace's face went ashen. "Then what? What is Bullet's mistake?"

"Bullet was Fanny's dog. Got his leg tangled in a trap. Bullet's mistake means we take a left dogleg turn." Actually, Bullet had caught his right leg in the trap, but Ace didn't need to know that. Ben was betting that he wouldn't make the first twenty minutes.

Plunkett gritted his teeth, then said, "All right, let's go."

"Jim, mark your watch."

The beginning of their descent into the tunnel was smooth and relatively level, but once they left the sunshine completely behind, the going got steeper. Ben could hear Ace's nervous panting behind him and he grinned. After about five minutes, Jim launched the plan they had fashioned. "Ben, hold on. Do you smell that?"

Ben made a show of sniffing the air. "Smell what? I don't smell anything."

"It's a sulfur smell. Very faint. Not a good sign. Mr. Plunkett? How about you? Do you smell it?"

Ace inhaled a deep breath. "Yeah. Yeah, I think I do. What does it mean?"

"Danger. I don't think we should go on. The flames in our lanterns could set the air afire. That happened to me once before and I barely got out alive."

"Hmm..." Ben rubbed the back of his neck. "Guess we'll have to turn back then. Ace, you can tell Fanny that—"

"No. You two go ahead. I'll stay here ready to help if you need me."

That part of the plan worked like a charm. Once they left Ace behind, Ben and Jim made very good time. At the twenty-minute mark, they noted a tunnel to the right and took it for seventy-three paces. There, they stopped and held their lanterns high.

They stood at the edge of a ledge. Beyond lay an empty darkness. Ben broke the tip off one of the jutting rocks beside him, tossed it into the dark and counted. At eight, he heard a faint splash. "Hmm..."

"Look, Ben." Jim pointed to their right where the ledge disappeared into another opening. "What do you think? The clue is N-thirty-seven. Think that way is north? Maybe thirty-seven paces."

Ben checked his compass and grinned. "You're a bright one, Jim."

They took the path and counted their steps. At thirty-seven, Ben stopped and explained. "When we waited for the Abilene score we squeezed into this narrow passage and waited for a stage."

"Like that?" Jim pointed toward a crack in the cavern wall.

Ben nodded and led the way into a chamber. Against one wall sat a stack of trunks, bags and strongboxes.

IN ANOTHER CAVE, on another day, Will exclaimed, "Geronimo's Treasure!"

"Could be," Ben said. "Or, it could be that the richest strike in the West is still waiting to be found in the Guadalupes. Nevertheless, Shotgun's gold came in the form of coins, not nuggets. Tens of thousands of them. Papers inside one of the boxes dates 'em back to wartime. Since this was Apache land at the time and judging by some other items stored with the gold, I suspect what we have is a storage cave of items taken during stagecoach raids."

Logan asked, "So, do the Plunketts have the gold now?"

"Hell, no. We went back and handed Ace a 'clue' that I said we found at the end of the tunnel. It was an Indian pipe I'd brought along with me, and then I spun a story that led us to another tunnel Jim had told me about and the search continued. The gold is waiting right where we found it."

Caroline frowned. "Is that why you're here now, Ben? Please tell me Deuce Plunkett's brother isn't waiting right around a bend in a tunnel."

"Don't worry, ma'am," Jim said. "Ace is in the saloon in town drowning his sorrows. His mama's not talking to him because he let Ben get killed."

"I fell into a bottomless pit, don't you know."

Jim nodded. "Ace heard the whole thing happen, so there wasn't any doubt."

Ben chuckled as he explained, "Jim knew of a section of caves that distorts voices. We staged a fall in one of them yesterday, then during the night, Jim led me to this section of caves. They connect to the cavern he's been exploring north of here. About a hundred yards to the east of here is a tunnel that leads up to a sheltered area on top of the cliff. It gives a perfect view of the desert below. We saw y'all coming hours ago."

"You did? But we hugged the base of the mountains to avoid being noticed." Caroline whipped her head around and stared worriedly at Logan. "What about the sentries?"

"If they'd seen us, we would never have made it this far," he replied.

"He's right," Ben agreed. "I've counted the days since Deuce left the canyon and I knew you were due so we kept a close watch. We were ready to go down and intercept you, but once you started coming this way, we thought the safest thing was to watch and see where you were headed. Jim knew about this crack—he'd found it from the inside a few days ago. This entire mountain is just a maze of caves. He brought me here from the other chamber once we realized your intentions."

"So, let me get this straight." Caroline reached for Logan's hand.

"Will is safe. Ben is safe. Suzanne's murderer is dead. It's over. We can go home."

Ben scratched the back of his head. "Well now, honey. I don't know about that. Deuce might have done the killing and the kidnapping, but Fanny was behind it all. It goes against my grain to let her get away with it."

"She's not getting away with it," Logan said flatly. "She preyed upon my family. I'll see her in jail."

"Or dead," Ben suggested. "She killed Caroline's mother."

"Or dead," Logan agreed.

Caroline's heart dropped to her toes. "Logan..." she warned.

He squeezed her hand, then dropped it. "Jim, you know any sneaky ways into Devil's Rest?"

PICKING his way down the cliff by moonlight, dodging the needles and spines of cholla, prickly pear and Spanish dagger by luck alone, Logan waited for his trouble sense to quiver. He was very well aware that he might be about to make one of the biggest mistakes of his life. But two things propelled him toward the collection of buildings built originally by a rancher, then usurped by a loose-knit gang of outlaws and renamed Devil's Rest. First, the Plunketts deserved justice. Second, he'd spied the yellow bandanna tied to an agave stalk near the entrance to the canyon. While it could be a coincidence, Logan didn't believe that was the case. It was a signal, one that dated back to his childhood, the flag on their tree house in the Piney Woods.

He'd bet his last bullet that Holt Driscoll had come to Black Shadow Canyon to help.

The idea made sense. After getting Cade to Fort Worth, where he would have medical help and the assistance of other friends such as Dair MacRae, Holt would have continued the mission. He easily could have arrived before Logan, considering the delays he and Caroline had experienced on the trail. If Holt had come to Devil's Rest to help him, Logan couldn't sneak his family out the back door, so to speak, and leave Holt behind to figure it out. He needed to find his friend or confirm that the signal wasn't a signal at all.

So, while he might be making a huge mistake, he truly had no choice. He'd do anything to help his friend. Sort of like Caroline and her old ornery outlaw.

Now that he'd met the man, seen the love in his eyes as he gazed at Caroline and Will, Logan had a hard time keeping an angry on for the fellow. Sure, with his quest for vengeance, Ben Whitaker had thrown Logan's life for a loop. But he'd been there for Caroline and Will when Logan wasn't around. For that and that alone, Logan owed him.

Those thoughts hovered in Logan's mind as he made his way to the canyon floor at the point where desert conditions transitioned to a more fertile zone. Here, trees and shrubs offered concealment and he paused beneath the spreading branches of an alligator juniper to observe activity around the small settlement.

They'd added two buildings since his last visit, bringing the total up to eight. In addition to the combination saloon and whorehouse, Devil's Rest boasted a bunk-house, a store of sorts, a mess hall, stable, and corral. The rest of the buildings were private residences, one of which served as the Plunkett family home.

Logan studied the house Jim had indicated to be Fanny's. Lamplight burned in a single window. Someone was home. Probably Fanny, likely alone. He could slip inside and kill her and be done with it. Heaven knew she deserved it.

Considering all the evil she'd wrought, he probably was a fool to hesitate, but Logan had never killed a woman. The thought of doing so left him feeling twitchy. Arresting her and dragging her off to jail without rising the residents of Black Shadow Canyon against him would take good planning and even better luck. First and foremost, Logan intended to keep his family safe. If he did have a Texas Ranger here to help, the situation got a whole lot easier.

He shifted his focus to the saloon from which the tinny notes of a piano drifted into the night air. Lights shone in every window, including all the upstairs rooms. The place was hopping tonight. While he wouldn't expect to find Holt sitting at a table drinking a whiskey—Holt's face was even more recognizable by this group of miscreants than his own—that's undoubtedly where Holt would expect to find him, since the town saloon was always the best place to gather information. If Holt was in Black Shadow Canyon, he'd be in a place where he could watch the entrance to the saloon.

Therefore, Logan had to make an appearance of some kind. The question was how to do it without revealing his identity.

He needed a disguise, something better than this sweat-stained serape and oversize hat he'd used on the trail. What could he—

Hiss came a sound from behind him. "Logan?" Caroline.

Logan went stiff as a fence post. He whipped his head around. "What the hell are you doing here?"

"I'm watching your back, just like I vowed."

Rage flashed like fire inside him. "You need to get your cute little butt back up to that cave, Caroline Grey. Right now."

"Let me put this simply. No. You can't walk into Devil's Rest as Logan Grey."

"I don't intend to. This disguise has held up so far."

"Yes, but that was the trail and this is Devil's Rest. You're too threatening in that serape. Someone—probably more than one someone—will shoot you on sight. You need me to be a distraction and you need to wear this." She shoved a businessman's suit into his arms.

"The hell I do. I'd look like a banker. I'd be mobbed with men trying to rob me. Where did you get this?"

"Not a banker. You'll look like a newsman. The suit is Ben's. You're of a similar size. When I heard Will mention how scary he thought you look in the serape, I began to worry. This isn't as good as the orange pants and purple vest, but you'll be a less threatening companion for me in a business suit. We can say you worked at the Artesia *Standard* with Ben and that's why you accompanied me. Now hurry, Logan."

Recognizing that she had a point and glad to be rid of the hot serape, he shed the blanket and donned the suit. It was tight across the shoulders and the pant legs were too short, but that helped make his appearance less threatening. Damn, but the woman was smart. Then she put one of those silly little bowler hats on top of his head and he scowled.

"We're wasting time," she said. "Either we go in together, or we don't go in at all."

"Why are you being so damned hardheaded?"

"Because I love you, Logan, and I don't want anything to happen to you. This began as my fight, and it's still my fight. I think I'll be safe enough if I arrive looking for Ben because Will has disappeared. The Plunketts can't know about Deuce's demise as of yet. They won't shoot me on sight. And you will be much safer slipping limpidly into Devil's Rest while I'm making a grand entrance."

"Limpidly! I told you..." He blew out a breath. "You are the most infuriating woman."

"We make a good team. Oh, I almost forgot. It's the crowning glory." She took his hat off, tugged a round tin from her pocket, opened it and smeared greasy stuff in his hair. From the other pocket she took a comb and slicked back his hair, then handed him back the stupid little hat. "Now, what is the plan?"

"I don't have a plan that involves you," he snapped, messing with his hair. He absolutely hated pomade.

"Then let's make one." She slapped his hand away from his head. "Leave it alone. You don't look at all like yourself. I should have thought of this before." Then, moving on to another subject, she asked, "Now, what is your goal here, Logan? Just what exactly do you intend to do to the Plunketts?"

He argued with himself for another moment, then admitted she was right. They did make a good team.

"I'm not as concerned about the Plunketts as I am about Holt." He explained about the bandanna signal and his suspicion that they had unexpected help.

"So you don't want to kill them?" she asked, the hope in her voice obvious.

"I suspect we'd be leaving ourselves open to retaliation in the future if we don't deal with them now, but if I have the choice, I'll be happy to get everyone out of this canyon safe and sound."

"Then let's do that." He saw the flash of her smile in the moonlight, then she leaned forward and kissed him lightly on the mouth before taking a step back.

Well, that just teased him. Wanting more, he pulled her against him and kissed her hard. "When we're done with this, we need to find an opportunity to be alone."

"I won't argue with that."

"Finally. Something she won't argue about." He kissed the back of her hand, then said, "Okay, here's what I think we should do."

Ten minutes later, her neckline pulled just a tiny bit lower than normal, her hips swaying just a little broader than usual, Caroline sashayed into Devil's Rest Saloon with Logan a few steps behind her. Speaking in a melodramatic tone, she clasped her hands in front of her and said, "I'm looking for my father, Ben Whitaker."

Before she could continue her prepared spiel, a stranger about Logan's age shot from his chair and rushed toward her saying, "Darling, you've finally arrived. I've been so worried!"

When he took her in his arms and kissed her, Logan reconsidered his decision not to kill.

CAROLINE WAS PREPARED FOR GUNS, knives, and considering this had been Apache country, even bows and arrows. She wasn't prepared for a kiss.

As a result, she stood frozen in shock as the stranger kissed her lavishly, then embraced her, whispering in her ear. "Holt Driscoll sent me."

"Oh." She smiled against his shoulder, well aware of the avid attention of the others in the room.

Logan stepped forward, menace in his tone. "You let her go."

The stranger glanced up and met Logan's gaze. "Hello, Thurgood."

Caroline figured she was the only one who noted the flash of speculation in Logan's eyes and the brief hesitation before he replied. "What are you doing here?"

"Looking for Caroline, of course." He kept his arm slung around Caroline's shoulder as he faced Logan and raked him with a scathing gaze. "When I heard that she left town with the likes of you I knew I had to come after her. Honey?" He gave Caroline a quick glance "What were you thinking, making this trip with the town drunk? Why, if you'd run across trouble in the desert ol' Thurgood here would have been worthless as a pail of hot spit."

Caroline took a fast glance around at the suspicious faces in the saloon and decided they'd spent enough time on Act One. "Thurgood is not the town drunk. That's a medical condition that makes him stumble a lot. You be nice to Thurgood. I had to get here fast and he was kind enough to accompany me." Raising her voice, she said, "Excuse me, do any of you know where I can find my father, Ben Whitaker? Or perhaps you've noticed a new boy in town? I think my son, Will Grey, ran away from home to find him."

Half the men in the saloon and all three females looked toward a table in the back corner. Caroline followed their gazes and her knees turned to water. He looked exactly like his brother, down to the cruelty in his expression. Ace Plunkett.

He lifted his stare from his beer and said, "Ben Whitaker? That son of a bitch is dead."

Even though she knew it to be a lie, hearing those words come from that man's mouth shocked Caroline and made it easier for her to play her role. She gasped and clutched her hands against her breasts. "Wh-wh-what?"

"Deader'n a beaver hat," Plunkett returned, drunkenly slurring his words.

"And...and...my boy?"

Plunkett swiped up his beer glass and threw it at her, exploding, "What the hell good is he gonna do us with Whitaker dead?"

Caroline ducked and the glass crashed against the wall behind her, shattering and sliding to the floor. Deciding he'd given her the perfect cue to make her exit, she burst into fake sobs, turned and rushed out the door, confident that Logan and the stranger would follow.

Outside, Logan led her away to a spot where they wouldn't be overheard. Acting solicitous to Caroline, he spoke to the stranger. "Holt sent you?"

"He said you'd recognize the code name. He brought me. He's keeping a low profile since half the outlaws in this place know him. I'm new blood in the company. My name is Tom Wilkerson."

"You a Ranger, too?"

"I have a bright, shiny badge."

"I appreciate your help. Look, I need to talk to Holt. We've had a few developments."

"He's waiting for you up by the big yucca behind the saloon. He said you'd know which one he meant."

As Logan nodded, Caroline pictured the tall yucca plant that stood like a sentinel on one of the hills behind the makeshift town. She and Will had discussed its size earlier, estimating it to be almost thirty feet tall.

Tom Wilkerson tipped his hat toward Caroline. "My apologies for acting forward, ma'am. Holt and I thought that my claiming to be your beau provided the best excuse for my hanging around. Also, my condolences on the loss of Mr. Whitaker."

"No apologies necessary, Mr. Wilkerson," she replied, offering him a smile.

"Sure they are," Logan muttered.

"And as far as Ben goes, he's one of the developments Logan mentioned."

Logan gazed up the hill to where the yucca stood reflected in the moonlight. "Wilkerson, can I trust you to guard my wife until I get back?"

"Yessir."

"And keep your hands—and mouth—off her."

"Yessir...although, remember I'm supposed to be comforting her."

Logan's eyes glittered like a cat's in the moonlight. "I reckon a man has to be nervy to become a Texas Ranger, but you watch your step, boyo."

Caroline gave Logan's hand a squeeze, told him to be careful, then watched him fade into the darkness. For the next ten minutes or so, she sat waiting with the ranger, softly making small talk and acting distraught and upset whenever anyone happened by. She kept a close watch on the door of the saloon, hoping to avoid another encounter with Ace Plunkett. She was aware, but not overly nervous. After all, she had two Texas Rangers and a range detective to protect her. How much trouble could she possibly get into?

She no sooner noticed Tom Wilkerson stiffen when a feminine voice spoke. "Caroline? Caroline Grey? I'm an old friend of Ben and Suzanne's. My name is Fanny Plunkett and I'm just so sorry about what's happened. Why don't you come to my house, dear, and we'll share a spot of tea."

Caroline offered the brassy-haired, curvaceous-figured outlaw queen a shaky smile. How much possible trouble?

Plenty.

CHAPTER FIFTEEN

Logan thought his heart might just jump out of his chest when he saw Fanny Plunkett tuck her arm through Caroline's and walk her down the street. He let out a string of curses and struck out at Holt. "What the hell kind of Ranger is he?"

"A good one," Holt assured. "He will protect her. And besides, Fanny isn't going to do anything bad to her. She's probably hoping that Ben shared information with Caroline about the map, and that Caroline can help her find the treasure."

All right. Holt had a point. If Logan could just get his heart back down in his chest where it belonged, he might be able to appreciate it. "Hell, Holt. I'm scared as a rabbit in a coyote's hind pocket. What do we do?"

"You love her, don't you?"

Logan wasn't going near that. "I'd love to paddle her behind. If only she'd stayed in that cave where she belonged..."

"Well, she didn't and we have to plan accordingly. C'mon, Lucky, get your head together. This isn't like you. We need to figure out what we're doing. Sooner we do that, the sooner you can go after her."

"You're right. You're right." Logan tried to recall where they'd left off. After greeting his friend and being updated on Cade's condition, he'd brought Holt up to date on events that occurred since the tornado. They'd been debating whether to pursue the Plunketts now or come back for them at a later date when they didn't have precious baggage to protect.

He swallowed the lump that formed in his throat when he watched Caroline enter Fanny Plunkett's lair. "My gut is telling me to deal with these folks now if it's possible. It's cleaner that way. Faster. I don't want Caroline and Will to have to watch over their shoulders for weeks. Plus, I think I know a way we can go about it—as long as Caroline doesn't say or do something while she's with Fanny that would prevent it. You don't have a problem with enclosed spaces, do you, Driscoll? Any idea how young Wilkerson is in that regard?"

"What do you have in mind?"

Logan told him as quickly and succinctly as possible. He was chomping at the bit to get back to Caroline.

After making arrangements to meet the following day, he made his way back down the hill and headed for Fanny's hoping his disguise held up. Just because Fanny Plunkett was a cruel killer didn't mean she wasn't intelligent. She'd be suspicious of any newcomer to the canyon. Luckily, he and Fanny had never met face-to-face, but he needed to appear as nonthreatening as possible when he was around the woman.

He strode up the front steps and knocked on Fanny's front door. Moments later, it swung open to reveal Tom Wilkerson. He didn't look surprised to see Logan. "Thurgood, you found us."

Gazing past Wilkerson's shoulder to where he could see Caroline and Fanny sitting in a parlor and sipping from cups and saucers, he spoke loudly. "Even better, I think I found Will!"

Both women's heads jerked toward him. Briefly, Caroline's mouth gaped and a shocked what-in-the-world-are-you-doing expression flashed in her eyes, but she recovered quickly. Fanny pursed her painted lips in speculation.

Caroline set down her cup and stood. "Thank goodness. I've been so worried. Where is he?"

"He ran off up into the hills. I called his name, but he didn't respond, Miss Caroline. I know he heard me, though."

Fanny Plunkett approached. "Who are you?"

"Thurgood, ma'am." Logan kept his gaze lowered. "I work for Ben Whitaker at the newspaper." Then, struck by a flash of inspiration, he added, "I'm his biographer." Her interest obviously piqued, Fanny repeated, "Biographer?"

Logan smiled, the wheels in his mind turning like a locomotive's as he spun his story. "The Whitakers lived exciting lives, but then you would know that, of course. I hope you'll afford me the opportunity to interview you while I'm here. Ben told me a lot about the Sunshine Gang days, but I'd love to hear another perspective."

"You know about his past," she stated.

He could almost see her wheels turning, too. He nodded. "I write articles about the West. I've had pieces printed in the *New York Times*. Perhaps you've read some of my stories? Oh, but wait. I'm being self-centered again. It's a fault of mine. Caroline is beside herself with worry over Will."

"Yes, I am." She moved toward Logan. "Tell me exactly what you saw."

"Well. I'm not positive the boy was Will, mind you. It's dark outside and he was wearing a hat, but how many boys hang around Black Shadow Canyon?"

"There is one," Fanny said. "He's a cowboy who works for a rancher in the area. He likes to explore and he was also a friend of Ben's."

"Was he helping to look for the gold? If so, I hope he'll talk to me."

"You know about the gold?"

"Suzanne told me about it. We went over the map at Christmas, and we were contemplating an expedition to look for it when she died." Logan turned to Caroline. "If you'd like, I can show you where I last saw the boy. If it was Will, he won't ignore you. He's never liked me."

She took his hint and offered Fanny an anxious smile. "Please excuse me. I simply must find out if this boy is my son."

"Of course, of course. Now, it's getting late." Fanny smiled at Tom. "Do y'all have a place to stay tonight?"

"Yes'm," Tom replied. "I rented rooms in the house at the north end of town. I understand the usual residents are away."

She nodded. "I do believe the Jones brothers are out, um, working.

You will be comfortable there. I do hope you'll join me and my son for breakfast in the morning, say at eight o'clock? I have something important I wish to discuss with you."

Excellent. Logan met Fanny Plunkett's gaze and nodded. "I can't speak for Caroline and her beau, but I'll be pleased to join you."

"Actually," Fanny said, taking a step closer to Logan. She reached out and trailed her finger down his arm, then suggestively licked her lips, batted her eyes toward him. "The Jones boys' house is cramped. Why don't you stay with me?"

Logan struggled mightily to hide his shudder of revulsion and the words he needed to make a graceful escape simply wouldn't come.

Caroline stepped into the breach. She took hold of Logan's arm and said, "He is pretty to look at, isn't he? I'm afraid you're wasting your time, Fanny. Thurgood only likes men. You should see the bright orange pants he has in his carpetbag!"

The denial rose automatically to his lips, but Logan hadn't gone completely brainless. He smiled limpidly and added, "They're not orange, they're puce."

Following an abbreviated night's sleep, Caroline led Holt and Tom Wilkerson away from Devil's Rest, and they slipped into the cave just before dawn. With a long stretch of uneventful waiting ahead of them, they all attempted to get a few more hours of sleep. Aware that Logan would soon be walking into the Black Widow's lair without backup, Caroline enjoyed only minimal success, tossing and turning atop the thick blanket of her bed while the others' snores echoed in the cavern. Eventually, exhaustion overtook her, and, influenced by the darkness in the cave, she didn't awake until mid-morning.

Holt informed her that Will and Jim had left to see to their part of this plan an hour before. Jim was to lead her son on the path through the mountain out of Black Shadow Canyon where they'd make their way first to the horses Logan had hidden, and then to the ranch where Jim worked to purchase needed supplies for the trip home. They were to wait at the designated rendezvous for the rest of the party to arrive.

The morning passed slowly, as did the early afternoon. As the appointed lookout, Tom was able to report that Logan and Ace Plunkett had indeed made their way into the cavern where Ben "died." So far so good, Caroline thought upon hearing the news that indicated Logan's plan was on track.

As the hours stretched on Caroline took advantage of the time to try to win Ben over to Logan's side. Ben Whitaker had despised Logan Grey since she had broken down in Suzanne's kitchen and confessed that she was expecting, and nothing she said could change his mind.

"I don't care what his excuses are," Ben groused. "I don't care what heroic deeds he's done lately or that I am in his debt for killing Deuce, the man isn't good enough for you. No man is."

"Now, Ben. Logan is a good man."

"Hah. Good men don't abandon their brides after getting them with child. He had to go off and play posse and outlaws. Now that he has that out of his system he wants to play daddy? Well, you don't know him and neither does Will."

She kissed his cheek. "I love you, too, Ben. You are the protective father that my papa should have been and I value you more than you'll ever know. But do you think if I can convince him to give our marriage a try that you could give him a chance? I know it would be difficult for you to adjust to having another man in the house, but he could be a lot of help to you, too."

"Ah, honey. About that." He twisted up his lips and scratched at his beard. "I, um, I don't think I can. I don't want to go back to that house. In fact, if I have my druthers, I'd rather stay here."

Shocked, she drew herself up. "Here? In Black Shadow Canyon?"

"Here in the Guadalupes. I'm intrigued by these caverns, honey. Jim and I are having the times of our lives exploring them. In some of these tunnels you see signs of life and you know that some other fella has been here before you. But in others, you leave a footprint in the dust, and you know you might well be the first man in history who has ever set foot there. It's humbling."

"But...it's the middle of nowhere."

"And I love that. It sounds strange, I know, but I feel close to my Suz out here. It's like she's with me. I don't know if that's because this is where we met and fell in love, or what. But sometimes when I'm wandering around these mountains, I feel as if she's walking right beside me. At home, I felt alone. Empty. I don't want to go back to that."

His words bruised Caroline's feelings. She understood what he was saying, but she couldn't help being hurt and a little angry. To have gone through all the trials and tribulations of the past few weeks and he wasn't even coming back? A part of her was furious. The better part of her understood. In Black Shadow Canyon, Ben and Suzanne were together.

The fact that she understood his reasoning didn't negate the fact that she'd lost Suzanne. Now she was losing Ben. "Will and I love you, Ben."

"And I love you, too, but you don't need me, not like you did in the past. Will is almost grown and you're still young. You don't need to hang around nursing an old man whose heart is battered and broken. Hell, maybe it's meant to be this way. If that numbskull Grey finds his brain and figures out he can't live without you, then it'll be good for the three of you to find your way as a family without having me around. Although, just because I'm willing to be open about all this because I love you doesn't mean I'm not still pissed at the pecker-wood. If Logan Grey hurts you again, I'll wipe the floor with him."

"I'll count on that, Ben."

"Now, don't think I won't keep an eye on you. I plan to visit. Who knows, maybe I'll make some spectacular discovery in these hills and you can interview me for the newspaper and we can both become famous."

Caroline didn't want to be famous and she didn't want to lose Ben. She folded her arms and pouted until he chuckled and reached over to affectionately tug on her ear. She sighed and leaned her head against his shoulder. "I'll worry about you, maybe not as much as when you left us because I know you're happy, but still...I'll miss you, Ben."

"I'll miss you, too." He paused a moment, then added, "So, you won't give me trouble about this?"

"I guess not. Not too much trouble, anyway. Although, I have one condition. You can't stay unless the threat of the Plunketts has been eliminated one way or another."

"Oh, that is gonna happen even if I have to hide out and play sniper. In fact, I almost like that plan better than leaving retribution for Suzanne's murder up to somebody else. That should be my job."

"But you don't have a badge. Logan and Holt and Tom Wilkerson do. For my peace of mind, let them handle this, all right?"

"I'll defend myself—and you and Will—if necessary, but yeah, I'll let the young whippersnappers do the work."

"Let's just hope Logan's plan works," Caroline said. "You will go with us to the rendezvous, won't you? You have to say goodbye to Will."

"Of course I'll see you off. Besides the fact that I'll want my goodbye hugs, I want to see the Plunketts in handcuffs—or even better, in graves. What a beautiful sight that will be."

Caroline couldn't argue otherwise.

ACE PLUNKETT WAS all gurgle and no guts from what Logan could tell. The grown man was afraid of the dark—and that couldn't have worked out better.

"Ma is not going to like this," he muttered as he followed Logan down the hill after spending much of the morning in the caves. Or at least on Ace's part, just inside the caves.

Logan had studied the map Fanny had given him over breakfast that morning and pretended to follow it. Instead, once Ace refused to follow him farther into the cave, he'd spent a good amount of time viewing the pictographs on the wall of one section of the tunnel and taking a nap in another. The goal was to make their way past the Black Shadow Canyon sentries just after dark, giving them most of the night to put distance between themselves and any possible pursuit. With the timeline in mind, he'd returned to Ace's position a short time later and explained that he needed Fanny's assistance. He arrived at her house, checked his watch and reassessed his schedule. Right on time. Excellent.

Fanny answered the door with avarice in her eyes. "You're back early. Did you find something?"

"In a manner of speaking. I need your help."

"*My* help."

"Yes, ma'am. Like I mentioned before, when Ben went over the map with me, he wasn't too certain about a couple of the earlier clues. Now that I've checked things over, I'm thinking he must have made a mistake—a terrible mistake—to end up dead on the floor of a bottomless pit."

"If it's bottomless, it doesn't have a floor," Ace said with a sneer.

Ace for ass, Logan decided. "Guess he fell all the way to Hell, in that case." To Fanny, he continued, "My hope is that you will be able to look at the first few landmarks in the cave, and with your knowledge of his and Shotgun Reese's past, discover just where he misinterpreted the map and point us in the right direction."

"You want *me* to go into the caverns," she stated flatly.

Logan nodded, then added some incentive. "I understand that Geronimo's Treasure gold mine is rumored to be bigger than the Comstock strike in California."

"Let me change my clothes."

That took a bit longer than Logan would have liked and she walked slow as molasses in January, so they were running about a half hour behind schedule when they finally reached the opening of the cave. Then Ace attempted to talk his way out of going inside, which took up more time and had Logan reconsidering an earlier decision not to pull his gun and plug the bastard. Finally, his mother demanded Ace shut up and move forward and apparently she was one person he would not cross.

Logan lit the three lanterns he'd positioned earlier and led them into the cavern, hoping this plan he'd concocted wasn't another huge mistake in his life, one that ranked right up there with the other two whoppers he'd committed—leaving the Wilson brothers alive in Mexico so they could track down Maria and sweet little Elena, and leaving Caroline the morning after their wedding night.

As they descended into the cave, moving deeper into the darkness, Logan's worries began to haunt him. *Maybe I am making a mistake. Maybe*

I should draw and fire right this second. No one would know otherwise if I called it self-defense. Why in the hell am I taking this risk? Didn't I learn my lesson in the past? Why would I trust the Plunketts to the legal system and leave my family in danger?

As they entered one of the larger, dome-shaped caverns on their route, Logan shifted his lantern from his right hand to his left, then his free hand hovered just above his six-shooter. Old demons made his palms itch. Old regrets all but brought him to his knees.

"What is that?" questioned Fanny Plunkett.

They'd reached the first landmark on Shotgun Reese's gold map. It was a colossal wonder, a stalagmite that rose from the cavern floor almost twenty feet. It was thick and round and flattened on top as if a giant had strolled by and went *splat* with his fist. "Do you recall the first clue on the map?"

She quoted without hesitation. "Done in by him, we fled to distant climes."

"Look at the shape, ma'am." Logan held up his lantern and gestured for Ace to do the same. "What does that remind you of?"

She pursed her lips and walked in a semicircle around the stalagmite. "A gentleman's hat?"

"A stovepipe hat. Like the one worn by Abraham Lincoln."

"Done in by him..." she repeated in a murmur. "Shotgun came West after the War Between the States."

"I think it's safe to say that Ben was right in identifying this as the first landmark on the map."

"The map has fourteen landmarks." She glanced at her son, whose complexion appeared bloodless in the lamplight. "Which one was Whitaker looking for when he died?"

"Uh..." Ace's lantern rattled as his hand shook.

Logan could tell ol' Ace didn't have a clue. Though he would have liked to let him stew, time was ticking by. "Number ten. I don't expect you to go that far, ma'am. Actually it's number six that has me most concerned."

"Well, then, let us proceed to number six."

Ace made a sound that combined a groan and a moan. His mother ignored him. Logan allowed himself a grin hidden by the darkness as he led them from the domed chamber following landmarks Ben had pointed out as they honed the plan the previous day.

The trek took them deeper and deeper into the caverns along a rocky trail that sometimes sloped gradually, sometimes climbed steeply, and always remained dark as a tomb. The trio seldom spoke between stops so every sound was magnified. Their footsteps, the sound of their breathing. Ace Plunkett's tiny whimpers. Finally, his mother rounded on him. "What is *wrong* with you?"

"I just…I just…I don't like this place."

"Act like a man, would you?"

"The sixth landmark is just ahead," Logan quickly interrupted. The last thing he needed was for Ace Plunkett to find his manhood now.

The next part of the plan was mostly Ben's idea. The man wanted —hell, he needed—to have his revenge on Fanny and her son. While Logan would have preferred to keep the process straightforward and clean, he understood Ben's motivation. Sympathized with it, too. Fanny and Ace deserved a lot worse than what they had planned for them.

They deserved to die.

Kill 'em now, the protective male in him whispered. *This is your last chance before you join the others. Do it and the problem is solved and no one is the wiser.*

But they'd wonder. Caroline and Will might even ask. Her, he could lie to—he owed her a big one, after all. But could he look Will in the eyes and deny he'd acted as jury, judge and executioner? He didn't want to destroy the boy's opinion of him right off the bat. Shooting Ace and Fanny here and now wouldn't be like killing Deuce. Ace didn't push Suzanne Whitaker down the stairs. Neither did Fanny. She planned Will's kidnapping, true, but his son was still alive. Could he murder her in cold blood? Sure. But could he admit as much to his son?

"No."

"What was that?" Fanny asked.

"We're almost to the sixth landmark," he lied. Actually, Fanny and her son would never see the sixth landmark, because the ambush spot was just around the next curve.

Surreptitiously, he checked his watch. Forty minutes late. *I hope they haven't given up on me.*

He coughed loudly, sounding the signal.

THE DARKNESS ENVELOPED LIKE A TOMB, a total and complete absence of light. Despite her preparation, despite the ready source of light at her feet, Caroline couldn't prevent the anxious unease that crawled up her spine.

Then the soft yellow glow of lantern light appeared just where expected. One. Two. Three. She focused on the comforting flickers and quieted her breath.

"This is it." Logan's voice echoed hollowly off the walls. "It's a little bit tricky. We have to position our lights just right. Ma'am, if you'll step here?"

From her hiding spot, Caroline watched him position the older woman. A sudden, unexpected flash of pure fury washed through her. Evil had joined her in this cave.

"Ace, you'll need to stand here."

"What's over there?" he replied, his voice pitched high and shaky. "I don't like it. I'm fine here."

"Get your ass over there, boy," snapped his mother. "I swear I knew you were useless, but I never realized you were such a yellow-bellied coward."

"Now, Mama."

"Oh, shut up."

Logan managed to place Ace into position, then he took his own, drew a deep breath, then said, "All right, set your lanterns on the ground on your right side and look straight up. See, up above you? It looks like a ceiling of diamonds."

The pair looked up. Holt's and Tom's arms extended from their hiding spots. Logan said, "Now."

The lanterns went out and the world went black.

Ace screamed. Fanny cried out, her voice riddled with fear. "What happened? Thurgood Hall? What's going on?"

From out of the darkness came the disembodied voice. A ghost's voice, saying, "I'll tell you what's going on, Fanny. You're going to Hell."

"Mama!" Ace whimpered.

"You should have left my family alone."

Fanny exclaimed, "Whitaker!"

"You're dead!" Ace cried out.

"Hell isn't a very nice place," Ben continued. "As you are soon to see."

"A ghost. He's a ghost." The man was blubbering now. Then he cried out again, "What's that? Who's there? Lord, save me! Hell's demons are touching me."

Caroline heard Fanny Plunkett breathing hard and the sounds of scuffling. "What the—"

"Got him," came Holt's voice.

"Her, too," said Tom.

"Handcuffs," Fanny scoffed. "What is this? Do you fools think you're going to arrest me?"

Ace sobbed. "You can arrest me. Just get me out of here. Arrest me. Arrest me."

Ben spoke. "This darkness is absolute, isn't it? Like no darkness I've ever seen before. Like death. Suzanne didn't deserve this darkness. She was all goodness and light. I think it's only right that you know what it's like to be alone in the darkness, trapped and unable to find your way into the light. Good luck finding your way out of here. I believe at this point we're some five hundred feet below the surface. Men, let's go."

Caroline heard the sound of footsteps and knew that Logan, Holt and Tom used the rope guide to move into position. She started counting. Fanny Plunkett began cursing, ugly words coming from an ugly heart. Her son's cries faded to whimpers.

Caroline had sided with Logan when he'd argued against Ben's desire for revenge. What they were doing was cruel and it bordered on torture. Ben felt that five minutes of believing themselves trapped in the dark constituted letting the Plunketts off easy, and he'd rattled off a litany of sins including bank robberies and stage robberies and cold-blooded murders the pair had committed in addition to their crimes against him to bolster his argument. At Holt's suggestion, they'd compromised on three minutes. Caroline's part was to light her lantern at the appropriate time.

Counting down, she readied her match. There. Three minutes. She struck the match, lit the lantern's candle and rose from behind the boulder that concealed her just as Logan called out her name in a warning tone...

And the gunshot sounded. The bullet hit the cavern wall beside her, then ricocheted off the wall. "Bring that lantern over here now or you're dead," came Fanny's voice.

"Damn," Tom said from a short distance away. "She had a gun? I missed a gun?"

"And you handcuffed her hands in front of her rather than behind, you greenhorn," Holt scoffed.

"Give her the lantern," Logan called, a thread of fear in his voice.

"And the keys to these cuff's," Fanny added.

"Mama?" Ace whimpered. "Mama, I want some light. Get me out of here, Mama."

"Oh, shut the hell up. You disgust me. I never knew you were such a pantywaist."

Then, to Caroline's horror, she pointed her gun in the direction of her son's voice and pulled the trigger. He made a grunt of pain, then nothing. "You shot him. You shot your own son."

"A weak seed," she said coldly. "I don't tolerate weakness. Good riddance to him. Now, come here, girl." She shoved Caroline in front of her and kept her gun stuck in Caroline's side. "Ben Whitaker? You come here and lead the way out of here. One false move and I'll kill her. You know I will."

Caroline figured that all four men had guns pointed at Fanny and she was a little surprised that none of them had yet taken a shot. Was it the fear of ricochet stopping them? The lack of a clear shot? Fear they might hit her instead of Fanny?

"All right. Here I come," Ben said.

Fanny demanded, "Light your lantern."

It was as she heard the match being struck that Caroline first noted the sound. A faint hum, but not exactly a hum. More like a whine from far away. From far below.

And it was coming closer.

Tension thickened the air and Caroline shifted uneasily. Dread and trepidation filled her and had little to do with the gun against her side. Fanny was an evil she recognized, one she trusted Logan to deal with. The hair on the back of her neck rose as she waited for what, she didn't know.

The superstitious part of her wondered if maybe it *was* demons from below coming for wicked souls. She wished she hadn't skipped church last Sunday.

Fanny didn't appear to notice anything untoward because she poked the gun against Caroline hard and said, "Let's go, Whitaker. Move."

"I'm going. I'm going. Don't hurt her." Ben strode out of the widened chamber and back into the narrowed tunnel, which led to the nearest cavern exit.

Caroline jumped when she felt the first whoosh of something skimming past her. Even as she realized that, another and another and another joined the first, and the whine bore down upon them. Barreled past them. Brushed her skin.

Fanny cried, "What...?"

"Bats!" Logan hollered just as Caroline figured it out on her own.

It was a stream of bats, a river of them, squeaking and shrieking in her ears, swishing past and occasionally thumping against her. They came and they came and they came—hundreds and thousands and more, gushing into the narrow tunnel and filling it from wall to wall, ceiling to floor. The musty smell grew overpowering, and the age-old fear of humans for the tiny mammals made her forget about Fanny and her gun. The lantern lights extinguished, leaving them once again in total darkness, and Caroline heard herself whimper.

Vaguely, she realized Fanny was screaming and shooting her little revolver, long past the time she'd emptied its chambers of rounds.

Then something big and hard pushed against her. A body. A hand grabbed her, found her arm and tugged her against the fearsome stream. Logan. A leathery wing hit her face and she shut her eyes, following blindly. Blind as a bat. A hysterical little laugh escaped her. Then he shoved her down against a thick stalagmite.

"Curl up, honey," he instructed, hollering to be heard. "Think of a rock in a stream bed—the water will flow around us."

Then he knelt in front of her and shielded her body with his, and Caroline felt safe.

When he kissed her, it shocked her almost as much as had the bats and she jerked her head away. "What are you doing?"

"Protecting you." He nuzzled her neck. "Distracting you."

"Oh. Well. Carry on."

She never completely lost track of time or place, but he did take the terror out of the moment. The bat flight lasted a long, long, long time—more than half an hour— and when the sounds finally died, the movements finally died, Logan lifted his head and whispered, "Stay here."

She wouldn't dream of doing anything else.

He said, "Sound off."

"Here," Holt said.

"Yo," came Tom's voice.

"Holy heaven above," breathed Ben. "Where's Caroline?"

"I'm here," she called out. "I'm fine."

Logan let out an audible sigh of relief. "Anybody hurt?"

Each man answered in the negative, then Tom asked, "Where's the witch?"

"I don't know," Logan grimly replied. "But unless she has a gun belt strapped on somewhere out of sight, she's out of bullets. Can anyone find their lantern?"

"I'm looking for mine," Holt called back. "Hard."

Tom discovered his first, and when the soft glow of candlelight bloomed in the darkness, the collective sigh of relief caused everyone to laugh.

"What in Hades happened here?" Tom asked once the rest of the lanterns were located and lit. "I've never seen nor imagined the likes of such a thing."

"Sunset," Ben explained. "The bats leave their roost at sunset to hunt. I've been in the caves at this time of the evening, but never in this particular section. We ended up between the bats' roost and their exit."

"Scared the bejezus out of me," the young Ranger confessed. "Miz Caroline, I am powerful sorry that my mistake put you at risk."

"That's all right," Caroline said.

"No, it's really not," Logan fired back. "I expect you to make up for it by guarding her with your life while we go find the murdering whore. I don't care if a pride of mountain lions comes through here next, you and Ben damn well better keep her safe. Holt, you up to going with me to find Fanny?"

"Not gonna be necessary, partner," Holt replied. Once his lantern was lit, he'd moved down toward where she'd last been seen. "I followed the footsteps in the dust. Look." Caroline refused to let loose Logan's hand, so he tugged her along the path with him to where Holt stood. "Careful. There's a drop-off." Holt held out his lantern and illuminated the black space.

Caroline sucked in a breath. Fanny Plunkett hadn't fallen far, but she'd fallen hard. Her eyes were open and glassy, her expression one of bone-chilled terror. Her head rested in a plate-size pool of blood.

Beside Caroline, Ben Whitaker said, "Now that was an ugly death. Good. The old bat got what she deserved. May she rot in hell and get spattered in bat droppings twice a day for eternity."

"Amen," said the men, one after another.

Caroline wrapped her arms around Logan's waist and hugged him hard. "It's done. It's over. Now, let's go home."

CHAPTER SIXTEEN

Fort Worth, Texas

Logan walked through the doors of Doctor Peter Daggett's private hospital into the sunshine, lifted his face to the warmth and gave a silent little prayer of thanks. He'd never been much of a churchgoing man, but after the events of the past weeks, he was beginning to think he should look into it.

He, Holt, Caroline and Will had made the hospital their first stop upon arriving in town this morning. Holt had warned them what to expect, but nothing could have prepared them for what they found. Logan had taken one look at Cade, and for the first time since Maria and Elena died, damned near broke into tears.

His scars were savage. His attitude...well...Logan couldn't quite read it. He said the right things, smiled and joked and acted positive, but Logan wasn't sure he bought it. His injuries, the pain, the forced incapacitation had all taken a toll on the Cade he knew like a brother. Something more was there. Something he wasn't talking about—not even when the others had left them for a little private conversation during which Logan attempted to apologize and Cade refused to listen.

Yet, Dr. Daggett claimed he would recover. Cade's bones were healing, his cuts closing, and the infections were just about whipped. The news was something to celebrate.

Nevertheless, Logan felt a powerful need to kick something.

Glancing around the bustling front lawn, he spied Caroline and Will sitting on a bench beneath the shading branches of a cottonwood tree. He wasn't surprised to see her crying. He could tell when she'd walked into Cade's hospital room that she had trouble holding in her emotions.

Will saw him and waved, said something to his mother, then walked over to Logan, his expression troubled. "Is he really gonna be okay, sir? Mama is fit to be tied."

Logan fitted his hat onto his head and blew out a heavy breath. He'd tried to talk Caroline into getting off the train at the Artesia stop, but she'd been determined to check on Cade herself. "Cade will pull out of this. He has a long road ahead of him, but in the end, I truly believe he will be all right."

Will's expression went solemn. "It's our fault."

"No, it's not," Logan reassured him. *It's mine.* "Look, Cade doesn't blame anyone for what happened. He told me a few minutes ago that it was his choice to be on that train and his bad luck to be swept away by that cloud. If he believes that, then we should make a good effort to do likewise. I know one thing...he was happy as a flea in a doghouse to meet you."

"Maybe I can visit him again. He said he had lots of stories he wanted to tell me about you."

"I'll just bet he does," Logan replied, wincing at the thought. Then, giving the area another sweep, he asked, "So, where did Holt run off to?"

"He went to see his captain. He said he wanted to make sure Tom didn't blow the mistake he'd made with Fanny Plunkett all out of proportion, and he asked me to tell you that he'd see you tonight at the MacRaes."

Dair had met them at the station this morning for a quick exchange of information and an invitation to dinner at his and Emma's new home. With the new caretakers settled in well at the orphanage, and Emma missing her parents and siblings, the MacRaes had decided to make Fort Worth their permanent residence. When a perfect house came on the market the same day the tornado struck the train, Dair made a cash purchase and they'd moved in immediately. Their home was in the same neighborhood where Logan had purchased a house last fall, an investment, since a man with his job didn't have much use for a house.

Of course, back then he didn't know he had a wife and son. The house would come in handy until he and Caroline figured out how they should handle this marriage and fatherhood thing.

He slung his arm around his son's shoulder and said, "Will, let's see your mother to my place. It's been a hard few days of traveling, and I know she's longing for a bath."

Twenty minutes later, he opened the gate to the white picket fence and led them up the front walk to a large, two-story home with a wraparound porch on the front and a backyard made for playing catch. "This is your house?" Will breathed, his eyes round with wonder. "It's a mansion!"

"Well, that depends how you define *mansion*," Logan replied with a laugh. "I don't have much in the way of furniture."

Caroline stepped inside, glanced around and laughed. "Not much in the way of furniture? You have a chair, Logan. One."

He shrugged. "I only need one. There's just one of me. Although..." He dragged a hand down his face. He hadn't been thinking. "I guess I'd better get hold of one of the furniture stores in town and get a bed delivered for Will."

Glancing around, he looked at the bare interior with new eyes. "In fact, would you make a list, Caroline? Whatever you think we need."

Following a long moment's pause, she stared him straight in the eyes and repeated, "We?"

He shrugged and tried to act as if he didn't know what she meant by glossing over the question. "I don't even have a kitchen table. I never cook for myself when I'm here."

"You eat in restaurants all the time? Don't you get tired of that and want a home-cooked meal?"

"Then I usually beg a meal off one of my friends' wives."

But Caroline wasn't about to let it go. "Are you inviting us to stay, Logan?"

He opened his mouth to speak, but he didn't know what words he wanted to say. He hemmed. He hawed. He shuffled his feet.

Caroline sighed and said, "Will? Will you excuse us, please?"

"Gladly." The boy looked at Logan with disapproval in his eyes and maybe just a little disgust.

Logan blinked. So much for the boy being awestruck with him. When it came to his mother, he was a bear.

Logan's natural response to the moment was to reach for his wallet and offer him money. "There's a candy shop in town. Indulgences, it's called. I recommend the Chocolate Teases."

"I'll just bet you do," Will grumbled as he accepted the bills, kissed his mother's cheek. He didn't so much as look at Logan when he left.

"Boy can fill with vinegar fast, can't he?" Logan observed.

The hard shut of the door seemed to echo through the empty house. Emotion he didn't want to name—hell, he didn't know if he *could* put a name to it—welled up inside him. All he knew for certain was that he didn't want her to go…but he couldn't ask her to stay.

He waited for her to speak first, but she outsmarted him by repeating her question. "Logan, are you inviting us to stay?"

He shoved his hands in his pockets and rocked back on his heels. "Ah, Caroline, nothing has changed. I'll give you my house, my money, whatever you need. If you want to live here, that's fine. It'll be easier for me to see more of Will that way than if y'all stay in Artesia. But my warning is the same. Don't ask, don't expect more from me. Like I told you before, I'm not offering you a family."

"We already are a family, Logan. Whether you like it or not."

"No, we're not!" The unknown, unnamed emotion rolled and bubbled and burned. "Even if I had any doubts, which I don't, what happened in that cave would have put them to rest. Look, you need to get that through your head, woman, once and for all. You were damned lucky in that cavern. I should have killed Fanny before she ever had a chance to put a gun on you."

She blinked. "Let me get this straight. You think we are not a family because Fanny Plunkett threatened to shoot me?"

"My families die, Caroline!" That time his voice did echo through the empty rooms.

Caroline closed her eyes and her mouth set in a grim line. Logan realized his heart was racing like a Thoroughbred at the half-mile turn. That was before Caroline shocked him speechless by shrugging out of her traveling jacket and lifting her fingers to the buttons on her blouse.

His mouth went dry when she slipped off her shirt. His hands fisted at his sides when she dropped her skirt. By the time she stripped away her underwear, his pecker was hard enough to drive nails. Finally, he found his voice, "Why?"

"I want a bath. I assume you have one of those?"

"Yeah...sure...upstairs. The house has a shower, too," he replied, distracted by the wondrous sight of high, full breasts tipped in delicate coral, the narrow waist and flaring hips and tawny triangle. She was beautiful and...sneaky. This was blatant seduction, and he hadn't a clue how it was that they'd gone from discussing buying furniture to this. Making one last extremely weak effort at resistance, he asked, "But, Caroline...why?"

"Because I've been traveling and honestly, Logan, you can use one, too. Why don't you join me?"

"Well, I do need a good washing."

"Oh, honey." Damned if she didn't wink at him. "Good doesn't begin to describe what I have in mind."

Forty-five minutes, one bath and two showers later, he lay sprawled across his bed, naked and spent, his mind still drifting in a sensual haze. It occurred to him that they hadn't settled anything, but in that moment, in the exhausted wake of her wild and tempestuous loving, he couldn't find it in himself to care.

So he allowed the subject to drop for the rest of the day, then for a week, then for an entire month. Three months passed and he never once broached the topic. Logan Grey was happy.

"Lucky Logan Grey is the saddest excuse for a disciplinarian I have ever seen," Mari Prescott said, shaking her head in wonder from her seat on Logan's back porch where she and her sisters watched him attempt a stern look while scolding the children for recklessly swinging from one oak tree to another.

"He's new at it," Kat Kimball said in his defense even as she laughed at the way her own little Caroline batted her eyes up at the man while she twirled a long auburn curl around her finger. "He'll learn."

"He can say no to Will upon a rare occasion." Caroline grinned as she set a plate of assorted cookies in the center of the white wicker porch table for the women to share. "When it comes to little girls, he's mush."

Emma chose a ginger snap. "He's happy. Now that Cade is out of the hospital the last of the shadows are gone from his eyes."

At that, Caroline's smile faltered. Now if she could just do something about the shadows in his heart. "Seeing Cade discharged was a huge relief for Logan."

"What is he going to do with his time now that he won't be spending it all at the hospital?"

"I don't know. He doesn't say." Caroline attempted nonchalance as she added, "I expect he might take a job and leave here. Those boots of his do tend to wander."

"Does he recognize that you are making him a home, Caroline?"

"Yes, I think he does. And that will be what sends him running, I'm afraid."

The sisters shared a look, then Mari took her hand. "He loves you, Caroline. It's as plain to see as Emma's belly."

"Well," scoffed Emma, placing a protective hand on her recently visible pregnancy.

Caroline rewarded Mari's attempt to coax a smile from her. But it didn't last. "I know he loves me. Will knows he loves us both. I think everyone in Fort Worth knows it after Wilhemina Peters wrote that special report in the newspaper. I didn't mind giving her an eyewitness account of the tornado, but did she have to include how Logan went crazy buying us gifts at the general store both before and afterward?"

"Don't pay any attention to Mrs. Peters. She's plagued us all our lives, and we're none the worse. Well, not *too* much the worse. If you're a citizen of Fort Worth, she's your cross to bear."

"The question is how long will I be a citizen," Caroline responded. "School starts soon. Will has made friends here, but if Logan is going to leave, I think he'd rather go home to Artesia and his friend Danny."

"Why would Logan leave?" Mari asked. "It makes no sense."

"Dair thinks something happened to him during those years where no one kept up with one another," Emma said.

"It's his story to tell," Caroline said. "I won't betray his confidence more than to say that yes, he has reason to flee from what I have to offer him. Maybe not a good reason, but an understandable one."

At that point the man under discussion suddenly lifted his head like a hunting dog on point. His gaze swept the yard and the children who played there, then turned toward the porch. She wasn't certain, but she thought he was counting heads.

From inside the house came the ring of the telephone. Caroline saw Logan start toward the house as she excused herself to answer it, wondering who could be calling and why.

It was the why that had her uneasy.

She lifted the receiver and spoke into the mouthpiece. "Hello?"

A man's voice replied, "Mrs. Grey?"

"Yes."

"This is Deputy Stevens and I'm looking for Sheriff Prescott. May I speak to him, please? We have us an emergency."

"Certainly, Deputy. I'll get him right away."

"Thank you, ma'am."

Caroline set down the receiver and hurried out to the back porch where she stopped and met Logan's worried gaze as she called out to the men circled around the barbecue pit. "Luke? You have a telephone call from Deputy Stevens. He says there's an emergency."

Logan's scowl deepened, but he didn't comment as Luke handed his drink to Jake Kimball and stretched his long legs into a run. The other men followed at a slower pace until the four couples and Holt Driscoll congregated by the back steps. Prodded by an instinct she didn't understand, Caroline descended the steps to stand beside Logan. She took hold of his hand just as Luke Prescott opened the back door.

Logan gripped Caroline's hand hard even before the white-faced sheriff began to speak. "Men, someone needs to get Lucky and Caroline to the hospital. Will has run into some trouble." He raised his voice to be heard over the gasps as he added, "It's not a life-threatening wound, but the boy has been stabbed."

"Stabbed!" exclaimed Holt. "What happened?"

"I need the rest of you to get your guns. It's possible we have some major troublemakers in town. Looks like Lucky's boy tried to make a citizen's arrest and it backfired."

"Arrest? Who did he try to arrest?"

Luke grimaced, briefly dropped his head, then met Logan's and Caroline's stare head-on. "Harvey Logan."

The name meant nothing to Caroline, but all the men reacted in a way that scared her half to death.

Holt cleared his throat and said, "You mean *the* Harvey Logan? Otherwise known as Kid Curry?"

Grim faced, Luke nodded. "Lucky, your son just tried to arrest the Wild Bunch's executioner. The good news is that he's going to live to tell about it. Looks like your good luck has rubbed off on your son."

Logan muttered so low that only Caroline heard it. "Lord help us all."

———

"I HATE THIS PLACE," Logan muttered as they rushed up the steps of the hospital. "I absolutely hate this place."

"Thank God it is here," Caroline replied, her voice tight. "We don't have a hospital in Artesia."

They burst through the front doors and Logan zeroed in on the man with a badge. "Will Grey?"

"This way."

As the deputy led them down a short hallway, Logan heard Will's excited voice. The knot of tension inside him began to ease.

"I studied outlaws because of my pa," Will was saying. "He's the famous range detective Lucky Logan Grey. He's brought dozens and dozens of outlaws to justice."

"So you thought you'd follow in his footsteps?" the doctor asked.

"I want to be like my father," Will said, just as his parents entered the room.

Hearing the sentiment as his gaze fell upon his son's bloody shirt, Logan felt as if he'd been stabbed through the heart.

"William!" Caroline said, rushing forward. "Are you all right?"

"Yeah, I was lucky, though. Just like Pa." He grinned, his young eyes wide with excitement. "I sensed he was fixin' to turn and I jumped back so the knife just sliced my belly instead of sticking me. Doc Daggett gave me twelve stitches. I guess I should have shot my gun, but I reckon killing a man is something you've got to get used to. I couldn't make myself pull the trigger, so he got away."

"Oh, my." Caroline tossed an accusatory look toward Logan, then grabbed the back of a nearby chair for support.

Logan went cold inside and he had to work to keep his voice level. "Let me clarify. You were carrying a gun?"

Sheepishly, Will nodded.

"The Colt I bought for you?"

Again, a nod.

"Did you have permission to carry that gun?"

A wince. "No, sir."

"In fact, weren't you specifically forbidden to touch that gun unless I was with you?"

"Yes, sir."

"William Grey, you are in so much trouble!" Caroline declared.

"But, Ma, it was Kid Curry! The entire Wild Bunch is here in town! See, I was walking by Swartz View Company and noticed the big photograph in the window. It hadn't been there the day before when I walked by. I couldn't believe it. There they were— Butch Cassidy, the Sundance Kid, Will Carver, Ben Kilpatrick and Kid Curry. While I stood there gawking, who walked out of Swartz's but none other than Kid Curry. He was staring at a big old stack of prints of the photograph in his hand. Didn't even spare me a glance."

Logan's stomach rolled and he thought he might lose his lunch.

Caroline spoke with a touch of hysteria in her voice. "So you decided to pull a gun on a vicious killer? Will, why would you do such a thing?"

The boy shrugged. "The sheriff's office was just around the corner. I'm as big as Kid Curry. I thought I could get him that far."

"He could have killed you, Will!" Caroline exclaimed. "You could be dead right now. The thought of that makes me...Oh, son."

His mother's obvious fright and concern finally doused Will's excitement and his expression filled with dismay. "I'm sorry, Ma. I didn't mean to worry you. I didn't think. I just...I wanted to make Pa proud."

Instinctively, Logan backed away.

Will continued, "I guess I messed up bad, didn't I? Kid Curry got away because I was bleeding and everyone's attention was on me. He'll warn the others." Will seemed to collapse in on himself at that. "Instead of me catching the Wild Bunch, I'll be responsible for letting them get away." There were tears in his eyes as he looked up at Logan. "Instead of making you proud, I've shamed you."

The urge to flee pounded like a pulse, and it took every bit of self-control Logan possessed not to turn and run. But his son needed words from him now, and Logan summoned his strength and said them. "Don't be stupid, Will. I'm not ashamed of you. I understand what you tried to do and why you tried to do it. However, that doesn't mean that I'm not mad enough to bite the head off a hammer. You broke my rule by carrying the gun, then you compounded the problem by using it in a reckless manner. You came within a fraction of an inch of breaking your mother's heart."

"I'm sorry, Ma. I'm sorry, Pa."

"Oh, baby." Caroline carefully wrapped her arms around Will's shoulders and hugged him tenderly. "If you ever do something so foolish again I'll be the one who kills you."

"Yes, ma'am. I won't. I promise."

She turned to the doctor then and fired off a round of questions regarding wound care and rest. Once the physician reassured them both that their son should fully recover and was free to return home with his parents, Logan took his leave, using the Wild Bunch as an excuse.

While he did go directly to Luke Prescott's office to join the search for Butch Cassidy and his gang, he was, in truth, reacting rather than acting. He couldn't handle seeing Will in bloodstained britches and his mother worried half to death. He'd have done anything to get away from Caroline and the boy at that moment. Joining the hunt for the Wild Bunch simply provided an escape.

The Fort Worth police united with the sheriff's office and Logan in a massive manhunt for the outlaws. They tracked the gang to a boardinghouse in the heart of the Acre where they discovered loot from the First National Bank of Winnemucca, Nevada, but no robbers. As the news spread, Pinkerton detectives, Wells Fargo agents and Union Pacific railroad detectives joined the search. It soon became clear that the Wild Bunch had skipped town.

After working with Range Detective Logan Grey, every one of the law enforcement agencies offered him a job to hunt down the West's most successful outlaw gang.

For three days Caroline waited for Logan to come home. She knew he was busy with the search, understood that he had a personal stake in the outcome, but she also suspected that his absence went on longer than necessary. She hadn't missed how withdrawn he'd been at the hospital.

He'd been shaken by the attack on Will, that much had been obvious. As had the way he'd begun to pull away from them from the moment he saw that Will was all right.

As she crawled into bed on the third night after the incident, she wondered if he'd ever come home again.

She lay in bed reading a novel when she heard the front door open, then shut, and his familiar footsteps climb the stairs. She set aside her book, licked her suddenly dry lips and braced herself.

The moment she saw him, she knew that he was leaving.

"Hi," he said, looking at her but not quite meeting her eyes.

"Hello."

"How is Will doing?"

"He's fine. A little sore. Unhappy at being grounded for two weeks."

"Good. He got off easy. My vote was for six months."

"Six months?" She laughed. 'Trust me, having him cooped up for six months would have been a bigger punishment for me. You're still new at this parenting business. A bit more practice and you'll learn."

He froze just for an instant in the midst of unbuckling his gun belt and Caroline knew in that moment. *He's not going to be a parent.*

Logan crossed the room and draped his guns over the back of a chair. As he emptied his pockets and tossed the contents into a wooden bowl atop his dresser, he asked, "You did get my messages?"

"Yes. Thanks for letting me know not to expect you. Did y'all have any luck?"

"No. They're long gone. It looks like they've split up, too." He paused as if he wanted to say something, then he briefly closed his eyes and said, "I...uh...need a bath."

He disappeared down the hall to the bathroom and Caroline allowed herself one little shudder of sorrow, a single tear and a lone sniffle. She was losing him. These last months were all she would ever have. He didn't care enough about her, about their family, to conquer his fear. She wanted to bury her head in her pillow and weep, but instead she worked to rid herself of self-pity. By the time he returned, she'd assured herself that she'd strengthened her resolve and banished the sadness.

He wore a towel wrapped around his waist and nothing else. His hair was damp and finger-combed, his skin tanned and toned. Caroline spoke from the heart rather than her mind when she said, "I've missed you."

His immediate stiffening proved she'd made a poor choice of words.

At that point, despite her best efforts, grief overwhelmed her. "Oh, stop it. I'm not a fool, Logan Grey. I know what's happening here."

Defensiveness sharpened his voice. "What do you mean? Nothing's happening here except that I'm going to bed. It's been a hard few days and I'm whipped."

"Don't lie to me."

"What the hell are you talking about?"

She spied the awareness in his eyes, so his continued dishonesty fired her temper even more. "Maybe I am a fool after all. A fool for loving a man who is such a fraud."

"Fraud!"

"Lucky Logan Grey," she said, her voice scathing. "Fearless range detective who has fought dozens of gun battles, hunted down countless criminals, met the most evil of men face-to-face and never faltered. Yes, a fraud. Because he's too afraid to face his own feelings."

"Dammit, Caroline."

"You're leaving, aren't you?"

His mouth set in a grim line. "Tomorrow. Wells Fargo hired me to follow up a lead on Kid Curry. Looks like he's gone East. I'm leaving because of the job, Caroline."

"No, you're not. You're leaving because you're afraid. Afraid of your own family. Afraid to make a home. Afraid of love. Because you had all that in the past and you lost it."

He sucked in a breath past gritted teeth. "You don't know..."

"Don't I? I've suffered my own losses, Logan. My mother died when I was just a girl. My father never shared his heart. The man I married ran out on me."

Now he sputtered a litany of curses beneath his breath.

"Were your losses really any worse than mine, Logan? A loss is a loss. A broken heart is a broken heart. But I'm not afraid to love you, Logan Grey. And I'm not afraid to let you go."

He closed his eyes, acknowledging the blow, and she forged ahead. "I'm a survivor. I managed with Will when I was little more than a child myself, alone and afraid. I can manage now. I want you, but I don't need you in order to survive. You go on and exist, Logan. Will and I will live."

The color drained from his expression and he dropped his chin to his chest, his breaths coming harsh and fast as if he'd run for miles. Or rather, years. He had been running for years, hadn't he?

At that, Caroline's anger drained away. She hadn't walked in his shoes. It wasn't fair of her or right of her to compare the intensity of their losses. He'd lost a child he loved. How would she react if, God forbid, she ever lost Will?

Tears stung her eyes as she grieved for him, for herself, and for their son. "I'm sorry, Logan. I—"

"No. It's okay. You're right, Caroline." He swallowed hard, then confessed, "I'm afraid to stay."

She looked away, blinked back the tears and braced herself to continue. In a soft, composed voice, she said, "I know, and my heart breaks, but not for me as much as for you. I did fine without you all these years, and I'll do fine without you again. And it's the same for Will. We will miss you, but we'll get along all right by ourselves because we will have each other."

"That's good."

"Yes, it is. For us. But you...you will be alone again. That's what breaks my heart. Because whether you know it or not, whether you can admit it or not, you love us. You love me."

His eyes were jade-colored pools of pain, his voice gruff and rough as he said, "Kill me now, Caroline. Pick up my gun and shoot me. It would be kinder than what you are doing to me with your words."

She managed a bittersweet smile. "Don't worry. I've said all I need to say. I'm done talking. It's time to act." She reached out a hand toward him. "Lie with me, Logan. Lie with me and tell me goodbye."

CHAPTER SEVENTEEN

Every ounce of self-preservation he possessed told Logan to grab his britches and leave right then. Even as he told himself to go, that this was a mistake, he walked toward her, let her take his hand and pull him down to her. The mattress dipped, the sheet rustled, his towel fell away and he was in her arms.

In her arms, where he needed to be.

She looked up at him, the emotion naked in her eyes. In those violet depths, he saw a reflection of his heart. The power of the moment hit him hard and his chest tightened, stealing his ability to breathe.

"Logan?"

He couldn't reply for the lump in his throat. Instead, he pulled her up and swallowed the tiny gasp of surprise. With sensual purpose, he kissed her. Long, delicate kisses that bespoke a man who knew it might be the last time. He tasted the sweetness that was hers alone, twining his tongue with hers, exploring...wishing.

If only he could stay.

You could stay. You could stay like this forever. Be a family. Be a husband. Be hers.

Then reality crashed back upon him and he knew that couldn't happen. No matter how much he wanted.. .how much he wished. No. He couldn't. Will's accident had brought it all home. He simply couldn't. So for right now, he'd take what she offered and he would be grateful, for it was far more than he deserved.

He steeped himself in the scent of her, the flavor of her, the texture of her skin. He lost himself in the pleasure of sumptuous curves and sleek valleys. He abandoned himself to the heaven that was Caroline. He was slow. He was gentle. He was achingly tender. He kissed her, a deep, soulful kiss full of longing and desire, passion and apology. Caroline deserved more, deserved better than he had to give.

Trailing kisses down her throat, he nuzzled at her breast with gentle insistence. A moan of pleasure slipped from her parted lips and she delved her fingers into his hair, urging him to capture a nipple. He sucked deeply, slowly. First one, then the other, drawing them deep into his mouth.

He needed this, needed her, more than he'd ever needed anyone in all his life.

Above him, she made sweet sounds of pleasure that ripped through him, swelling his arousal even more. When her hips arched instinctively, driving his need to the brink, Logan fought the urge to take her then and there. He wanted to make this good for her, wanted her to be mindless and melting in his arms. Wanted her to have a piece of his heart in the only way he knew how to give it.

He brushed soft, openmouthed kisses along her belly, dipping his tongue into her navel. Desire coursed through Logan, made him tremble and ache with something he couldn't quite define. Never in his life had he been this way, almost desperate. He could barely breathe for wanting her. His every sense felt stretched and heightened to an almost painful intensity. He was loving her with his body, but somehow, the act went deeper than the physical. What they found with each other was beyond that, beyond description, beyond words. It wasn't just sex, he knew. It was more. It was...

The last time. It was all they'd ever have.

This was the end.

Dark emotions tugged on his heart, yet he stamped them down

again. With Caroline, he would find heaven in this moment, this night, and let morning take care of itself.

And he savored.

With slow hands, he reached down and cupped her hips. His mouth followed the path of his hands, dancing along the sensitive skin of her inner thigh as he spread her apart. He glanced up and saw the shock blending with anticipation in her fevered gaze when she realized his intent. Her legs tensed, her body stiffened.

"Let me love you, Caro."

Coaxing her to relax, he kissed her mound until he felt her muscles slacken. Then without another word, he claimed her. Using his mouth in ways he never had before, he stroked, licked and branded until she arched off the bed with a shriek that touched his soul. It was hard and fast and like nothing he'd ever shared with a woman before.

As she came back to earth, Logan's pride prompted him to smile up at her and start all over again.

This time, he built the intensity slowly, gently, letting her mindless whimpers wash over him like warm rain.

He loved the noises she made. He loved her open, genuine enjoyment of sex. He loved that she held nothing back.

He wondered how he would have the strength to go on living without her in his life.

When she collapsed again, panting and shaken, she pleaded, "No more. I can't. Please, I can't."

"Sure you can."

Crawling up beside her, he brushed the damp hair from her cheek and slipped an arm beneath her. In one movement, he positioned himself so she sat in a straddle atop him.

Still breathless, Caroline leaned down and kissed him sweetly, once and then again. "I guess you're right."

Then with a slow, enigmatic smile, she lowered herself onto him, binding him to the core of her body.

Logan trembled and closed his eyes. This was perfect. A man couldn't ask for anything more. He gripped her bottom and held her still, reveling in the connection. *God, give me the strength to walk away from her.*

As if she understood, Caroline reached down and pulled at his shoulders, holding on as if for dear life. Her breasts perched before him, taunting him with their pretty hardened tips. Tempted beyond reason, he pushed up and took one in his mouth.

A throaty moan escaped her as she started to move, slowly, finding a rhythm that soon turned their bodies into a slick, hot meld of flesh on flesh.

Logan could barely breathe for wanting his wife. He clung to her, sucking one nipple, pulling the other with his fingers.

It was like nothing on earth, watching her writhe and moan and arch and keen. To see her like this, free and abandoned, her head tossed back, her skin flushed with passion, drove him up to the highest of heights. Need curled inside him, hot and demanding. The urge to toss her down and drive into her hot, wet warmth was a pounding heat in his blood.

But he didn't want it to end. Not yet.

"Caroline," he murmured, wanting, needing her to look at him. Her lashes lifted and he gazed deeply into those enormous violet pools, silently telling her the words his lips could not form.

"Logan," she whispered, the sweet sound like a prayer and the mood changed. Deepened.

She folded down onto him and he rolled her over onto her back and rose above her. Their hands clasped. Their gazes didn't shift from one another as time continued in a slow haze.

They were as one. The rasp of her breath heavy with passion was his breath. The honeyed taste of her kiss, his kiss. The warm, wet yield of her body as he thrust within her and the tight clasp of velvet muscles as she rose to meet him wasn't simply a physical union, but a joining of souls.

It was heaven. It was hell. It was life at its most basic. He wanted it to last forever, but the slow erotic friction eventually took its toll. Pressure built at the base of his spine and as she cried out her pleasure, as those inner waves of ecstasy clamped around him, he had no choice but to lose himself within her, to give himself to her in both sadness and in joy.

He clung to her damp body, wishing away the heaviness in his heart. Her name slipped from his lips in a sigh as he cuddled Caroline closer and kissed her temple.

Exhausted, he sank down into the pillows, taking her with him. She snuggled up against him, kissing his shoulder. With a trust he didn't deserve, she buried her face in the crook of his neck. It was then he felt the tears. "Caroline?"

"Don't," she whispered with a soft sniffle. "Let's just leave it be. For tonight."

Even now, when he knew her heart was breaking, she tried so hard to be strong. Logan's heart constricted. "Honey, I wish that I—"

"Please," she begged. "Don't say anything. Just hold me. For now, just hold me, Logan. It's all I want."

His insides twisted painfully at the raw anguish in her tone, but he could no more deny her request than he could leave the bed. All she wanted was her husband. Tonight, at least, he could give her that.

After a bit, she slept. He lay awake, all his senses alive. He heard the faint bark of a dog, noted the scent of beeswax and lemon and lovemaking on the air. He tasted salt from her tears and felt the warm wisp of a breeze drifting through their open window and skimming across his bare skin.

Mostly, he focused on her. He listened to her breathe, steady and sated. He was so attuned to her body, knew her pulses, her heartbeat and her movements. He knew the flash in her eyes when she was happy, angry and about to find heaven in his arms.

He also knew she loved him.

Letting his hand run a soft caress along her back, Logan looked to the window and stared out into the moonless night sky. So dark, he thought absently. Colorless and empty. No moon, no stars.

Was that what he had to look forward to? Darkness? Solitude? No Caroline. No Will. How would he manage without them? How could he walk away and live with nothing when everything was right here?

But when a man had nothing, he had nothing to lose. He'd had everything before and it damn near killed him. Twice.

He would manage nothing. It was the only choice he could make.

Caroline awoke the next morning determined to treat the day like any other. As usual, she woke before him and indulged in a few moments simply lying beside him, watching the sunlight strengthen through the window and enjoying the sensation of having her man in her bed. This day, the last day, she took an extra minute before silently rising to wash and dress and prepare herself to face the hours ahead.

How would she get through them? She liked to believe she was strong, but was she really? How could she stand there and watch the man she loved walk away? How could she let him go without a fight?

Because the fight isn't yours, but his. His fears went deep and no one could conquer them but Logan.

So she wouldn't make demands. She wouldn't beg. She wouldn't cry. What she would do was pick up the pieces of her broken heart while trying not to think of her own fears.

She decided to make waffles for breakfast. They were Will's favorite and she wanted to pamper him today. Logan's leaving would be hard for him and while she couldn't protect him from the pain, the mother in her needed to make a gesture. She heard sounds of movement upstairs as she stirred her mix and her heart caught, but she shook it off. Moments later, she heard Sly come bounding downstairs and she moved to the door to let him out.

He vaulted out into the backyard with enthusiasm, ready for another exciting day of life. Watching him sniff and explore the space still new to him, Caroline was struck by two things. First, thank goodness they'd sent for the dog instead of waiting for Will's planned visit with Daniel later this month, and second, how nice it would be to trade places with Sly for a day. What she wouldn't give to spend today sniffing and digging and worrying about chasing butterflies rather than comforting her son and remaining strong herself when Logan Grey said goodbye.

The two males in her life came downstairs together, Will peppering his father with questions about the search for the Wild Bunch. 'Tell you what, son. Let's wait until after breakfast to get into that, shall we? Thinking about Kid Curry and his knife is bound to give me indigestion."

With his questions shut down, Will spent his time on his other favorite topic—attempting to finagle his way out of the home-confinement part of his punishment. He offered up a few creative alternatives, she had to admit, though he posed them to his father, who responded with simply a helpless look at Caroline. She said, "The idea of you helping Doctor Daggett at his hospital does have some appeal. Let me think about it, and we'll discuss it after lunch."

His eyes widened in surprise. Caroline had never rescinded a grounding in the past, and while she could see he had a question, he wasn't about to voice it. "Okay. Thanks, Ma. Great waffles." Then he dabbed his mouth with his napkin, and said, "May I be excused to do my morning chores?"

"You may. Start by weeding my vegetable patch, please. The dandelions are about to take over."

"Yes, ma'am." Seconds later, the screen door slammed behind him and she heard him call out, "Sly! Fetch the ball, Sly!"

"Can I help you with the dishes?" Logan asked, standing and speaking his first words to her that day.

"No, thanks. You have things of your own to do."

He hesitated as though he wanted to say more, then he gave an almost imperceptible shrug, turned and headed upstairs.

Caroline's fingers trembled just a little as she washed, dried and put away the dishes. She worked to keep her mind blank and her emotions encased in a block of ice, but she managed it. When she climbed the stairs once her kitchen work was done and she'd made a brief detour into the library, she was calm, collected and cool as a winter morn.

Their bedroom door was open. She stopped just inside the room. His suitcase lay open on the bed, the clothing that had hung next to hers in the chifforobe now packed neatly inside. He stood at the window, gazing out at Will on his hands and knees amongst her summer squash. "You gonna modify his punishment?"

"Probably. It'll be good for him to be around other people the next few days, I think."

He nodded slowly, his eyes never leaving the scene below. Caroline felt the ice around her heart start to crack, so she quickly forged ahead. "It looks like you're just about packed."

"Yeah...I travel light." Finally, he turned around. "My train leaves in less than an hour."

She forced a smile and made it look good. "Well, you'd best hurry, then. You'll need a few minutes with Will before you go."

"Caroline—"

"I wondered if you might like to take this with you," she interrupted when it appeared as if he thought to rehash the discussion from the previous night. She handed him a framed tintype of Will. "Mr. Swartz felt so bad about what happened to Will that he offered to make it at no charge."

"He's a fine-looking boy," Logan said, staring down at the photo. "Thanks. I'll treasure this. But...I need one of you, too."

Caroline swallowed hard. "I didn't have one made. Now, can I help you with your packing? Did you remember your razor from the bathroom? And your work boots are down in the mud room. I don't know if you'll want those or not."

His voice held a bit of an edge as he said, "You're taking this better than I figured."

She almost lost her control then, but she took a moment to settle before she replied. "Did you want me to cry and carry on and beg you to stay? Would that make this easier for you? Are you hoping that I do exactly that so that you feel you must stay, and then you can spend the next ten, twenty, fifty years holding it against me? Is that what you want, Logan?"

"No, of course not."

She continued as if he hadn't spoken. "Well, if it is, you are officially out of luck. That doesn't suit me. Believe me, I've put a lot of thought into it. Yes, I want you to stay, but that's not enough. *You* need to want to stay. *You* need to be certain. You need to be with me and with Will of your own free will, not because I coerced you with tears or because I told you I—"

She broke off abruptly, then took a deep, calming breath and finished. "You need to choose us because you know that being with us is right, you know it all the way down to your bones. Any other reason will poison what we have, and that is the one thing that would break my heart irreparably."

He had words bottled up inside him, that she could tell by the pain in his eyes, the line of his jaw, the grimace on his face. Yet, he said only, "I'm leaving, Caroline. I have to leave."

"I know that," she snapped back. "You've explained it to me. I might not agree with it, but I understand. Now, go explain it to your son."

His jaw hardened even more as he shut the suitcase and fixed the buckles. Caroline straightened her spine and squared her shoulders as he grabbed the case and walked past her. "Are you coming with me?"

"No. This is something you need to do on your own."

She remained in their bedroom as he went downstairs, his footfalls sounding heavy and loud against the wooden steps. When she heard the back screen door bang shut, she moved toward the window. Though she'd prefer not to eavesdrop on this conversation, her son's welfare compelled her to do so. She pushed the window open wider and waited.

"Will?" Logan called. "I need to talk to you for a moment."

"Yessir."

Caroline watched her son stand and brush the dirt off the knees of his jeans. "I'm sorry, buddy," she murmured softly. "I wish I could have spared you this."

Logan shoved his hands in his pockets and rocked back on his heels. Will loped up to him and asked, "Ah, man. You've got that look on your face. What did I do now?"

"Nothing. I, um, I took a job with Wells Fargo. I'm going after the Wild Bunch."

"You are!" Will's excitement quickly faded. "I guess that means you'll be gone for a bit."

"Um, longer than a bit, Will. I'm off to Tennessee first, and after that, who knows."

Now Will stuck his hands in his pockets as he faced his father, the two looking so much alike that Caroline let out a little moan. "I don't understand. I thought range detectives were free to take whatever jobs they want."

"They are."

"So...you want to take this job?" Without giving Logan a real chance to answer, he added, "You want to leave us?"

Logan raked his fingers through his hair. "This is something I need to do."

"Because of me?" Will's voice sounded stricken. "Do you feel you have to seek revenge because of what Kid Curry did to me?"

"No, son. I didn't take the job because of you."

"Have you run out of money, then? Look, I can take some of that stuff you bought me back."

"No." Logan grimaced and frustration tightened his voice. "Money isn't a problem. I'm wealthy. I took it because...well...it was time."

"Time for what?"

"For me to leave."

"Why?" Will's brow furrowed in confusion and in pain. "I don't understand!"

"It's complicated. Look, what you need to know is that no matter where I am, I will always be your father. I am not abandoning you. You must understand that. Any time you want to contact me, let 'em know at the local Wells Fargo office and they'll track me down. If you really need me, I'll do my best to get back here for you."

"Track you down? You mean, you really aren't coming back unless I need you to?"

As Will stared up at Logan, his expression appeared to collapse in on itself. The admiration, the respect, even the love simply crumbled. Will yanked his hands from his pockets and fisted them at his sides. "I won't need you."

Logan turned his head as if he'd taken a blow to the chin.

Will took a step back, and now when he looked at his father, his gaze was a glare, his smile a grim line and the tone of his voice a scathing attack.

"Fine. I get it. I understand. It's time for you to leave. You're tired of us. It's just like the last time. You left Mama. Ben was right about you all along, I guess. I should have known. Mom warned me, but I thought she was crazy. What kind of man wouldn't want what she has —what we have—to offer? Only a fool or maybe a coward. What are you, Logan Grey? A fool or a coward? I think it's both. You're a fool *and* a coward."

Logan opened his mouth, then shut it abruptly without responding.

"I looked up to you," Will continued. "Guess that makes me a fool, too. But, I'm not a coward. I'll tell you what I think of you. You're supposed to be the luckiest man in Texas. Well, I think that's true. It was your good luck to have my Mama marry you."

"Now that's true," Logan agreed. "Your mother is the best thing that ever happened to me. Because of her, I have you. I never thought I'd be lucky enough to have a son."

Will snorted. "A son you are happy as a clam to throw away."

"Dammit, that isn't true! Look, Will, I don't expect you to understand, but...well...the truth is that, for the most part, I'm plagued by bad luck." He threw a glance up toward the house and Caroline thought he might be looking to be rescued. Well, this time, he'd simply have to sink or swim. Will deserved to have his say.

"To put it bluntly, Pa, that's bullshit. Mama loves you! Because of that alone, you're the luckiest man on earth."

"I know that."

"Then why are you leaving her?" Will screamed, his pain and anguish ringing in his voice. Caroline knew he was trying to be strong, but his voice broke when he asked, "Why are you leaving me?"

"I don't want to, son." Logan hung his head in misery. "I just can't stay."

"Then what Mrs. Peters needs to write about in her paper is that you're also the dumbest man in Texas because you are too blind to see your good luck. You're throwing away your family. You don't want us? Well, we don't want you, either. You may be the man who made me, but you're not my father."

Logan's head snapped up. "I will always be your father, William."

"No, you won't. If you were really a father, you'd want to stay. All you are is the man who wanted to pass some time with my mama, but didn't have the guts to stay around." Will dragged his sleeve beneath his nose, wiping away the evidence of his tears, then pointed toward the horizon. "So go. Just go. To hell with you, Lucky Logan Grey. Don't let the door hit you on the ass on your way out."

Will turned away from Logan and ran to the back of the yard where Sly was busy digging in the dirt. Will dropped to his knees, wrapped his arms around his dog's neck and with shoulders shaking, buried his face in his best friend's fur.

Logan spat an ugly-curse, then kicked the dog toy lying in the grass, sending it flying.

Caroline turned away from the window, glanced in the mirror and found a handkerchief to dab at her own watery eyes. Those two poor, brokenhearted boys.

She refused to think about her own broken heart.

As she made her way downstairs, her gaze focused on his suitcase waiting at the foot of the staircase. When a lump formed in her throat, she swallowed hard. Was she doing the right thing for this family she loved? Should she ask him to stay?

Logan entered the hallway from the kitchen looking as if Will had ripped his heart out. *Oh, Logan.*

"Well, that went well," he said with a rueful, crooked smile that broke her heart all over again.

"He has a hair-trigger temper just like his mama, I'm afraid, but he gets over it quickly, too."

Logan nodded, sighed, then picked up his suitcase. "Caroline, I'm going to miss you."

"I should hope so," she said with a quick grin she didn't feel to lighten the moment as much for herself as for him. Otherwise, she might break down and bawl and that simply wouldn't do.

She went to him, hugged him hard, then pressed a quick, light kiss against his lips. "Godspeed and safe journey, Logan Grey. I hope you find Butch Cassidy and whatever else it is that you're searching for."

He closed his eyes and pressed his forehead against hers. "Thanks." He cleared his throat. "Caroline, um, take care. You and the boy, take care. If you need me, send for me, and I'll come back and fix the problem."

Then you'll go again. You'll just keep going, keep running. You'll never stop. You'll never stay. Her hands hidden by the folds of her skirt, she clasped them so hard that her knuckles turned white. "You'd better go or you'll miss your train."

He nodded and took two steps toward the front door before he pivoted, dropped his suitcase and pulled her into his arms. He gave her a long, thorough, heartbreaking kiss. When he finally lifted his head, he tugged his medallion from around his neck and slipped it over hers. Gruffly, he said, "Goodbye, Caroline."

Using her last bit of strength, she stood in the doorway watching as he strode down the street. At the corner, he paused and looked back. The look on his face crushed her, and Caroline knew she would remember it for the rest of her life. *He's the loneliest man I've ever seen.*

Knowing what he needed from her, Caroline smiled and waved. Then calmly, she stepped inside and shut the door. That's when the pain hit, fast and furious. Holding his medallion in a white-knuckled grip, she gasped a breath, whimpered and slid down the door to the ground. Bitterly, she wept. Foolishly, she wondered. Had she made the right choice?

He would have stayed if she'd told him about the baby.

CHAPTER EIGHTEEN

SIX MONTHS LATER, NEW YORK CITY

Logan wondered if he might not be growing a tumor in his chest like the one that had grown in Dair MacRae's head. Seemed like he walked around with a weight in his chest all the damned time.

He was tired in a way he'd never been before, his tail always dragging the ground. Of course, that might well be from lack of sleep. He didn't think he'd slept the night through since leaving Fort Worth. Dreams plagued him. Nightmares, really. Made him think of those awful dreams Caroline had when Will was in trouble. He'd telegraphed her the first time or two he'd suffered them, but after they became a regular fixture of his nights, he'd settled for promises from his friends to let him know if trouble occurred.

A gust of bitter wind whipped down the city street, and Logan hunched his shoulders and pulled his coat tight. He hated this place, the crowded streets, the way everyone rushed to wherever they were going. He missed the wide-open spaces and the big sky and the slower pace of life. He missed the clean scent of the air and the taste of beef barbecued in a man's own back-yard. A man bumped into him from behind, knocking him into a woman. He tipped his hat and said,

"Pardon me, ma'am." She replied with a scathing look, then hurried on her way.

He missed Caroline.

Logan sighed as he spied the shipping office that was his destination. After running Kid Curry to ground in Tennessee, he'd picked up the trail of the Wild Bunch's leaders and tracked Sundance, Butch and his woman, Etta Place, here to New York. While he'd yet to lay eyes on the trio, he had found someone who claimed they intended to leave the United States entirely within the week. Logan had spent the morning visiting shipping offices and studying passenger lists and telling himself it wasn't really cold enough to freeze ducks to a pond in this damned overcrowded city.

Inside the office, he showed his credentials to the clerk and ten minutes later, found his men and the woman. He checked his pocket watch. "Did the *Annabelle* sail on time this morning?"

"That she did," replied the clerk. "We pride ourselves on punctuality."

"I missed them by three hours."

The clerk dragged a hand down his whiskered jaw. "The Wild Bunch, hmm? I've been reading about them in the newspaper for a few years now. It'd be really something to catch Butch Cassidy."

"I didn't catch him. I missed him."

"The Blankenship Line has a ship leaving for South America in the morning. They wouldn't be too far ahead of you."

"Great," Logan said with a total lack of enthusiasm.

"You want me to call over and secure a ticket for you? It's a woolly day out there. That would keep you from having to make the trek in the cold."

And secure a ticket commission for the clerk, no doubt. He'd already visited the offices of the Blankenship Line that morning, so he knew where to go. "No, thanks. I need to check with my bosses before I take off for a foreign country. Appreciate the effort, though."

As Logan opened the door to leave, the clerk called, "Good luck, sir."

Logan waved and muttered, "Luck. Hell."

He shoved his hands into his pockets and headed up the avenue in the general direction of the other shipping office. He'd lied to the clerk. He didn't need to get permission before following the Wild Bunch to Bolivia. He just needed to work up his own desire to do so.

"I don't want to go," he murmured. To be perfectly honest, he didn't care all that much if Butch and Sundance got away scot-free. They'd robbed banks and trains and stages, but they'd never physically hurt anyone. They weren't killers like Kid Curry. They were South America's problem now, not Wells Fargo's.

But if he didn't go to South America, where would he go? What would he do?

The tumor in his chest seemed to grow another pound in a heartbeat as he trudged up the street buffeted by the wind. Another tumor popped up in his throat. He coughed and muttered, "I need to buy a ticket and get on that ship."

Then a little voice whispered inside him. *You could go home. Home to your wife and son.*

Logan halted abruptly. He closed his eyes and turned to one side, putting his back toward the wind.

Home. Wife. Son.

Family.

The tears trickling down his cheeks were caused by the cold, bitter wind, were they not? *The cold, bitter wind inside you.*

The wind gusted, almost blowing him over, sweeping him back into the past when the wagon began to tip and his mother and sister screamed. Then from somewhere nearby came the hard bang of a shutter. It sounded like a gunshot and he was back in the house in Oklahoma, the Wilsons dead at his feet, Maria and Elena on the floor beside them. Then from out of nowhere came the echo of Will's voice. *You're a fool and a coward. A fool. A coward. The luckiest man in Texas. You're throwing away your family.*

Your family.

Pain roared up inside him, bending him over double. Logan braced his hands on his knees, wondering if his body would explode from tumors that had grown too big to be contained.

Then he opened his eyes and his gaze fell upon an item on display behind the plate-glass picture window.

In that moment, Logan knew what he had to do.

CAROLINE SAT on the settee in her living room surrounded by gaily wrapped boxes and dear friends. An hour ago her women friends had surprised her by descending on her home bringing baby gifts, desserts and more laughter than this house had seen in months.

Not that she and Will had a bad life, because they didn't. He liked school and he'd made new friends. He enjoyed living in the bigger city. She had filled a hole in her life by writing book reviews and covering local elections for the *Daily Democrat*.

Another hole—the hole in her heart—continued to plague her, paining her even more as the baby's birth approached. But Caroline was a strong woman and she dealt with the ache, all the while aware that she was better off than Logan. She had Will and the baby. Logan, wherever he was, whoever he was with, was alone.

She untied a big yellow bow and opened the box. "Oh, they are beautiful," she said, pulling out a multicolored receiving blanket and a pair of baby booties knitted from the softest of yarns. "Wilhemina, did you make these yourself?"

"I did," she said with a satisfied sniff. "Now that Mr. Peters has grown so persnickety about my retirement from the newspaper, I have time on my hands."

"Well, they're lovely and I will put them to very good use."

"I treasure the blanket you made for me, Wilhemina," Emma MacRae observed. "You have true talent with knitting needles."

Kat Kimball glanced up from the notepad where she kept track of gifts and givers so Caroline could pen her thank-you notes and nodded. "Mama is a wonderful seamstress, but you have her beat when it comes to knitted goods. But don't tell her I said that."

"I heard you, Katrina," Jenny McBride called from the kitchen where she was refilling the coffeepot.

All the women laughed, then Maribeth Prescott handed Caroline another gift saying, "At risk of sounding like one of the children, open mine next, Caro. Open mine."

It was a huge box intricately wrapped. "Who in the world tied these knots?"

"Kat's daughters. They had entirely too much fun wrapping the gifts."

Her concentration on the ribbons, she only vaguely noted the quieting of conversation around her. "I should have asked Will to leave me his knife before he went off with the men to the stock show," she said, picking at a knot with her fingernails.

A pocketknife appeared before her. "Here, use mine." Logan.

Caroline gasped, her gaze jerking up, her hand lifting to clasp the medallion she never took off. Sure enough, Logan Grey stood beside her. He handed her the knife, but it slipped through her fingers.

She realized that the room filled with a dozen females had grown as quiet as a church. "Logan," she breathed.

"Hello, Caroline." He picked up Wilhemina Peters's baby booties and studied them with a warm gleam in his eyes. "Whoa, those are tiny. Pretty, but tiny."

"Logan," Caroline repeated.

Kat Kimball's impatient voice called, "Is that all you have to say?"

Logan chuckled, then said, "See, the thing about that is that Caroline isn't the one who needs to talk first. That would be me. Her explanation of why she hadn't bothered to inform me of the pending arrival can wait. Unless, how pending, Caro?"

"T-t-two weeks."

"Okay. Two weeks I can deal with. From the size of her stomach, I was worrying I only had two minutes."

He moved around in front of her and went down on his knees, taking her hands in his. His expression intense, his eyes glowing with emotion that was sure and proud and fierce, he said, "Caroline Grey, I love you. Will you be my wife? Be the mother of my children? Will you be my family and make me, once and for all, the luckiest man in Texas?"

Wilhemina Peters hissed toward Maribeth Prescott. "Aren't they already married?"

"Yes. Hush," Mari snapped back.

Caroline had to clear her throat to speak. "Oh, Logan. Are you sure?"

"Sweetheart, you can paint it on the barn."

"We don't have a barn."

"On the side of the house, then. Hell, you can tattoo it on that stomach of yours. There's plenty of room."

"Quit making cracks about my stomach!"

"I love your stomach and the baby growing inside—the baby I didn't know about—but we'll talk about that later."

"You mentioned that."

"I love Will and Sly and this home you have made for me. I love our family, Caroline. I love you. For now and forever, for however long forever turns out to be."

Jenny McBride sighed. "I'm going to cry."

Emma MacRae sniffed. "It's so romantic."

Caroline Grey steepled her hands over her mouth, then asked with suspicion. "No one told you? You didn't come back because of the baby?"

"No one told me. I came back because I finally figured out that this is where I belong. Here, with you and our children. You are my heart and my home, Caroline, and I'm sorry, so very sorry, that it took me so long to admit it. Our son was right when he called me a fool and a coward, but I think I needed to leave to find my courage. I did that, honey, on a street in New York City, of all places."

"What was in New York City?" she asked.

"Answer my question and I'll show you."

"What question?"

Logan let out a little frustrated laugh, then touched his forehead to hers. "Can I come home, Caroline?"

"Yes! Oh, yes!" She threw her arms around him then and started to cry as she pressed kisses on his cheeks, his nose, his forehead and finally, as her lips hovered above his, she said, "Welcome home, Logan Grey." With the kiss, the hurt inside them healed.

When they finally broke apart, Logan said, "You can call me Lucky."

Caroline laughed and fumbled for a handkerchief and wiped the tears from her face, feeling the warmth of a blush in her cheeks as her friends cooed and clapped their approval until Kat Kimball spoke up. "Wait. What about her question? What about New York?"

"Oh." Logan grinned and the front door opened as he rolled to his feet. "You know, the minute I saw it, I knew it was a sign. Still, I never figured it was as big a sign as it turned out to be."

He turned to leave the room when Will let out a yelp. "Ouch! Who left this thing sitting in the middle of the hallway? Gotta be more careful, you know. We don't want my mama tripping over it."

Carrying a wooden rocking horse in his hands, he stopped in the doorway and gaped at his father.

Logan shrugged and said, "When I was a boy I had a rocking horse named Racer."

NEWSLETTER

Emily March invites you to join her monthly newsletter for information about new releases, giveaways, and book sales.

Please register at www.emilymarch.com

ALSO BY EMILY MARCH

The Bad Luck Wedding Historical Romance Series

THE BAD LUCK WEDDING DRESS

THE BAD LUCK WEDDING CAKE

Bad Luck Abroad Trilogy

SIMMER ALL NIGHT

SIZZLE ALL DAY

THE BAD LUCK WEDDING NIGHT

Bad Luck Brides Quartet

HER BODYGUARD

HER SCOUNDREL

HER OUTLAW

THE LONER

The Republic of Texas Duo

THE WIDOW'S RAFFLE

THE WEDDING RANSOM

Stand Alone Historical Romances

THE TEXAN'S BRIDE

CAPTURE THE NIGHT

THE SCOUNDREL'S BRIDE

THE COWBOY'S RUNAWAY BRIDE

The Brazos Bend Contemporary Romance Series

MY BIG OLD TEXAS HEARTACHE

THE LAST BACHELOR IN TEXAS

The Callahan Brothers Trilogy

LUKE—The Callahan Brothers

MATT—The Callahan Brothers

MARK—The Callahan Brothers

A CALLAHAN CAROL

Read more about the Callahan Brothers in

ANGEL'S REST

an Eternity Springs novel.

The Eternity Springs Contemporary Romance Series

ANGEL'S REST

HUMMINGBIRD LAKE

HEARTACHE FALLS

MISTLETOE MINE

LOVER'S LEAP

NIGHTINGALE WAY

REFLECTION POINT

MIRACLE ROAD

DREAMWEAVER TRAIL

TEARDROP LANE

HEARTSONG COTTAGE

REUNION PASS

CHRISTMAS IN ETERNITY SPRINGS

A STARDANCE SUMMER

THE FIRST KISS OF SPRING

THE CHRISTMAS WISHING TREE

JACKSON

TUCKER

BOONE

ABOUT THE AUTHOR

Emily March is the *New York Times, Publishers Weekly*, and *USA Today* bestselling author of over thirty novels, including the critically acclaimed Eternity Springs series. Publishers Weekly calls March a "master of delightful banter," and her heartwarming, emotionally charged stories have been named to Best of the Year lists by *Publishers Weekly, Library Journal,* and Romance Writers of America. A graduate of Texas A&M University, Emily is an avid fan of Aggie sports and her recipe for jalapeño relish has made her a tailgating legend.

Join Emily March online
www.emilymarch.com
emily@emilymarch.com

Made in United States
North Haven, CT
19 September 2022